*Irish Stories and Tales*

is one of a number of fine anthologies of
fiction available in handsome paper-bound
editions. We recommend for your pleasure:
*Famous Chinese Short Stories*, retold by Lin
Yutang; *The Great Short Stories of Robert
Louis Stevenson; A Pocket Book of Modern
American Short Stories*, edited by Philip Van
Doren Stern; *Mid-Century*, a collection of
contemporary American short stories edited
by Orville Prescott; *German Stories and Tales*,
edited by Robert Pick; *French Stories and
Tales*, edited by Stanley Geist; *The Great
Short Stories of Guy de Maupassant; Tales
from the Decameron*, selected by Herbert
Alexander; *Tales from the Arabian Nights*,
selected by P. H. Newby; *Spanish Stories and
Tales*, edited by Harriet de Onís and a
somewhat longer version in Spanish of that
book: *Cuentos y narraciones en lengua
española.*

WS
ⵔⵒⵍ

# IRISH STORIES
# AND TALES

•

*Edited by Devin A. Garrity*

WASHINGTON SQUARE PRESS, INC.  •  NEW YORK

# IRISH STORIES & TALES

## 1961

A new edition of a distinguished
literary work now made available in
an inexpensive, well-designed format

**L**

Published by
Washington Square Press, Inc.: Executive Offices, 630 Fifth Avenue;
University Press Division, 32 Washington Place, New York, N.Y.

WASHINGTON SQUARE PRESS editions are distributed in the U.S. by
Affiliated Publishers, Inc., 630 Fifth Avenue, New York 20, N.Y.

# Acknowledgments

✳

Brandt & Brandt for permission to reprint "Come Back, My Love" by Maurice Walsh, from TAKE YOUR CHOICE, J. B. Lippincott Co.; copyright 1953 by The Curtis Publishing Co.

Paul Vincent Carroll and Richard J. Madden Play Co., Inc., for permission to reprint "She Went by Gently," from *Irish Writing*.

Desmond Clarke for permission to reprint "The Islandman," from the *Dublin Magazine*.

Maurice Crain and the author for permission to reprint "The World Outside" by Val Mulkerns, from *Irish Writing*.

Eric Cross for permission to reprint "Saint Bakeoven," from *Irish Writing*.

Curtis Brown, Ltd., for permission to reprint "Bell Wethers" by Jim Phelan, from BOG BLOSSOM STORIES, Sidgwick & Jackson, Ltd.

The Devin-Adair Co. for permission to reprint "The Return" by Daniel Corkery, from THE WAGER AND OTHER STORIES, copyright 1950 by The Devin-Adair Co.; "The Kith of the Elf-folk" by Lord Dunsany, from THE SWORD OF WELLERAN, copyright 1954 by Lord Dunsany; "Weep for Our Pride" by James Plunkett, from THE TRUSTING AND THE MAIMED, copyright 1955 by James Plunkett; "The Wild Duck's Nest" by Michael McLaverty, from THE GAME COCK AND OTHER STORIES, copyright 1947 by The Devin-Adair Co.; "Teresa," by Sean O'Faolain, from THE MAN WHO INVENTED SIN, copyright 1948 by The Devin-Adair Co.; "The Tent," by Liam O'Flaherty, from THE SHORT STORIES OF LIAM O'FLAHERTY, copyright 1955 by Liam O'Flaherty.

E. P. Dutton & Co., Inc., for permission to reprint "The Cat and the Corn-field," by Bryan MacMahon, from THE RED PETTICOAT; copyright 1953 by *The Sign*.

St. John Ervine for permission to reprint "The Burial," from EIGHT O'CLOCK AND OTHER STUDIES, Maunsel & Co.

# ACKNOWLEDGMENTS

Padraic Fallon for permission to reprint "Something in a Boat," from CELTIC STORY, edited by Aled Vaughan, Pendulum.

Frank Gallagher for permission to reprint "The Leaping Trout," from THE CHALLENGE OF THE SENTRY, The Talbot Press.

Arnold Hill for permission to reprint "Miss Gillespie and the Micks," from *The Bell*.

Patrick Kavanagh for permission to reprint "Football," from *Envoy*, August, 1950.

Alfred A. Knopf, Inc., for permission to reprint, from THE STORIES OF FRANK O'CONNOR, "The Drunkard," originally published in *The New Yorker;* copyright 1948, 1952 by Frank O'Connor.

The Macmillan Co. for permission to reprint "Red Hanrahan" by William Butler Yeats, from THE STORIES OF RED HANRAHAN.

M.C.A. Management, Ltd., for permission to reprint "All the Sweet Buttermilk" by Donagh MacDonagh, from CELTIC STORY, Pendulum.

New Frontiers Press and the author for permission to reprint "The Story of the Widow's Son" by Mary Lavin, from IRISH HARVEST.

Brian O'Nolan for permission to reprint "The Martyr's Crown," from *Envoy*, February, 1950.

Edward Sheehy for permission to reprint "The Black Mare," from the *Dublin Magazine*, October, 1953.

Mrs. James Stephens for permission to reprint "A Rhinoceros, Some Ladies and a Horse," from *Irish Writing*.

Alphonsus Sweeney for permission to reprint "Michael and Mary" by Seumas O'Kelly, from THE GOLDEN BARQUE, The Talbot Press.

The Talbot Press for permission to reprint "The Devil and O'Flaherty," by Padraic O Conaire, from THE WOMAN AT THE WINDOW AND OTHER STORIES, translated from the Irish by Eamonn O'Neill.

The Viking Press, Inc., for permission to reprint "Araby" by James Joyce, from DUBLINERS, included in THE PORTABLE JAMES JOYCE; copyright 1946, 1947 by The Viking Press, Inc.

C.A.M. West for permission to reprint "Myself and a Rabbit" from *The Bell*, January, 1946.

# Introduction

*

The Irish have always had a way with words. Long ago they took on a language not their own and learned to rework it into pure magic. Nowhere is this magic more in evidence than in their short stories—stories that combine lyricism, humor and tragedy with rare imagination set in simple backgrounds, without resort to props.

The seemingly effortless art of the best Irish writers has an appeal that is naive and highly sophisticated at the same time; the disarming simplicity with which the tales are spun being somewhat misleading at first reading.

The stories in this collection should be read for enjoyment rather than for critical evaluation. No attempt has been made to comb the output of the twentieth-century Irish writers for the "best." That would be a most difficult task; for almost everyone in Ireland writes a poem or two, a play and a short story, at one time or another. And while the poems and plays have received considerable attention in recent years, the Irish stories, by and large, have not. Many fine examples can still be found buried in the pages of the "little" magazines which appear in Ireland periodically and as quickly disappear, never having broken the Irish barrier. *Irish Writing*, edited by David Marcus; Seumas O'Sullivan's *Dublin Magazine; Envoy*, and *The Bell*, edited by Sean O'Faolain and later by Peadar O'Donnell, gave many of the young writers their start.

More than half the stories are published here for the first

time in America. They have been collected over the past decade and reread at intervals to see if they retained their peculiar magic. Each of the present gathering has stood that test well.

"Irish genius," someone has said, "works best, if not solely, in short explosions." But even in short bursts, variety is desirable and an effort has been made to avoid sameness—a quality which can be as boring in a gathering of the elect as among any other group.

—*Devin A. Garrity*

# Contents

✳

# IRISH STORIES
# AND TALES

PAUL VINCENT CARROLL

# She Went by Gently

\*

It was close on three when the knock came in the night.
She was out of bed on the instant in her old flannelette
nightgown, with her silver-gray hair tossed down her back.
The night-light was flickering quietly as, in the shadows
by the elm tree outside, she discerned Manahan's unshaven
face under the battered hat.

"The pains is bad on the girl," came his voice. "I think
maybe it's surely her time."

"Go before me fast and have plenty of hot water," she
answered. "I'll be at your heels with Frank."

She heard his foot in the night hurrying off as she drew on
her heavy dress over the nightgown. Himself stirred and put
his beard irascibly outside the blankets.

"You'll go none," he snapped. "A slut like that, that gets
her child outside of priest and law. Four miles uphill on a
mountain road and the mists swarmin'."

"I'll go," she said quietly, and crossing, she ruffled Frank's
unruly hair on the little camp bed. "Be risin', Frank, and
let you carry the lantern for me to Manahan's."

"If there was just a drop o' tay before we'd start, ma," he
protested sleepily.

"There's no time, son."

"A grand pass we've come to, in this country," grumbled
himself. "Encouragin' the huzzies and the sluts to be shame-

From *Irish Writing*.

1

less. I'd let her suffer. A good bellyful o' sufferin' would keep her from doin' it again."

He moved coughingly into the deep warm hollow she had vacated in the bed. The strictures of his uncharitable piety followed her into the silver and ebony of the mountainy night. She went gently . . . her feet almost noiseless. There was an inward grace in her that spilt out and over her physical lineaments, lending them a strange litheness and beauty of movement. Frank was a little ahead of her, swinging the storm lantern. He was munching a currant scone plastered with butter. His sturdy little legs took the steep sharp-pebbled incline with careless grace. Now and again, he mannishly kicked a stone from his path and whistled in the dark.

"Careful now, Frank, in case you'd slip over the bank in the dark," she admonished.

"Och, ma," he protested, "the way you talk! You'd think I wasn't grew up. It makes little of a fella."

She smiled and watched him lovingly in the silver dark. He was her youngest. The others had all followed the swallows into the mighty world. Martin was in America, Annie in England, Matthew in Glasgow, Paddy in the Navy, Mary Kate a nursemaid in Canada, Michael was at rest somewhere in Italy. His C.O. had said in a letter that he had died well. If that meant that he had had the priest in his last hours, then God be praised, for he was her wayward one. She preferred him dying full of grace to dying full of glory. . . . But Frank was still with her. He had her eyes and gentleness and the winning tilt of the head. It would be good to have him to close her weary eyes at the end of all . . .

They had now crossed the cockeyed little bridge over a dashing tawny stream and the mountains came near her and about her like mighty elephants gathered in a mystic circle for some high purpose. Everywhere in the vast silvery empire of the dark there was the deep silence of the eternal, except for the rebellious chattering of the mountain streams racing with madcap abandon to the lough below. They were the *enfants terribles* of the mighty house, keeping it awake and uneasy. Now and again a cottage lifted a sleepy eye out of its feathery thatch, smiled at her knowingly and slumbered again. All of them knew her . . . knew of her heroism, her quiet skilled hands, her chiding, coaxing voice in the moments of peril. . . . In each of them she had been the leading actress in the great primitive drama of birth.

The climb was now gruelling and Frank took her arm pantingly. The lantern threw its yellow ray merrily ahead. All would be well.

She ruffled his hair playfully, and smiled secretively under the black mask of the night.

At a mischievous bend on the mountain path, the Manahan cottage suddenly jumped out of the mist like a sheep dog and welcomed them with a blaze of wild, flowering creepers. Inside, the middle-aged labourer was bending over a dark deep chimney nook. A turf fire burned underneath on the floor. From a sooty hook far up, a rude chain hung down and supported a large pot of boiling water. She nodded approvingly and donning her overalls moved away in the direction of the highly-pitched cries from an inner room.

"If there's anythin' else I can do . . ." he called, half-shyly, after her.

"Keep a saucepan of gruel thin and hot," she answered. "And put the bottle of olive oil on the hob in case we'd need it. Play about, Frank, and behave yourself till I call you."

She went smilingly to the bed and looked down at the flushed tearful face, the big bloodshot eyes and the glossy tossed hair of the girl. No more than eighteen, she thought, but a well-developed little lass with a full luscious mouth and firm shapely breasts. Jim Cleary who skipped to England in time had had a conquest worth his while. . . . The little rebel, caught in the ruthless trap of Nature, grabbed her hands beseechingly, held on to them hysterically and yelled.

"Oh, Maura, ma'am, please, please, please . . ." she sobbed.

Maura chaffed her hands, soothed her gently, clacked her tongue admonishingly and pretended to be very disappointed at her behaviour.

"Now, now, now, Sadie," she reproved her. "A fine soldier

*you* are! When I was here at *your* comin', your mother, God rest her, bit her lip hard and said no word at all. Come on now, and be your mother's daughter."

"Ah, sure how could I be like me poor dead mother, and me like this, and all agin me?" sobbed Sadie.

"Am *I* agin ye, child?" soothed Maura, "and I after walkin' four miles of darkness to be with you!"

The tears came now but silently, as Maura's skilful hands warmed to her work . . .

Frank remained in the kitchen at a loss until suddenly the door opened and a large nanny goat sailed in with perfect equanimity and balefully contemplated this stranger on home ground. Frank looked askance at her full-length beard and her formidable pair of horns, but this was of small consequence to the goat which advanced on Frank and in the wink of an eye had whipped his handkerchief out of his top pocket and stuffed it in her mouth. Frank's protest brought an assurance from Manahan who was stooped over the fire bringing the gruel to the boil.

"She'll not touch you," he said without turning his head.

"But she has me handkerchief," protested Frank.

"Ah, sure isn't she only playing with you!" returned Manahan heedlessly.

But by this time the goat had consumed the handkerchief with terrific relish, and was about to make a direct attack on the sleeve of his jersey. Frank dashed for the door with the goat after him. In the little yard he dived behind the water barrel that caught the rain-water from the roof. The goat snuffed past him in the darkness, and Frank hastily retraced his steps to the kitchen and barred the door.

He was just in time to see his mother put a generous spoonful of butter into a bowl of thin steaming gruel.

"Go in and feed this to your daughter, and coax her to take it," she directed Manahan. "She's quiet and aisy now and all will be well." He obeyed her shyly and without a word.

"You must be a big grown-up fella tonight and help your ma, Frank," she said.

"Anythin' you say, ma," he answered. "What is it?"

The baby had come forth without a cry. It was limp and devoid of any sign of life. She carried it quickly but calmly to the open peat fire, as close to the grimy chain as the heat would allow. It was naked and upside down. Frank, under her calm directions, held it firmly by its miniature ankles.

"Be a good son now and don't let it fall," she warned him, and plastering her own hands with the warm olive oil, she started to work methodically on the tiny body. Up, down and across the little chest, lungs and buttocks went the skilful fingers rhythmically until the newborn skin glistened like a silver-wrought piece of gossamer. The long minutes went by heavily. The oil lamp flickered and went out, leaving the dancing rays and shadows of the fire to light this crude drama with its eternal theme. Five minutes, seven, ten . . . without fruit or the promise of fruit. . . . But the moving fingers went on with rhythmic ruthlessness, searching for the spark that must surely be hidden there in a fold of the descending darkness. Frank's face was flushed, his eyes gathered up with the pain of exertion, his breath coming in spasms. On his mother's forehead beads of sweat gathered, rivuletted down the gray gentle face and flowed on to the newborn body to be ruthlessly merged in the hot oily waves of her massaging.

Then suddenly, as the tension had reached almost to the unbearable, a thin, highly-pitched cry came from the tiny spume-filled lips. She seized the baby, pushed Frank from her, turned it upright, grabbed a chipped, handleless cup of cold water and even as the fluttering life hesitated on the miniature features for one solitary second to receive its divine passport and the symbol of its eternal heritage, she poured a little of the water on the tiny skull and said, "I baptise you, in the Name of the Father and of the Son and of the Holy Ghost."

She wrapped the little corpse in the remnant of a torn sheet, without tear or trace of any sentiment, placed it in a drawer she took from the crazy wardrobe, and having made the Sign of the Cross over it gave it no further attention.

When she saw that the bowl was almost empty of gruel,

she chased Manahan out with a gesture and settled the little mother comfortably. She was adjusting her wet, tearstained hair over her pillow when suddenly she felt Sadie's arms tightly about her neck. Her big eyes were quiet now and the pain and the travail were gone, but the tears came rushing from them again as Maura kissed and soothed her.

"I wish I had me mother," she sobbed. "Maura, ma'am, I'm goin' to be a good girl from now on."

"You have never been a bad one, darlin'," coaxed Maura, tucking the faded bedclothes into her back. "A wee bit foolish maybe, but the world and the years will learn ye. Sleep now and I'll see you tonight."

She re-donned her old black cloak in the kitchen.

"I'll tell Maloney to bring you up a white box," she said to Manahan. "It will save you the journey down."

On the mountain path she went noiselessly, with Frank a little ahead, carrying the extinguished lantern. The dawn greeted her from the heights with far-flung banners of amber and amethyst. The heights themselves ceased from their eternal brooding for a brief moment of time and gave her a series of benign obeisances. The racing rivulets tossed her name from one to the other on the Lord's commendation. The sun himself, new-risen and generous, sent a very special ray of light that caught up her tossed hair and rolled it in priceless silver.

"Why do men lie prone in their beds," she murmured, "and the great glory of God washin' the hills with holy fire?"

Shamus Dunne was taking in his two nanny goats for the milking as she passed his cottage.

"The blessin' o' God light on ye, woman," he said, touching his wind-swept hat.

"And on yourself too, Shamus," she answered. "How is the little fella now?"

"Ah, sure isn't he over a stone weight already. Ah, woman—oh, wasn't it the near thing that night? Ah, sure only for yourself, wasn't me whole world lost?"

"Arrah, men always think the worst at such times," she answered smilingly. "Sure, there was never any great fear

of the worst that night! Herself, within, is much too good a
soldier for that!"

Frank had now discovered a salmon tin and was kicking it
vigorously before him. She took out her rosary at the bend
where the path dips perilously between two ageless boulders,
and as she trudged along, she began counting the beads
effortlessly. There on the heights at dawn, caught between
the gold and the deepening blue of day, she might have been
a pilgrim out of a Europe that has long since vanished, or
maybe a Ruth garnering the lost and discredited straws of the
age-old Christian thought.

Frank had now lobbed his salmon tin on the lofty fork
of a tree, and when she caught up with him, he took her arm
undemonstratively. Himself would be up now, she thought,
with his braces hanging, and maybe a hole in his sock that
she had overlooked. He wouldn't be able to find the soap and
the towel even if they were both staring at him, and of
course if he blew the fire, even with a thousand breaths, it
would never light for him. . . . But no matter now. Thanks be
to God, there was an egg left in the cracked bowl that would
do his breakfast. If the little white pullet in the barn laid in
the old butter box, Frank would have one, too, with the help
o' God. . . . When the cock himself laid an egg, Glory be,
*she'd* get one all to herself!

They crossed the rickety bridge, as the dawn was losing its
virgin colour. Frank saw a squirrel and rushed ahead of her.
She paused for a moment and contemplated the restless
waters. They took to her like a rich tawny wine poured out
of some capacious barrel by some high ruthless hand who
had suddenly discovered the futility of all riches. A May
blossom rushed under the incongruous arch and emerged to
get caught between a moss-covered stone and a jagged piece
of rock. There was a turmoil and pain for a moment, and then
it freed itself and rushed on. She wondered if it was the little
soul she had lately saved, rushing on in a virgin panic to the
eternal waters. . . . Maybe it was. . . . Maybe she was just an
imaginative old fool. . . . Ah, sure what harm anyway to be

guessing at infinite mysteries, and she so small on a mountain road?

Himself met her in the stone-floored kitchen. Indeed, yes, he was trailing his braces, and the sulky fire was just giving a last gasp before expiring.

"I suppose you saved the slut's bastard," he commented acidly.

She bent on her knees to blow the fire aflame again.

"I saved him," she answered, and a flame leaped suddenly upwards and made a sweet and unforgettable picture of her face.

DESMOND CLARKE

# The Islandman

✳

The Islandman came zig-zagging down the mountain from his shelter high on Craughan, a shelter built of thick sods of earth and grass, roofed over with two sheets of galvanised tin, and bedded, deep and thick, with bracken and mountain moss.

He was a tall thin angular man, young and loose-limbed. His face, firm and unsmiling, was bronzed a deep brown and weather-beaten; a tousled mass of black curly hair waved in the breeze like the unclipped mane of a young filly.

He was dressed like a fisherman in a thick loose-fitting jersey of navy blue with a high collar reaching to his chin, and long sleeves doubled over his wrists. He wore rough grey homespun trousers, the seams thick, like pieces of rope. The pampooties on his feet were wet with the morning dew.

He came to the pier sheltering the small unused harbour at the foot of the mountain, a pier jutting out to the sea shaped like a large crooked L. He stood still for a while, shading his eyes against the bright glare of the early morning sun thinly suspended over the distant blue water, and watched the cork markers of his line bob gently up and down.

The morning was very quiet and still; the little village across the bay was asleep. As yet no smoke poured from the blackened chimneys of the cottages huddled closely together. Along the beach upturned curraghs lay, their black bottoms to the sky like a line of giant beetles asleep.

Quite suddenly he jerked his head to one side, and screwed

From *The Dublin Magazine*.

his eyes tightly together, for the noisy agitated flight of a flock of gulls disturbed the calm peace of the morning. He watched the gulls pour from the cliffs in a great stream and wheel excitedly over the sea. He followed their flight to where they wheeled and gathered in a mass, and then he saw a moving patch of sea bubble up like a boiling pot. The gulls wheeled and circled over it, and screaming loudly dived, one after another, into the water.

The mackerel shoal moved quickly round the rocky head. The young man watched the sea and gulls for a while longer, then he nodded his head thoughtfully up and down, a faint sarcastic smile gathering at the corners of his tight mouth. He turned and looked over at the sleepy village, then at the upturned curraghs on the beach, and the long nets hanging from upright poles.

He dropped lightly from the pier and walked across the shingle, his long arms swinging loosely by his sides. His small curragh lay in a bed of stones close to the water's edge. Deftly he turned it over and dragged it into the sea, the water swilling about the end of his trousers and covering his feet. Carefully he manoeuvred round the end of the pier out into the shafts of golden light that cut deeply through the water revealing the rocky weed-covered bottom.

A quarter of a mile out, the row of corks bobbed gracefully up and down in line. The Islandman slew the curragh round in a wide sweep and brought it to the end of the line. Very carefully he reached over the side and drew the first pot into the boat. There were a few lobsters in it and he emptied them into the bottom of the curragh, returning the pot to the sea. The curragh drifted slowly along the line as he played it through his hand stopping just to take each pot and empty it.

The Islandman then rowed shore-wise. His face had grown softer, and he whistled quietly to himself. There was a fair heap of milling lobsters disentangling themselves in the bottom of his curragh. He stopped whistling and counted them roughly. Close on four dozen lobsters he had. They'd be worth at least sixpence apiece, maybe more, for the fishermen reckoned it was a poor season, and blamed everybody and everything for it, everybody and everything but their own innate laziness.

The curragh grated once more on the shingle and the Islandman dragged it gently to its bed of stones. He gathered the lobsters into a sack, leaving aside those he considered too small and immature.

Across the bay the cluster of white cottages came to life. Smoke curled thickly from all the chimneys. The women were raking out the dead ashes, uncovering the still glowing embers and building a fresh fire for the day. Children had gathered about the open kitchen doors, and two young girls were milking tethered goats by the gable end of a cottage.

The young Islandman wiped his forehead on the back of his hand, and gathering his sack of lobsters over his shoulder he climbed in a slow zig-zag fashion up the mountainside. Outside his sod-built cabin he made a fire of brushwood and dead bracken and brewed a can of strong tea. He ate a thick chunk of dry bread, washing it down with hot unmilked tea. Then he rested.

The sun had moved round in the heavens when he came down the mountain again. There was plenty of movement in the village like an uncovered ants' nest. Only a few curraghs still lay on the beach, the sun glinting brightly on their black bottoms. Many more were at sea moving quickly towards the shore, whilst far out a few were riding motionlessly like small specks on a polished board.

The Islandman, his sack slung across his shoulder, crossed the beach running by the village. The station, a dingy low-sized shed, lay farther round and was slightly obscured by the cottages. The young man walked on, his head down. He looked neither to the left nor right, neither did he bid the time of the day to the men and women who watched him with cold unblinking eyes. He could feel the cold eyes on him and in his ears he could hear what they were saying about him; he could only partly understand them but he sensed their feelings deeply. He was an Islandman from Innishcloghan, and the sea, the sea that washed their shores, was their sea, their very own.

Yes, he was a foreigner to them, an outsider, a strange, un-spoken, deep sort of fellow who lived for a few months each year in a sod-built shelter on the mountainside, snug in a hol-low against the wind, with a bed of brushwood and dry moss to lie upon.

At the station gossiping fishermen hung about, their legs dangling from stacked empty mackerel cases. They were smoking and spitting and talking in loud deep voices. The Islandman walked past them and entered the low dark build-ing smelling strongly of fish and brine.

The agent was in his shirt sleeves, standing at a desk, and writing with a stub of a pencil which he wet every now and then with his tongue. He was a big chested man, red faced and almost bald; he had a big belly held in with a thick leather belt, hole-punched every inch or so. He turned his head. "'Morrow," he said gruffly, and then "What have ye got to-day?"

The Islandman told him, and planted his sack on the wet concrete floor. He rubbed his numbed hand up and down the coarse seam of his trouser. He stood painfully at ease whilst the agent opened the mouth of the sack and poked amongst the lobsters with a piece of stick.

"Not bad, not bad at all," he muttered to himself. Then he straightened up with a grunt and crooked his thumbs in the broad belt across his belly. "How d'ye manage it at all?" he asked queerly, and he looked hard at the Islandman.

The young man grinned foolishly, not quite understanding. The agent took the piece of pencil from behind his ear and sucked it for a moment or two.

"What are ye askin' for them?" he said, his eyes narrowing shrewdly, and his lips sucked into his mouth.

"Sixpence apiece," the Islandman told him.

The agent grunted and frowned a little.

"The lot for a pound—twenty shillings," the Islandman said.

"A tidy lot for lobsters, son. A tidy lot."

Three or four fishermen came in. They nodded in a friendly way to the agent. "What's he got?" one of them asked.

"A handy case of lobsters," the agent said.

The fishermen were silent then and stood about with their hands deep in their pockets.

The Islandman felt uneasy; he bent down and gathered the neck of the sack in his hands. "D'ye want them, mister?" he asked simply.

The agent took the sack from him. "Sure. Of course I want them. But, son, your price isn't reasonable, ye're askin' a bit much, aren't ye?"

The Islandman shook his head. For a moment he was at a loss for a word then he said, "They're scarce, very scarce."

The fishermen laughed loudly and one of them said in a hard voice, "Not so scarce with you, lad, eh?"

The agent was grunting and mumbling to himself. "A tanner apiece son? It's a bit steep, isn't it?"

The Islandman shook his head blankly.

One of the fishermen detached himself from the group and opened the sack. He poked a thick tobacco stained finger amongst the lobsters. The Islandman looked at him, his brow darkening and his mouth twisting to one side. The fisherman was grinning and looking at the agent. "Not worth a tanner apiece, Johnny. They're smalls," he said.

The other fishermen gathered round and mumbled together in deep voices. The Islandman, his face flushed, pushed them aside and gathered up the neck of the sack. "They're mine," he said warningly, and turning towards the agent he asked, "Are *you* taking them, mister?"

The fishermen stood back their eyes fixed darkly on him. "Ye're an uncivil bloody man," one of them said, and another said he should go back to the island he came from.

"Are ye takin' them, mister?" the young man asked again, and he dragged the sack towards himself.

The agent nodded. "I'll take them. A quid for the lot, an' if ye ask me anything it's a divil of a lot of money to be handin' out."

The Islandman hauled the sack across the shed and tipped the lobsters into a box. He could hear the fishermen whispering and mumbling among themselves, and he knew they were talking about him.

The agent handed him a pound note, crumpled and dirty, which the Islandman folded and placed in a small leather purse.

"Ye gave too much for them lobsters, too bloody much," he heard one of the fishermen say as he went out.

"I'd like to know where he gets them," another said.

"Don't we all know," a third said in a loud voice.

The young man stopped, and turned and faced the men in the shed. For a moment he stared them hard, his eyes bright and burning like small red coals, he was thinking out the words he wanted to say. "I catch them honest," he cried. "No one can say I don't. No one! No one!" A lock of hair had fallen curl-wise over his forehead, and he tossed it back with a defiant jerk of his head. "There's plenty, plenty of them, and fish too," he said remembering the shoal of mackerel passing round the head when the village slept under the morning sun. "Plenty, be God!" he cried. The men were grinning at him so he turned around and went out.

The sun was just a bright red ball with a blunted side, resting on the distant sea, when the Islandman pulled his curragh out to the row of corks, resting peacefully on a flaccid sea, a sea stained with gold and purple stripes. Leisurely, as though it were a pleasant easy task, the young man drew in each pot, examined it carefully, and then baited it liberally.

In the same leisurely way, with long slow strokes, he pulled his curragh to the shore, dragging it lightly over the shingle, deftly up-ending it, and then placing large stones against the gunwale to hold it in place for the night.

He was thinking all the time, thinking in a slow unhappy kind of way. He sat down beside the curragh; his eyes narrowed slightly as he fixed them on the dimly-dark outline of the island, a ragged and discordant rent in the unbroken skyline like a great tear. Gradually the broad expanse seemed to narrow, the sea between the shore and the rocky island faded to a thin line like a road between.

A feeling of loneliness surged about him and then swept over him like a great encompassing wave. A choking lump tightened in his throat and his mouth felt dry. He swallowed hard, and then buried his face in his hands. His island home never seemed so near and yet, yet a sea swept between them.

For an instant he thought of the upturned curragh beside him, and how easy it would be—O so easy—to draw it out to sea and row swiftly steadily homewards to warmth and friendliness and . . . He set his face hard against the temptation, after all a few months lobster catching, even from an inhospitable shore, was all he had. A few months to earn enough to sustain him through a winter, to roof the half-built stone cottage on a rock-strewn acre from which a few unwilling potatoes grew, and where there was only sparse feeding for his goat. A few pounds to complete and furnish the cottage, and then pay the priest for making Maireadh his wife.

Maireadh! Maireadh of the curling jet black hair, of the creamy complexion, and the fresh young breasts rising firm and enticing from her body like ripe apples. His thoughts dwelt pleasurably on Maireadh, on the rough stone cottage in the shielding of Ballyvoggy Head. His thoughts were satisfying, like a pleasant dream, and he was happy. Then grating footsteps on the shingle disturbed him and he turned his head sharply, startled like one awakening suddenly.

There was a woman standing close by him. A tall, thin wizen creature with torn unlaced boots, a torn shawl about her head and clutched tightly against her scrawny breasts. Her black skirt was badly torn and frayed all round the end. She leaned heavily on a hobbly stick, bent and gnarled like herself.

"God and Mary bless ye," she croaked a greeting in Gaelic.

The young Islandman was frowning but his face softened, and he stared the strange creature wide-eyed. Nobody on the mainland had ever addressed him in the tongue of his island home. He returned the old hag's greeting.

"You're a stranger here, *avico*," she said, eyeing him closely. He nodded.

"You sleep on the hill beyant?" She jerked her stick towards the mountain.

"Yes."

"Your home is there, there on the island beyant, eh?"

"Yes, over there," he told her, pointing to the blurred mass fading into the darkening sky.

"Innishcloghan, *avico*, Innishcloghan," she cried in a high squeaky voice, and she nodded her head. "Sure I know it, know it well, *avico*."

He jumped quickly to his feet and stood close to the withered old woman, lank and lean like a hungry scarecrow. "Dhia!" he cried like one reunited to an old friend.

"Aye, I know it, *avico*," the old woman croaked, "but 'tis many the year since I set foot there, many and many the year long before you were borned, *avico*. I've travelled a bit since then, many a lane, many a road, aye and many a land, but sure 'tis on'y a cross, cantankerous woman I am, an old bothered woman of the roads with ne'er a roof over me head, an' ne'er the chick or child to offer one, but . . ."

"You can have my cabin for the night," he interrupted quickly, adding apologetically, "It's not much, woman, but 'tis warm an' dry."

She laughed loudly, harshly, her whole frame shaking, her hobbly stick dancing on the stones. The Islandman stared her, a puzzled expression clouding his face.

She stopped laughing and touched him with a cold hand. "You've the generous warm heart of an islandman, *avico*, a kind good heart, but . . ." she wagged her head from side to side and laughed again, not so loud though.

"What are ye laughin' at?" he asked.

"Yerrah 'tis the innocent ye are," she said, her voice harsh, "the innocent without eyes to see, without ears to hear. What d'ye think they'd be sayin' across the bay there? Aye, what would they be sayin'?"

He was amazed at the harshness of her voice, a harshness with venom pouring from a toothless mouth and thin indrawn lips.

"Aye, I know what they'd be sayin'. Aye, I know for I've ears that hear and eyes that see. Liz, mad Liz, sleepin' in the stealer's shack, the stealer from the island who takes our lobsters from our pots, and . . ."

"A stealer! A stealer!" the young man cried, his face ugly with anger. He turned his head and looked across the bay to the village growing dark and hazy in the fading light, then he turned on the old hag gripping her roughly by the shoulders.

She shook herself free. "Don't heed them, *avico*, don't heed them, for they're a hard bitter people," she said in a voice that was acid with hate. She shook her head from side to side. "They talk to me, me," she said, "for they don't mind me. Hi. Hi. I'm just Liz, a harmless bothered old woman of the road. Duine le Dhia, moryah! A woman of God. But 'tis me that knows them, knows what they say, an' what they think, knows the schemes they plan deep down in their hard hearts. Ye're not the first man they broke, son. There are them that went before ye, *avico*. Aye, them that went before ye," she said, in a quiet faraway voice like one recalling a memory dimmed with the forgetfulness of years. Then the venom poured from her thin drawn lips again and she pointed a scrawny finger to the cottages. " 'Tis the badness in them, the badness in their hearts, and, *avico*, they'll come in the night, an' you high in the mountain there, an' cut the pots from the line, an' lay them adrift."

"Why should they, woman?" the young man cried, his face close to hers. "Why should they? What have I done? What?" he cried, his dark eyes ablaze deep in his head.

He looked hard at the ugly line-seamed face of the old woman whose eyes were screwed up into tight little knots. She's mad, mad, he told himself.

"A stealer, a thief from the island, that is what they say," she told him, pouring the words out close to his ear. "Ye take the lobsters from their pots, the mackerel from their nets, the herrin's and plaice from their lines, the . . ."

The Islandman drew back and laughed loudly, a harsh forced laugh. For an instant the absurdity of it struck him as funny, but then very slowly he began to understand. She was not mad, she spoke the truth, didn't they always look at him with strange sidelong glances, didn't they whisper and mumble to one another, didn't they interfere with him, come be-

tween him and the agent and make fun of his catch. He
turned on her, his mind bitter. "It's a lie! A lie!" he cried.
"When did I ever have herrin's, mackerel, plaice? When?
When?"

"Easy, *avico*. Easy," she said, a strange gentleness creeping
into her croaking voice.

"I've only lobsters, lobsters," the young man told her. "I
have them because . . . because . . ."

He sighed deeply and turned away.

It had grown dark. The sun had slipped far down beyond
the rim of the sea, leaving a faint halo of crimson and purple
like the last red embers of a great fire. On the earth's edge the
sea was still alight burning softly, and high overhead small
dark clouds chased one another unguided by a single star.
On the sky-merged island a long beam of light moved round
in a great circle tearing a long bright gash across the calm
water.

The Islandman turned his head. "Good-night, woman,"
he said. "God and Mary be with you on your way."

"God and Mary and Patrick bless ye," she said, and he
heard her stick grate on the stones as she walked into the
night.


The sun was lying low in the east, pale and watery, and
across the bay the white cottages were huddled coldly in a
grey mist.

The Islandman picked his steps slowly and carefully down
the mountain. The water from the wet bracken seeped into
his pampooties, and he made a loud squelching noise as the
weight of his body came down on each foot; the thick upturned ends of his trousers were wet and heavy.

He stood for a while by his curragh, one hand resting on
the bottom. He looked out over the grey sea, undecided. The
tide was flowing strongly, a turbulent undercurrent agitating
it somewhat. A cold shiver passed through his body as the
damp air gathered thickly in minute blobs on his jersey.

He brushed a recalcitrant lock of hair back from his forehead, and then dragged the curragh roughly into the water,

pushing himself out with an oar. The water was fairly calm in the shielding of the pier, but beyond that the sea was rough, and beat noisily against the wall of stone.

The Islandman bent his back and pulled strongly to the line of corks bobbing frantically ahead of him, straining hard from their mooring. The curragh danced and reared violently so that he had to dip and hold his oars tightly to steady the frail craft. With a knowledge born of experience he pulled the line in on the tip of his oar carrying it across his bow.

His face grimly set, his lips drawn tightly together, he gathered the line in his hand and drew in each pot. He did not empty them for he was thinking of Mad Liz and the fishermen in the row of cottages by the beach. There were lobsters aplenty in the pots, large greedy fellows locked together, but the Islandman tried not to see them. Instead he piled the pots in a neat heap in his curragh, drew in the line and cut the anchoring stones away.

The young man was tired, and he rested for a while, his oars dug deeply into the water, and gripped against his side. Across from him the row of cottages were blurred in the mist, and away out far where the sun peered blearily from a bank of watery clouds the island was shrouded in a thick curtain of dull gray, cold and forlorn; it was like a death visited house.

On the shore in the shelter of the pier Mad Liz clutched her shawl tightly to her shrivelled breast. She peered through rheumy eyes at the bent figure of the young man lying idly on his oars. She saw the curragh drift shore-wise, rising on the crest of one wave, and then disappearing in its slough, but all the time coming nearer and nearer to the shore with the incoming tide.

Then, quite suddenly, life seemed to jump into the bent body. With a quick strong pull on one oar he turned the curragh round. And as the heavy clouds gathered overhead, and the swell rose along the beach she saw him pull swiftly away.

She clawed the shawl tightly against her breast, and opened her mouth to cry out. The rain started, pouring down heavily. The woman turned towards the Islandman's track up the mountain. Half way up she stopped and looked. The curragh seemed far away, a lone frail thing like a bobbing cork. "God be with ye, young man," she said half aloud, then shaking her clenched fist towards the village she muttered a low curse through her tight bloodless lips.

DANIEL CORKERY

# The Return

✻

Where Ankle Lane joins Blarney Street there are four high houses, dark-looking and very old, of that sort lane-dwellers call "fabrics" or "castles." The number of inhabitants varies from day to day: tricky-men in for the races will stay two nights, cattle-drovers only one; in periods of idleness a group of coal-porters sometimes attains to a certain solidarity—the same figures go in and out the doors day after day—but, just as happens in a factory, change sets in with prosperity; new faces come and go; and the next period of idleness sees a new colony, the same in its general characteristics, though made up of quite different individuals, repeat the fortunes of the last.

The largest, the darkest of these four houses was kept by a widow named Tynan; Bonnety Tynan she was called, from a wisp of a bonnet that clung to her scanty hairs; the other lodging-house keepers wore shawls. Her face was crabbed, shut like a fist against craft, reduced to its smallest and toughest by dint of years of hard-dealing. And her bonnet was equally shorn of its beams; this, too, was now not much bigger than a fist, but the legend still held that it was the lodging-house keeper's money-box. Sometimes she would have as many as thirty men under her roof, most of them idle, so her hardness, her aloofness were needed. How else could she have managed them? The Law?—it was too complicated; and besides, she kept too irregular a house to care to invoke it.

From THE WAGER, New York, The Devin-Adair Co.

She had laws and ejectment-processes of her own. Sometimes she conceived suspicion of a lodger; she waited till his back was turned; then she would slap a few buckets of water over his bed; he returned to find it sodden; and she went on with her washing while he stamped and cursed.

In the beginning of winter one evening towards six o'clock, as she shuffled in along the dark hall, she was surprised to see a glare of firelight breaking out towards her from the kitchen; she had been out of the house for some hours and hoped for nothing better than a spark in the bottom of the grate.

Opening the squeaking door she was still more surprised: a great figure, a darkness, sat on a stool before the fire; she noticed the curving width of his back; the huge head bent forward—he was asleep. She went silently up to him, bending to see his face: it was tanned; she glanced at his hands: they were dark with tar, knobby, and had blue rings and flags tattooed on them; but it was the hard, exaggerated-looking creases in his serge clothes that spoke his trade most clearly—these clothes had been folded tightly for weeks, perhaps for months, in the bottom of a seaman's chest. She shook him: "Come on now—wake up, who are 'oo? who are 'oo?"

He growled; then his voice softened; he rose and stretched himself, very much at his ease; a light came into his sea-bleared eyes; he examined the old woman's face with interest, with amusement apparently. "You're not changed a ha'p'orth," he said, "not a ha'p'orth."

She stared up; he was handsome in such a place.

"Sit down," she said, "I can't call to mind what your name is—'tis after escaping me memory."

With a seaman's license he put his great arm about her, drew her towards the glowing fire, and said again:

"You're not changed a ha'p'orth."

"I don't know you," she snapped out, breaking away.

"If you don't there's not a soul in Cork to say who I am—I'm Jim Daunt that was."

A memory or two, quite unimportant, stirred in her brain:

"So you are, so you are; you're welcome; how long will you be staying?"

"Till half-past eleven, anyway," he said.

"Where's the boat—Queenstown?"

"No—the Jetties," he answered, "and I must be aboard for midnight."

## II

She treated him well; she gave him a couple of eggs and many rounds of bread; yet for a seaman he made but a scanty meal.

"You're not doing well?" she said.

"If I only had it yesterday," he said, "you'd see the death I'd give it."

She moved about in the silent way of a woman who is accustomed to keep people at a distance. It was he who spoke:

"Isn't this a quare thing," he said, "I was never a bit lonesome wherever I was on sea or land—thousands of miles away —never a bit lonesome till this evening sitting there on that there stool."

She believed him; for she knew these sailormen well; and how any shelter that has the look, or even the name of home, stirs them.

"You were a great long time out," he continued, half complaining.

"How did I know you'd be here?"

"When did you leave the house?"

"Near four, I expect."

"Well, now, look at that," he said. "You mustn't have been well round the corner when I came in; and here I stopped, for I couldn't go away again—couldn't go away. Was I asleep when you came in?"

A lodger they called Brother entered; Mrs. Tynan made the two men known to each other. The sailorman wanted drink to be sent for; Bonnety, however, wouldn't have it: there was plenty of time, and, besides, drink was no food for a man after a day's work. Brother seconded her; Saturday Night would be coming in soon, and he was the best of company; 'twas company a man wanted after being shut up for

months in a wind-bag, "Wasn't it, matey?" he said, taking
the seaman's hand. A radiance had come into Brother's face:
unexpected joy is straight from the hands of the gods: exhausted, heavy in all his limbs from climbing with a laden
hod forty-foot ladders from early morning—terrible work—he
had hoped for nothing beyond a single drink in Miss Nora's,
and lo! the pleasures of a revel were emerging in his imagination.

"Have you enough of it?" he said.

"Of what?"

"The say?"

"God knows an' I have," said the sailor, with unexpected
earnestness, "but isn't it a quare thing to say that I was never
a bit lonesome till this evening sitting there on that there
stool?"

"How so?" said Brother.

And then with lingering detail the sailor told how he had
kept watch while Mrs. Tynan was down in Miss Nora's.

### III

Saturday Night came in after a few moments; in every fea-
ture, in every limb he had become misshapen by dint of com-
bat; his most restful attitude challenged; yet in Brother's
words he was the best of company: spirit is spirit.

Brother, introducing the men, mentioned the sailor's former
connection with the house: "There's no house like the old
house," he said, and Saturday Night, gripping the sailor's
hand, told him that though he had never met him before, he
felt they were old friends already: "There's something draws
me to you," he said, and the sailor answered: "A fellow don't
hear words like them from foreigners."

And three minutes afterwards he told Saturday Night that
he had never known what it was to be down-hearted till that
evening, sitting on that there stool before the fire. And, in-
dicating Brother, "Himself will tell you," he answered Saturday Night's look of inquiry.

Again he wanted to send out for drink; but again the landlady blanked the proposal: "What hurry was there? wasn't the night long enough? couldn't they wait for Johnny Swaine at least?"

Instead of Johnny Swaine came Katty Sullivan, saying as her first word:

"Isn't Johnny here?"

"Not yet," and they bade her sit down.

"By James, I might as well," she said: the form of swear she had invented herself, and its use seemed to lift her above the common throng; yet she needed no such aid; by nature she was above her surroundings. Strong and happy, with full, firm flesh, her face colored like ripe corn, her eyes blue and bright as the skies that go with it, she was large-hearted, and merry and frank because of her fearlessness, of her consciousness of power.

"Here's a lonely sailorman wouldn't object to a bit of company," said Saturday Night, and " 'tis a thing no wan objects to," she answered, in a tone that had as much daring as pity in it. Her words seemed to take the sailorman off his guard; the impudence in his face withered before her eyes. She had laid her spell on him; but everyone saw that some weakness of spirit denied his rising to it: he looked like a sick sportsman who, on a morning of sunshine, suddenly discovers that he is unable to lift his body from the bed. The moment's unrest was swallowed in a whirl of words, for Katty Sullivan was one they all liked to talk with. She was one of those who, though they might give a man a "wipe" across the mouth, never get on their dignity, an attitude that takes all heart out of a night's merriment. Soon Johnny Swaine came seeking Katty, even as she had been seeking him; and the sailor saw at once that he was her accepted lover, and with the knowledge a touch of daring came back into his look; his eyes, in spite of himself, as it were, would now find themselves resting on Johnny's face. Brother was sent for drink; he returned with two friends; " 'twould go to me heart to refuse them," he explained to the sailor.

The sailor drank nothing but raw whiskey, and it soon

appeared that his loneliness had gone from him; so, too, had his hold on himself. He became aggressive; when Brother was telling his champion tale of a sailor who, having deserted, signed on again in the self-same ship under stress of drink, the sailor stopped him half-way, and in his mouth the story from being a mere fill-gap became wild and thrilling. And almost without a pause he went on to tell the story of a parson's daughter of Adelaide, the girl who hid herself in a ship's hold for the sake of a young captain—how she might now be met with in the cities of the South American seaboard, in Buenos Aires or Rio—the sailors speak of her as the Australian Rose. He had seen her himself. His voice became higher and louder; he seemed to be talking against time, and his eyes shifted continually from face to face. He twitted Brother on his powers of drinking; he joked Saturday Night on his wounds; yet somehow his merriment was not contagious; and they all sniffed trouble when he began to raise bad blood between the lovers, for they could see that Katty's eyes were rife for mischief.

Johnny, she said, would have gone sailoring himself only for the wetness of the sea and his love for his mother; anyway, he wouldn't like to be pickled as well as drownded and, by James! she wouldn't care to see him pickled herself; "he'd be a terrible sight!" Then the sailor, with great concern, asked her what would she do if Johnny went off with another girl? She laughed, bent with laughter at the idea, and the whole room laughed uneasily with her. And so Johnny Swaine, made scapegoat for the company, sat by the girl's side, looking with glum eyes at his unfinished drink. But at the end of a bout of merriment the sailor stretched his hand to him saying that a joke was a joke; Johnny would not even look at the proffered hand. "Anyway, fetch us the measure," the sailor continued with some diplomacy; and Swaine, thinking of peace with honor, rose from his place and made for the gallon. Without a sound the sailor sprang into the vacant space at the girl's side, and Johnny, turning, found him there. A roar of laughter addled him, maddened him. He flung the gallon about the floor, squared out, and his voice rose above the jubilee: "Stand up, if you're a man."

"Miss Sullivan," the sailor's voice was heard saying in the sudden, expectant silence, "isn't it lovely weather?"

"Stand up, I say."

"A beautiful night?"

"Will you stand up?"

And the girl's eyes danced to see such spirit in her lover.

"You won't, won't you?" and Johnny's open hand met the sailor's cheek with a ringing blow. In a flash the two men were dancing at each other, the sailor all activity, his voice jerking out the best known of all the chanties:

> Ranzo was no sailor;
> Ranzo, boys, Ranzo.

And every time he came to "Ranzo" in the refrain—the word on which the rope is dragged as they hoist sail—he struck or rather touched Johnny's face or side or ears: he played with the landsman, dancing round him, tipping him wherever he wished.

> Ranzo was no sailor;
> Ranzo, boys, Ranzo.
> The mate he was a good man;
> Ranzo, boys, Ranzo!

The company, seeing that he did not mean to punish his man, let their mirth loose; they began to cry out: "Go it, Johnny, go it, old man." But after some time the sailor became over-confident, became careless; Johnny, on the other hand, had recovered his self-possession. Seeing a chance, he stood statue-still for a moment; then, making a wild charge, struck full in the sailor's face. The sea-blood fired up; song and dance ceased; with swift, careful drives he drove Johnny back, back, almost into the fire-grate. The room had become silent. Both men seemed to be fighting for life. They panted; their feet scraped the floor. Katty stood up: "Sir," she said, in a breathy voice that was scarcely audible, "Sir, sir"; but neither fighters nor onlookers heard her at all.

Suddenly shuffling steps were heard coming in the hall, and "Police," whispered Brother; for policemen walk into such houses in the same manner as factory-inspectors enter factories. At the word the sailor's face went white; he turned half-round from his man towards the room door; and Johnny, who had not perhaps heard Brother's warning, battered him right and left with great will.

"Wait awhile," said the sailor, all confusion, still staring at the door.

"Come on," shouted Johnny, wondering what had happened.

All faces were on the door; some of the men were gripping others by the shoulders. It was old Ned Mulcahy, the mason, who stuck in his head. The next moment the sailor was dancing once more around Johnny.

> *He gave him five and twenty;*
> *Ranzo, boys, Ranzo.*

His terror had lifted; he resumed his antics, and soon he had Johnny hemmed into a corner, where he kept him until he had his nose pumping blood. Then the combatants were separated.

"He's a game fighter, anyway," said the sailor, releasing him; and Katty Sullivan, passing the defeated man a handkerchief, thought in her heart of hearts that she wouldn't give him for all the tanned-faced sailors on the sea.

IV

It was now high time for the sailor to be going if he was to make his ship by midnight; yet he dawdled to hear the end of a story, to turn a joke, to look at Johnny's nose. He lingered too long, for Saturday Night suddenly began to tell the tale he always reserved till he had become quite emotional in his drink. They were unloading the *Cyclamen*, he said, and the first glimmer of dawn was coming on the river and, merciful

God! he saw a woman floating down the tide, her golden hair spread out on top of the water. They got her into a boat—the handsomest woman he ever laid eyes on, and he tried to persuade the men to say nothing at all about the matter, only just take the corpse up to Burnt Lane on a shutter and give her a decent wake with candles, and Christian burial in the Gardens; but they wouldn't, they were afraid of the law; and the police came, and the first words the sergeant said were (and Saturday Night wept to repeat them): "What do you know about this *person?*" "What do you know about this *person?*" Saturday Night spoke the words again, turning towards the sailor; and "Was that what he said?" the sailor gasped out, but his voice was so strange that the whole room on the instant forgot the story; the sailor's jaw had become locked, his neck rigid, his head looked as if carved in hardwood, the eyes unskilfully painted—a blank stare. But he lifted himself up, and "I'll be late," he said, in a voice that beseeched them not to question or hinder him; he had broken down; he could not explain himself—at least, this is what they would think.

"Good night," he said, putting out his hand to Katty Sullivan in a sudden, jerky way, his eyes meanwhile turned away from all the faces. She took no notice; she let on to be speaking to Johnny, who was now once more at her side. Without another word the sailor vanished from their midst.

After a pause the old woman spoke in her hardest voice: "Did any of ye see that fellow coming in here?"

No one spoke; in the silence Brother cracked a match on the bowl of his pipe.

"He said he came here to-day after I wint out."

"And sure he might."

"I'd like to know," the old woman rejoined, and she lit two candles—a signal for them to retire.

"He said he was asleep," she added, "he was no more asleep than I was."

"Holy Mother!" said Katty Sullivan, as she rose to go, "I'm sorry I iver laid eyes on him."

V

Now, I think that the sailor, as he stumbled down the deserted hillside streets towards the river, shook himself and stood still a moment here, stood still a moment elsewhere, saying at every pause: " 'Twill be all right—what a fool I am!"

Anyway, he got to his ship; made to walk up the plank with his head in the air, and—who knows how the end came?

But the next day they brought up two dead bodies from between his ship and the quay-wall; one of them, the second mate it was, had a knife-wound in the right lung and another in the back below the lung; the second body, bearing no signs of struggle on it, was our sailorman, Jim Daunt; and it was proved by the stopping of their watches and otherwise that one body had been a couple of hours longer in the water than the other. Saturday Night says that as he went up the plank maybe he heard a voice saying "What do you know about this *person?*" but Brother says that 'tis how he threw himself in, for he saw that the whole race of men were turning against him—look at how Katty Sullivan, with no reason at all, *couldn't* shake hands with him. Johnny Swaine says they all came well out of it, as if a murderer has evil spirits at his beck and call.

But what brought the sailorman up to Bonnety Tynan's at all? Was he trying to prove an alibi? Or was it that the word Home was ringing in his brain?

ERIC CROSS

# Saint Bakeoven

❋

I don't pretend to be musical, apart, of course, from knowing
a good tune when I hear it—the sort of thing that a fellow can
whistle in his bath. It does so happen, however, that I was
almost responsible for what might have been one of the
musical sensations of the century, and, before I forget it, I'd
better make some record of it for future generations.

I used to spend a part of each year fishing in Kerry in those
days. On one occasion, while I was returning from a mountain
lake, I ran into a terrific thunderstorm. Below me in the valley
I spotted an isolated farmhouse and I worked my way down
to it as quickly as possible. I had barely knocked at the door
when it was opened by an old man who ushered me in as
though I were the prodigal son returning home. He helped
me off with my coat, drew up a chair to the fire for me, and,
in general, treated me with even more eager hospitality than
you usually meet in Kerry.

"You must find it a bit lonely tucked away back here," I
suggested, once the preambles of hospitality were settled.

"Yerra—lonely, is it?" replied the old man, whose name,
by the way, was Johnny Quill. "The divil a bit lonely am I
ever," he went on. "To tell God's truth, 'tis just the other
way about."

"How come?" I quite naturally asked, considering the
situation of the place.

" 'Tis the fairies," he replied, in a matter of fact way. "Them

From *Irish Writing*.

divils do be at me pestering and worrying and annoying and bothering me all hours of the day and night. 'Tis only when a Christian, such as yourself, comes along that the sight of him drives them out and I have a bit of peace and ease for myself as it is now. But the moment you'll be gone them divils will be back again with their whispering and their rustling like mice round a corn bin. They have me patience worn out. There should be a law passed against them by those useless people up in Dublin and then put the police onto them. But, oh, no—they're much too busy passing laws to make hens lay eggs by act of Parliament to have the time to do anything useful. I tell you that the fairies are the plaguiest, most pestering and bewildering form of creation that man was ever burdened with."

"Yes," I agreed, for, after all, an old man's fancies break no bones. "I am sure that you must find them a bit of a nuisance."

"Nuisance! Nuisance!" bellowed Johnny. "Why, the divils have me near driven mad. I lambaste them with the handle of a broom. I give them a histe of my boot and a skelp of my tongue, but it's all a waste of energy. A few minutes later and they will be back at their old comether again: whispering hocus pocus; mislaying things and upsetting things on me. There's all classes of them," he continued, "but there is one of them—the plaguiest one of me whole pick of divils, who comes mainly by night. A sort of a foreigner, I'd say he would be, and a damned bad-tempered one at that. There's some of them all mischief, but with this one the game is all music. Whenever he puts his face inside the kitchen, the whole house does be filled with the sound of music as though it was the air of the place. Then he tries to be telling me something, but I can't make head or tail of the queer language he speaks and that only seems to make him madder and he shakes the great head of him and holds the great fists of him in the air, with the fingers spread out like a dealer trying to buy a beast in a fair for ten pounds from a slow witted man.

" 'Saint! Saint! Saint!' he yells. Then 'Bakeoven! Bakeoven! Bakeoven!' and I can't make sense of that at all for the divil a bit does he look like a saint and the divil a bit do I know what he means by his 'Bakeoven' unless it be one of these newfangled fakes that they have in the towns for the lazy women to bake in.

" 'To hell with you and your "bakeoven," ' I yell at him, 'if it's a "bakeoven" that you are trying to sell me or persuade me to buy. It was on the cake from the bastable pot that I was reared and on the same I'll finish my days.' Then the music starts all over again till my head is like a hive of bees ready to swarm with the sound of it."

"All very interesting," I agreed. "It looks as though the worst of the storm is over. I think that I'll be pushing on." I said goodbye to Johnny and thanked him, and, as far as I was concerned, that would have been the end of the business, for fairies aren't particularly in my line.

It so happened, however, that there was a professor of music johnny, from Oxford, staying in the hotel, collecting 'folk music,' whatever that may be. Naturally he was a difficult subject for conversation and that night I happened to mention the rigmarole Johnny had told me that day, by way of being sociable.

The professor johnny, whose name was Peterson, pricked up his ears almost immediately and showed more signs of life than I had seen so far in him, when I told him the yarn. I went away to bed and naturally had forgotten all about it by the following morning but it seemed that this fellow Peterson had, overnight, made a mountain of the story. He had worked out some crazy notion from it about a German composer called Beethoven, who had composed nine symphonies and died before he had finished his tenth; and he had come back in ghost form to worry poor old Johnny Quill about it.

Peterson had worked out that Johnny's 'Saint' was the German for 'tenth' and his 'Bakeoven' was really 'Beethoven' —the composer's name, and the music Johnny heard, was, of course, the music of the tenth symphony, now finished. It didn't seem to be dripping with sense to me.

I happened to go into the bar before lunch for an appetizer

and who should be there but Johnny Quill himself, celebrating a deal in sheep. We had a drink together and I left him to it and went off in search of food. But in the dining room I ran into Peterson, bubbling over with some new brainwave on Johnny's story. In the hope of finishing the matter off, as far as I was concerned, I led him out and introduced him to Johnny himself, the fount of inspiration. But it wasn't my lucky day, for in spite of his knowledge of music he could not make anything of Johnny's accent, no more than Johnny could make of his, so I had to stand in as interpreter.

I opened the ball with the first round of drinks, Peterson having lemonade and going straight into action, instructing me to ask Johnny to describe the appearance of the ghost or fairy or whatever it was, in detail.

"Tell him," said Johnny, "that he is a stout block of a bucko with a great stook of hair on his head as though he is in dispute with the barber—and that might well be, for he has a fierce, bad tempered jowl on him. His clothes? . . . Yerra, he does mostly wear some sort of an ould swally tail coat with an ould choker round his neck and the knee breeches they used to wear in the time of the caroline hats."

"Hm!" snorted Peterson, like the man who had found the piece of kidney in the pie, when I translated this for him. "Ask him now what language his fairy or whatever it is speaks."

"The divil be from me but how would I know that," replied Johnny. "Tell the man of the lemonade that 'tis neither English nor Irish but some gibberish makeup of his own and that the only words that I can make out at all are his 'Saint' and his 'Bakeoven,' and to hell with him and his 'bakeovens.' I'll stick to me bastable pot."

Peterson was studying Johnny intently as he put him through the third degree. "Ask him now," ordered Peterson, "if anyone else sees this apparition or hears the music."

"Only the divil himself could answer that," snorted Johnny, "but 'tis not likely for ould Bakeoven wouldn't have the time left to be annoying anyone else after all the time that he spends annoying me. He'd scarcely have the time left to wash himself . . . and will you add to that," Johnny continued, "that I will answer no more questions till the gentleman puts away the lemonade and has a glass of whiskey with me like a Christian."

Peterson, in spite of protests, had to yield. Johnny, as the oracle, could call the tune and he called it quickly.

"Would it be possible for me to hear the music and see this ghost if I went along to the house?" was Peterson's next query.

"It might and it might not," was Johnny's answer to this. "But mostly I'd be saying against it for I do notice that when anyone comes into the house to me the music stops and ould Bakeoven goes up the chimney or out of the window. But tell the gentleman that he's welcome anytime and if he can salt the ould divil and take him away with him to foreign parts there will be no man was ever so welcome."

The party spirit was getting into its stride by now. Peterson disappeared for a few minutes and I was hoping that we could adjourn *sine die* but it wasn't to be. He had only been up to his room and he returned with an illustrated history of music. He instructed me to hand it to Johnny and to tell him to look through it and to see if there was a picture in it at all like his 'fairy.'

Johnny licked his thumb and started to turn the pages one by one. I did not translate all his remarks and comments on the pictures of famous composers he saw, though they were amusing. I had doubts if this Peterson fellow had any sense of humor at all.

After thumbing about half way through the book Johnny let out a yell, putting his finger down on a picture of Beethoven.

"The pesky ould divil himself," he whooped. "The living split image of him! Saint Bakeoven and the great ugly puss of him!" At this Peterson went up in the air. He ordered another round of drinks immediately. Even I began to wonder if there might be something in it after all.

"Ask him now," said Peterson, as pleased as Punch, "if he could describe or remember the music he hears."

"Could I remember the music!" exclaimed Johnny. "Indeed, but it would be the day of the greatest aise to me when the day dawns that I disremember every screech of it. As for describing of it," he continued, after some head-scratching, "will you tell him that it would be beyond the powers of the worst poet yet born to put words to it. 'Tis such a roaring and a buzzing and a banging and a beating: such a twirling of trumpets and a tweaking of flutes and a scattering of the scraping of fiddles that the like of it was never heard before in the history of the world. 'Tis like the bellowings of dumb animals in pain and the howling of infants in divilment and the scolding of women in crossness and in the midst of it all there is this ould divil of a queer one, waving his hands up and down and about in the air as though the sound was all running out of the ends of his fingers like porter out of a tap.

"Only once did I hear the match of it in my life and that was in the days of the ould militia in the town of Kenmare when someone had treated the band with decency and the band had treated themselves with equal decency and they marched through the town 'stocious' and every man of them doing his best to outblow the other fellow."

Johnny now ordered a round and Peterson replied with another question, asking if Johnny could hum or whistle the music or give some actual idea of it. Johnny was now most ready to oblige.

"I'd give you more than an idee of it, with a heart and a half, and good riddance to it," said he, "but that it is a class of music that has no sense at all to it at all at all. 'Tis what you might call a porridge of a music—not like the 'Blackbird' or 'The Coolin'' or 'The Wind that Shakes the Barley' or any of the decent civilized tunes that wake a man's heart and set his feet tapping. But I will do the best I can to accommodate the gentleman for he is turning out to be a better class of a man than my first judgment of him. 'Tis something like this that it goes."

With that Johnny drained his glass, threw back his head, fixed his eyes on a spot on the ceiling and started to screech and to bawl and to roar and to groan until, after a couple of minutes, even Peterson, with all his interest in music, had had enough of Johnny Quill's version of Beethoven's Tenth Symphony. It was a thirst-provoking effort and Peterson thought the game worth while but demanded a *quid* for his *quo*.

"Ask him if there is any musical instrument that he can play, with which he might be able to reproduce some of the music he hears."

After probing into the nature of Johnny's polite accomplishments, the only thing that I could discover was that when he was young—and that was a long time ago—he had been able to play the bagpipes—but not very well. About here the party broke up.

The following morning, when Peterson had recovered after a good night's sleep, he had worked out a plan of campaign, for there wasn't any doubt now in his mind, on the circumstantial evidence so far produced. He was on the verge of the most amazing musical discovery of the century. The weather wasn't too good for fishing and as there wasn't much else to do I continued as *aide de camp* and the general adviser and interpreter.

The first thing that we did was to visit Johnny's house and we soon found that we were quite definitely not allergic to fairies. Even Peterson did not hear a note. According to Johnny the moment we entered the house both the fairy and his music faded away. Naturally Peterson was a bit hurt about this but he was quite certain that Johnny was speaking the truth and quite incapable of pulling Peterson's leg on his home ground, as you might say.

This meant that we had to fall back on Johnny himself as medium, interpreter or what you will. And that meant that, by hook or crook, he would have to reproduce what he heard by means of the only musical instrument he knew—the bagpipes. Peterson wasn't at all in favor of my suggestion, my quite practical suggestion, of bringing a band along and letting Johnny conduct it. He even suspected that I was pulling his leg and not treating the matter with sufficient gravity.

So the problem, or rather the practical solution to it, was narrowed down to bagpipes. Somewhere in the district there was reputed to be a pair or set or whatever it is of them but when it came to finding them, they were as elusive as the end of a rainbow, flitting ahead of us from valley to valley and house to house. At last we caught up with them. Johnny regarded them carefully, seriously and ruefully. With all his native gift of courtesy he could find little good to say about them. There was a whistle or a tweeter or some such vital part missing. One of the protruding flutes or whatever they were was most obviously cracked. More apparent still was a great rent in the windbag. But, with optimism, a dash of glue, some twine and wire, a splash of tar and a bit of an old tire, Johnny thought that he might be able to make a job of them.

Eventually, with the help of the 'smith and the carpenter and a man who was a great hand at tying a fly and another man who had an uncle in America who, in his day, had been a famous piper, so that he had claims to being an expert, one place removed, we got the contraption fixed up. As Johnny tactfully described it—"they worked in a kind of a class of a way." Now all that he needed was a few days' practice to get his wind and fingers into trim.

The appointed night arrived and with it rain in sheets and floods and torrents. This seemed to me to be a warning to let well alone and sleeping spirits lie. It seemed just any other kind of night rather than one to set off into the darkness and the wetness of a desolate mountain valley to hear the first performance of a symphony played on bagpipes—or played any way at all for that matter. Peterson's mind, however, was made up and I decided that being in for a penny I might as well be in for a pound.

We borrowed the hotel proprietor's car. I took along a bottle of whiskey and a couple of rugs. As luggage Peterson had a wad of music paper. Long before we arrived at the concert hall it was obvious, even above the storm, that

Johnny had entered into the spirit of the occasion and was already having a preliminary canter. It seems that somehow the fairy or ghost had got an inkling of what was in the wind and had readily co-operated with the notion. In fact they had already a dress rehearsal and come to a common understanding of the procedure to be adopted. Beethoven would conduct a few bars and while they still lingered in Johnny's ears he would have a skirl or whatever the musical term is for a dash at it and so they would progress from bar to bar.

Johnny himself was by this time so taken up with the idea and the possible hope of ridding himself of his musical lodger, that he was taking the matter almost as seriously as Peterson himself. He wouldn't even have a drink before we started. "Only a dart, now and again, of the purest of spring water," he said, pointing to a bottle at his side, "just for the wind's sake, until the gentleman is satisfied."

Still we were not *personae gratae* with fairies and while we were within the kitchen Johnny said there would not be a note of music. When you think of all the trouble that Peterson was giving himself and other people, it did really seem a bit inconsiderate on the part of Beethoven, but judging by the picture of him it was about what you might be led to expect from him. So it meant that we—or rather Peterson —would have to eavesdrop through the window.

I, never having been much of an enthusiast for symphonies or bagpipes, retired to the shelter of the car. I wrapped myself up in the rugs and opened the bottle of whiskey. Unfortunately I was still within earshot of the bedlam which was let loose when the performance started, but as the storm increased the howling of the wind and the lashing rain toned it down somewhat. There would be a squealing and a screeching from the kitchen as though a score of pigs were being slaughtered. There was Peterson huddled up against the window ledge, with the rain cascading over him from the roof, while he scribbled down crotchets and quavers. Now and again he would bawl through the window for a repeat. Now and again there would be a lull in the noise, as

Johnny took a swig of the purest spring water for his wind's sake.

Mercifully after a short while I fell into a doze. What woke me wasn't a noise. It was the absence of a noise. I came to, conscious that now there was only the howling of the wind and the roar of the swollen mountain torrents around me. There wasn't a sound from Johnny's kitchen. The door was open and Peterson was missing. I made a dash for the house to find Johnny on the flat of his back on the floor, as he would describe it, 'stocious.' The bottle of the 'finest of spring water' lay smashed beside him and from the trickle which was left in it there came a smell which might be mistaken for whiskey. It is not unknown in Kerry where so many improbable things seem to be possible for 'the finest of spring water' to have such a smell. Beside the fragments of the bottle lay the corpse of the bagpipes in a heap.

"Busht! Busht and be damned!" were Johnny's last words as he gave himself up to the soundest sleep that ever fell on any man. The description aptly covered all—Johnny, the bottle and the bagpipes. We made Johnny comfortable for the night in his bed. There was nothing more that we could do. The performance was ended. The carriage awaited at the door.

Peterson was quite happy but very wet. There wasn't a doubt now in his mind. It was the true, authentic Beethoven music alright, recognizable even through the medium of bagpipes. A few score nights such as this and he would have the whole thing down in crotchets and quavers. A few months of work on it and it would be ready to astonish the world.

It seemed unfortunate that Peterson developed a high temperature during the night and had to be rushed off to a nursing home the following morning with pneumonia. But all's well that ends well and a few days later Johnny himself had to be taken to the county hospital. The combination of the finest of spring water, the excitement and the strenuous exercises of bagpipe blowing had not been the best treatment for the heart of his age. So, as it turned out, Peterson would not have been able to do anything more, and anyway the bagpipes were quite beyond any further repair.

I had quite a busy time between the two invalids: writing letters for Peterson, when he turned the corner, and doing a few odd things for Johnny. The doctor had advised Johnny to stay on in the hospital and he wasn't at all unwilling. I arranged the settling of his bit of land to a relative so that Johnny would be able to draw the old age pension and so have no further worry.

As soon as Peterson was well enough, I drove him over to see Johnny and, needless to say, Peterson had only one interest in the visit.

"Ould Bakeoven and his music? . . . Yerra, thank God that I have neither sight nor sound of him since the blessed day that I came in here—and good riddance, for at last after all these years I have peace and ease for myself and am able to call my soul my own."

"But, manalive!" almost shrieked Peterson, "don't you remember the music?"

"The divil a note of it," answered Johnny, puffing contentedly away at his pipe. "The divil a note of it have I heard since I came in and the divil a note of it will I hear to the end of my days for I have handed the place and the cow and the sheep to a nephew of mine and I have no mind to budge from here till they carry me out feet foremost. I'll live the rest of my life like a fine civil servant, at the country's expense, taking my aise like a lord, instead of being at the beck and call of a pack of fairies like a boots in an hotel."

Peterson cajoled, bribed, bullied, pleaded, wheedled and argued but Johnny would listen to no argument and no persuasion. The last thing that he said to Peterson when we came to say goodbye was: "If you should happen to see Ould Bakeoven at any time during your travels will you tell him from me that I did him a great harm and a great injustice and that I am sorry for it, for after all he was right. 'Tis the new-fangled 'bakeovens' that they use in this place for their breadmaking and you never in all your life tasted sweeter or grander or nuttier bread."

# The Kith of the Elf-folk

✳

The North Wind was blowing, and red and golden the last days of Autumn were streaming hence. Solemn and cold over the marshes arose the evening.

It became very still.

Then the last pigeon went home to the trees on the dry land in the distance, whose shapes already had taken upon themselves a mystery in the haze.

Then all was still again.

As the light faded and the haze deepened, mystery crept nearer from every side.

Then the green plover came in crying, and all alighted.

And again it became still, save when one of the plover arose and flew a little way uttering the cry of the waste. And hushed and silent became the earth, expecting the first star. Then the duck came in, and the widgeon, company by company: and all the light of day faded out of the sky saving one red band of light. Across the light appeared, black and huge, the wings of a flock of geese beating up wind to the marshes. These too went down among the rushes.

Then the stars appeared and shone in the stillness, and there was silence in the great spaces of the night.

Suddenly the bells of the cathedral in the marshes broke out, calling to evensong.

Eight centuries ago, on the edge of the marsh, men had built the huge cathedral, or it may have been seven cen-

From THE SWORD OF WELLERAN, New York, The Devin-Adair Co.

turies ago, or perhaps nine; it was all one to the Wild Things.

So evensong was held, and candles lighted, and the lights through the windows shone red and green in the water, and the sound of the organ went roaring over the marshes. But from the deep and perilous places, edged with bright mosses, the Wild Things came leaping up to dance on the reflection of the stars, and over their heads as they danced the marshlights rose and fell.

The Wild Things are somewhat human in appearance, only all brown of skin and barely two feet high. Their ears are pointed like the squirrel's, only far larger, and they leap to prodigious heights. They live all day under deep pools in the loneliest marshes, but at night they come up and dance. Each Wild Thing has over its head a marsh-light, which moves as the Wild Thing moves; they have no souls, and cannot die, and are of the kith of the Elf-folk.

All night they dance over the marshes, treading upon the reflection of the stars (for the bare surface of the water will not hold them by itself); but when the stars begin to pale, they sink down one by one into the pools of their home. Or if they tarry longer, sitting upon the rushes, their bodies fade from view as the marsh-fires pale in the light, and by daylight none may see the Wild Things of the kith of the Elf-folk. Neither may any see them even at night unless they were born, as I was, in the hour of dusk, just at the moment when the first star appears.

Now, on the night that I tell of, a little Wild Thing had gone drifting over the waste, till it came right up to the walls of the cathedral and danced upon the images of the colored saints as they lay in the water among the reflection of the stars. And as it leaped in its fantastic dance, it saw through the painted windows to where the people prayed, and heard the organ roaring over the marshes. The sound of the organ roared over the marshes, but the song and prayers of the people streamed up from the cathedral's highest tower like thin gold chains, and reached to Paradise, and up and down them went the angels from Paradise to the people, and from the people to Paradise again.

Then something akin to discontent troubled the Wild Thing for the first time since the making of the marshes; and the soft gray ooze and the chill of the deep water seemed to be not enough, nor the first arrival from northwards of the tumultuous geese, nor the wild rejoicing of the wings of the wildfowl when every feather sings, nor the wonder of the calm ice that comes when the snipe depart and beards the rushes with frost and clothes the hushed waste with a mysterious haze where the sun goes red and low, nor even the dance of the Wild Things in the marvelous night; and the little Wild Thing longed to have a soul, and to go and worship God.

And when evensong was over and the lights were out, it went back crying to its kith.

But on the next night, as soon as the images of the stars appeared in the water, it went leaping away from star to star to the farthest edge of the marshlands, where a great wood grew where dwelt the Oldest of the Wild Things.

And it found the Oldest of the Wild Things sitting under a tree, sheltering itself from the moon.

And the little Wild Thing said: "I want to have a soul to worship God, and to know the meaning of music, and to see the inner beauty of the marshlands and to imagine Paradise."

And the Oldest of the Wild Things said to it: "What have we to do with God? We are only Wild Things, and of the kith of the Elf-folk."

But it only answered, "I want to have a soul."

Then the Oldest of the Wild Things said: "I have no soul to give you; but if you got a soul, one day you would have to die, and if you knew the meaning of music you would learn the meaning of sorrow, and it is better to be a Wild Thing and not to die."

So it went weeping away.

But they that were kin to the Elf-folk were sorry for the little Wild Thing; and though the Wild Things cannot sorrow long, having no souls to sorrow with, yet they felt for awhile a soreness where their souls should be, when they saw the grief of their comrade.

So the kith of the Elf-folk went abroad by night to make a soul for the little Wild Thing. And they went over the marshes till they came to the high fields among the flowers and grasses. And there they gathered a large piece of gossamer that the spider had laid by twilight; and the dew was on it.

Into this dew had shone all the lights of the long banks of the ribbed sky, as all the colors changed in the restful spaces of evening. And over it the marvelous night had gleamed with all its stars.

Then the Wild Things went with their dew-bespangled gossamer down to the edge of their home. And there they gathered a piece of the gray mist that lies by night over the marshlands. And into it they put the melody of the waste that is borne up and down the marshes in the evening on the wings of the golden plover. And they put into it too the mournful song that the reeds are compelled to sing before the presence of the arrogant North Wind. Then each of the Wild Things gave some treasured memory of the old marshes, "For we can spare it," they said. And to all this they added a few images of the stars that they gathered out of the water. Still the soul that the kith of the Elf-folk were making had no life.

Then they put into it the low voices of two lovers that went walking in the night, wandering late alone. And after that they waited for the dawn. And the queenly dawn appeared, and the marsh-lights of the Wild Things paled in the glare, and their bodies faded from view; and still they waited by the marsh's edge. And to them waiting came over field and marsh, from the ground and out of the sky, the myriad song of the birds.

This too the Wild Things put into the piece of haze that they had gathered in the marshlands, and wrapped it all up in their dew-bespangled gossamer. Then the soul lived.

And there it lay in the hands of the Wild Things no larger than a hedgehog; and wonderful lights were in it, green and blue; and they changed ceaselessly, going round and round, and in the gray midst of it was a purple flare.

And the next night they came to the little Wild Thing and showed her the gleaming soul. And they said to her: "If you must have a soul and go and worship God, and become a mortal and die, place this to your left breast a little above the heart, and it will enter and you will become a human. But if you take it you can never be rid of it to become immortal again unless you pluck it out and give it to another; and *we* will not take it, and most of the humans have a soul already. And if you cannot find a human without a soul you will one day die, and your soul cannot go to Paradise, because it was only made in the marshes."

Far away the little Wild Thing saw the cathedral windows alight for evensong, and the song of the people mounting up to Paradise, and all the angels going up and down. So it bid farewell with tears and thanks to the Wild Things of the kith of Elf-folk, and went leaping away towards the green dry land, holding the soul in its hands.

And the Wild Things were sorry that it had gone, but could not be sorry long, because they had no souls.

At the marsh's edge the little Wild Thing gazed for some moments over the water to where the marsh-fires were leaping up and down, and then pressed the soul against its left breast a little above the heart.

Instantly it became a young and beautiful woman, who was cold and frightened. She clad herself somehow with bundles of reeds, and went towards the lights of a house that stood close by. And she pushed open the door and entered, and found a farmer and a farmer's wife sitting over their supper.

And the farmer's wife took the little Wild Thing with the soul of the marshes up to her room, and clothed her and braided her hair, and brought her down again, and gave her the first food that she had ever eaten. Then the farmer's wife asked many questions.

"Where have you come from?" she said.

"Over the marshes."

"From what direction?" said the farmer's wife.

"South," said the little Wild Thing with the new soul.

"But none can come over the marshes from the south," said the farmer's wife.

"No, they can't do that," said the farmer.

"I lived in the marshes."

"Who are you?" asked the farmer's wife.

"I am a Wild Thing, and have found a soul in the marshes, and we are kin to the Elf-folk."

Talking it over afterwards, the farmer and his wife agreed that she must be a gipsy who had been lost, and that she was queer with hunger and exposure.

So that night the little Wild Thing slept in the farmer's house, but her new soul stayed awake the whole night long dreaming of the beauty of the marshes.

As soon as dawn came over the waste and shone on the farmer's house, she looked from the window towards the glittering waters, and saw the inner beauty of the marsh. For the Wild Things only love the marsh and know its haunts, but now she perceived the mystery of its distances and the glamor of its perilous pools, with their fair and deadly mosses, and felt the marvel of the North Wind who comes dominant out of unknown icy lands, and the wonder of that ebb and flow of life when the wildfowl whirl in at evening to the marshlands and at dawn pass out to sea. And she knew that over her head above the farmer's house stretched wide Paradise, where perhaps God was now imagining a sunrise while angels played low on lutes, and the sun came rising up on the world below to gladden fields and marsh.

And all that heaven thought, the marsh thought too; for the blue of the marsh was as the blue of heaven, and the great cloud shapes in heaven became the shapes in the marsh, and through each ran momentary rivers of purple, errant between banks of gold. And the stalwart army of reeds appeared out of the gloom with all their pennons waving as far as the eye could see. And from another window she saw the vast cathedral gathering its ponderous strength together, and lifting it up in towers out of the marshlands.

She said, "I will never, never leave the marsh."

An hour later she dressed with great difficulty and went down to eat the second meal of her life. The farmer and his wife were kindly folk, and taught her how to eat.

"I suppose the gipsies don't have knives and forks," one said to the other afterwards.

After breakfast the farmer went and saw the Dean, who lived near his cathedral, and presently returned and brought back to the Dean's house the little Wild Thing with the new soul.

"This is the lady," said the farmer. "This is Dean Murnith." Then he went away.

"Ah," said the Dean, "I understand you were lost the other night in the marshes. It was a terrible night to be lost in the marshes."

"I love the marshes," said the little Wild Thing with the new soul.

"Indeed! How old are you?" said the Dean.

"I don't know," she answered.

"You must know about how old you are," he said.

"Oh, about ninety," she said, "or more."

"Ninety years!" exclaimed the Dean.

"No, ninety centuries," she said; "I am as old as the marshes."

Then she told her story—how she had longed to be a human and go and worship God, and have a soul and see the beauty of the world, and how all the Wild Things had made her a soul of gossamer and mist and music and strange memories.

"But if this is true," said Dean Murnith, "this is very wrong. God cannot have intended you to have a soul.

"What is your name?"

"I have no name," she answered.

"We must find a Christian name and a surname for you. What would you like to be called?"

"Song of the Rushes," she said.

"That won't do at all," said the Dean.

"Then I would like to be called Terrible North Wind, or Star in the Waters," she said.

"No, no, no," said Dean Murnith; "that is quite impossible. We could call you Miss Rush if you like. How would Mary Rush do? Perhaps you had better have another name—say Mary Jane Rush."

So the little Wild Thing with the soul of the marshes took the names that were offered her, and became Mary Jane Rush.

"And we must find something for you to do," said Dean Murnith. "Meanwhile we can give you a room here."

"I don't want to do anything," replied Mary Jane; "I want to worship God in the cathedral and live beside the marshes."

Then Mrs. Murnith came in, and for the rest of that day Mary Jane stayed at the house of the Dean.

And there with her new soul she perceived the beauty of the world; for it came gray and level out of misty distances, and widened into grassy fields and ploughlands right up to the edge of an old gabled town; and solitary in the fields far off an ancient windmill stood, and his honest handmade sails went round and round in the free East Anglian winds. Close by, the gabled houses leaned out over the streets, planted fair upon sturdy timbers that grew in the olden time, all glorying among themselves upon their beauty. And out of them, buttress by buttress, growing and going upwards, aspiring tower by tower, rose the cathedral.

And she saw the people moving in the streets all leisurely and slow, and unseen among them, whispering to each other, unheard by living men and concerned only with bygone things, drifted the ghosts of very long ago. And wherever the streets ran eastwards, wherever were gaps in the houses, always there broke into view the sight of the great marshes, like to some bar of music weird and strange that haunts a melody, arising again and again, played on the violin by one musician only, who plays no other bar, and he is swart and lank about the hair and bearded about the lips, and his mustache droops long and low, and no one knows the land from which he comes.

All these were good things for a new soul to see.

Then the sun set over green fields and ploughland, and the night came up. One by one the merry lights of cheery lamp-lit windows took their stations in the solemn night.

Then the bells rang, far up in a cathedral tower, and their melody fell on the roofs of the old houses and poured over their eaves until the streets were full, and then flooded away over green fields and plough, till it came to the sturdy mill and brought the miller trudging to evensong, and far away eastwards and seawards the sound rang out over the remoter marshes. And it was all as yesterday to the old ghosts in the streets.

Then the Dean's wife took Mary Jane to evening service, and she saw three hundred candles filling all the aisle with light. But sturdy pillars stood there in unlit vastnesses; great colonnades going away into the gloom, where evening and morning, year in year out, they did their work in the dark, holding the cathedral roof aloft. And it was stiller than the marshes are still when the ice has come and the wind that brought it has fallen.

Suddenly into this stillness rushed the sound of the organ, roaring, and presently the people prayed and sang.

No longer could Mary Jane see their prayers ascending like thin gold chains, for that was but an elfin fancy, but she imagined clear in her new soul the seraphs passing in the ways of Paradise, and the angels changing guard to watch the World by night.

When the Dean had finished service, a young curate, Mr. Millings, went up into the pulpit.

He spoke of Abana and Pharpar, rivers of Damascus: and Mary Jane was glad that there were rivers having such names, and heard with wonder of Nineveh, that great city, and many things strange and new.

And the light of the candles shone on the curate's fair hair, and his voice went ringing down the aisle, and Mary Jane rejoiced that he was there.

But when his voice stopped she felt a sudden loneliness, such as she had not felt since the making of the marshes;

for the Wild Things never are lonely and never unhappy, but dance all night on the reflection of the stars, and, having no souls, desire nothing more.

After the collection was made, before any one moved to go, Mary Jane walked up the aisle to Mr. Millings.

"I love you," she said.

Nobody sympathized with Mary Jane.

"So unfortunate for Mr. Millings," every one said; "such a promising young man."

Mary Jane was sent away to a great manufacturing city of the Midlands, where work had been found for her in a cloth factory. And there was nothing in that town that was good for a soul to see. For it did not know that beauty was to be desired; so it made many things by machinery, and became hurried in all its ways, and boasted its superiority over other cities and became richer and richer, and there was none to pity it.

In this city Mary Jane had had lodgings found for her near the factory.

At six o'clock on those November mornings, about the time that, far away from the city, the wildfowl rose up out of the calm marshes and passed to the troubled spaces of the sea, at six o'clock the factory uttered a prolonged howl and gathered the workers together, and there they worked, saving two hours for food, the whole of the daylit hours and into the dark till the bells tolled six again.

There Mary Jane worked with other girls in a long dreary room, where giants sat pounding wool into a long thread-like strip with iron, rasping hands. And all day long they roared as they sat at their soulless work. But the work of Mary Jane was not with these, only their roar was ever in her ears as their clattering iron limbs went to and fro.

Her work was to tend a creature smaller, but infinitely more cunning.

It took the strip of wool that the giants had threshed, and whirled it round and round until it had twisted it into hard thin thread. Then it would make a clutch with fingers of steel at the thread that it had gathered, and waddle away about five yards and come back with more.

It had mastered all the subtlety of skilled workers, and had gradually displaced them; one thing only it could not do, it was unable to pick up the ends if a piece of the thread broke, in order to tie them together again. For this a human soul was required, and it was Mary Jane's business to pick up broken ends; and the moment she placed them together the busy soulless creature tied them for itself.

All here was ugly; even the green wool as it whirled round and round was neither the green of the grass nor yet the green of the rushes, but a sorry muddy green that befitted a sullen city under a murky sky.

When she looked out over the roofs of the town, there too was ugliness; and well the houses knew it, for with hideous stucco they aped in grotesque mimicry the pillars and temples of old Greece, pretending to one another to be that which they were not. And emerging from these houses and going in, and seeing the pretense of paint and stucco year after year until it all peeled away, the souls of the poor owners of those houses sought to be other souls until they grew weary of it.

At evening Mary Jane went back to her lodgings. Only then, after the dark had fallen, could the soul of Mary Jane perceive any beauty in that city, when the lamps were lit and here and there a star shone through the smoke. Then she would have gone abroad and beheld the night, but this the old woman to whom she was confided would not let her do. And the days multiplied themselves by seven and became weeks, and the weeks passed by, and all days were the same. And all the while the soul of Mary Jane was crying for beautiful things, and found not one, saving on Sundays, when she went to church, and left it to find the city grayer than before.

One day she decided that it was better to be a Wild Thing in the lovely marshes, than to have a soul that cried for beautiful things and found not one. From that day she determined to be rid of her soul, so she told her story to one of the factory girls, and said to her:

"The other girls are poorly clad and they do soulless work; surely some of them have no souls and would take mine."

But the factory girl said to her: "All the poor have souls. It is all they have."

Then Mary Jane watched the rich whenever she saw them, and vainly sought for some one without a soul.

One day at the hour when the machines rested and the human beings that tended them rested too, the wind being at that time from the direction of the marshlands, the soul of Mary Jane lamented bitterly. Then, as she stood outside the factory gates, the soul irresistibly compelled her to sing, and a wild song came from her lips, hymning the marshlands. And into her song came crying her yearning for home, and for the sound of the shout of the North Wind, masterful and proud, with his lovely lady the Snow; and she sang of tales that the rushes murmured to one another, tales that the teal knew and the watchful heron. And over the crowded streets her song went crying away, the song of waste places and of wild free lands, full of wonder and magic, for she had in her elf-made soul the song of the birds and the roar of the organ in the marshes.

At this moment Signor Thompsoni, the well-known English tenor, happened to go by with a friend. They stopped and listened; every one stopped and listened.

"There has been nothing like this in Europe in my time," said Signor Thompsoni.

So a change came into the life of Mary Jane.

People were written to, and finally it was arranged that she should take a leading part in the Covent Garden Opera in a few weeks.

So she went to London to learn.

London and singing lessons were better than the City of the Midlands and those terrible machines. Yet still Mary Jane was not free to go and live as she liked by the edge of the marshlands, and she was still determined to be rid of her soul, but could find no one that had not a soul of their own.

One day she was told that the English people would not listen to her as Miss Rush, and was asked what more suitable name she would like to be called by.

"I would like to be called Terrible North Wind," said Mary Jane, "or Song of the Rushes."

When she was told that this was impossible and Signorina Maria Russiano was suggested, she acquiesced at once, as she had acquiesced when they took her away from her curate; she knew nothing of the ways of humans.

At last the day of the Opera came round, and it was a cold day of the winter.

And Signorina Russiano appeared on the stage before a crowded house.

And Signorina Russiano sang.

And into the song went all the longing of her soul, the soul that could not go to Paradise, but could only worship God and know the meaning of music, and the longing pervaded that Italian song as the infinite mystery of the hills is borne along the sound of distant sheep-bells. Then in the souls that were in that crowded house arose little memories of a great while since that were quite quite dead, and lived awhile again during that marvelous song.

And a strange chill went into the blood of all that listened, as though they stood on the border of bleak marshes and the North Wind blew.

And some it moved to sorrow and some to regret, and some to an unearthly joy. Then suddenly the song went wailing away, like the winds of the winter from the marshlands when Spring appears from the South.

So it ended. And a great silence fell foglike over all that house, breaking in upon the end of a chatty conversation that a lady was enjoying with a friend.

In the dead hush Signorina Russiano rushed from the stage; she appeared again running among the audience, and dashed up to the lady.

"Take my soul," she said; "it is a beautiful soul. It can worship God, and knows the meaning of music and can imagine Paradise. And if you go to the marshlands with it you will see beautiful things; there is an old town there built of lovely timbers, with ghosts in its streets."

The lady stared. Every one was standing up. "See," said Signorina Russiano, "it is a beautiful soul."

And she clutched at her left breast a little above the heart, and there was the soul shining in her hand, with the green and blue lights going round and round and the purple flare in the midst.

"Take it," she said, "and you will love all that is beautiful, and know the four winds, each one by his name, and the songs of the birds at dawn. I do not want it, because I am not free. Put it to your left breast a little above the heart."

Still everybody was standing up, and the lady felt uncomfortable.

"Please offer it to some one else," she said.

"But they all have souls already," said Signorina Russiano.

And everybody went on standing up. And the lady took the soul in her hand.

"Perhaps it is lucky," she said.

She felt that she wanted to pray.

She half-closed her eyes, and said "Unberufen." Then she put the soul to her left breast a little above the heart, and hoped that the people would sit down and the singer go away.

Instantly a heap of clothes collapsed before her. For a moment, in the shadow among the seats, those who were born in the dusk hour might have seen a little brown thing leaping free from the clothes; then it sprang into the bright light of the hall, and became invisible to any human eye.

It dashed about for a little, then found the door, and presently was in the lamplit streets.

To those that were born in the dusk hour it might have been seen leaping rapidly wherever the streets ran northwards and eastwards, disappearing from human sight as it passed under the lamps, and appearing again beyond them with a marsh-light over its head.

Once a dog perceived it and gave chase, and was left far behind.

The cats of London, who are all born in the dusk hour, howled fearfully as it went by.

Presently it came to the meaner streets, where the houses are smaller. Then it went due northeastwards, leaping from roof to roof. And so in a few minutes it came to more open spaces, and then to the desolate lands, where market gardens grow, which are neither town nor country. Till at last the good black trees came into view, with their demoniac shapes in the night, and the grass was cold and wet, and the night-mist floated over it. And a great white owl came by, going up and down in the dark. And at all these things the little Wild Thing rejoiced elvishly.

And it left London far behind it, reddening the sky, and could distinguish no longer its unlovely roar, but heard again the noises of the night.

And now it would come through a hamlet glowing and comfortable in the night; and now to the dark, wet, open fields again; and many an owl it overtook as they drifted through the night, a people friendly to the Elf-folk. Sometimes it crossed wide rivers, leaping from star to star; and, choosing its way as it went, to avoid the hard rough roads, came before midnight to the East Anglian lands.

And it heard there the shout of the North Wind, who was dominant and angry, as he drove southwards his adventurous geese; while the rushes bent before him chaunting plaintively and low, like enslaved rowers of some fabulous trireme, bending and swinging under blows of the lash, and singing all the while a doleful song.

And it felt the good dank air that clothes by night the broad East Anglian lands, and came again to some old perilous pool where the soft green mosses grew, and there plunged downward and downward into the dear dark water, till it felt the homely ooze once more coming up between its toes. Thence, out of the lovely chill that is in the heart of the ooze, it arose renewed and rejoicing to dance upon the image of the stars.

I chanced to stand that night by the marsh's edge, forgetting in my mind the affairs of men; and I saw the marsh-fires come leaping up from all the perilous places. And they came up by flocks the whole night long to the number of a great multitude, and danced away together over the marshes.

And I believe that there was a great rejoicing all that night among the kith of the Elf-folk.

ST. JOHN ERVINE

# The Burial

\*

The funeral procession from the girl's home to the graveyard was due to begin at half-past two, but long before that
hour the crowd of mourners began to collect. They stood
about the entrance to the lane leading to the churchyard,
and waited. The home of the dead girl faced the lane, and
the procession, therefore, would reach its journey's end in a
few moments from the time when it began to move. Towns-
men and neighbours mingled with men from the country
and the hills, and fishermen from the bay where the girl was
drowned; and each man, as he came up to a group of his
acquaintances, spoke of the terribleness of the disaster, and
then the talk circled round the affairs of the small town.

John Mawhinney came along the old road to Ballyshannon,
and when he was by the lane he hailed James O'Hara.

"How're ye, James?" he said.

James O'Hara, a lean, foxy-looking man, turned at the
sound of Mawhinney's voice. "Och, I'm just middlin'," he
replied, "I've the quare cowl on me! How is yourself?"

"Ah, I'm not so bad. Man-a-dear, this is a tarr'ble sad thing
about this young girl!"

"Aye, it is that. Man, I mind her when she was that height,
the same wee girl!" He allowed his hand to fall to the level
of his knees as he spoke. "An' a smart wee girl she was, too!
Aye! She always had an answer for ye, whatever ye said,
she was that sharp!"

From Eight O'Clock and Other Studies, Dublin, Maunsel.

He looked up as he spoke, and saw John McClurg approaching. "Is that you, John?" he said.

McClurg, a large, moon-faced man, with little, smiling eyes, came puffing up to them.

"It is surely," he replied to O'Hara's greeting.

"I saw ye in the market the fair day," said Mawhinney, "but ye wurn't lukkin', an' ye didden see me. Did ye do well wi' yer cattle?"

"Ah, I didden do so bad. I might 'a' done better, an' I might 'a' done worse!"

"Did ye sell thon wee heifer ye had wi' ye?"

"I did not. I wudden take the price——"

O'Hara tapped him on the arm. "I s'pose ye come to the funer'l?" he said.

John McClurg glanced across the road to the door of the house where the dead girl lay. "Well," he said, "I thought I wud just dander into the town an' show me respect til the dead, God rest her sowl!" The three men raised their hats at his prayer. "What time does it begin?" he asked.

"They wur talkin' about half-after-two," replied Mawhinney, "but I'm thinkin' it'll be later'n that. Sure, the mail train's not in thrum Bilfast yet, an' there's fren's comin' thrum there an' thrum Derry, too, an' they'll be wantin' their denner when they git here. It'll be three o'clock afore iver they stir out o' the dure!"

"Aye, it will that," said James O'Hara, and then he turned and spoke to John McClurg. "Wur ye wantin' much for yer wee heifer?" he asked.

McClurg bit a piece of tobacco off a long twist of dark villainous stuff, and when he had chewed it in his mouth a while, he spat yellow juice over the kerb, and then said: "You might think I was wantin' too much, an' I might think meself I was wantin' too little!"

"I saw her meself," exclaimed Mawhinney, "afore she went intil the sea, laughin' an' jokin' like annythin'! Aw, God save us all thrum a death the like o' her death!"

"They wur a quare long time findin' her!"

"They wur."

"Wud ye be wantin' five poun's fur yer wee heifer, John McClurg?" said James O'Hara.

"I wud, indeed, an' a bit more on top of it!"

"They foun' her jus' where she went down," continued Mawhinney, in the voice of a man who is reciting an oft-told tale. "Man, it's quare the way the body returns like that!"

"Aye!"

"Who's thon man wi' the tall hat an' the long coat on him, d'ye know?" asked one that stood by of Mawhinney, as a man in a frock-coat knocked at the door.

"I nivir seen him afore," replied Mawhinney. "He's a stranger in this town, I'm thinkin'. D'ye know him, James?"

"I do not," replied O'Hara. "Mebbe he's come be the train. The mail's in now. Thonder's Patrick Magrath with the mail-cart comin' roun' the corner!"

"Ye're mebbe right!" Mawhinney resumed the recital of his tale. "Did ye see the piece in the Derry paper about her?" he said. "Thon was the quare bit. An' there was a piece of portry be the young wumman in the post affice!"

"Aye, I saw that. It was quare an' nice. I didden know thon wumman cud do the like o' that!"

"Ah, sure she's in Government sarvice, issen she? . . ."

"The paper said she was the quare, clivir, wee girl, an' tuk a lotta prizes at the school in Derry her da sent her to. They must 'a' spent a power o' money on her trainin'!"

"They did that. They nivir grudged her nathin'. It's a quare pity of them!"

"Aye, it only shows ye shudden make a god of yer child-her! . . ."

Two young men, one of whom carried a costly wreath in his hands, went up to the door, and presently were admitted to the house.

"Fur dear sake, luk at thon wreath!" exclaimed John Mawhinney. "Man, thon must 'a' cost somethin'!"

"Aye, it's thrum the young men at the Y.M.C.A. She was goin' to be married to one o' them. Did ye nivir hear about it?"

"Naw. What was his name?"

"I think it wus young McCracken!"

"What! Thon lad?"

"Aye. It'll be a cut-up for him, this! . . . John McClurg, will ye take six poun' ten for yer heifer?"

"Mebbe I wud if it was affered to me! . . ."

"There's manny a Cathlik would be willin' to give a wreath, too, I'm thinkin'!" said John Mawhinney.

"Aye, that's true enough. Sure, there's no room for bigitry where death is! . . . Wur ye thinkin' o' makin' me the affer, James?"

O'Hara walked a little way from the group, and then, squirting tobacco juice before him, returned to it. "Ah, I was just wondherin' if ye wud take it if it was affered t' ye. I wudden affer more'n five poun' for it meself! . . ."

"Ah, well, it wudden be no good you afferin' that amount. I wudden part wi' it fur the money!"

"There's a brave crowd here now," said O'Hara, turning towards the crowd. "It'll be a big procession, I'm thinkin'!"

"It will that. But I've seen bigger. There was the time Dr. Cochrane died. D'ye mind that? That was a procession an' a half!"

"Aye, it was indeed. Near a mile long that was! . . ."

The door of the house opened, and a number of persons entered.

"They'll be startin' soon," said Mawhinney.

"Ah, well, God help her, she'll soon be oura all this. It's the long sleep til the Day o' Judgement!"

"Ye're right there. Ye are indeed! . . ."

The door slowly re-opened, and men came forth bearing the yellow coffin on their shoulders. A great quietness descended upon the village street, and each man in it removed his hat and, if he were a Catholic, crossed himself and prayed for the repose of the dead girl's soul. Here and there a woman wrapped her shawl about her face and wept. The bearers carried the coffin across the street to the lane leading to the churchyard, and the people in the street fell in behind, and marched slowly towards the grave. A bell tolled softly, and in the house from which the body had just been borne a woman was heard crying and lamenting.

"I'll give ye six poun's fur yer wee heifer," said James O'Hara, as the body went by.

"Ah, God rest her sowl!" murmured McClurg, marking himself with the sign of the cross on the head and breast. "I cudden take less nor six poun' ten!"

"I cudden give more nor six poun'! . . ."

"Well, ye'll not get it fur the price. It's six poun' ten or nathin'!"

"Ye're the hard man to bargain wi'! . . ."

"I'm not hard at all! . . . Mebbe, they're better dead young nor dead oul'!"

"Will ye not budge yer price?"

"I will not!"

"They're in the graveyard now. . . . Come on down til Maloney's public-house, an' I'll sale the bargain wi' ye."

PADRAIC FALLON

# Something in a Boat

*

The Whittys lived in the Crook, a southerly niche of sun, the best farm, and the best dwelling house, in the Island. It was known as "Mary the Burrows," though Mary's husband, Jack Tom, was the legal owner, to whom Mary brought nothing as a dowry but a couple of stony fields on a hill-top where she had ground her strength like a razor in the three years of her first marriage.

Mary should have been happy. She had Jack Tom, a slow, strong, humorous man, who could warm a house on any kind of a night, and a son, John, who might have been spat out of his father's mouth. Yet, on the night of a station, when the priest was praising the place she had, the fine weather-slated house with its byres and piggeries and white dairies, and said that she must be a very happy woman, she looked at him in amazement, and then at Jack Tom, who knocked out his pipe on the hob and laughed at her.

"D'you know, Father," Jack Tom said, "the poor woman was born with a worm in her."

"A worm, Jack?"

"The worm of Care, Father. He gives her no rest. Night, noon and morning she finds something to worry her."

"I wouldn't think that of her, then."

"How would you, and that peaceful face on her? She's sitting there now forninst you, and you'd think her bit of knitting was all she had in her mind, but give her five

From CELTIC STORY, edited by Aled Vaughan, London, Pendulum.

minutes and she'll be wondering if the geese are hanging long
enough to be tender for your dinner tomorrow and she'll be
out to the dairy to pinch them, or she'll be upstairs to see
if your bed is all right, or she'll be out in the valley-field to
see if the sheep haven't picked a way into the oats . . ."

And Mary smiled while they all laughed at her. But five
minutes later she had left her knitting on the chair and disappeared.

That was the way with her. She gave herself to the life
around her like a mother does. Her nerves went out delicately into the weather and the fields. She went up and down
with the mercury. For husband and son and farm she had a
sixth sense. She never intruded on them. She drew them together instead, as if they had to pass through her mind to
become real to themselves. She knew what they wanted before they did, and when son and husband were alone with
her at night before they went to bed, she watched them out
of her dark eyes without seeming to watch, speaking very
little herself, just looking up from her knitting now and then
as if to make sure that they lived outside of her as well as
inside her.

It didn't take her long to feel the new restlessness that
came over her son. She didn't speak of it until she saw there
was no sign of it leaving him. And even then she waited,
denying its existence to herself until Jack Tom opened the
subject himself one night at the fire when John came in late.

"I suppose you were over in Murtagh's, Johnny."

"I was not."

"Or in Glynn's?"

"No. Why would I be?"

Jack Tom put a spit neatly into the fire. "Well, isn't it
time you put a rope on some good girl? Time you made your
mother a grandmother?"

Mary looked up, startled, to find her husband's slow wink
waiting for her. Her eyes went to John, but he was filling his
pipe and showing no sign of confusion.

"She'll have to wait a while longer, then," he said. "For
it's on me mind to see a bit of the world first. I suppose you'll

be able to manage without me for a month. I want to have a look at the city. Dear God, it's staring me in the face every day from the other side of the bay since I was a foot high, and would you believe it's not until a month ago that I began to wonder what kind of a world at all was behind the two drowned steeples we see from the Hill."

He lit his pipe from a red turf. Jack Tom smoked on comfortably. But Mary's knitting lay idle in her lap. John went on, warming up. "I counted six steamers yesterday going up the bay, and eight coming out. There must be a great stir in a city like that, and I'm ashamed of me life I haven't put a foot there yet to see what it's like."

"You're no different from another, then," Mary put in quickly, too quickly. "It's few people from the Island ever see the city. And those that do are no better off for it."

He didn't answer her directly. Jack Tom said, "It does nobody any harm to know the world." And Mary glanced at him bleakly.

"What good'll it do him, either?"

John said nothing for a while. He puffed away at his pipe as if he hadn't heard her. She waited for him, her knitting still idle on her lap, but his eyes were on the fire. Outside, the sea was sounding as the ebb turned against the breeze. There would be a faint haze of light over the waters where the city stood.

"I'm thinking you spent your evening on the hill," she prodded. "You could find better things to do than be watching a couple of lamps across the bay. What would you do in the city for a whole month?"

He turned to her. "That's what I was wondering tonight. And I think it best that I go and see. I'll set off on Monday. The hay is up, and the turnips thinned, and I think ye can do without me for a while."

He went off on Monday morning before the sun. She made him his breakfast, still stiff with opposition. But before he went out the door, she blest him three times with holy water, and gave him a hard peck of a kiss. And when he had gone, she went up the hill where she could watch him walk the only road out of the island. She saw the smoke rising from the chimney of her house, and from other chimneys, and the sun stir and strike on the grey morning like a match; she saw the day waken round her in a way that was both sudden and slow, bringing people out of their houses, and cattle out of the fields, and when he had disappeared into the rocks of the cause-way, she came down only half-thinking of all the daily chores she had before her.

Jack Tom was puffing his first pipe at the gate. "You saw him off?" His face was kindly, but untroubled. She stood before him stiffly.

"If you had spoken one word he'd have put his nonsense away from him and stayed at home."

"God be good to you, woman," he said. "It's not to America he's going. Every young thing has its hour of play."

"It's no play to leave him go into a strange city."

"Wisha! Is it a babby in a box you want to make of him? Milk the cows, woman, and don't be always setting fire to yourself!"

He eyed her for a minute, his eyes soft, and a little shy. "He's a good boy," he said, "and we should thank God for him."

II

It was a month before he came back. She was the first to see him. She was coming in from the yard with two cans of milk, when the calves, nosing the bar off the gate, made a rush for her. She had time to step through the outer gate, and bang it shut, before they caught up on her; but then she had to go right round the house and in through the front door. She was turning the gable when she caught sight of him. She waited just as she was, the cans in her hands. He whistled, and hurried his stride, his face flushing as he came up to her. She didn't know what to say to him when he took the cans out of her hands and kissed her.

He was bubbling over with things to tell. He'd had a great

time of it. She sliced bacon for him and fried it with eggs, and all the time he talked of things he had seen and people he had met, she watching him and making him eat, rather than listening. She didn't want to hear, she was satisfied to look at him.

It was an hour later when she thought of the calves roaming the yard, and the byre door opening a way for them into the cows. By that time, three or four neighbouring men had turned up for an evening's conversation, so she went out herself to turn the calves into the haggard and lead out the cows. When she returned, the kitchen was full of neighbours and full of talk. She lit the lamp, and took her knitting to the hob, her face peaceful again. Now and again, she would throw a secret eye on her son, smiling mechanically when he laughed or when somebody else laughed, or she put a friendly question to some of the neighbours, just to make him feel welcome. No one had ever seen her so pleasant.

The whole atmosphere of the house, indeed, altered from that evening. The neighbours began to make a habit of dropping in for a talk, and she recovered the habit of listening that she had lost with her first marriage when she lived back in the hill. She became anxious to put people at their ease with her, so she rose sufficiently above her own pre-occupations to take some part in the slow saga of the neighbourhood that unwound itself out of the talk around her every night. Names came up out of the past, and she might remember them in her father's mouth, and think back to this event or that, nodding her head, sometimes, even, giving her version of it in her calm slow voice. Men began to like her a little, even to poke a joke at her now and then in Jack Tom's fashion. She would smile at them quietly and go on with her knitting, accepting the fact that it was John and Jack Tom who were at the centre of things and not herself, but very glad that the Island was building itself in talk all around her son. He would find it hard to break a net of that kind, hard to break away from a warm, friendly nest where he had his place. So she welcomed the men who cluttered up her floor; and dredged in her mind

for her share of memories. She would light the lamp, and
watch her dresser light up with delph and the cover-dishes
sparkle on the walls, and take her knitting again to the hob,
smiling gently out of her great reserve at the unshaven faces
round her, at the talkers and their talk, and the great rings and
clouds of pipe-smoke that made blue haloes over each head.
She wanted the Island to get such a grip on her son that he
would never dream of leaving it.

The Island, actually, was not an island at all, but a
peninsula that sprang out of the land at the entrance to the
bay, and after a couple of miles became as narrow as a jetty,
and then blew itself out like green glass into a fertile globe of
grass and tillage. Visitors were few. They stayed at the little
fishing port on the mainland that was also the market-town for
the Island; few faced the rough ten-mile road to the scattered
village, fewer still the great ugly rip of water to the little jetty.
So Mary was surprised one evening when a hatless, young
fellow faced her on her threshold, and blessing the house in
good Irish, asked for her son. She put him sitting down immediately, and filled him a mug of milk, and then began
cautiously to question him. He was talkative and gay, but
insisted on speaking to her in the Irish she had all but forgotten. She could make nothing out of him except that he had
met John in the city, and had spent many evenings with him,
and had now come to see him. He had sailed out from the
city. He laughed.

"John told me I wouldn't learn to sail a boat in a twelve-
month. Where's the big-mouth at all, Ma'am, until I take him
by the scruff of the neck and tug him to the jetty. I'll stuff
every word he said to me down his throttle."

His humorous violence drew a polite smile from her. But
her face changed when she saw the cockle-shell with the
too-tall mast he had moored to the little wall below.

"It's no boat for open water, I'm thinking," she said, "and
you all alone in it."

"Ah, sure, that's the sport of it, Ma'am. Danger is the goad
in things—"

He stopped abruptly before the look that came over her face. But she said nothing. She had it in mind to fling at him an old Gaelic proverb about the fool and the sea, but she closed her mouth, partly because of island courtesy, partly because the proverb itself touched too closely on memories of her own. She had heard an old man hurl it through his beard the night they brought her father home in an old sail, and she had heard it many times since, when young men, rotten with death and salt water, were laid down in the old graveyard near the Lighthouse.

"A boy can find death easily enough," she said, "without looking that hard for it. I'm thinking you're maybe a bit of a trial to your mother."

His face was masked for a moment. Then, he shrugged. "Maybe I am," he replied. "But a man must live his own life after all, not that of an old woman." He broke into a smile once more. "Only God's apron-strings are long enough for me." His hands went out in a magnificent gesture and his eyes lit. "God in Heaven, woman, what is a man to do but to burst out of himself into the great, wide world. Look at it! It's like a door always open, waiting for you to do something—to—to—I declare to God, I'm on the old hobby-horse again, and you must be thinking I'm mad. Tell me where John is, Ma'am, and I'll take meself after him!"

She was pondering him as she led him into the fields, too courteous to give him a hint of how he had affected her. Only once on the way, as they turned the hill and met the full vista of sea and far mountain together, did she lose her faint, hospitable smile. The boy had stopped suddenly, filled to the eyes with the summer day. "This is the grandest place in the whole world," he muttered. "Look at that sea!"

Then she spoke in spite of herself. "Those that get their living out of it," she said, "have looked their enough at it. Ah, *A Bhuachaill*, let those bargain with it who have to, for when it breaks a bargain there's no court will serve a summons on it."

She was surprised at the way John received the young man.

In his surprise, he almost folded him in his arms. His eyes shone. Then, the conventions of the Island took him, and he grew still and courteous after the Island fashion. She could see he was very happy. She left them unobtrusively, and hurried home to get a bed ready.

For the ten days the Stranger lived in her house, he never knew he was to her, still, *THE STRANGER*. He never guessed that she disliked him, or, more accurately, feared him, she was so quietly elaborate in the ways she tended his comfort, so suavely hospitable in obedience to the island code. He impressed her more than she wished. Outside, in the fields, where he lent a helping hand with the oats, he was not nearly the equal of Jack Tom or John, or any other man on the Island, but indoors, by the fire, when the neighbours foregathered after darkfall, his keen mind went leaping about like a swordsman. He danced through the histories of things and ripped them wide open. He gave them book-facts, and annotated their private sagas. He put things back in a schedule of time, and hung events up before them in colored calendars. They became alive to their background. He gave them word-for-word accounts of famous Fenian trials, and quoted long speeches that Irishmen had made before packed Juries. Then he moved into modern days, and told them of the new movement towards liberation that was beginning to stir all over the country. He made them conscious of Ireland in a new way, of a struggle that was not over, but beginning; he roused them into an awareness of things outside their immediate lives. Before he left, nearly every young man on the Island wanted to join the Volunteers. But he wouldn't have it. He told them to think it over for a couple of months, and John could come and see him about it.

He went off in his little boat, after a breath-taking jibe at the end of the jetty that made every island man there wince and roar instructions at him. In reply, he ran up a little flag that they hadn't seen until then. It was a Tricolour, Green, and White, and Gold, and the tiny craft bobbed away with it over the southerly swell with a nice breeze on her port quarter.

III

But when he had gone, Mary found he had left himself, or plenty of himself, behind. The Island seemed to remember it was not really an island at all but a part of the mainland where things were happening or about to happen. The young men started to gather on the hill of an evening, feeling that on a thousand other hills throughout Ireland, young men were gathering, too. They began to learn the rudiments of drill, and John spent hours under the lamp pondering a little book. Sometimes, forty or fifty young lads in fours would swing around her gable. Sometimes, she would see them creeping on their bellies through the fields. Sometimes, she would hear shouted words of command out in the dark, and know John's voice. And she didn't like it. But she never said anything. It was only a new kind of a play, she told herself, that was all. And Jack Tom laughed. "The Island," he said, with a spit, "is only a babby-house nowadays."

"Will it bring the police after them?" she queried.

"Sure, all Ireland is drilling, Woman, and they'll stop it there first if they're going to stop it at all."

That eased her for a while. Then, John started to bring home a weekly paper, and the reading disturbed her afresh. Big battles in Europe, English victories, German victories, the Russian Steamroller. It brought things to her door, and when she heard the drilling still go on in the loud winter evenings, with plover and oyster-catcher piping above the strand, she had moments of blind terror. The newspaper counted the dead in paper figures that meant nothing to her, but when John shouted *HALT!* and *GROUND ARMS!* on the hill, she had wit enough to sense that there was a point where drilling turned into war and death. So, one night, she forced herself to speak to him.

"I don't like that newspaper coming into the house, John."

"And why not, Mother?"

"It's too full of a troubled world. We're safe from the big

war here," she went on significantly, "that is, if we stay quiet."
And she repeated, to get her hint clear, "If we stay quiet."

He was unlacing his boots, his pipe going. "I suppose you
don't like me to be drilling? Is that it?"

"Drilling is only the beginning," she said. "The beginning
of war. And what war would we be fighting in the Island
here? Aren't we as well off as we want to be?"

His words came slowly. "While the English hold us," he
said, "we're not men except we fight to put them out."

"I don't see any English on the Island, John."

"They're in Ireland, Mother, and what are we, only a part
of Ireland. We're as good a people as they are. There's no reason why we should let them rule us."

Her knitting lay idle on her lap. Her eyes were unhappy
and grave as she searched for the words that would convince
him. "England is too strong for you to beat," she said at last.
"You'll only be one of those men that die in gaol or at the end
of the hangman's rope. Will you give up the drill for my sake?
I can ask that, for it's well I earned you in bringing you into
the world."

He pondered for a bit, his open face showing that he was
giving her more than a courteous consideration. Then he
shook his head. "I can't, Mother. I'd be ashamed before myself if I didn't do what was laid on me to do."

They were silent for a while, and the silence embarrassed
both of them. A cockerel gave a choked and sleepy crow in the
hen-house outside, the room filled with the heavy thunder of
the sea. Inside, in the west room, Jack Tom knocked the
dottle out of his last pipe and drawled, "If ye've settled the
world now between ye, maybe ye'd go to bed and let me
settle meself." Mary stood up. " 'Tis time we did go to bed,"
she said. She started to cover the fire with ash, so as to preserve the red seed until the morning, but before she had
finished it, she was speaking once more. "I'll have to talk to
The Stranger about you," she said. "He led you into this
thing, and I'll see that he leads you out again. He'll be out on
Sunday, won't he?"

He rose and knocked out his pipe. "He'll be out, indeed,"

he answered. "But you'll only waste your breath. I'm a full-grown man, and I'm not going back to babby-clothes for anybody."

He turned from her and went into his room.

IV

She got no chance to speak to The Stranger, for on Sunday, instead of breezing in, with half the young men of the Island at his heels, he was making his way by bicycle through the suburbs of Dublin, and on Monday he was in the General Post Office with a rifle on his shoulder, on Friday a bullet shattered the same shoulder, and on the following Monday, he found himself in a prison hospital, and three months later in a prison camp in England. It was, as a matter of fact, exactly two years later when he turned up, and then she said nothing to him beyond the traditional words of welcome and the traditional enquiry after his family. He stayed for three months that time. He had three stiff fingers, but he earned his keep in the fields, working with Jack Tom and John until dewfall. John and himself would disappear then. Sometimes they came home from the sea with a string of codling or bass, John laughing, the other full of humorous complaint.

"Mother in Heaven!" John might say. "A sailor needs no flag to tell him where the wind is. What's the skin on his face for, Man? Can't he feel it there, or if it's aft of him, on the back of his neck?"

And The Stranger would turn a wry and laughing face to Mary. "I jibed her again, Ma'am. We nearly had to swim for it."

Her heart missed a beat. "John can't swim," she said.

"Then we'd have a great time drowning each other."

"Why don't you give it up, Salmon?" John would laugh. "You have a good future as a farm labourer, now that they've taken the school off you, but in a boat, man, you've no future at all, for you're a natural born suicide." And John, now that The Stranger was a stranger no longer, would go off into a fit of laughter at his own wit.

Often, Mary was tempted to ask them where they spent the other evenings, the evenings when they came home late and missed the Rosary that was said in the kitchen every night. She didn't. She daren't force an open break on this new John of hers who went his own way so calmly. He was so complete in himself. He was the same as ever to her, but he had dropped something like a space between them. It was as if he had moved out of her mind into his own. She watched him all the time, and weighed him in her dark, still eyes, their nerves touching in the tension that was between them, and decided to do nothing for a while. After all, the defeat of Easter Week and the years in prison must surely have taught The Stranger some sense. And there was no drilling. She was certain of that.

Then, one day, a week after The Stranger had left for the city in his little boat, two big police constables in bottle-green uniform came into the kitchen on top of her, ostensibly to take particulars of the year's tillage, in reality, as she was to learn in a minute or two, on a more dubious business. One of them sat at the table and took out his bundle of forms, the other carted his bulk to the sugawn chair on the hearth, and pushing the regulation baton askew, ensconced himself comfortably therein. Both took off their caps, and both accepted with dignity the big mugs of buttermilk she proffered them, for the sun was a dead gold over the earth and the land sweated dust.

" 'Tis a grand dwelling you have here, Ma'am," the pompous man on the sugawn said after a bit, when the buttermilk had watered him down.

" 'Tis a modest good holding, sir," she answered, pleased in spite of herself. "But we're good contrivers and we manage, thanks be to God."

"Is there many in the family, Ma'am?"

"I have one son, sir, but he's as good as two. And a husband that's not far behind in spite of the years that are on him."

" 'Tis a great thing to have a good son. A great thing, indeed."

The other constable had his pencil poised. He rubbed a spit on it, and asked her how many acres of potatoes, and how many acres of oats she had, and her full name, and her husband's full name. While he was writing it all down slowly, the pompous one loosened his collar and took his ease.

"It's a great blessing, indeed," he said, "to have a good son about the house, and a credit to any woman in those times if she's able to keep him good. The great thing, I say, is to keep an eye on him, and to direct him. There's an old saying that says, *as the twig is bent, so does the grown tree incline*. There's a power of wisdom in that, mind you, a power of wisdom. What are the boy's predilections, Ma'am?"

"His what, sir?"

"What does he incline for, Ma'am?"

"I don't know, sir, except for hard work and maybe a rabbit hunt of a Sunday."

"Hah! Sound and solid predilections, indeed, Ma'am. I remember meself, before I joined the Force, and the way I took me pleasure of a Sunday in a likewise manner. Keep him to that, Ma'am, and he's safe from trouble, safe from the law. But it's only wisdom to keep your eye on him, for those are bad times. You never know but he might fall in with one of those codgers who're walking the land secretly, fomenting civil war and making fools of decent boys with their claptrap about Irish Freedom. And we never as free as we are this day, masters of our farms for a rent that's only a tithe of what we had to pay one time. Thim boyos should have known the days that are gone, days that you might remember, Ma'am, when there was a rent on your back like a load of stones. Who freed us of that but England? In open Parliament she did it. Isn't that true, Ma'am?"

"It might be," she replied. "Though it's a different story the way I heard it. If ye'd like a cup of tea, now, I'd take pleasure in putting on the kettle for ye. It's no trouble."

"It's no day for tea," the pompous one said. "But I was ever and always a martyr to a good cup of tea."

She made tea for the two Peelers, while they tried to draw

her out cunningly. They were unsuccessful, and in the end, the pompous fellow came to the point suddenly.

"I hear you had a queer fellow staying with you lately, Ma'am."

"We had a boy working," she admitted.

"A buck from the city, eh? An organizer of devilment."

"If he's that," she asked, "why isn't he in gaol?"

"There may be reasons, Ma'am, state reasons for that."

"Are ye looking for him?"

"We might be, Ma'am. And we might not. Is he here now?"

"He is not, not since last Sunday."

"Hum. That agrees with our own information. Do you know his new habitation, Ma'am?"

"I do not."

The constables stood up, and the kitchen seemed to fill with them, and overflow out of doors. They put on their caps, and stooped through the door into the sunlight. They had bicycles, she saw.

"Well, welll" the pompous one grunted. "We'll be saying good-day to ye. And maybe I should be leaving you a little bit of advice, for you're a decent woman. Keep that fly-by-night out of your house and away from your son, or it's a nice sting he'll leave in you."

When they took themselves off into the still sunshine, they left a very frightened woman behind them. She forgot their stupidity, and remembered only the gross cunning with which they had filled her kitchen. Behind those big uniforms, like a threat, loomed a history of death and gaol-house, and now it had come suddenly alive before her, actively malignant in the privacy of her own dwelling. She sat down for a long time, savoring shadows; then, she gathered herself and went about her work, a little tighter in the face, a little quicker and more definite in her movements.

When she stirred out for the cows, a black steamer was moving up the sound, riding down its own smoke. Wind south-east, she decided automatically, and enough of it. A beam wind from the city. She was thinking of The Stranger again. The Island had nick-named him the Salmon, because that was the name of his little boat, but he would be The Stranger to her always, the bolt from the blue, the evil chance inside the *pishoge*. And as if he were answering her thought, his little boat came round from under the steamer's quarters, riding her wake perilously, the wind rocked and knocked out of its small sails. Her heart stopped for a moment before the boy's danger and her own native horror of the sea. Then, as a lucky puff took him due aft and he squared away before it with a filled mainsail, she thought to herself that it would have been an easy way out for herself and her son had he taken the sea over the side and gone under. And the thought went with her as she rounded up the cows, and went to seek her son. And even before she met him, it had ceased to shock her.

"He's not to come into the house," she told John. "The Police are looking for him."

He answered her calmly. "They're looking a long time for him. Now that they've had a look here, they won't come again for a while. It'll be safe enough to give him a bed."

She looked at him with terrible eyes, her mouth as grim as granite. "If he puts a foot in my house," she said, "I'll inform the police."

"You'll do as you wish," he answered, his face going grim, too. "There'll be enough houses in the Island to welcome him."

That night, John was late home, without The Stranger. In the morning she asked him where The Stranger was. He wouldn't answer her.

The police came back a week later, this time in force, and with rifles on their backs. They searched her house and the outhouses, and three or four other houses in the neighbourhood, and they took John away with them. In the two days that he was gone she suffered agonies. She was standing at the door when he returned, but instead of meeting him as she wanted to, with her arms wide and her mouth stiff, she sat down by the fire and turned her head away from him. He knew the way it was with her, however, and turned her face round for his kiss. She kept her mask on, though her eyes startled him with their wild brilliance.

That night she said to him, "You'll have to give up all this folly, John. I'm not able for it."

It was the first confession of personal weakness she had ever made. He looked at her sadly, pushing the cap back on his skull till the lamplight caught the peak and made it a halo over him. "I know, Mother," he said awkwardly. "I know. There'll be more of it, too. A lot more, I'm thinking. And there's nothing I can do about it."

He pushed back his chair at that, and went to bed.

v

From that out, she found herself watching the Sound for the little sail-boat. Sometimes, she did see it; more often, she guessed from John's behavior that it had arrived. It sailed no longer from the city, but from one of the many creeks within the bay, so she formed the habit of walking towards the jetty of an evening to look for it before she settled in for the night. She didn't think of The Stranger as a person any more. He was only some odd kind of force that had struck into her life. His face was rubbed out of her consciousness. Sometimes, he had a man's form in her mind, more often he was just a sail, a boat that came and went with evil purpose. She thought of him no longer as someone she had fed and cared for under her roof. She found it difficult to think that she had ever known him at all. And, maybe, that is why she was able, in the end, to do what she did.

For one night, when the little craft was drawn up on the slipway out of the flood, she moved down to it with a couple of obscure tools, some tarred paper, and a handful of corks. She wasn't more than a half-hour doing whatever she did do, but when that was done, the boat was just sufficiently sea-worthy to be a deathtrap.

She said the Rosary as usual with Jack Tom, but she didn't go to bed. She sat on the hob with her knitting, listening to the breeze come stronger from the south-west, feeling with her nerves how the tide was dropping back against the wind and the way the sea was turning outside the shelter of the

land. It might be happening, all of it, inside her, for she spread
out over the night until the sea was breaking in her and birds
wading on her strands. Three swans flew low over the house,
and their wings plucked music out of her as they passed
through her breast. And then she fell asleep.

She awoke, shocked. Something had happened within her
that she couldn't bring to consciousness. She had to ponder
for a minute before she could remember where she was or
why she was there. The old chains of the clock on the wall
were the first to catch her eye. And then, the clockface. And
then, the hour.

She knew then. Knew everything.

Yet, she didn't scream, or make a sound that would waken
Jack Tom out of his sleep in the room within. She stood up
slowly, as if she were balancing a basket on her head, looked
into John's empty room, then made for the door, and out.
There she began to run. Little splutters of rain soused her
face, a wet star was burning low-down in the south-east. The
glimmering outlines of things rose before her. She ran and
ran.

And all the time she knew what she would find. And still
she hurried, turning into one great prayer that soared from
the earth towards heaven; she flowed up, dissolving like a
fountain, gasping. And she came to the jetty.

The boat was gone.

In the first house, they told her what she knew already.
Yes, John had gone with the Salmon, seeing the sea was a bit
too much for a bad sailor like him. They couldn't understand
why she took on, why she went rambling out towards the
shore, keening like a tramp-woman, till the dogs were out for
miles around the village. Still, being Island people, the women
stirred up their fires, and the men got out of bed and put
their clothes on and laced their boots. It wouldn't be the first
time a mother had dreamed of her son's death on the sea, and
more often than not the dream had proved a reality.

So, they were waiting on the hill when the dawn came up
on the horizon like the grey back of a whale. But, they saw

nothing. And they found nothing. Not even Mary the Burrows found anything, though she stood on the hill and walked the strands for three years afterwards, until she died.

And, maybe, 'twas as well.

ARNOLD HILL

# Miss Gillespie and the Micks

✳

We called her old Miss Gillespie, although I do not suppose she was more than forty-five or fifty. She was a big stout woman with rosy cheeks and red hair and an enormous bosom. She always seemed to wear far too many clothes and always appeared to be very warm and out of breath. She had practised midwifery until her fondness for drink caused people to lose faith in her. They pitied her, but would not have her attend them in childbirth. Still the brass plate remained on the doorframe of her house: Miss Gillespie, Certified Midwife.

She lived with her brother, a retired sea-captain, in a little house on the outskirts of the village. Her brother was a short, stocky man with a red face and a sailor's roll. He was very quiet and spent most of his time working about the garden, but occasionally he would come down to Johnston's pub and sit in a corner drinking beer and telling yarns about his sea-faring days. He had served his apprenticeship under sail, and always spoke with contempt of the steamship, maintaining that any landlubber could be a sailor nowadays. "It was a sad day," he used to say, "the day they traded a clean spread of canvas for a splutterin', stinkin' donkey-engine."

Our favorite prank used to be letting down the back tire of her bicycle. She always cycled down to Johnston's on Saturday night and left the bicycle outside while she got drunk in the bar parlour. It was a strange thing, but she always seemed to ride much better when she came out of Johnston's. At other

From *The Bell*.

times her method of riding was slow and wobbly and uncertain, as if she were on a bicycle for the first time. But on leaving the pub on Saturday nights she would heave her huge body on to the saddle and go pedalling furiously up the narrow street, weaving in and out among carts and dogs and herds of cattle, narrowly missing other cyclists and shouting at anyone who got in the way.

If, however, we had previously removed the valve from the back tire, she would pull up before she had gone more than a few yards, hop clumsily off the saddle and begin to shout at the top of her voice, standing in the middle of the street with one foot on the ground and the other supported on the pedal. The anger and the shouting made her very red in the face, and we who crouched giggling in some nearby doorway could almost have sworn that her hair became redder, too.

Some of the men who always stood about Johnston's would come over to her and ask her what was the trouble. "Och, it's them children again," she would shout. "Sure they'd break a body's heart. They haven't left me what air in me back tire would blow out a candle. Bad cess to them! Of all the meddlin', interferin' wee brats that ever were let into this world, them in this place takes the cake! I'll put the polis on them. Declare to God I will; I'll put the polis on them and have them banished from the country. A pack of common thieves and rogues and liars, that's what they are. A decent, respectable body doesn't get a chance with the likes of them around, so they don't."

Then she would begin to cry and would have to be taken back into Johnston's for consolation while someone repaired her flattened tire.

Half an hour later they would bring her out, blear-eyed and breathing heavily through her nose, help her on her bicycle and send up a ragged cheer as she shot off up the street, stiff and solid as a rock, her mouth grim with determination.

Never slackening her pace for a moment, she would push up the hill, past the post-office and the Orange Hall, round the corner and along the straight, wide road to the church. Turning to the right, where the houses of the village began to thin out and to be separated by little plots and patches of meadow, she would come to the home of the O'Hagans, sitting back from the roadway, with dirty children playing around the door, the washing on the hedge and peat-smoke filtering from the slanting chimney.

Invariably, she would ride past the house, looking neither right nor left; then, as though some thought had suddenly occurred to her, she would pull up, leaning to one side and gripping savagely at the inefficient brake, and slowly circle round in the roadway.

The O'Hagans were the largest, and perhaps the poorest, family in the district. The father was a tall, quiet man, who seemed to spend all his time working with a few chickens and a meagre plot behind the house. He was very shy, and was rarely seen in the village. The mother was a little harassed, anxious woman, who only appeared outside the house to draw water from the nearby pump or hang huge quantities of washing on the hedge. They had seven children, the eldest of whom could not have been more than ten years old at that time. They were a very devout couple, and I think now it may have been this very quality of devoutness and passive acceptance of life's hardships that inflamed Miss Gillespie against them.

Pedalling back to the O'Hagans' place, she would hop to the ground and stand astride her bicycle, one foot on the road, the other on the pedal. "Hi, there!" she would call to the children. "Away in and tell yer da I want a word with him. A lot of words! Tell him to come on out here till I give him his character. Go on, ye wee Fenian brats!"

At this the children would run into the house and close the door, and Miss Gillespie's fury would increase. "Are ye never away yet, O'Hagan? Take you and your snivellin' wife and your brood of whelps and brats and away you go—over the Border where ye belong. Away with the lot of ye—you've contaminated the landscape long enough, God knows. Away back to yer chapels and yer Popery and leave honest Christian

folk to live in peace. This is a civilized, Protestant country—
we want none of your kind here."

She would keep this up for perhaps ten minutes, until
hoarseness and shortage of breath forced her to cease. There
was never any attempt made to stop her. Passers-by only
laughed and teased her into stronger invective. The house
presented a blank face to her abuse. We youngsters, crouching behind the hedge, whistled and jeered and threw pieces of
clay and dried cowdung at her, but so intense was her absorption in the O'Hagans that she seemed not to notice anything
else. When it was over she would remount her bicycle and,
still muttering threats and imprecations, ride off up the road
toward her own house. Shortly afterwards, the O'Hagans'
front door would open and the children would come out to
resume their playing, as if nothing had happened.

Some of the older people tried from time to time to break
her of this habit (as they also tried to stop her from drinking).
Their intentions were good, but their efforts were in vain.
Miss Gillespie would not listen to reason. Her personal pride
and integrity were as strong as her powers of hatred. She
refused to accept instructions from anyone on how to conduct
her life. Even the frequent appeals of the local Methodist
minister were without effect. "What business is it of yours,
how I behave myself?" she said to him once. "You go on
preachin' your wee sermons on Sundays and leave us stipend-
payers to look after our own lives. What do you care, as long
as the money keeps comin' in? Away and convert them
heathen O'Hagans and let us good Christian folks alone!"

One week early in Spring there was very heavy snow, and
two or three other boys and I went to the door and asked Captain Gillespie if we could clean his path, hoping to earn a
few coppers. We didn't get the money, but when we had done
he invited us into the house for tea. It was a tidy little house,
full of bits of ship's gear and bottled schooners. This was
Captain Gillespie's hobby, and he explained the delicate
process by which the apparently impossible feat of getting a
four-masted ship through the narrow neck of a bottle is ac-
complished.

Miss Gillespie, who presided at the tea-table, appeared to be in a very irritable mood. Evidently she was annoyed with her brother for having invited us in. She had been baking in the afternoon, and we had big warm farls of soda-bread, oozing with melted butter, and tea which could have supported the original of any of the captain's models. She herself ate and drank little, and, when she had finished, sat glaring and grunting at us while Captain Gillespie recounted one of his interminable tales of adventure in a clipper off Cape Horn.

While we were sitting there, a timid knock was heard at the front door. The captain rose to answer it. We could hear a young, eager voice, and the captain's deep rumbling replies.

Suddenly she looked at the door and shouted, making us jump.

"Who is it, Albert?"

The door opened and her brother came in, closing it after him. He looked rather uncomfortable.

"Er—it's one of the O'Hagan children. He says his father sent him to ask if you'd come down there right away." He coughed nervously. "Mrs. O'Hagan's going to have a baby. They—can't get the doctor. The road's snowed up."

He stood there waiting, watching her from under his frowning, bushy eyebrows.

At first Miss Gillespie was unable to speak. Only her reddening face registered her rising anger. Then she said:

"Well, of all the impertinence! Of all the unbelievable impertinence! The likes of *them*, daring to send for me."

"I think you'd better go, Bertha," said her brother. "The woman must be pretty ill."

"Go? Here, go out and tell that brat to go home and tell his da I wouldn't lift a finger to help them, not if they were havin' triplets! The idea of it!" She was shaking like a jelly. Big tears began to roll down her cheeks. "The very idea— them sendin' to *me* for help. Well, don't stand there with yer mouth open. Go and tell him what I said. Chase him out of here before I go out and beat the lugs off him!"

He shrugged his shoulders and went back to the waiting boy. Miss Gillespie seemed to have forgotten our existence.

She sat with her hands in her lap and sobs shook her big body. The tears trickled over her fat cheeks and ran down the sides of her nose. "The idea of it," she kept saying, staring at the tablecloth in front of her. "Just fancy, them sendin' for me!" Her voice was thick with tears.

We sat in a cloud of embarrassment, then, as if we had all had the idea at the same moment, rose and hurried outside. The captain stood at the door, gazing after young O'Hagan as he walked slowly down the road. We thanked him for the tea and, once we were out in the roadway, shed our discomfort and began to laugh at the big woman sitting there crying over the tablecloth. We followed the O'Hagan boy and hung about outside the house, full of curiosity. We could hear the woman groaning and wailing inside. There were none of the children playing round the door.

We began to build a snowman by the roadside, and I climbed into a field and got an old bowler hat off a scarecrow to set on his head. The eldest boy came out and told us his father said not to make so much noise, because his mother was sick. We pelted him with snowballs, and he had to run into the house again.

We got tired waiting, and were about to go back into the village when we saw Miss Gillespie cycling down the road. She was wobbling along the narrow lane between the banks of snow, and we expected at any moment to see her hit the side and tumble off. We waited on the verge of laughter. She did not fall, however, and when she reached us she hopped off and asked angrily what we were doing there. Her black straw hat sat on top of her head, secured by a long pin at each side. Her eyelids were red and swollen. You could hardly see her eyes.

"Away off with ye!" she cried. "Away out of this, before I beat the ears off you with my own two hands."

She pushed the bicycle at us, and we scampered off down the road, jeering and whistling.

Miss Gillespie made as if to mount her bicycle again, hesitated, and then, with a sudden impatient movement, placed it against the low wall at the front of the O'Hagans' house and marched up to the door. We waited no longer, but ran down to the village to tell what we had heard and seen. It was perhaps an hour later when Miss Gillespie came riding down the street, drew up outside Johnston's pub and went into the bar parlour. A few moments later Joe, Mr. Johnston's assistant, came out and wheeled her bicycle inside. It was not long before the word went round that shortly after her arrival Mrs. O'Hagan had given birth to another son.

She stayed later than usual in the pub that night, and then she came pedalling furiously up the hill past the house, puffing and panting, and did not as much as turn her head. Then, twenty yards farther up the road, she suddenly pulled up, made a precarious turn between the snowbanks, and came cycling back. She stopped outside the quiet house, where a dim yellow light shone from the kitchen window. She stood with one foot on the road and the other on the pedal, holding the bicycle up under her.

"Hello there, O'Hagan," she called. "Come out, O'Hagan. Come out here till I tell you what I think of ye. Are ye never away yet, you dirty Fenian dog? Why don't you clear out an' take your yelpin' pups along with ye? We don't want you here, among decent Christian people. Clear out, an' take your woman and her brood with ye!"

She began to cry and to shake the handlebars of her bicycle in impotent rage.

"D'you hear me, you dirty Mick?" she howled. "Away back where you belong, the lot of ye." She paused, as though waiting for some reply, then began to sob and moan in great distress. "Ah, God forgive me!" she wailed. "God forgive me this night, that ever lent a hand to bring a Papish brat into the world!"

DAVID HOGAN

# The Leaping Trout

*

Michael Davin was sitting at the end of a narrow, roughly-made pier of stones which stretched into the brown waters of Lough Dan. He had come that day post-haste from Dublin and this peace was sweet to him. After the toil of cycling over the tortuous mountain roads, so little used that whenever he turned a corner a score of rabbits hurled themselves in a flash of white into their burrows, after the jolting the rugged ground gave him in that long ride, after the strain of riding past half-a-dozen police barracks with three rifles tied along the cross-bar of his bicycle—from such a day the silence, the infinite placidity of the lake was exquisite retreat.

It was evening time in early June. The surface of the lake was broken now and then by a sudden breeze which put its hand upon the water and stretched long fingers out. Whenever these fingers were lifted the lake was a mirror marvellously filled with the reflection of hills and trees and the whiteness of the evening sky. From his throne of stones Michael could see the lake bottom through the brown waters. A little farther out the dancing of the flies fascinated him. He watched them land upon the water, sail a little, and then leap into the air to dance again. Dreamily watching that dance, he heard a trout jump close to him. He thought it was close until he saw the widening circle in the water half way across the broad lake. Everything was so still.

Again came the "hullop" of a jumping fish, and Michael

From THE CHALLENGE OF THE SENTRY, Dublin, The Talbot Press.

saw that a number of rings had begun to appear on that mirror surface. The trout were feeding. Every time the sound came it was the call of a lover to him, and, half-dreaming still, he undid the boat which lay by the simple pier and soon was moving slowly over the quiet lake. Though a fisherman born, he did not want to fish now—just to drift upon the waters, lying back in the boat, seeing only the sky, hearing the faint sounds from the lake-shore, listening to the music of the feeding trout.

At an extra big splash he said to himself: "That was a whopper, surely." And he raised himself slightly in the boat to watch for the next leap. He saw the first circle, well-marked, widening rapidly. As he watched it grow another spout of water leaped into the air, and Michael Davin knew then that it was a stone. In a second the whole furtiveness of a rebel's life repossessed him. He became again nervous, supersensitive, eager, anxious. He crouched back into the boat wondering whence the stone had come, who had thrown it, what was its meaning. Why did not the thrower shout?

Inside the boat he got the oars into position for swift use and began to scan the shore near which the drifting of his boat had carried him. He could see nothing, nobody. The fear that he was being watched by enemy eyes filled him: he could feel them on him. Yet there was nothing to be seen along that shadowy bank except the groups of wind-formed trees that stood along the water's edge. His eyes were drawn towards one of those groups—four twisted trunks standing on a tiny peninsula mirrored in the surrounding waters faintly now for night was coming on. But save four twisted trees he could see nothing. In the breathless hush of the whole world he could hear the trout jumping in the centre of the lake and then from the group of trees which hypnotized him he heard a faint metallic click.

Quicker than thought the oars were out and Michael Davin was pulling wildly away from the shore. His whole being waited for another sound, a sound that would shout its way across from hill to hill, from shore to shore, up the valleys, into the wooded heights, bringing many a waiting column what word? As he waited for that sound Michael Davin had a strange sensation. He felt that he was standing before a great church whose pillars slowly bent forward and began to break into little fragments of dust and stones, the heralds of a mighty fall. He had the illusion that he was watching the great copper dome with its towering golden cross slipping slowly towards him and that in a moment the world would be shaken with the fall of it. It seemed to him that unless he rowed ever more swiftly the tottering church would overwhelm him.

That was his illusion as he pulled like a madman across the darkening lake, pulling away from the sound he knew so well, the sound he had heard behind that group of twisted trees—the click of a magazine being replaced in a rifle. That was what he had heard. He knew it was nothing else. For two years he had drilled and marched and fought with the East Wicklow column of the I.R.A. and knew every sound that a rifle gives. Whoever had thrown that stone had wanted him to sit up, that he might be seen—and shot. The click behind the trees meant that whoever held the rifle was determined to take no chances. He was not going to rely on one shot, he had filled his magazine to make sure. But he had not fired. That, Michael could not understand. He had loaded his magazine because he had meant to fire. As Michael sent his light craft skimming over the lake he forgot his expectant fear in meditating on the mystery of the rifle that did not speak.

The night was coming rapidly. Looking again for the clump of trees Michael found that they had melted into the black heights that now encircled the lake. A thought came to him then and he purposely steered the boat across the light that still hovered in the centre of the lake. As he passed from the shadows of one side, across the brightness, steering towards the shadows of the other, he waited again for a shot. It did not come, and soon Michael's boat must have been lost to the silent watcher on the farther shore. To make doubly sure, Michael drew his boat up to the pier, rattled the iron ring as if he were making her fast, walked loudly upon the stones, knowing that all those sounds would travel over the waters to the unseen rifleman who stood among the trees. Then with the noiselessness of a cat he crept down to his boat, slid it out into the lake again, and lying in the prow drove it forward silently with his hands as oars. As a mother duck, bringing her brood for their first long swim and sensing always the eye of the hovering hawk, hugs the tree-rimmed shore, so Michael stole from shadow to shadow, round the edge of the lake, across to that side whence the ominous sound had come, and then moved slowly downward towards the treed peninsula. When two hundred yards from it, he silently beached his boat and went forward on foot.

In the oval opening of the hills was the last faint glow of daylight, but the stars had broken through it and the new moon rose above Mullaghcleevaun mountain like the diadem of a fairy queen walking upon its summit. But the light of the stars and the sickle moon could not pierce the shadows of the lake-shore. Michael knew how to walk noiselessly. More than once even in daylight he had gone forward undiscovered to the very elbows of some bivouacking column of the R.I.C. to count their numbers and note their positions. And nobody sitting by that still lake would have heard any sound from that moving thing which stole from tree to tree. At last Michael could see before him the four twisted trunks. His heart leaping within him, he stared at them. After a while he thought he could see gleaming very faintly in the darkness a round of silver. He was not sure, but what he saw seemed like the badge of a constabulary cap. He waited, but the little round of silver did not move. And Michael began to go forward again.

II

What sixth sense is it that enables us to perceive the unseen, to feel the intangible? What mysterious power dominates those moments when we can tell the secret thoughts of our friends, hear the coming of death, feel the world about us full of a presence which the eye sees not nor the ear hears?

Whatever it be, that strange other-world knowledge overwhelmed Michael Davin as he was about to step from the cover of the bushes and go towards the silver circle that

glowed in the heart of the twisted trunks. It was so powerful a message that it checked his step, brought him sharply
to a halt, and sent him crouching back into the shadows. The
four twisted trunks stood before him, and in their midst was
the mystery he must solve. Yet it was not towards them he was
looking now. Some distance back from the lake-shore, immediately under the ebony cliff that ringed the lake, was a patch
of furze. The furze was not visible except as a shadow against
the deeper shadow of the hills behind; but towards it Michael
found himself gazing expectantly, fearfully.

No sound had come from there or anywhere. The silence
of the great lake was supreme. The waters shone faintly in the
tremulous light, the black hills stood in a stooping circle
about them. Waters and hills were silent as death is silent.
Yet Michael knew that the clump of furze had a meaning for
him greater even than the silver circle which shone in the
midst of the twisted trunks. There was somebody in that
clump of furze—somebody who lived. He waited, wondering
and afraid.

A twig snapped, and the sound sent the blood drumming
in Michael's ears. A moment later he was not sure if he had
really seen something move against the black hills. It had no
form, no color. It was not so dark as the hills behind it, he
thought . . . Yes, it was moving. It was coming nearer, very
slowly, ready to fly, full of hesitation. Michael drew back
further into the shadow, his eyes always on the wraith which
as yet was like the reflection of a cloud passing over the sea
at night. He heard last autumn's leaves rustle under a step.
The moving form began to take shape, take color. He could
see the white shadow of a face, the fainter grey of a dress
. . . it was a girl! With cautious, dreading steps she was going
towards the four twisted trunks, towards the cap-badge that
caught the starlight.

From the security of his cover Michael watched this drama
of an unlit stage. He was thrilled, awed. He stared again at
the place to which the girl was going. Was his imagination on
fire, or could he now really see a man leaning against one of
the trunks, a tall burly man, whose head silhouetted against

some momentary brightness on the surface of the lake appeared to hang forward, as if he were asleep, or drunk—or dead? A stir brought his gaze back to the other character in the play. She was still only a shadow, but he could see that she was standing quietly, looking in amongst those four trees. She was a few yards from them, and Michael knew that she must have pierced the secret that they held. Yet she did not show it in her stand. She took another step forward like a wild thing creeping upon its prey. Then, suddenly, she started back, stiffened, stood still. He heard her draw in her breath sharply. He saw that she remained in the crouching position in which she had been creeping forward—as if she had been turned to stone by what she saw.

It seemed hours before she moved again. She fell on her knees and buried her face in her hands. Michael could hear her sobbing. He tried to think of a way to make his presence known without adding to her terror. He must have made some movement, for her hands fell from her face, the sobs ended in a little cry, and she leaped to her feet. Before Michael could think of what to do she had fled back towards the clump of furze, falling once or twice in the blind terror that was on her. She did not hear him call "Mary, Mary," as she ran.

When the last echo of those running steps had been swallowed up in the great silence, Michael himself crept forward to the four twisted trunks . . . Sergeant Edward Hayden of the Laragh barracks was lying dead against the trees. Michael knew him well and knew that for months the sergeant had wanted to capture or kill him, for there was a reward and promotion to be had from the Government for either.

And lying on the ground by his feet Michael found the sergeant's carbine. It seemed to have fallen suddenly from his hands. The magazine was full. The muzzle of the rifle was pointing towards where he had looked up when the splash of the stone woke him from his day dreams. It must have been pointing in that way, too, when death—a death whose wings nobody had heard—swooped down silently upon him. Michael was on his knees by the rifle when he thought of the constabulary cap whose silver badge had spoken to him from the darkness. He found it caught on a branch, and as he stretched out his hand to take it he saw between the sergeant's shoulders the shaft, as it were, of a great arrow.

Overcoming his nausea, Michael drew the arrow out. Even in the faint light of the stars he could see the crimson upon its bronze head. He stood gazing at it for a long time, and then, having washed it in the brown water of the lake, he carefully broke its long shaft into many pieces. Going some distance from the body he bent over the water and scooped a hole in the lake bottom. Having placed the pieces there, he covered them with a stone, and without turning back to where the dead sergeant looked upon the sleeping lake, he walked quietly towards the clump of furze.

He could piece the story in his own mind now. He knew where the arrow had come from. Only one house in the Glen had a weapon like that. Tim O'Dowd's house. Tim in his young days was a miner out in Africa, and it was often he told Michael of the Zulu chief who had given him a great bow and a quiver of bronze-headed arrows. Old Tim learnt that the English meant to kill this Zulu chief and warned him; the gift was the chieftain's thanks. Since the trouble started in Ireland Tim had kept the bow and arrow out of sight, and Michael was sure the R.I.C. knew nothing of them. They would never learn now how Sergeant Hayden died, unless the pieces he had buried in the lake were found.

All this Michael was thinking to himself as he strode the path that led over the mountain to Tim O'Dowd's little house. All this and more. For he was thinking of the girl whom he had last seen running and falling, like a wounded fawn. She must have learned by some way that he was upon the lake and was coming to him with some message, or with no message at all. Perhaps she had taken the bow and arrow for them both to fool with. Perhaps she had seen Sergeant Hayden and by intuition knew his mission. She would have followed him then to the lake side, for long ago Michael had taught her to scout and shadow and track a foe. Perhaps as she lay hidden by the clump of furze watching the Sergeant throwing stones near his boat she saw him get the rifle ready for the shot that would make him a Head Constable. And then as the magazine clicked into position and the head leant forward to get the sights into line there came the twang of a bow-string, a little faint noise like one note of a harp, and the tragedy had been given another ending . . .

Old Tim O'Dowd was brought to the door of his cottage by the sound of steps coming down the stony path. When he saw it was Michael Davin he called in to his daughter that "himself" was coming.

# Araby

\*

North Richmond Street, being blind, was a quiet street except
at the hour when the Christian Brothers' School set the boys
free. An uninhabited house of two storeys stood at the blind
end, detached from its neighbours in a square ground. The
other houses of the street, conscious of decent lives within
them, gazed at one another with brown imperturbable faces.

The former tenant of our house, a priest, had died in the
back drawing-room. Air, musty from having been long enclosed, hung in all the rooms, and the waste room behind the
kitchen was littered with old useless papers. Among these I
found a few paper-covered books, the pages of which were
curled and damp: *The Abbot,* by Walter Scott, *The Devout
Communicant* and *The Memoirs of Vidocq.* I liked the last
best because its leaves were yellow. The wild garden behind
the house contained a central apple-tree and a few straggling
bushes under one of which I found the late tenant's rusty
bicycle-pump. He had been a very charitable priest; in his
will he had left all his money to institutions and the furniture
of his house to his sister.

When the short days of winter came, dusk fell before we
had well eaten our dinners. When we met in the street the
houses had grown somber. The space of sky above us was the
color of everchanging violet and towards it the lamps of the
street lifted their feeble lanterns. The cold air stung us and we
played till our bodies glowed. Our shouts echoed in the silent

From DUBLINERS, New York, The Viking Press.

street. The career of our play brought us through the dark muddy lanes behind the houses where we ran the gauntlet of the rough tribes from the cottages, to the back doors of the dark dripping gardens where odors arose from the ashpits, to the dark odorous stables where a coachman smoothed and combed the horse or shook music from the buckled harness. When we returned to the street, light from the kitchen windows had filled the areas. If my uncle was seen turning the corner we hid in the shadow until we had seen him safely housed. Or if Mangan's sister came out on the doorstep to call her brother in to his tea we watched her from our shadow peer up and down the street. We waited to see whether she would remain or go in and, if she remained, we left our shadow and walked up to Mangan's steps resignedly. She was waiting for us, her figure defined by the light from the half-opened door. Her brother always teased her before he obeyed and I stood by the railings looking at her. Her dress swung as she moved her body and the soft rope of her hair tossed from side to side.

Every morning I lay on the floor in the front parlor watching her door. The blind was pulled down to within an inch of the sash so that I could not be seen. When she came out on the doorstep my heart leaped. I ran to the hall, seized my books and followed her. I kept her brown figure always in my eye and, when we came near the point at which our ways diverged, I quickened my pace and passed her. This happened morning after morning. I had never spoken to her, except for a few casual words, and yet her name was like a summons to all my foolish blood.

Her image accompanied me even in places the most hostile to romance. On Saturday evenings when my aunt went marketing I had to go to carry some of the parcels. We walked through the flaring streets, jostled by drunken men and bargaining women, amid the curses of laborers, the shrill litanies of shop-boys who stood on guard by the barrels of pigs' cheeks, the nasal chanting of street-singers, who sang a *come-all-you* about O'Donovan Rossa, or a ballad about the troubles in our native land. These noises converged in a single sensation of life for me: I imagined that I bore my chalice safely through a throng of foes. Her name sprang to my lips at moments in strange prayers and praises which I myself did not understand. My eyes were often full of tears (I could not tell why) and at times a flood from my heart seemed to pour itself out into my bosom. I thought little of the future. I did not know whether I would ever speak to her or not or, if I spoke to her, how I could tell her of my confused adoration. But my body was like a harp and her words and gestures were like fingers running upon the wires.

One evening I went into the back drawing-room in which the priest had died. It was a dark rainy evening and there was no sound in the house. Through one of the broken panes I heard the rain impinge upon the earth, the fine incessant needles of water playing in the sodden beds. Some distant lamp or lighted window gleamed below me. I was thankful that I could see so little. All my senses seemed to desire to veil themselves and, feeling that I was about to slip from them, I pressed the palms of my hands together until they trembled, murmuring: *"O love! O love!"* many times.

At last she spoke to me. When she addressed the first words to me I was so confused that I did not know what to answer. She asked me was I going to *Araby.* I forgot whether I answered yes or no. It would be a splendid bazaar, she said she would love to go.

"And why can't you?" I asked.

While she spoke she turned a silver bracelet round and round her wrist. She could not go, she said, because there would be a retreat that week in her convent. Her brother and two other boys were fighting for their caps and I was alone at the railings. She held one of the spikes, bowing her head towards me. The light from the lamp opposite our door caught the white curve of her neck, lit up her hair that rested there and, falling, lit up the hand upon the railing. It fell over one side of her dress and caught the white border of a petticoat, just visible as she stood at ease.

"It's well for you," she said.

"If I go," I said, "I will bring you something."

What innumerable follies laid waste my waking and sleeping thoughts after that evening! I wished to annihilate the tedious intervening days. I chafed against the work of school. At night in my bedroom and by day in the classroom her image came between me and the page I strove to read. The syllables of the word *Araby* were called to me through the silence in which my soul luxuriated and cast an Eastern enchantment over me. I asked for leave to go to the bazaar on Saturday night. My aunt was surprised and hoped it was not some Freemason affair. I answered few questions in class. I watched my master's face pass from amiability to sternness; he hoped I was not beginning to idle. I could not call my wandering thoughts together. I had hardly any patience with the serious work of life which, now that it stood between me and my desire, seemed to me child's play, ugly monotonous child's play.

On Saturday morning I reminded my uncle that I wished to go to the bazaar in the evening. He was fussing at the hall-stand, looking for the hat-brush, and answered me curtly:

"Yes, boy, I know."

As he was in the hall I could not go into the front parlor and lie at the window. I left the house in bad humor and walked slowly towards the school. The air was pitilessly raw and already my heart misgave me.

When I came home to dinner my uncle had not yet been home. Still it was early. I sat staring at the clock for some time and, when its ticking began to irritate me, I left the room. I mounted the staircase and gained the upper part of the house. The high, cold, empty gloomy rooms liberated me and I went from room to room singing. From the front window I saw my companions playing below in the street. Their cries reached me weakened and indistinct and, leaning my forehead against the cool glass, I looked over at the dark house where she lived. I may have stood there for an hour, seeing nothing but the brown-clad figure cast by my imagination, touched discreetly by the lamplight at the curved neck, at the hand upon the railings and at the border below the dress.

When I came downstairs again I found Mrs. Mercer sitting

at the fire. She was an old garrulous woman, a pawnbroker's widow, who collected used stamps for some pious purpose. I had to endure the gossip of the tea-table. The meal was prolonged beyond an hour and still my uncle did not come. Mrs. Mercer stood up to go: she was sorry she couldn't wait any longer, but it was after eight o'clock and she did not like to be out late, as the night air was bad for her. When she had gone I began to walk up and down the room, clenching my fists. My aunt said:

"I'm afraid you may put off your bazaar for this night of Our Lord."

At nine o'clock I heard my uncle's latchkey in the halldoor. I heard him talking to himself and heard the hallstand rocking when it had received the weight of his overcoat. I could interpret these signs. When he was midway through his dinner I asked him to give me the money to go to the bazaar. He had forgotten.

"The people are in bed and after their first sleep now," he said.

I did not smile. My aunt said to him energetically:

"Can't you give him the money and let him go? You've kept him late enough as it is."

My uncle said he was very sorry he had forgotten. He said he believed in the old saying: "All work and no play makes Jack a dull boy." He asked me where I was going and, when I had told him a second time he asked me did I know *The Arab's Farewell to his Steed*. When I left the kitchen he was about to recite the opening lines of the piece to my aunt.

I held a florin tightly in my hand as I strode down Buckingham Street towards the station. The sight of the streets thronged with buyers and glaring with gas recalled to me the purpose of my journey. I took my seat in a third-class carriage of a deserted train. After an intolerable delay the train moved out of the station slowly. It crept onward among ruinous houses and over the twinkling river. At Westland Row Station a crowd of people pressed to the carriage doors; but the porters moved them back, saying that it was a special train for the bazaar. I remained alone in the bare carriage. In a few

minutes the train drew up beside an improvised wooden platform. I passed out on to the road and saw by the lighted dial
of a clock that it was ten minutes to ten. In front of me was a
large building which displayed the magical name.

I could not find any sixpenny entrance and, fearing that
the bazaar would be closed, I passed in quickly through a
turnstile, handing a shilling to a weary-looking man. I found
myself in a big hall girdled at half its height by a gallery.
Nearly all the stalls were closed and the greater part of the
hall was in darkness. I recognised a silence like that which
pervades a church after a service. I walked into the center of
the bazaar timidly. A few people were gathered about the
stalls which were still open. Before a curtain, over which the
words *Café Chantant* were written in colored lamps, two men
were counting money on a salver. I listened to the fall of the
coins.

Remembering with difficulty why I had come I went over to
one of the stalls and examined porcelain vases and flowered
tea-sets. At the door of the stall a young lady was talking and
laughing with two young gentlemen. I remarked their English
accents and listened vaguely to their conversation.

"O, I never said such a thing!"

"O, but you did!"

"O, but I didn't!"

"Didn't she say that?"

"Yes. I heard her."

"O, there's a . . . fib!"

Observing me the young lady came over and asked me did
I wish to buy anything. The tone of her voice was not en-
couraging; she seemed to have spoken to me out of a sense
of duty. I looked humbly at the great jars that stood like
eastern guards at either side of the dark entrance to the stall
and murmured:

"No, thank you."

The young lady changed the position of one of the vases
and went back to the two young men. They began to talk of
the same subject. Once or twice the young lady glanced at
me over her shoulder.

I lingered before her stall, though I knew my stay was useless, to make my interest in her wares seem the more real. Then I turned away slowly and walked down the middle of the bazaar. I allowed the two pennies to fall against the sixpence in my pocket. I heard a voice call from one end of the gallery that the light was out. The upper part of the hall was now completely dark.

Gazing up into the darkness I saw myself as a creature driven and derided by vanity; and my eyes burned with anguish and anger.

PATRICK KAVANAGH

# Football

\*

"Go on our Micky—"
"Gut yer man—"
"Bog him—"

A football match is in progress in my imagination, and I
must admit that I am not a spectator but in there, ploughing
all around me, making myself famous in the parish as a man
that never "cowed" even at the risk of a broken neck.

"Aw, Kavanagh, the dhirty eejut."

"How could he be an eejut and him a poet?" one of our
supporters replied, and my traducer had no comeback.

The battle raged up and down the stony field. The team
we were playing was a disgusting class of a team who used
every form of psychological warfare. For instance, when one
of them was knocked down he rolled on the ground and
bawled like a bull a-gelding.

Then there was the time when I put the ball over the goal-
line and a most useful non-playing member of the opposing
team kicked it back into play. We argued and there was the
normal row.

The referee came up and interviewed the non-playing
member of the opposition, and that man replied: "I never
even saw the ball. Do you think I'd tell a lie and me at
Holy Communion this morning?"

What could we say to that?

From *Envoy*.

Of course we had our own methods. We never finished a game if towards the end we were a-batin'. We always found an excuse to rise a row and get the field invaded.

Ah, them was the times.

For one year I was virtual dictator of that team, being captain of the team and secretary and treasurer of the club. There was no means of checking up on my cash which gave rise to a lot of ill-founded suspicion. I remember I kept the money in an attaché-case under my bed. It is possible that every so often I visited it for the price of a packet of cigarettes, but nothing serious.

I once went as the club's representative to the County Board. We had to defend ourselves from a protest against us being awarded a certain game on the grounds that the list of players wasn't on water-marked Irish paper. I pointed out that the list was written on the inside of a large Player packet and that Players packets were made in Ireland. This did not impress. Nothing I said impressed as I hadn't the clichés off. It took a good deal of conspiring to depose me from my dictatorial post. Members of the team met in secret groups to know what could be done, but as soon as I got wind of the conspiracy I fired every man of them.

In the end they got rid of me but it was a job.

The man responsible for my deposition was a huge fellow, a blacksmith, a sort of Hindenburg whose word carried weight. He was a great master of the cliché, but sometimes he broke into originality as when the time we were going for the county final he wouldn't let us touch a ball for a week previous as he wanted us to be "ball hungry."

Ball hungry as we may have been we lost the match, and I was blamed, for I was "in the sticks," and let a ball roll through my legs.

The crowd roared in anguish: "Go home and put an apron on you." And various other unfriendly remarks were made such as "Me oul' mother would make a better goalier."

Somebody has said that no man can adequately describe Irish life who ignores the Gaelic Athletic Association, which is true in a way, for football runs women a hard race as a topic for conversation.

The popular newspaper has driven out the football ballad which at one time gave fairly literal accounts of famous matches—

> *At half-past two the whistle blew*
> *And the ball it was thrown in,*
> *The haro Murphy sazed it and*
> *He kicked it with the win'*

Then there was a ballad singer who used to sing—*"The catching and the kickin' was mar-veel-e-us for to see."*

After the ballad came the local paper where we were all Trojans in defence and wizards in attack. I once got a lot of kudos from a report which described me as "incisive around goal." No one knew the meaning of the word incisive but it sounded good.

These reminiscences have been inspired by a Dublin barman—a native of my own district—who said to me: "I often wonder you never wrote about the time you were playing football for the Grattans. Do you mind the Sunday we played yous below in Jackie's meada beside the river? and big Hughie on the side-line with an ashplant ready to cut the head of e'er a man that kem 'ithin a mile of him?"

"Vaguely," I said.

"Aw, you must remember. Weren't you playing that day?" Then it came back.

She was a brave mother who willingly allowed her son to play football. Most mothers would "be out of their minds" worried over their sons on the playing fields, never knowing when he'd come back to her a "limither for life."

"Many's the good man the same football put an end to. How I remember the poor Poochy Maguire that got the boot in the bottom of the belly and never overed it. If you'd take a fool's advice that you never took you'd lave the football alone."

"Things have changed since them days."

"That'll do you, now. What about young Kiernan of Cross that was killed in Cavan?"

As soon as the player came home he was scrutinized by his mother. She had sharp eyes as a rule and was able to see the deep cut over his eye which he had been trying to conceal with a lock of hair.

"You got a kick?"

"That's only a little thing."

"Little thing! Aw, God knows but it's me that's the unfortunate woman. I heard the roaring down there in that stony meada of Jackie's, and I didn't know at what minute you'd be brought home to me half dead. Did yous win atself?"

"A draw."

"Yous were never able for Donaghmoyne—with all your bummin. Get the black porringer from under the stairs and put them pair of eggs in it. . . . No, never during soot were yous fit to bate Donaghmoyne."

"Only for the referee——"

"Only for something the sky id fall. Yes, only for something the sky id fall."

For all this my imagination finds difficulty in focusing on this period—and one should always trust the imagination to light up vital things. All sporting subjects are superficial. The emotion is a momentary puff of gas, not an experience, and I know now why I have been unable to write about it at length.

One reads a lot about life in England but one hardly ever comes across a novel in which soccer is interwoven—or even cricket, which has been built into an art on the level of music. At the moment we have a poet, John Arlott—who did write a good poem on cricket—pumping out books about that game. Then there are Nevill Cardus and C. B. Fry, all straining for an artistic allusion in their descriptions of Washbrook's drive through the slips or some one else's æsthetic catch at silly point.

I have noted that in *Ulysses*, that compendium of common-place emotions and goings on, only the punter speculating on the result of the Ascot Gold Cup comes into the theme. So sport can't have been very vital, for Joyce had a mind like a sponge. But all these opinions of mine are barren. It is none of my business, and one should always try to extract the comedy from life and not see it moralisingly.

"Hello."

"Hello."

"How are you after the game last Sunday?"

"A stiff leg."

"I know what that means."

"You're right. Can't sit down without the leg straight out in front. Shocking bleddy nuisance. We were in very bad luck. Sure, Paddy Keegan had an open goal in front of him and he shot forty yards wide. The man that id miss that id miss the parish if he fired at the chapel."

"Bad all right."

"Desperate. Pity Trainer wasn't playing. Mother won't let him."

So the two men on opposite sides of a stone fence talk on.

My brother was telling me how one lovely Sunday morning he was taking a stroll outside San Francisco on the edge of the Pacific when he saw hurrying with little bundles under their oxters men of a rural Irish complex.

Sometime later he came upon a Gaelic football match in progress. Everything was as at home: There were the men running up and down the unpaled side-line slicing at the toes which encroached, with hurleys and crying: "Keep back there now, keep back there now." And all around the pitch the familiar battle cries of the Dalcassians were to be heard.

"Gut yer man . . ."

"Bog into him."

Not a man of them had ever left home and the mysterious Pacific was just a bog-hole, gurgling with eels and frogs. Yet, there was something queer and wonderful about the sight, or the thought.

*Then Inniskeen came on the field and they were stuffed*
    *with pride,*
*They fell before the Fontenoys like grass before a scythe.*
Yes, says he, they fell before the Fontenoys like grass be-
fore a scythe.

MARY LAVIN

# The Story of the Widow's Son

※

This is the story of a widow's son, but it is a story that has two endings.

There was once a widow, living in a small neglected village at the foot of a steep hill. She had only one son, but he was the meaning of her life. She lived for his sake. She wore herself out working for him. Every day she made a hundred sacrifices in order to keep him at a good school in the town, four miles away, because there was a better teacher there than the village dullard that had taught herself.

She made great plans for Packy, but she did not tell him about her plans. Instead she threatened him, day and night, that if he didn't turn out well, she would put him to work on the roads, or in the quarry under the hill.

But as the years went by, everyone in the village, and even Packy himself, could tell by the way she watched him out of sight in the morning, and watched to see him come into sight in the evening, that he was the beat of her heart, and that her gruff words were only a cover for her pride and her joy in him.

It was for Packy's sake that she walked for hours along the road, letting her cow graze the long acre of the wayside grass, in order to spare the few poor blades that pushed up through the stones in her own field. It was for his sake she walked back and forth to the town to sell a few cabbages as soon as ever they were fit. It was for his sake that she got

From IRISH HARVEST, edited by Robert Greacen, Dublin, New Frontiers Press.

up in the cold dawning hours to gather mushrooms that would take the place of foods that had to be bought with money. She bent her back daily to make every penny she could, and as often happens, she made more by industry, out of her few bald acres, than many of the farmers around her made out of their great bearded meadows. Out of the money she made by selling eggs alone, she paid for Packy's clothes and for the greater number of his books.

When Packy was fourteen, he was in the last class in the school, and the master had great hopes of his winning a scholarship to a big college in the city. He was getting to be a tall lad, and his features were beginning to take a strong cast. His character was strengthening too, under his mother's sharp tongue. The people of the village were beginning to give him the same respect they gave to the sons of the farmers who came from their fine colleges in the summer, with blue suits and bright ties. And whenever they spoke to the widow they praised him up to the skies.

One day in June, when the air was so heavy the scent that rose up from the grass was imprisoned under the low clouds and hung in the air, the widow was waiting at the gate for Packy. There had been no rain for some days and the hens and chickens were pecking irritably at the dry ground and wandering up and down the road in bewilderment.

A neighbour passed.

"Waiting for Packy?" said the neighbour, pleasantly, and he stood for a minute to take off his hat and wipe the sweat of the day from his face. He was an old man.

"It's a hot day!" he said. "It will be a hard push for Packy on that battered old bike of his. I wouldn't like to have to face into four miles on a day like this!"

"Packy would travel three times that distance if there was a book at the other end of the road!" said the widow, with the pride of those who cannot read more than a line or two without wearying.

The minutes went by slowly. The widow kept looking up at the sun.

"I suppose the heat is better than the rain!" she said, at last.

"The heat can do a lot of harm, too, though," said the neighbour, absent-mindedly, as he pulled a long blade of grass from between the stones of the wall and began to chew the end of it. "You could get sunstroke on a day like this!" He looked up at the sun. "The sun is a terror," he said. "It could cause you to drop down dead like a stone!"

The widow strained out further over the gate. She looked up the hill in the direction of the town.

"He will have a good cool breeze on his face coming down the hill, at any rate," she said.

The man looked up the hill. "That's true. On the hottest day of the year you would get a cool breeze coming down that hill on a bicycle. You would feel the air streaming past your cheeks like silk. And in the winter it's like two knives flashing to either side of you, and peeling off your skin like you'd peel the bark off a sally-rod." He chewed the grass meditatively. "That must be one of the steepest hills in Ireland," he said. "That hill is a hill worthy of the name of a hill." He took the grass out of his mouth. "It's my belief," he said, earnestly looking at the widow—"it's my belief that that hill is to be found marked with a name in the Ordnance Survey map!"

"If that's the case," said the widow, "Packy will be able to tell you all about it. When it isn't a book he has in his hand it's a map."

"Is that so?" said the man. "That's interesting. A map is a great thing. A map is not an ordinary thing. It isn't everyone can make out a map."

The widow wasn't listening.

"I think I see Packy!" she said, and she opened the wooden gate and stepped out into the roadway.

At the top of the hill there was a glitter of spokes as a bicycle came into sight. Then there was a flash of blue jersey as Packy came flying downward, gripping the handlebars of the bike, with his bright hair blown back from his forehead. The hill was so steep, and he came down so fast, that it seemed to the man and woman at the bottom of the hill that he was not moving at all, but that it was the bright trees and bushes, the bright ditches and wayside grasses that were streaming away to either side of him.

The hens and chickens clucked and squawked and ran along the road looking for a safe place in the ditches. They ran to either side with feminine fuss and chatter. Packy waved to his mother. He came nearer and nearer. They could see the freckles on his face.

"Shoo!" cried Packy, at the squawking hens that had not yet left the roadway. They ran with their long necks straining forward.

"Shoo!" said Packy's mother, lifting her apron and flapping it in the air to frighten them out of his way.

It was only afterwards, when the harm was done, that the widow began to think that it might, perhaps, have been the flapping of her own apron that frightened the old clucking hen, and sent her flying out over the garden wall into the middle of the road.

The old hen appeared suddenly on top of the grassy ditch and looked with a distraught eye at the hens and chickens as they ran to right and left. Her own feathers began to stand out from her. She craned her neck forward and gave a distracted squawk, and fluttered down into the middle of the hot dusty road.

Packy jammed on the brakes. The widow screamed. There was a flurry of white feathers and a spurt of blood. The bicycle swerved and fell. Packy was thrown over the handlebars.

It was such a simple accident that, although the widow screamed, and although the old man looked around to see if there was help near, neither of them thought that Packy was very badly hurt, but when they ran over and lifted his head, and saw that he could not speak, they wiped the blood from his face and looked around, desperately, to measure the distance they would have to carry him.

It was only a few yards to the door of the cottage, but Packy was dead before they got him across the threshold.

"He's only in a weakness!" screamed the widow, and she urged the crowd that had gathered outside the door to do something for him. "Get a doctor!" she cried, pushing a young labourer towards the door. "Hurry! Hurry! The doctor will bring him around."

But the neighbours that kept coming in the door, quickly, from all sides, were crossing themselves, one after another, and falling on their knees, as soon as they laid eyes on the boy, stretched out flat on the bed, with the dust and dirt and the sweat marks of life on his dead face.

When at last the widow was convinced that her son was dead, the other women had to hold her down. She waved her arms and cried out aloud, and wrestled to get free. She wanted to wring the neck of every hen in the yard.

"I'll kill every one of them. What good are they to me, now? All the hens in the world aren't worth one drop of human blood. That old clucking hen wasn't worth more than six shillings, at the very most. What is six shillings? Is it worth poor Packy's life?"

But after a time she stopped raving, and looked from one face to another.

"Why didn't he ride over the old hen?" she asked. "Why did he try to save an old hen that wasn't worth more than six shillings? Didn't he know he was worth more to his mother than an old hen that would be going into the pot one of these days? Why did he do it? Why did he put on the brakes going down one of the worst hills in the country? Why? Why?"

The neighbours patted her arm.

"There now!" they said. "There now!" and that was all they could think of saying, and they said it over and over again. "There now! There now!"

And years afterwards, whenever the widow spoke of her son Packy to the neighbours who dropped in to keep her company for an hour or two, she always had the same question to ask; the same tireless question.

"Why did he put the price of an old clucking hen above the price of his own life?"

And the people always gave the same answer.

"There now!" they said, "There now!" And they sat as silently as the widow herself, looking into the fire.

But surely some of those neighbours must have been stirred to wonder what would have happened had Packy not yielded to his impulse of fear, and had, instead, ridden boldly over the old clucking hen? And surely some of them must have stared into the flames and pictured the scene of the accident again, altering a detail here and there as they did so, and giving the story a different end. For these people knew the widow, and they knew Packy, and when you know people well it is as easy to guess what they would say and do in certain circumstances as it is to remember what they actually did say and do in other circumstances. In fact it is sometimes easier to invent than to remember accurately, and were this not so two great branches of creative art would wither in an hour: the art of the story-teller and the art of the gossip. So, perhaps, if I try to tell you what I myself think might have happened had Packy killed that cackling old hen, you will not accuse me of abusing my privileges as a writer. After all, what I am about to tell you is no more of a fiction than what I have already told, and I lean no heavier now upon your credulity than, with your full consent, I did in the first instance.

And moreover, in many respects the new story is the same as the old.

It begins in the same way too. There is the widow grazing her cow by the wayside, and walking the long roads to the town, weighted down with sacks of cabbages that will pay for Packy's schooling. There she is, fussing over Packy in the mornings in case he would be late for school. There she is in the evening watching the battered clock on the dresser for the hour when he will appear on the top of the hill at his return. And there too, on a hot day in June, is the old labouring man coming up the road, and pausing to talk to her, as she stood at the door. There he is dragging a blade of grass from between the stones of the wall, and putting it between his teeth to chew, before he opens his mouth.

And when he opens his mouth at last it is to utter the same remark.

"Waiting for Packy?" said the old man, and then he took off his hat and wiped the sweat from his forehead. It will be remembered that he was an old man. "It's a hot day," he said.

"It's very hot," said the widow, looking anxiously up the hill. "It's a hot day to push a bicycle four miles along a bad road with the dust rising to choke you, and sun striking spikes off the handlebars!"

"The heat is better than the rain, all the same," said the old man.

"I suppose it is," said the widow. "All the same, there were days when Packy came home with the rain dried into his clothes so bad they stood up stiff like boards when he took them off. They stood up stiff like boards against the wall, for all the world as if he was still standing in them!"

"Is that so?" said the old man. "You may be sure he got a good petting on those days. There is no son like a widow's son. A ewe lamb!"

"Is it Packy?" said the widow, in disgust. "Packy never got a day's petting since the day he was born. I made up my mind from the first that I'd never make a soft one out of him."

The widow looked up the hill again, and set herself to raking the gravel outside the gate as if she were in the road for no other purpose. Then she gave another look up the hill.

"Here he is now!" she said, and she raised such a cloud of dust with the rake that they could hardly see the glitter of the bicycle spokes, and the flash of blue jersey as Packy came down the hill at a breakneck speed.

Nearer and nearer he came, faster and faster, waving his hand to the widow, shouting at the hens to leave the way!

The hens ran for the ditches, stretching their necks in gawky terror. And then, as the last hen squawked into the ditch, the way was clear for a moment before the whirling silver spokes.

Then, unexpectedly, up from nowhere it seemed, came an old clucking hen and, clucking despairingly, it stood for a moment on the top of the wall and then rose into the air with the clumsy flight of a ground fowl.

Packy stopped whistling. The widow screamed. Packy yelled and the widow flapped her apron. Then Packy swerved the bicycle, and a cloud of dust rose from the braked wheel.

For a minute it could not be seen what exactly had happened, but Packy put his foot down and dragged it along the ground in the dust till he brought the bicycle to a sharp stop. He threw the bicycle down with a clatter on the hard road and ran back. The widow could not bear to look. She threw her apron over her head.

"He's killed the clucking hen!" she said. "He's killed her! He's killed her!" and then she let the apron fall back into place, and began to run up the hill herself. The old man spat out the blade of grass that he had been chewing and ran after the woman.

"Did you kill it?" screamed the widow, and as she got near enough to see the blood and feathers she raised her arm over her head, and her fist was clenched till the knuckles shone white. Packy cowered down over the carcass of the fowl and hunched up his shoulders as if to shield himself from a blow. His legs were spattered with blood, and the brown and white feathers of the dead hen were stuck to his hands, and stuck to his clothes, and they were strewn all over the road. Some of the short white inner feathers were still swirling with the dust in the air.

"I couldn't help it, Mother. I couldn't help it. I didn't see her till it was too late!"

The widow caught up the hen and examined it all over, holding it by the bone of the breast, and letting the long neck dangle. Then, catching it by the leg, she raised it suddenly above her head, and brought down the bleeding body on the boy's back, in blow after blow, spattering the blood all over his face and his hands, over his clothes and over the white dust of the road around him.

"How dare you lie to me!" she screamed, gaspingly, between the blows. "You saw the hen. I know you saw it. You stopped whistling! You called out! We were watching you. We saw." She turned upon the old man. "Isn't that right?" she demanded. "He saw the hen, didn't he? He saw it?"

"It looked that way," said the old man, uncertainly, his eye on the dangling fowl in the widow's hand.

"There you are!" said the widow. She threw the hen down on the road. "You saw the hen in front of you on the road, as plain as you see it now," she accused, "but you wouldn't stop to save it because you were in too big a hurry home to fill your belly! Isn't that so?"

"No, Mother. No! I saw her all right but it was too late to do anything."

"He admits now that he saw it," said the widow, turning and nodding triumphantly at the onlookers who had gathered at the sound of the shouting.

"I never denied seeing it!" said the boy, appealing to the onlookers as to his judges.

"He doesn't deny it!" screamed the widow. "He stands there as brazen as you like, and admits for all the world to hear that he saw the hen as plain as the nose on his face, and he rode over it without a thought!"

"But what else could I do?" said the boy, throwing out his hand; appealing to the crowd now, and now appealing to the widow. "If I'd put on the brakes going down the hill at such a speed I would have been put over the handlebars!"

"And what harm would that have done you?" screamed the widow. "I often saw you taking a toss when you were wrestling with Jimmy Mack and I heard no complaints afterwards, although your elbows and knees would be running blood, and your face scraped like a gridiron!" She turned to the crowd. "That's as true as God. I often saw him come in with his nose spouting blood like a pump, and one eye closed as tight as the eye of a corpse. My hand was often stiff for a week from sopping out wet cloths to put poultices

on him and try to bring his face back to rights again." She
swung back to Packy again. "You're not afraid of a fall
when you go climbing trees, are you? You're not afraid to go
up on the roof after a cat, are you? Oh, there's more in this
than you want me to know. I can see that. You killed that
hen on purpose—that's what I believe! You're tired of going
to school. You want to get out of going away to college.
That's it! You think if you kill the few poor hens we have
there will be no money in the box when the time comes to
pay for books and classes. That's it!" Packy began to redden.

"It's late in the day for me to be thinking of things like
that," he said. "It's long ago I should have started those tricks
if that was the way I felt. But it's not true. I want to go to
college. The reason I was coming down the hill so fast was
to tell you that I got the scholarship. The teacher told me
as I was leaving the schoolhouse. That's why I was pedalling
so hard. That's why I was whistling. That's why I was waving
my hand. Didn't you see me waving my hand from once I
came in sight at the top of the hill?"

The widow's hands fell to her sides. The wind of words
died down within her and left her flat and limp. She didn't
know what to say. She could feel the neighbours staring at
her. She wished that they were gone away about their business. She wanted to throw out her arms to the boy, to drag
him against her heart and hug him like a small child. But
she thought of how the crowd would look at each other and
nod and snigger. A ewe lamb! She didn't want to satisfy
them. If she gave in to her feelings now they would know
how much she had been counting on his getting the scholarship. She wouldn't please them! She wouldn't satisfy them!

She looked at Packy, and when she saw him standing
there before her, spattered with the furious feathers and
crude blood of the dead hen, she felt a fierce disappointment
for the boy's own disappointment, and a fierce resentment
against him for killing the hen on this day of all days, and
spoiling the great news of his success.

Her mind was in confusion. She started at the blood on his
face, and all at once it seemed as if the blood was a bad

omen of the future that was for him. Disappointment, fear, resentment, and above all defiance, raised themselves within her like screeching animals. She looked from Packy to the onlookers.

"Scholarship! Scholarship!" she sneered, putting as much derision as she could into her voice and expression.

"I suppose you think you are a great fellow now? I suppose you think you are independent now? I suppose you think you can go off with yourself now, and look down on your poor slave of a mother who scraped and sweated for you with her cabbages and her hens? I suppose you think to yourself that it doesn't matter now whether the hens are alive or dead? Is that the way? Well, let me tell you this! You're not as independent as you think. The scholarship may pay for your books and your teacher's fees but who will pay for your clothes? Ah-ha, you forgot that, didn't you?" She put her hands on her hips. Packy hung his head. He no longer appealed to the gawking neighbours. They might have been able to save him from blows but he knew enough about life to know that no one could save him from shame.

The widow's heart burned at sight of his shamed face, as her heart burned with grief, but her temper too burned fiercer and fiercer, and she came to a point at which nothing could quell the blaze till it had burned itself out. "Who'll buy your suits?" she yelled. "Who'll buy your boots?" She paused to think of more humiliating accusations. "Who'll buy your breeches?" She paused again and her teeth bit against each other. What would wound deepest? What shame could she drag upon him? "Who'll buy your nightshirts or will you sleep in your skin?"

The neighbours laughed at that, and the tension was broken. The widow herself laughed. She held her sides and laughed, and as she laughed everything seemed to take on a newer and simpler significance. Things were not as bad as they seemed a moment before. She wanted Packy to laugh too. She looked at him. But as she looked at Packy her heart turned cold with a strange new fear.

"Get into the house!" she said, giving him a push ahead

of her. She wanted him safe under her own roof. She wanted to get him away from the gaping neighbours. She hated them, man, woman and child. She felt that if they had not been there things would have been different. And she wanted to get away from the sight of the blood on the road. She wanted to mash a few potatoes and make a bit of potato cake for Packy. That would comfort him. He loved that.

Packy hardly touched the food. And even after he had washed and scrubbed himself there were stains of blood turning up in the most unexpected places: behind his ears, under his finger-nails, inside the cuff of his sleeve.

"Put on your good clothes," said the widow, making a great effort to be gentle, but her manners had become as twisted and as hard as the branches of the trees across the road from her, and even the kindly offers she made sounded harsh. The boy sat on the chair in a slumped position that kept her nerves on edge and set up a further conflict of irritation and love in her heart. She hated to see him slumping there in the chair, not asking to go outside the door, but still she was uneasy whenever he as much as looked in the direction of the door. She felt safe while he was under the roof; inside the lintel; under her eyes.

Next day she went in to wake him for school, but his room was empty; his bed had not been slept in, and when she ran out into the yard and called him everywhere there was no answer. She ran up and down. She called at the houses of the neighbours but he was not in any house. And she thought she could hear sniggering behind her in each house that she left, as she ran to another one. He wasn't in the village. He wasn't in the town. The master of the school said that she should let the police have a description of him. He said he never met a boy as sensitive as Packy. A boy like that took strange notions into his head from time to time.

The police did their best but there was no news of Packy that night. A few days later there was a letter saying that he was well. He asked his mother to notify the master that he would not be coming back, so that some other boy could claim the scholarship. He said that he would send the price of the hen as soon as he made some money.

Another letter in a few weeks said that he had got a job on a trawler, and that he would not be able to write very often but that he would put aside some of his pay every week and send it to his mother whenever he got into port. He said that he wanted to pay her back for all she had done for him. He gave no address. He kept his promise about the money but he never gave any address when he wrote.

. . . . And so the people may have let their thoughts run on, as they sat by the fire with the widow, many a night, listening to her complaining voice saying the same thing over and over. "Why did he put the price of an old hen above the price of his own life?" And it is possible that their version of the story has a certain element of truth about it too. Perhaps all our actions have this double quality about them; this possibility of alternative, and that it is only by careful watching and absolute sincerity, that we follow the path that is destined for us, and, no matter how tragic that may be, it is better than the tragedy we bring upon ourselves.

# DONAGH MAC DONAGH

# "All the Sweet Buttermilk . . ."

The most lonesome place I was ever posted to was a little town twenty miles from the nearest railway, in the County Mayo, where there was neither cinema, theater nor anything else; the only entertainment was a chat and a smoke, a drink and an occasional dance. I was always a great one to fish and take life easy, so it suited me fine, but the Sergeant didn't fancy it at all.

Sergeant Finnegan was a dour looking man and very close. I never rightly discovered what it was had him shifted to that place, but it can't have been want of zeal. He was the most energetic man and the most enthusiastic man in his search for crime that ever I met. Of course he was wasting his time looking for crime in Coolnamara, but what he couldn't find he invented.

Hanlon and Flaherty and myself used to have a grand easy life of it in old Sergeant Moloney's time; there wasn't a bicycle lamp in the district, the pubs closed when the last customer went home, and that was earlier than you'd think, and if there was any poteen made nobody came worrying us about it. But Sergeant Finnegan soon changed all that. He wasn't a month in the place till every lad in the county had a lamp on his bike, I even bought one myself; and there was such a row kicked up about the pubs staying open that nobody went home till midnight. They suddenly realized that there must be a great charm in after-hours drinking.

From CELTIC STORY, edited by Aled Vaughan, London, Pendulum.

The Sergeant used to have me cross-eyed chasing round the country in search of illicit stills, and as soon as ever I'd get settled down for the evening with my pipe going nicely and the wireless behind my head, he'd be in with some new list of outrages, cattle straying on the road, a camp of tinkers that whipped a couple of chickens, or some nonsense like that.

"Take your feet down off that mantelpiece," he'd say, "and get out on patrol. Who knows what malicious damage or burglary or larceny is going on under the cover of night!" And up I'd have to get, put on my coat and go in next door to listen to the news.

He was a great man for objecting to dance-hall licences, and if he'd had his way there wouldn't have been a foot put on a floor within the four walls of Ireland. On the night of a dance he'd be snooping around to see was there any infringement of the regulations, and his finger itching on the pencil to make notes for a prosecution.

One night there was an all-night dance over in Ballyduv and he sent me over to keep an eye on it.

"I think I better go in mufti, Sergeant," says I. "There's no use in drawing their attention to the Civic Guards being present."

"True. True. Quite true!" says he. So up I went and changed, chuckling to myself. I could have worn a beard and a major-general's outfit and every hog, dog and devil in the place would have known me. But I always enjoyed a dance and I didn't want to be encumbered with a uniform for the stretch of the evening.

When I got to the dance-hall it was about half-ten but hardly anyone had arrived yet. At an all-night dance they're never in much of a hurry to get started, and besides the lads have to get washed and changed after the day's work. I stood chatting to Callaghan, that owned the hall, for a bit, and then we went over to Hennessy's for a couple of pints. Of course it was well after hours by this time, but with the Sergeant safe in Coolnamara nobody was worrying too much about that. Around about half-eleven we heard the band getting into its stride, so we came back to see how the fun was going.

As soon as I stepped in through the door I saw the grandest looking girl you'd want to see, bronze colored hair, green eyes, and an American dress that was made for her figure.

"Who's that?" says I to Callaghan. "She must be down from Dublin."

"Dublin nothing!" says he, "she's from the mountain beyond. There's a whole family of them, and they're as wild as a lot of mountain goats. Lynch's they are."

"Give us a knock-down," says I, "I'll surely die if I don't meet that one!"

"I will," says he, "but I better say nothing about you being in the Guards."

"And why not?"

"Now never mind. It's what I'm telling you." So he brought me over and introduced me to her.

Well, we got on grand. There was a waltz just starting and I asked her out, and we danced from that out without a break, and when we were tired dancing we went out for a bit of a walk, and I can tell you I wasn't wasting my time.

She told me all about the sister in America, and how anxious she was to get to Dublin, and I could see she was dying down dead to find out what I was, but after Jack Callaghan's warning I made her no wiser.

On about one o'clock we were whirling around when what should I see sloping in through the door but the Sergeant, and he in mufti, too. He gave me a very cold nod and I didn't pretend to take the least bit of notice of him.

"Who's your friend?" says she. "I never saw him before."

"Any more than you saw me!" says I, giving her a squeeze and avoiding the question.

"Who is he, though?" she said again, so I saw there was no way out of it.

"That's Sergeant Finnegan from Coolnamara," says I, "and a greater trouble maker there isn't in the country."

"And what else would he be only a trouble maker, if he's a Guard. If there's one thing I hate in this world it's a

Guard, and if there's a thing I hate more it's a Sergeant." I could see I was on very delicate ground and took all the trouble I could not to be any way awkward with my big feet.

"And why is that?" says I, but she only tossed her head and shot the Sergeant dead with both her green eyes.

After a bit some great gawk of a countryman managed to prise her away from me, and off she went, though I felt she'd rather stay. No sooner had she gone than I could feel the Sergeant breathing down the back of my neck.

"Come outside here till I talk to you," says he, and I could see she had her eyes buried in us as we went out the door.

"Do you know who that is?" says he.

"That's a girl called Maeve Lynch," says I. "Isn't she a grand looking thing."

"Her father's the greatest poteen maker in the County of Mayo, and I thought you were long enough in the county to know that."

"Well, that's news to me. He was never prosecuted in my time. How do you know?"

"From information received. Now you keep away from that girl, or it might be worse for you. And keep your mind on your business. Don't you know you have no right to be dancing?"

"I was just seeing could I pick up any information. But things are very quiet."

"Things are never as quiet as they appear. I hope you investigated Hennessy's after closing time."

"You can be bound I did!" says I without a smile.

We went back into the hall, and as soon as I got the Sergeant's back turned I gave Maeve the beck to come on out. As she passed the Sergeant she gave him a glare that must have rocked him back on his heels.

"Are you not going to dance?" says she to me, but instead of answering I drew her out into the dark and slipped an arm around her. We walked along for a while without saying a word. Then she gave my hand a squeeze.

"What did the Sergeant want with you?"

"Ah, he was just chatting."

"You seem to be terrible great with him."

"I wouldn't say that. I just know him."

"Did he say anything about me?"

"What would he say? He doesn't know you, does he?"

"Oh, the dear knows. They're a very nosey crowd, the Guards. Come on back and dance."

"No," I said, "I'm tired. Let's sit down." So we sat down.

When we got back to the dance it was near breaking up and the Sergeant was gone. I was all for taking her home, but there were some cousins of hers there who said they'd take her in a trap, so I arranged to meet her the next Sunday at a dance a few miles away, and away I went singing "The Red Haired Girl" and whistling back at the birds.

I had an early breakfast and was off to the lake with my rod and line long before the Sergeant or Hanlon or Flaherty were stirring. I spent half the day fishing and half the day dreaming, and when I got back in the afternoon the Sergeant was fit to be tied.

"Where were you all day?" says he, "I'll report you to the Superintendent for being absent without leave."

"Oh, indeed I wasn't, Sergeant," says I, "I was on duty all day. I was down at the lake keeping an eye open for poachers." It was fortunate that I had left the half-dozen trout down the town on my way home.

"Poachers!" says he. "And who ever heard of poachers on Cool Lake?"

"You never know when they might start. I took the precaution of bringing along a rod as a camouflage!" I could see he was only half convinced, but he let it go.

"Get up on your bike there," says he. "We have work to do." But I told him I'd have to get something to eat first. I had such an appetite that minute that I'd have nearly eaten the sour face off himself. I downed a good meal in record time and the two of us started off.

For a couple of miles the Sergeant never said a word, and I said no more. After a bit I realised we were heading up towards the mountains, a part of the world I wasn't very well acquainted with.

"Where are we off to, Sergeant?" says I.

"We're off on a job that may get you your Sergeant's stripes if you play your cards right. It's that old Maurice Lynch. I have information that he's after running enough poteen to set the whole countryside drunk. He thinks he's as safe as Gibraltar, stuck up here on his mountainside, but it isn't old Sergeant Moloney he has to deal with now. Callaghan told me last night the daughter didn't know about you being in the Guards."

"That's true enough."

"Well, maybe it's just as well you were so busy chasing after her. You'll be able to keep them in chat while I have a look around. You can pretend you came on a social call."

I cursed my day's fishing when I realized that it was too late now to get any word to Maeve. If I'd been in the station when the Sergeant first decided on this expedition I could have sent a message through Callaghan, but here I was now on an empty bog road with the Sergeant glued to my side and every stroke on the pedals bringing us nearer. There was a big push being made against poteen all through the country, and I knew it would go hard with old Lynch if he was caught.

At last we got into the mountains, and after a while we had to get down and walk, and heavy climbing it was.

"There it is now," says the Sergeant. "We'll have to dump the bikes and take to the fields. But you go ahead and I'll follow after at a safe distance."

Here's my chance, said I to myself, and I started hot-foot for the farmhouse. Just as I got up to the gate, a fine handsome girl with red hair came out the door and leaned against the jamb, showing off her figure. I was just going to wave to her when I realized that it wasn't Maeve.

"What can we do for you?" says she, looking very bold at me.

"Listen!" says I, "this is urgent. If you have any poteen about the place, for God's sake tell me where it is till I get rid of it. There's a Sergeant of the Guards on his way across the fields now."

"Poteen?" says she. "Poteen? I seem to have heard of the stuff."

"Look!" I said, "this is no time for fooling. Show me where it is quick till I destroy it. God knows I'm taking enough risk." She stretched her arms over her head and yawned.

"Is your father here?" I said.

"He is not."

"Is Maeve?"

"She is not."

"Well then, show me where it is quick. The Sergeant will be in on top of us in a minute."

"He'll find nothing here."

"Very well then, I give up. But you'll be a sorry girl if your father gets six months or a year in jail."

"Be off with you now, you have the look of a spy about you. By the big boots I'd take you for a peeler. Go on now before I let out Shep."

I gave a sigh and turned out the gate again. The Sergeant was just coming up the field, his uniform standing out against the country like a scarecrow in the corn.

"Why aren't you inside keeping them out of the way?" says he.

"There's no one there."

"Better and better. Come on and help me now." And he was off like a retriever for the barn. I pretended to help him in his search, but he found no more than I did.

"I'll tell you a little trick I know," says he, and he caught up a dung-fork that was lying against the wall. "Come out here now and I'll show you." So I followed him out again. He went across to the heap of manure that was lying in the back yard and started to probe around in it with the fork. I was just standing, admiring the fine sight of a Sergeant at work when there was the noise of the fork striking something, and the next moment the Sergeant was standing up holding a two-gallon jar. He pulled out the cork and gave the first real smile I ever saw on his face.

"Poteen!" says he, and the way he said it you'd think it was a poem. Then he whipped it behind his back quick and I looked round and saw Maeve's sister just coming round the corner of the house. When she saw the Sergeant's uniform she shook her fist at the two of us.

"I knew what you were," she said, "I knew! Let you get out of this now before my father gets back or it'll be the worse for the pair of you."

"Be careful, young woman!" says the Sergeant. "It is a very dangerous thing to obstruct a Guard officer in the discharge of his duty. We are here in search of illicit spirits, and if there is any on the premises it is wiser to tell us now."

I was leaning against the door of the barn, looking out over the Mayo mountains, and wondering how long would poor old Lynch get at the District Court, when what should I see peeping up over the hedge but another red head. And this time it was Maeve sure enough. She had been there all the time watching every move. She gave me a wicked glare. I winked back. The Sergeant was standing with his back turned to her, rocking from his heels to his toes playing cat-and-mouse with the sister, and waggling the jar gently behind his back. There wasn't a prouder Sergeant on the soil of Ireland that minute.

I could see that Maeve wasn't quite sure whether I was just a pal of the Sergeant's that came out to keep him company, or a Guard on duty, and she kept glancing from me to the jar that the Sergeant was so busy hiding. She seemed to be asking me a question with her eyes. As there wasn't anything I could do to help her I gave her another wink and a big grin. She looked hard at me, then ducked out of sight behind the hedge. I was just beginning to wonder what had happened to her when she stood up straight, and my heart nearly stopped when I saw the big lump of a rock she had in her fist. I'm not a very narrow-minded man, and I had no particular regard for the Sergeant, but I wasn't going to have him murdered in cold blood before my eyes. If a thing like that came out at the inquest it would look very bad on my record. I was in two minds whether to shout out or not, weighing the trouble Maeve and her family would get into if I did against the trouble I'd get into if I didn't, when she drew back her arm, took wicked and deliberate aim, and let fly. I closed my eyes tight and turned away. When I heard a scream of agony from the Sergeant I closed them even tighter, but I opened them again when I heard what he was shouting.

"Blast it! Blast it! Blast it to hell!" he was roaring, and then I saw the heap of broken crockery at his feet. The sister was in kinks of laughter and there wasn't a sign of Maeve. There was a most delightful smell of the very best poteen on the air, and when the Sergeant threw the handle of the jar on the ground in a rage I realized that it was the jar and not the Sergeant's head that had received the blow. I burst out laughing.

"Who did that?" he shouted at me. "Who did that, you grinning imbecile?" But I shook my head.

"I was just day-dreaming," I said, "I didn't see a thing."

"You'll pay for this!" he said. "You'll pay dearly for this, you inefficient lout! Dereliction of duty! Gross imbecility! Crass stupidity! I'll have the coat off your back for this day's work!" Of course the poor man didn't know what he was saying, but in a way I was nearly sorry for him. He was so sure that he had the case all sewn up. But now, without the contents of the jar any chance of a prosecution was ballooned from the beginning. The Law requires very strict proof in these matters.

The Sergeant and myself searched all through the farm that day. And every day for a week afterwards Flaherty and Hanlon and myself searched it again. But it was labor in vain. It was great weather, though, and I used to spend most of the day lying out in the hay, and after the first day I managed to get Maeve to join me. I had a terrible job persuading her that all Guards aren't as bad as she thought, and that the Sergeant was quite exceptional. Fortunately, Flaherty and Hanlon were in no great hurry to get the searching finished, so I had plenty of time to devote to persuading her. For some reason old Lynch didn't seem to care if we searched till doomsday, and himself and myself struck up a great friendship when I told him about my conversation with Maeve's sister, Mary. So that when Maeve agreed to marry me he put up no objection.

The Sergeant did his level best to have me drummed out of the Guards for marrying a poteen-maker's daughter, but, as I pointed out to the Superintendent, there was no proof that Maurice Lynch ever ran a drop of poteen, and even if he did, wouldn't a Guard in the family be the greatest deterrent against illicit distilling. The Superintendent saw my point, but I'm not so sure that I was right. I've often said that my father-in-law makes the smoothest run of mountain dew it has ever been my good luck to taste.

It was just as well the Sergeant was moved soon after. He was very bitter about the broken jar and would have stopped at nothing to get a conviction. Things have been very quiet and peaceful since he left and crime has practically disappeared from the district.

MICHAEL MAC GRIAN

# Myself and a Rabbit

\*

The blackberry picker filled her small basket and departed. I hardly noticed her going. The strong sun-heat of afternoon had taken full possession and made all things still. All sound and movement had gone into the shadows to sleep.

I dozed in company with the trees until one sudden movement nearby broke the calm. I saw a rabbit and it was acting in a queer way. It ran around in circles and the erratic orbits grew smaller and smaller until it just ran up and down a few yards either way.

Then I saw another movement in the grass, an oiled keen movement showing flashes of rustbrown fur and I understood why the rabbit was acting so oddly.

The stoat was trailing by scent although only ten yards away, following the aimless circle of fear. The rabbit could not escape because the stoat scent was spun around it, etched indelibly on the still air by its own guideless movement. It might as well have been shut in a cage for it was powerless to break away to safety through the invisible web of dread.

I stood up. The stoat was very near and the rabbit was jerking about as if in a fit, small whimpering noises rasping in its throat. I knew the sequence. The squeals would increase to screams and then die away to snoring whimpers and the stoat would feed on the warm arterial blood, receiving the fearsoaked heartgush in its own throat.

From *The Bell*.

Maybe it was because my heart went out to the little beast in its grievous terror; maybe I felt its fear akin to something similar in myself: whatever bond had quickly tied us the rabbit hopped stiffly towards me, almost spent. I watched its coming, surprised and forgetting the trailing killer. It came right up to my feet and snuggled against my shoes.

The stoat was on the last hot scent. It saw the huddled form and leaped towards it with awkward little springs, undulating death movement swift as swift water. I snatched for the rabbit's ears and the stoat blundered against my hand.

I have felt the weight of water in a spating stream bearing against my body with a force irresistible; I have watched great breakers gouting through a narrow V of rock, churning and fuming; and I have experienced passion's culmination: I have dreamt dreams wherein I toppled from unknown heights down-rushing to some eternal abyss with the speed of light; and I can imagine the blind pressure of two dead ashed planets chafing lightly together in the gloom of space: but the shock of feeling that small stoat's bite on my forefinger, the blind a-human pressure behind the small white fangs driving their ivory points deep into flesh, gave more realization of force than any of these elemental things.

Instinctively I snatched up the rabbit with the stoat hanging momentarily from my finger. It dropped off, chattering with disappointment, tail bristling and eyes blowing. I made a kick at it, afraid of it, afraid even to touch it with my shoe.

"Go away!" I shouted. "Go away, you crazy wicked bastard!"

It ran around me twice, full of the hot scent and puzzled that it had not led to a kill, then it slipped away into the grass. The rabbit lay in my arms, the long ears close to its neck. It might die, I thought, die from terror, unscathed as it is.

I held it in my arms, sucking my finger and thinking. Soon I forgot about it altogether; all but its terror. I was just conscious of its heart under my fingers, conscious of the swift heart.

Lifting up my head I looked around. The silver lake below

me was serene with dappled cloud shadows. About me the
lush undergrowth clung to the shade. The wild flowers I
should have named drooped in the heat. The tall beeches
planted two hundred years before stood in straight immobile
lines waiting with terrible patience for their seasonal call.
The winding carriage track trebled its length in curves around
the edge of an inlet without thought for economy of the
cheap labor of a hundred semi-slaves now under the earth
they shovelled but did not own.

Myself and a rabbit looking down on that majestic landscape, on all the thick heavy beauty of a year's closing. Myself
and a rabbit, fearstricken by every mock shadow of the
day's designing, jumping nervously and apologetically at
the bark of every mongrel that lived by a law of instinctive
distrust.

To stand alone, I thought; to stand alone and unarmed,
unarmed but watchful; that was my wish—unarmed, fearful,
watchful; haunted perhaps by untold fears lodged in every
imagined shadow; mute as the rabbit was mute, and stalked
as it was stalked by one vast foolish braggart threat. . . .

The rabbit moved and brought me back. It was more peaceful. I walked down to the cottage, across the lawn, and deep
into the hazel thickets until I found a quiet place speckled
with green sunlight. There I released the animal.

It crouched close to the earth. Going softly downwind
I watched but it did not move. It may die, I thought, just like
that, and become a cold tight ball of fur.

When I clapped my hands it paid no heed and I could
not watch it any more. As I went back to the cottage I
thought about it and became irritated with it. It was a silly
animal. It was safe now, and free. To-morrow it might meet
the same or another stoat but to-day it was safe and free.

Going into the cottage I sat down, not thinking about
anything save of the rabbit in a confused way. My finger
was almost painless, less painful than the deep prick of a
thorn. It was marked by two punctures alongside the nail.

These were the only stigmata I could show to prove that
I had experienced a pressure as omnipotent as the hammer

of Thor. So I was led to wonder about the dark strength lying in the jaws of a lion, for instance, and what a fly must feel when nipped by a spider. And I wondered about all these dark a-human forces in nature, of the great and pitiless strength of a gale pressing against a flagging tree: by virtue of his humanity, apparently, man has been spared much of this confused and mighty scheme of existence.

Perhaps oddly enough I thought of the Lord's Prayer, listening again to my mother's voice when my hearing was far more developed than my speech. . . . Forgive us our debts, as we forgive our debtors. And lead us not into temptation, but deliver us from evil. . . .

I wanted to go back to the rabbit, hoping to find it gone. But I could not return for fear it was still crouching there quietly dying from complete terror, quietly dying in the green sunlight under the twisted hazels.

I grew angry at myself and rabbits, cursing them aloud for their silliness. Almost, I wanted to go back and kill the silly beast. I would take it up by the hind legs and bring down the edge of my right hand on its neck with a clean quick blow. It would leap wildly, twitch for a moment, and then lie still forever. Better that than thinking about it patiently dying.

I started to the door, hesitated, turned back. Going over to the camp bed I pulled out a suitcase and started packing.

Outside, the skiffs of wind crinkled patches of the lake's surface, leaving islands of calm dark water between. The tall bulrushes and reeds swayed over gracefully, the varnished green of the rushes catching the slanting sun on their plump rounded stems.

Ten high curlews scythed their way through the cooling air, heading westwards for the rich ripe ooze of the marshes into which they would plunge their curved bills with relish, casting abroad their liquid cry which was the sound of their shape and flight.

The breeze followed them, growing stronger and erasing all the calm dark patches, leapt among the bulrushes, raced over the hazels, and the trees whispered to the lake below.

MICHAEL MC LAVERTY

# The Wild Duck's Nest

\*

The sun was setting, spilling gold light on the low western hills of Rathlin Island. A small boy walked jauntily along a hoof-printed path that wriggled between the folds of these hills and opened out into a crater-like valley on the cliff-top. Presently he stopped as if remembering something, then suddenly he left the path, and began running up one of the hills. When he reached the top he was out of breath and stood watching streaks of light radiating from golden-edged clouds, the scene reminding him of a picture he had seen of the Transfiguration. A short distance below him was the cow standing at the edge of a reedy lake. Colm ran down to meet her waving his stick in the air, and the wind rumbling in his ears made him give an exultant whoop which splashed upon the hills in a shower of echoed sound. A flock of gulls lying on the short grass near the lake rose up languidly, drifting like blown snowflakes over the rim of the cliff.

The lake faced west and was fed by a stream, the drainings of the semi-circling hills. One side was open to the winds from the sea and in winter a little outlet trickled over the cliffs making a black vein in their gray sides. The boy lifted stones and began throwing them into the lake, weaving web after web on its calm surface. Then he skimmed the water with flat stones, some of them jumping the surface and coming to rest on the other side. He was delighted with himself and after listening to his echoing shouts of delight

From The Game Cock, New York, The Devin-Adair Co.

he ran to fetch his cow. Gently he tapped her on the side and reluctantly she went towards the brown-mudded path that led out of the valley. The boy was about to throw a final stone into the lake when a bird flew low over his head, its neck a-strain, and its orange-colored legs clear in the soft light. It was a wild duck. It circled the lake twice, thrice, coming lower each time and then with a nervous flapping of wings it skidded along the surface; its legs breaking the water into a series of silvery arcs. Its wings closed, it lit silently, gave a slight shiver, and began pecking indifferently at the water.

Colm, with dilated eyes, eagerly watched it making for the farther end of the lake. It meandered between tall bulrushes, its body black and solid as stone against the graying water. Then as if it had sunk it was gone. The boy ran stealthily along the bank looking away from the lake, pretending indifference. When he came opposite to where he had last seen the bird he stopped and peered through the sighing reeds whose shadows streaked the water in a maze of black strokes. In front of him was a soddy islet guarded by the spears of sedge and separated from the bank by a narrow channel of water. The water wasn't too deep—he could wade across with care.

Rolling up his short trousers he began to wade, his arms outstretched, and his legs brown and stunted in the mountain water. As he drew near the islet, his feet sank in the cold mud and bubbles winked up at him. He went more carefully and nervously. Then one trouser leg fell and dipped into the water; the boy dropped his hands to roll it up, he unbalanced, made a splashing sound, and the bird arose with a squawk and whirred away over the cliffs. For a moment the boy stood frightened. Then he clambered on to the wet-soaked sod of land, which was spattered with sea gulls' feathers and bits of wind-blown rushes.

Into each hummock he looked, pulling back the long grass. At last he came on the nest, facing seawards. Two flat rocks dimpled the face of the water and between them was a neck of land matted with coarse grass containing the nest. It was untidily built of dried rushes, straw and feathers, and in it lay one solitary egg. Colm was delighted. He looked around and saw no one. The nest was his. He lifted the egg, smooth and green as the sky, with a faint tinge of yellow like the reflected light from a buttercup; and then he felt he had done wrong. He put it back. He knew he shouldn't have touched it and he wondered would the bird forsake the nest. A vague sadness stole over him and he felt in his heart he had sinned. Carefully smoothing out his footprints he hurriedly left the islet and ran after his cow. The sun had now set and the cold shiver of evening enveloped him, chilling his body and saddening his mind.

In the morning he was up and away to school. He took the grass rut that edged the road for it was softer on the bare feet. His house was the last on the western headland and after a mile or so he was joined by Paddy McFall; both boys, dressed in similar hand-knitted blue jerseys and gray trousers, carried home-made school bags. Colm was full of the nest and as soon as he joined his companion he said eagerly: "Paddy, I've a nest—a wild duck's with one egg."

"And how do you know it's a wild duck's?" asked Paddy slightly jealous.

"Sure I saw her with my own two eyes, her brown speckled back with a crow's patch on it, and her yellow legs——"

"Where is it?" interrupted Paddy in a challenging tone.

"I'm not going to tell you, for you'd rob it!"

"Aach! I suppose it's a tame duck's you have or maybe an old gull's."

Colm put out his tongue at him. "A lot you know!" he said, "for a gull's egg has spots and this one is greenish-white, for I had it in my hand."

And then the words he didn't want to hear rushed from Paddy in a mocking chant, "You had it in your hand! . . . She'll forsake it! She'll forsake it! She'll forsake it!" he said, skipping along the road before him.

Colm felt as if he would choke or cry with vexation.

His mind told him that Paddy was right, but somehow he

couldn't give in to it and he replied: "She'll not forsake it! She'll not! I know she'll not!"

But in school his faith wavered. Through the windows he could see moving sheets of rain—rain that dribbled down the panes filling his mind with thoughts of the lake creased and chilled by wind; the nest sodden and black with wetness; and the egg cold as a cave stone. He shivered from the thoughts and fidgeted with the inkwell cover, sliding it backwards and forwards mechanically. The mischievous look had gone from his eyes and the school day dragged on interminably. But at last they were out in the rain, Colm rushing home as fast as he could.

He was no time at all at his dinner of potatoes and salted fish until he was out in the valley now smoky with drifts of slanting rain. Opposite the islet he entered the water. The wind was blowing into his face, rustling noisily the rushes heavy with the dust of rain. A moss-cheeper, swaying on a reed like a mouse, filled the air with light cries of loneliness.

The boy reached the islet, his heart thumping with excitement, wondering did the bird forsake. He went slowly, quietly, on to the strip of land that led to the nest. He rose on his toes, looking over the ledge to see if he could see her. And then every muscle tautened. She was on, her shoulders hunched up, and her bill lying on her breast as if she were asleep. Colm's heart hammered wildly in his ears. She hadn't forsaken. He was about to turn stealthily away. Something happened. The bird moved, her neck straightened, twitching nervously from side to side. The boy's head swam with lightness. He stood transfixed. The wild duck with a panicky flapping, rose heavily, and flew off towards the sea. . . . A guilty silence enveloped the boy. . . . He turned to go away, hesitated, and glanced back at the bare nest; it'd be no harm to have a look. Timidly he approached it, standing straight, and gazing over the edge. There in the nest lay two eggs. He drew in his breath with delight, splashed quickly from the island, and ran off whistling in the rain.

BRYAN MAC MAHON

# The Cat and the Cornfield

✳

In Ireland, all you need to make a story is two men with completed characters—say, a parish priest and his sexton. There at
once you have conflict. When, as a foil for the sexton, you
throw in a mature tinker girl, wild and lissom, love interest is
added to conflict. And when, finally, you supply a snow-white
cat, a cornfield, and a shrewish woman who asks three questions, the parts if properly put together should at least provide
a moderate tale.

The scene is laid in a village asleep on a summer hill: the
hour of the day is mid-morning. The village is made up of a
church that lacks a steeple, a pair of pubs—one thatched and
the other slated—with maybe a dozen higgledy-piggledy
houses divided equally as between thatch and slate. The
gaps between the houses yield glimpses of well-foliaged trees
beyond which the countryside falls away into loamy fields.

On the morning of our story, the sexton, a small grumpy
fellow of middle age with irregular red features, by name
Denny Furey, had just finished sweeping out the brown flag-
stones of the church porch. He then took up the wire mat at
the door and tried irritably but vainly to shake three pebbles
out of it.

At the sound of the rattling pebbles, the sexton's white
cat which was sitting on the sunny wall of the church beside
his master's cabin looked up and mewed soundlessly.

Denny glanced sourly at the cat. "Pangur Bán," he said,

From THE RED PETTICOAT, New York, E. P. Dutton.

"if you didn't sleep in my breeches and so have 'em warm before my shanks on frosty mornings, I'd have you drowned long 'go!" The cat—he had pale green eyes and a blotch on his nose—silently mewed his misunderstanding.

Suddenly there came a sound of harness bells. A tinker's spring-cart, painted bright green and blue, with a shaggy piebald cob between the shafts, drew slowly past the church gate. Sitting on the near wing of the cart was a tinker girl wearing a tartan dress and a bright shoulder-shawl. Eighteen, perhaps; more likely, nineteen. She had wild fair hair and a nut-brown complexion. Spying the sexton struggling with the mat, her eyes gleamed with puckish pleasure.

Meeting her gaze, Denny grimaced ill-temperedly and then half-turned his back on her. As on a thought he swung around to scowl her a reminder of her duty. Slowly the girl cut the sign of the Cross on herself.

Just beyond the church gateway, the cob's lazy motion came to a halt. The girl continued to stare at the sexton. Angrily Denny dropped the mat. Swiftly he raised his right hand as if he had been taken with a desire to shout: "Shoo! Be off with yourself at once!" The words refused to come.

Pangur Bán raised himself on shuddering legs, arched his back and sent a gracious but soundless mew of welcome in the girl's direction.

"That you may be lucky, master!" the tinker girl said. Then: "Your wife—have she e'er an old pair of shoes?"

"Wife! Wife! I've no wife!" Denny turned sharply away and snatched up his brush.

The girl watched as the sexton's movements of sweeping became indefinably jaunty. Then her smiling eyes roved and rested for a moment on the thatched cabin at the left of the church gate.

Without turning round, Denny shouted: "Nothing for you today!"

The girl was slow in replying. Her eyes still fast on the cabin, she said: "I know you've nothin' for me, master!" She did not draw upon the reins.

Denny stopped brushing. His stance indicated that again

he was struggling to say: "Be off!" Instead of speaking, he set his brush against the church wall, turned his head without moving his shoulders and looked fully at the girl. She answered his eyes with frankness. They kept looking at one another for a long time. At last, his altering gaze still locked in hers, Denny turned his body around.

As if caught in drowse Denny set aside his brush. He donned his hat, then walked slowly toward the church gate. Lost rosaries clinked as the white-painted iron yielded to his fingers. Denny looked to left and to right. Up to this their eyes had been bound fast to one another.

The sunlit village was asleep. Pangur Bán lay curled and still on the warm wall.

A strange tenderness glossed Denny's voice. "Where are you headin' for?" he asked. The gate latched shut behind him.

"Wherever the cob carries me!"

Again the girl's gaze swivelled to the cabin. "Is that your house?" she asked, and then, as she glanced again at the wall: "Is that your cat?"

"Ay! . . . Ay!"

For a long while the girl kept looking at the little house with its small deeply recessed windows. She noted well the dark-green half-door above which shone a latch of polished brass.

"Do you never tire of the road?" Denny asked.

"Do you never tire of being fettered?" the girl flashed. She had turned to look at him directly.

Both sighed fully and deeply. Under the black hat Denny's eyes had begun to smoulder.

Secretly the girl dragged on the rein. As the cob shifted from one leg to another, she uttered a small exclamation of annoyance. Her red and green skirt made a wheel as she leaped from the vehicle and advanced to make an obscure adjustment to the harness. This done she prepared to lead her animal away.

Denny glanced desperately around. Uproad stood a hissing gander with his flock of geese serried behind him.

"I'll convey you apass the gander!" he blurted.

The tinker girl glanced at the gander; her mouth-corners twitched in a smile. She made a great to-do about gathering up the reins and adjusting her shawl. As she led the animal away, Denny moved to the far side of the road and kept pace with her as she went. Walking thus, apart yet together, they left the village and stepped downhill. Once the sexton glanced fearfully over his shoulder; the village was not so much asleep as stone-dead.

As the white road twisted, the village on the hillock was unseen. The cob—a hairy, bony animal—moved swiftly on the declivity so that Denny had to hurry to keep up with the girl and her animal.

The splendor of the summer accompanied them. The gauds of the harness were winking in the bright light. The countryside was a silver shield inclining to gold. Their footfalls were muted in the limestone road dust. Muted also were the noise of the horse's unshod hooves and the ringing of the harness bells. At last they came to the foot of the hillock. Here the road ran between level fields. Denny looked over his shoulder and saw Pangur Bán fifty yards behind him walking stealthily on the road margin.

"Be off!" the sexton shouted.

Pangur Bán paused to utter his soundless mew.

The girl smiled. They walked on for a space. Again Denny turned. "Be off, you Judas!" he shouted. He snatched up a stone and flung it at the cat.

The instant the stone left the sexton's hand, Pangur judged that it was going to miss him. He remained utterly without movement. When the stone had gone singing away into stillness, the cat went over and smelled at a piece of road metal the bounding stone had disturbed. Pangur mewed his mystification into the sky; then spurted faithfully on.

The road again twisted. Now it was commanded by the entrance to the village on the hillock.

Here in a cornfield at the left-hand side of the road, the ripening corn was on the swing from green to gold. The field was a house of brightness open to the southern sky. Directly beside their boots a gap offered descent to the sown ground.

The cob stopped dead and began to crop the roadside grass.

"Let us sit in the sun," the sexton ventured. He indicated the remote corner of the cornfield.

The girl smiled in dreamy agreement. With slow movements she tied her cob to the butt of a whitethorn bush. The pair walked along by the edge of the corn and sat down on the grassy edge of the farthest headland. Here the corn screened them from the view of a person passing on the road. The fierceness and lushness of growth in this sun-trap had made the hedge behind them impenetrable. Denny set his hat back on his poll. Then he took the girl's hand in his and began to fondle it. Points of sweat appeared on his agitated face.

Twice already, from the top of the grassy fence, Pangur Bán had stretched out a paw in an attempt to descend into the cornfield. On each occasion thistles and thorns tipping his pads had dissuaded him from leaping. Through slim upended ovals of dark pupil the cat ruefully eyed the cropping horse, then turned to mew his upbraidings in the direction of his master. Tiring of this, he settled himself patiently to wait.

Pangur Bán sat with his tail curled around his front paws. His eyes were reluctant to open in the sunlight. His ears began to sift the natural sounds of the day.

Reading his Office, the huge old priest walked the village. Glancing up from his breviary, he noticed the brush idle against the church wall: he also spied the wire mat that lay almost concealed on the lawn grass. The impudence of the gander the priest punished with a wave of his blackthorn stick. Standing on the road in front of the sexton's cabin, he sang out: "Denny! Denny Furey!" There was no reply.

The priest shuffled to the church door and in a lowered voice again called for his sexton. At last, with an angry shrug of his shoulders, he again turned his attention to his breviary. Still reading, he sauntered downhill and out into the open country.

After a while he raised his eyes. First he saw the brown and white pony, then he spied the flame that was the cat burning white beside the olive cornfield.

The old man's face crinkled. He grunted. Imprisoning his

stick in his left armpit, he began to slouch in the direction of Pangur Bán. From time to time his eyes strayed over the gilt edging and the colored markers of his book.

Denny glanced up from his sober love-making.

"Divine God!" he exclaimed.

The girl was leaning back on the grass: her posture tautened a swath of green hay to silver. She was smiling up at the sky as she spaced her clean teeth along a grass stem.

Reaching the cat, the priest halted. "Pangur Bán," he wheedled in a low voice. His eyes were roving over the cornfield. The cat tilted his back against the lower may leaves, set his four paws together and drooped as if for a bout of languid gaiety.

For a moment or two the priest tricked with the cat. Then he threw back his shoulders. "To think that I don't see you, Denny Furey!" he clarioned.

Denny and the girl were silent and without movement. About them the minute living world asserted itself in the snip of grasshoppers.

Again the priest thundered: "Nice example for a sexton!"

The sweat beaded above Denny's eyebrows. His thighs began to shiver in the breeches his cat slept in. The girl peered at the priest through the altering lattice of the corn-heads. Her expression was quizzical as she glanced at Denny.

From the roadway came again the dreaded voice: "If it's the last thing I do, Denny Furey, I'll strip you of your black coat!"

At this moment a shrewish woman, wearing a black and green shawl, thrust around the bend of the road. She was resolutely headed for the village.

Seeing the woman approach, the priest quickly turned his face away from the cornfield and resumed his pacing along the road. His lips grew busy with the Latin psalms.

Peeping out and recognizing the newcomer, Denny Furey at first swore softly, then he began to moan. "The parish will be ringin' with the news before dark!" he sniffled.

The woman blessed the priest so as to break him from his

Office: then in a tone of voice that expressed thin concern: "Did I hear your voice raised, Father?"

The priest lowered his shaggy eyebrows. "Sermons don't sprout on bushes, my good woman!"

"Ah! Practisin' you were!"

Her crafty eyes alighted on the white cat. "Would it be bird-chasin' the sexton's cat is?"

"It could be, now that you mention it!"

There was a pause. The conversation of the wheat spars was only one step above silence. Flicking the cornfield and the cart with a single glance, the woman said, in a half whisper: "People say that tinker girls 'd pick the eye out of your head!"

"Did you never hear tell of the virtue of charity, woman?" the priest growled.

The woman made her crumbled excuses. It suited the priest not to accept them. Hurriedly she walked away. Resentment was implicit in the puffs of road-dust that spouted from beneath her toe-caps. Before the village swallowed her up, she looked over her shoulder. The priest was standing in mid-road waiting to parry this backward glance.

Again the priest turned his attention to the cornfield. With a sound half-grunt, half-chuckle, he untied the cob, and leading it by the head, turned away in the direction of the village.

The instant the harness bells began to ring, the tinker girl sprang to her feet and raced wildly but surefootedly along the edge of the cornfield. "Father!" she cried out. "Father!"

The priest came to a halt. Well out of the range of his stick, the girl stopped. "So I've drawn you, my vixen!" the priest said.

Breathlessly, the girl bobbed a half-curtsy.

"What're you goin' to do with my animal, Father?"

"Impounding him I am—unless you get that sexton o' mine out of the cornfield at once."

The girl leaped on to the low fence: "Come out o' the cornfield," she shouted, "I want to recover my cob!"

There was a pause. Then Denny shuffled to his feet. The cat stood up and mewed loyal greetings to his lord.

The priest stood at the horse's head. The angry girl was on

the fence; her arms akimbo. Shambling dismally, Denny drew nearer. When he had reached the roadway, the tinker girl cried out: "I was goin' my road, Father, when he coaxed me into the cornfield!"

Denny opened his mouth, but no words came. He began to blink his moist eyes. His mouth closed fast. He kept his distance from the priest's stick. As Pangur Bán began rubbing himself against the end of the beloved breeches, the sexton gave the cat the side of his long boot and sent him careening into the bushes.

"A *chait*, ou'r that!" he said.

"Aha, you scoundrel!" the priest reproved, "Can you do no better than abuse a dumb animal?"

Turning to the girl: "Take your cob! And if I catch you in this village again, by the Holy Man, I'll give you the length and breadth of my blackthorn!"

"He said he'd convey me apass the gander, Father!"

Three times she lunged forward. Three times her buttocks winced away. At last she mustered courage enough to grasp the winkers. Clutching the ring of the mouthpiece, she swung the pony downroad. When she had gained a few yards she leaped lightly on to the broad board on the side of the cart and slashed at the cob's rump with the free dangle of the reins. The animal leaped forward.

The priest, the sexton, the cat. The sunlit, rustling cornfield.

"Come on, me bucko!" the priest said grimly.

He began to lead the way home. The sexton trailed a miserable yard or two behind. Glory was gone out of his life. The wonderful day seemed to mock him. The future was a known road stretching before his leaden legs. What he had thought would prove a pleasant bauble had turned to a crown of thorns. In the past, whenever he had chafed against the drab nature of his existence, he had consoled himself thus: "One day, perhaps today, I'll run and buy me a hoop of bright colors."

Denny began to compare his soul to a pebble trapped in a wire mat of despair.

Gradually the priest became infected with Denny's moroseness. Side by side, the priest and his sexton continued to move homewards. In the faraway, the sound of the harness bells was a recessional song of adventure.

Behind the pair and at a discreet distance, Pangur Bán traveled quietly. Now and again he paused to mew his loyalty into the sunny world.

GEORGE MOORE

# Julia Cahill's Curse

✳

"And what has become of Margaret?"

"Ah, didn't her mother send her to America as soon as the baby was born? Once a woman is wake here she has to go. Hadn't Julia to go in the end, and she the only one that ever said she didn't mind the priest?"

"Julia who?" said I.

"Julia Cahill."

The name struck my fancy, and I asked the driver to tell me her story.

"Wasn't it Father Madden who had her put out of the parish? But she put her curse on it, and it's on it to this day."

"Do you believe in curses?"

"Bedad I do, sir. It's a terrible thing to put a curse on a man, and the curse that Julia put on Father Madden's parish was a bad one, the divil a worse. The sun was up at the time, and she on the hilltop raising both her hands. And the curse she put on the parish was that every year a roof must fall in and a family go to America. That was the curse, your honor, and every word of it has come true. You'll see for yourself as soon as we cross the mearing."

"And what became of Julia's baby?"

"I never heard she had one, sir."

He flicked his horse pensively with his whip, and it seemed to me that the disbelief I had expressed in the power of the curse disinclined him for further conversation.

From THE UNTILLED FIELD, Philadelphia, Lippincott.

"But," I said, "who is Julia Cahill, and how did she get the power to put a curse upon the village?"

"Didn't she go into the mountains every night to meet the fairies, and who else could've given her the power to put a curse on the village?"

"But she couldn't walk so far in one evening."

"Them that's in league with the fairies can walk that far and as much farther in an evening, your honor. A shepherd saw her; and you'll see the ruins of the cabins for yourself as soon as we cross the mearing, and I'll show you the cabin of the blind woman that Julia lived with before she went away."

"And how long is it since she went?"

"About twenty year, and there hasn't been a girl the like of her in these parts since. I was only a gossoon at the time, but I've heard tell she was as tall as I'm myself, and as straight as a poplar. She walked with a little swing in her walk, so that all the boys used to be looking after her, and she had fine black eyes, sir, and she was nearly always laughing. Father Madden had just come to the parish; and there was courting in these parts then, for aren't we the same as other people—we'd like to go out with a girl well enough if it was the custom of the country. Father Madden put down the ball alley because he said the boys stayed there instead of going into Mass, and he put down the crossroad dances because he said dancing was the cause of many a bastard, and he wanted none in his parish. Now there was no dancer like Julia; the boys used to gather about to see her dance, and who ever walked with her under the hedges in the summer could never think about another woman. The village was cracked about her. There was fighting, so I suppose the priest was right: he had to get rid of her. But I think he mightn't have been as hard on her as he was.

"One evening he went down to the house. Julia's people were well-to-do people, they kept a grocery store in the village; and when he came into the shop who should be there but the richest farmer in the country, Michael Moran by name, trying to get Julia for his wife. He didn't go straight to Julia, and that's what swept him. There are two counters in that shop, and Julia was at the one on the left hand as you go in. And many's the pound she had made for her parents at that counter. Michael Moran says to the father, 'Now, what fortune are you going to give with Julia?' And the father says there was many a man who would take her without any; and that's how they spoke, and Julia listening quietly all the while at the opposite counter. For Michael didn't know what a spirited girl she was, but went on arguing till he got the father to say fifty pounds, and thinking he had got him so far he said, 'I'll never drop a flap to her unless you give the two heifers.' Julia never said a word, she just sat listening. It was then that the priest came in. And over he goes to Julia; 'And now,' says he, 'aren't you proud to hear that you'll have such a fine fortune, and it's I that'll be glad to see you married, for I can't have any more of your goings-on in my parish. You're the encouragement of the dancing and courting here; but I'm going to put an end to it.' Julia didn't answer a word, and he went over to them that were arguing about the sixty pounds. 'Now why not make it fifty-five?' says he. So the father agreed to that since the priest had said it. And all three of them thought the marriage was settled. 'Now what will you be taking, Father Tom?' says Cahill, 'and you, Michael?' Sorra one of them thought of asking her if she was pleased with Michael; but little did they know what was passing in her mind, and when they came over to the counter to tell her what they had settled, she said, 'Well, I've just been listening to you, and 'tis well for you to be wasting your time talking about me,' and she tossed her head, saying she would just pick the boy out of the parish that pleased her best. And what angered the priest most of all was her way of saying it— that the boy that would marry her would be marrying herself and not the money that would be paid when the book was signed or when the first baby was born. Now it was agin girls marrying according to their fancy that Father Madden had set himself. He had said in his sermon the Sunday before that young people shouldn't be allowed out by themselves at all, but that the parents should make up the marriages for them. And he went fairly wild when Julia told him the example she was going to set. He tried to keep his temper, sir, but it was getting the better of him all the while, and Julia said, 'My boy isn't in the parish now, but maybe he is on his way here, and he may be here to-morrow or the next day.' And when Julia's father heard her speak like that he knew that no-one would turn her from what she was saying, and he said, 'Michael Moran, my good man, you may go your way: you'll never get her.' Then he went back to hear what Julia was saying to the priest, but it was the priest that was talking. 'Do you think,' says he, 'I am going to let you go on turning the head of every boy in the parish? Do you think,' says he, 'I'm going to see you gallavanting with one and then with the other? Do you think I'm going to see fighting and quarrelling for your like? Do you think I'm going to hear stories like I heard last week about poor Patsy Carey, who has gone out of his mind, they say, on account of your treatment? No,' says he, 'I'll have no more of that. I'll have you out of my parish, or I'll have you married.' Julia didn't answer the priest; she tossed her head, and went on making up parcels of tea and sugar and getting the steps and taking down candles, though she didn't want them, just to show the priest that she didn't mind what he was saying. And all the while her father trembling, not knowing what would happen, for the priest had a big stick, and there was no saying that he wouldn't strike her. Cahill tried to quiet the priest, he promising him that Julia shouldn't go out any more in the evenings, and bedad, sir, she was out the same evening with a young man and the priest saw them, and the next evening she was out with another and the priest saw them, nor was she minded at the end of the month to marry any of them. Then the priest went down to the shop to speak to her a second time, and he went down again a third time, though what he said the third time no-one knows, no-one being there at the time. And next Sunday he spoke out, saying that a disobedient daughter would have the worst devil in hell to attend on her. I've heard tell that he called her the evil spirit that set men mad. But most of the people that were there are dead or gone to America, and no-one rightly knows what he did say, only that the words came pouring out of his mouth, and the people when they saw Julia crossed themselves, and even the boys who were most mad after Julia were afraid to speak to her. Cahill had to put her out."

"Do you mean to say that the father put his daughter out?"

"Sure, didn't the priest threaten to turn him into a rabbit if he didn't, and no-one in the parish would speak to Julia, they were so afraid of Father Madden, and if it hadn't been for the blind woman that I was speaking about a while ago, sir, it is to the Poor House she'd have to go. The blind woman has a little cabin at the edge of the bog—I'll point it out to you, sir; we do be passing it by—and she was with the blind woman for nearly two years disowned by her own father. Her clothes wore out, but she was as beautiful without them as with them. The boys were told not to look back, but sure they couldn't help it.

"Ah, it was a long while before Father Madden could get shut of her. The blind woman said she wouldn't see Julia thrown out on the road-side, and she was as good as her word for wellnigh two years, till Julia went to America, so some do be saying, sir, whilst others do be saying she joined the fairies. But 'tis for sure, sir, that the day she left the parish Pat Quinn heard a knocking at his window and somebody asking if he would lend his cart to go to the railway station. Pat was a heavy sleeper and he didn't get up, and it is thought that it was Julia who wanted Pat's cart to take her to the station; it's a good ten mile; but she got there all the same!"

"You said something about a curse?"

"Yes, sir. You'll see the hill presently. A man who was taking some sheep to the fair saw her there. The sun was just getting up and he saw her cursing the village, raising both her hands, sir, up to the sun, and since that curse was spoken every year a roof has fallen in, sometimes two or three."

I could see he believed the story, and for the moment I, too, believed in an outcast Venus becoming the evil spirit of a village that would not accept her as divine.

"Look, sir, the woman coming down the road is Bridget Coyne. And that's her house," he said, and we passed a house built of loose stones without mortar, but a little better than the mud cabins I had seen in Father MacTurnan's parish.

"And now, sir, you will see the loneliest parish in Ireland."

And I noticed that though the land was good, there seemed to be few people on it, and what was more significant than the untilled fields were the ruins for they were not the cold ruins of twenty, or thirty, or forty years ago when the people were evicted and their tillage turned into pasture—the ruins I saw were the ruins of cabins that had been lately abandoned, and I said:

"It wasn't the landlord who evicted these people."

"Ah, it's the landlord who would be glad to have them back, but there's no getting them back. Everyone here will have to go, and 'tis said that the priest will say Mass in an empty chapel, sorra a one will be there but Bridget, and she'll be the last he'll give communion to. It's said, your honor, that Julia has been seen in America, and I'm going there this autumn. You may be sure I'll keep a lookout for her."

"But all this is twenty years ago. You won't know her. A woman changes a good deal in twenty years."

"There will be no change in her, your honor. Sure hasn't she been with the fairies?"

VAL MULKERNS

# The World Outside

❋

Most of the children were early that morning, creeping in
subdued and stiff in the unaccustomed shoes, their faces and
limbs shining from prolonged scrubbing. Some of the boys
looked unusually ugly because of having had their hair savagely attacked with scissors and bowl the previous night by
overzealous mothers, but the girls were glossy and braided and
comely, and looked much more confident than the boys, as if
handling inspectors would not be much trouble to them. The
school master scanned all the faces sharply, planning the
traditional reshuffle. Something nervous and trusting in the
general atmosphere prompted him to put them at ease, though
he was jumpy enough himself.

"Tell me, is it the same crowd at all I have before me, or is
it some swanky gang down from Dublin for the day?" he
grinned at them in Irish, and a relieved pleased ripple of
laughter went over the desks. "Let me see now, we'll have to
have yourself in the front, Mary Mannion, to show off that
brave red ribbon, and let you take yourself to the back desk,
Tomás Peig, where with God's help you'll get a chance to
show the Inspector how to do fractions." The point was that
Mary was easy on the eyes and utterly brainless, and Tomás
Peig was a bright lad and back benchers were inevitably ques-
tioned. "We'll have you over by the window, Muiris, and our
friend with the red head in the second row. Will you get
those boots back on you this minute, Tadg, and I'll flay the

From *Irish Writing*.

155

hide off you if I see them anywhere except where they're meant to be. Do you think now that it was to decorate the floor for me your mother went to Clifden last week and handed out a mint of money. No, Sir, well you may be sure the answer is No Sir, and take heed of what I said to you, if you value that hide of yours." But as the reshuffling went on, they understood the unusual bantering humor for what it was, an effort to put them at ease, and their faces beamed gratefully back at him. They were being examined, and God knew what horrible things would happen to them if they failed to please the inspector, and here was Boozy, the decent man, and he with nothing to fear being a Master, soft as butter with them to drive away their nervousness.

"Now listen to me the lot of you. If he speaks to you in Irish don't answer him back in a blast of English just to show that you know it. Answer him in Irish. Now if he speaks to you in English, what are you to do, Mary Mannion?"

"Answer him in Irish, sir," said Mary with a bright confident smile. There was a gale of laughter, and Mary was prodded incredulously by her neighbours.

" 'Tis a professor of Logic we'll make out of you. If he speaks to you in English, what will *you* do, tell her, Martin Flaherty?"

"Answer him in English, sir."

"Right. Now keep that in your heads. The next thing to remember is if he asks the class in general a question and you think you know the answer, put up your hands. Don't be afraid. He won't eat you if you happen to be wrong. He's probably a fine, well-fed man. The only people whose hands I don't want to see up for anything are Mary Mannion and Micilín Seán Mullen, because they have a job keeping up with the best of us, and we'll give them a rest to-day. Next year with the help of God they'll be ready for anything. Do you hear that now, the pair of you?"

"Yes, sir." Micilín Seán was beaming with relief and Mary Mannion was sulking.

"Right. Now the next thing to remember is—" his eyes suddenly caught sight of a figure at the gate—"that he's coming up the path this minute, and let you keep as still as mice while I call the register." There were sighs and gasps and rapid intakes of breath all around, and then utter petrified silence, and everybody answering "Annso, a Mhaighistear" in an unrecognizable whisper.

Mr. Mulvey was gray and hunched and small, with heavy-lidded gloomy eyes and a mouth turning down hopelessly at the corners. A first glance, before he opened his mouth, suggested that his voice would be a sick wind among the reeds, but in fact it was big and jolly and when he laughed, which was frequently, you had the fantastic impression that some enchantment had been worked before your eyes and that this was certainly not the man who had walked into the room. It was difficult to say whether his life had taken the form of a victorious battle against his natural temperament, or whether it was only his appearance which belied him. His clothes were silver gray and faultlessly pressed, and he carried a neatly rolled black umbrella and a black brief-case.

As he stepped into the room out of the thickening rain, the children scraped to their feet and stood looking at him with dismay. They were more used to fat tweedy red-faced inspectors with patches of leather down their jackets. He shook hands with and spoke a few pleasant words to Mr. McGlynn, and then turned to the pupils with his incredible smile, which showed square healthy white teeth, slightly prominent, and produced numbers of answering smiles. He was delighted to see them all, absolutely delighted, and hoped to learn more this morning than he had ever done at school. Would they sit down now, and attend to Mr. McGlynn's lesson, and later on he'd have a chat with them. He sat down on the chair which had been placed for him near the window, opened his brief-case, and became again, in a moment, the gloomy little gray man who had entered the room. The schoolmaster finished calling the register, closed the book, and sent Mary Mannion across with it to the inspector. Then the lesson began, Geography. The large map of Europe behind the master's desk was covered by a map of Mexico, and as was his usual custom, he began by giving them a general impression of the country itself, the color, the atmosphere, then something of its history. His words were alive and interesting, because omnivorous reading of everything from strictly technical works or anthropological works to things like Graham Greene's "The Lawless Roads" had produced complete familiarity. It happened to be Mexico to-day because that was the stage of the syllabus they had reached, but it was the same with everywhere, when he was sober, that is. The three maps which he drew with quick strokes, one of the physical regions, one of the climatic regions, and the third showing produce, were accurate and even beautiful with their lively blending colors. Then the class was set to work, an intricate business because of the different ages. Little working groups were put together, and a résumé of what in particular each had to tackle was given, and the older pupils were set some questions on the lesson.

All this time, the bent little depressed figure by the window appeared to be taking no notice. The register had been scrutinized and laid aside, and also some sample exercise books, and then he seemed to give all his attention to some private papers. The Arithmetic lesson went by, and the Irish grammar lesson, and then towards midday, when a rising wind was lashing the rain against the windows, he stood up and the transfiguring smile shone out.

"Well now, I suppose you're all fit for bed, after the work you've done this morning, what?" He drew the required laugh from them, and rubbed his small gray hands happily together. "But before we let you off home there are one or two things which have been puzzling me for some time." He changed rapidly to English. "Tell me, is Mexico in the Northern Hemisphere?" The hands shot up, and so did Mary Mannion's, but it was rapidly lowered. "I see my little friend here with the red ribbon knows and doesn't know. Which hemisphere is Mexico in, will you tell me now, like the sound woman you are?"

"The Southern Hemisphere, sir," said Mary Mannion with superb confidence and a shake of the head. There were the inevitable gasps from the class, and Mr. Mulvey smiled still more brilliantly.

"I don't think we all agree with you there, do we?" and there was an enthusiastic chorus of "No sir!" "The last time I was in Mexico," he went on, directly addressing Mary Mannion, who was smiling engagingly at him, "it was in the Northern Hemisphere. Will you remember that, because I don't think it's moved since then?"

"Yes, sir. No, sir," said Mary Mannion with another engaging smile.

"Well now there's another thing that's been puzzling me. A few weeks ago I went into the dining room of my house in Galway and two of the children had apples, nice big red ones. Seán said, 'Daddy, I'll give you half mine,' and Máire said, 'I'll give you three-eighths of mine, Daddy.' Now I thought a while before I decided which I'd take, and I want to think now. Which was the more decent offer of the two, Seán's or Máire's?" The hands went up slowly, three, four, six, then ten. "Difficult question to put to a poor simple father, wasn't it? How did I know which to take?" Again he was speaking Irish.

"I'd have taken the both of them, sir," said Mary Mannion in lamentable English, beside herself with the notice she had achieved.

"Ní thuigim," said Mr. Mulvey, with another brilliant smile, and then ignored her. "Well, will you tell me, the boy at the back, there?"

Tomás Peig, to the schoolmaster's joy, got smartly to his feet, held back his fair head and spoke up very clearly. "Seán's offer was the one you should have taken, sir, because he was giving you four-eighths (or a half) and Máire was only giving you three-eighths."

"Splendid. If I had been as bright as you now, I wouldn't have done myself out of the eighth of a fine apple."

Before they had quite finished laughing, the inspector turned to the schoolmaster and said, "I think the best thing we can do now is to send them off home for the rest of the day because they're too clever for us."

When they had all filed out into the cloakroom in clattering happiness, Mr. Mulvey's gloomy gray eyes roamed for a while about the schoolmaster's face before the smile broke again and he held out his hand. "That was the only Geography lesson in Ireland that's ever interested me," he said. He glanced quickly again at the schoolmaster's qualifications listed on the sheet before him, and asked sharply: "What are you doing here? We could do with plenty more of your kind in the national schools throughout the country but—?" He shrugged, half-smiling the question.

"It suits me here," Peter McGlynn said briefly, "I like it."

The inspector shrugged again. "If you ever wanted a change, my friend Dr. Linnane in Galway would jump at a man like you—preparing boys for University scholarships, that sort of thing."

"Thanks," the schoolmaster said without interest, "I'll remember if I ever decide to change. It's very kind of you."

"Nonsense," Mulvey replied, with an old-fashioned air, gathering his things together and fastening the brief-case. "You lived for some time in Mexico, I take it?"

"No. My Grand Tour took the form of a day trip to Liverpool. I never slept a night outside this country in my life."

"Remarkable. I taught, myself, for seven years in Mexico City and you brought it back into this classroom today, the heat, the filth, the color, the indolence, the preposterous fascination of the place. It's remarkable."

"No," Peter McGlynn smiled, "it's Baedeker, and a studious youth, and Graham Greene and a trick of the tongue. You'll not refuse a bite of lunch with me in our one and only hostelry, Pats Flaherty's?"

"I will now," said the inspector warmly, "I spend my life having lunch with clerical managers and a man can do with a bit of civilization now and again."

Pats' wife had clearly taken some trouble to see that the catering arrangements of Ballyconnolly would stand up to inspection quite as well as the school. As soon as she had received the schoolmaster's order two days previously, she had set to work, scouring and polishing the little square room off the bar, hunting out her best lace tablecloth, unused since the previous inspector's visit, and fixing a formidable array of family photographs along the mantelpiece. Despite these, the warm, low-ceilinged little room with its scarlet geraniums and looped lace curtains was welcoming to the two men as they stepped in out of the bitter wild morning. The place was permeated by the fragrance of roasting fowl, stewed apples and strong spirits, blending deliciously with the bitterness of turf-smoke. Kate Pats Flaherty bustled busily in and out, talking all the time.

" 'Tis frozen and demented the pair of you must be with the hunger, now. Ah, sure I often heard it said a man that works with his brain needs twice the feeding of a man that works with his body, and why wouldn't he, indeed? There was a cousin of my own, Mr. Mulvey, sir, and there he is before ye on the mantelpiece with the white face there in the middle, and hadn't they got him starved in the college above in Dublin and he going in for a priest. Night and day he was at the books, God pity him, and he no more than a lad, and there wasn't he only out a priest a few months, and his brother not even married, when he took a delicacy and died on his poor mother, God between us and all harm. 'Twas a fright to the world the way she took it, bawling and crying every time she'd look at a priest for years after. There she is for you now, Mr. McGlynn, on the bend of the mantelpiece with the feathery hat down near her nose, but sure God is good and didn't the second lad, a fine big puck of a boy, go in for a priest after, and he's a curate below in Kerry now. Another sup of that soup, Mr. Mulvey, sir? Or the Master? Well now, I'll have that bird on the table before you'll be finished licking your lips. There he is to your north now, Mr. Mulvey, sir, with the fine soft plucks on him and the holy book in his hands. We had him here now, and you could have seen him only a few weeks ago, and there was never a lad like him for feeding, and wouldn't he need it, I ask you, and him not to be dying on us like his poor brother, God rest his soul." Half of this oration was in English and half in Irish, and during journeys to the kitchen and to the bar the rich strong voice came clearly back to her guests, of whom she expected and desired no response. It was only when the last course had been cleared away and the bottle of whiskey ordered by the schoolmaster was between them on the table, and the smoke from their cigarettes was rising to the low ceiling, that Kate Pats Flaherty drew the door behind her, put her head around it again and said: "I'll leave ye now to yourselves to talk to your heart's content and if there's any other thing in the world ye want, leave a screech out of ye and I'll hear it."

She went, and the door closed at last. In the brief satisfied silence the rain beat in gusty blasts against the window, and the wind swept down the chimney to set the turf leaping and blazing. The hunched gray man in the gray clothes was the first to speak, lifting the gloomy eyes that were flecked now with a faint humor.

"There's Ireland for you now, McGlynn, all of it. Unending rain rattling the windows, and inside a kindly woman boasting about her clerical relations, and two men drinking whiskey, and outside the rest of the world. If Michelangelo painted the Resurrection on her smoky ceiling she wouldn't give it a look or him a thank-you if her portly cousin His Reverence were within miles of the place. Once upon a time we exported scholars and culture to the Continent. Now we export nothing but beasts and priests, God help us." And there began one of those inevitable discussions on what's wrong with the country, that never end and are more common in Ireland than discussions on religion or sex. But before the well-worn tracks had been followed to within reach of their muddy end, the talk under the direction of Mr. Mulvey took a turn to Mexico, and from there to Spain where he had found his wife, the daughter of a Spaniard who had a ballet company in Mexico but who had left his daughter in Spain to be educated. In the warm half-forgotten enchantment of good whiskey on which the brain floated away like a dead flower and only the senses and the imagination were taut and alive, the schoolmaster felt the sun like the caressing tongue of some fantastic animal, at once savage and tender, and smelled the fruit piled high in the narrow streets, and the bitterness of cheap wine, shivered at the sudden white chill inside the vaulted Cathedrals where black-eyed women chattered and laughed before Mass began and felt no urge to leave their personalities like gifts outside the church door, at which filthy mewling beggars held out diseased limbs; he watched the cypresses shooting eager and dark into warm, star-filled air tingling with the music of De Falla to which a girl was dancing like a flame, twisting and writhing in the dark agony of exorcism; narrow martyred faces of El Greco floated in a golden mist beside the warm sensual beauties of Velasquez and in a timeless jumble of history real and imagined the sweet sane voice of a woman saint blended with the fat bass of a wandering peasant demanding an island of his master; and over it all, rising and falling like a sea of sound, was the music of Albeniz, the "Iberia," of which every note was as familiar as the sound of rain beating on gray stone.

He had no clear memory of when exactly the little gray inspector left him, but only a vague impression of a warm handgrip and a voice urging him to visit the house in Galway to meet Maria, and look at some Spanish etchings and some Mexican carvings, and he vaguely remembered too standing at the door of Pats Flaherty's and watching the huddled gray figure disappearing through driving rain in the direction of his car, and then he remembered turning back into the fire-broken shadows of the bar, the tang of spirits and turf-smoke in his nostrils, and his head bemused with sunlight.

# The Devil and O'Flaherty

❋

"The devil and O'Flaherty couldn't do it; no, they couldn't," said the old carman to me when I told him that I had to be in Galway before ten o'clock. "Why, man, if we had a racehorse, we couldn't do it. You won't catch that train to-night, take my word for it."

The rain was coming down in torrents and the west wind blew a full gale from the sea. Where there were trees by the roadside the wind made the weirdest music in their bare branches. The full moon was somewhere up in the sky if the astronomers were to be believed, but it was completely hidden from us. I was wet to the skin, tired, weary and hungry. The driver was in no better condition. The horse was just dragging his legs after him and his head bobbed up and down like a child's toy horse. The wind shrieked, making a sound like devils' music. The horse started. The driver jumped down and, slowly as the horse went before, he now went very much slower, as the driver held him by the bridle and tried to coax him forward. I said a lot of things about that horse, about Galway carmen, about the weather, the place and other things, but I fear the printer would be ashamed to read them. The driver, however, paid no attention to what I said. Probably he had heard similar language pretty often before. In any case he went on in his own way, as he did not mount the car again until we had gone a couple of miles of the wet road, muddy and full of ruts.

From THE WOMAN AT THE WINDOW AND OTHER STORIES, translated from the Irish by Eamonn O'Neill, Dublin, The Talbot Press.

He was between me and the wind, and from time to time I heard him mutter something. "The Devil" was what I heard oftenest, but sometimes I caught the words "The Devil and O'Flaherty." Though I was swearing under my breath myself, I was becoming interested in the driver's mutterings. "O'Flaherty!" Who was O'Flaherty? What had he to do with the Devil? I thought of every story I had ever heard about devils assuming the form of men. Was O'Flaherty a devil in human form? Where did he live? When? What was his appearance? Did he leave any family? Did they take after the father who begot them, or the mother who bore them?

The sky cleared somewhat. The astronomers were right. The moon came out. The driver had been silent for some time.

"Over there on the top of the cliff he lived," he said suddenly.

I started.

"Who?" I said. "The Devil, was it?"

"No, but his heir. O'Flaherty Dubh."

I put him a few questions and soon he let himself go.

"Over there he lived," he said, "till the devil came for him in the end. He was a landlord but, even so, many a hundred pounds did he owe all over the country. God help you, man! If he had a couple of thousand a year itself, he was well able to get through it. Racehorses, gambling, dogs, eating and drinking, music and dancing by day and by night. Women—oh! shut up, man! He scandalized the whole countryside. He did, indeed!"

The driver lit his pipe, and I lit mine, but not without difficulty. The driver seemed willing to continue his story.

"Was he married, did you say?" he said, answering me. "Didn't I tell you he was? He wasn't much more than twenty when he married an earl's daughter from Munster—a kind, charitable, charming woman—but where's the wife who could live in the same house with a man who had a wife in every village from here to Dublin? After the birth of her fifth son she had to return to Munster. The child had not even

been baptized when seven carriages drove up to her
door one night. O'Flaherty himself was in the first carriage.
All the occupants—men and women—were under the influence of drink and were singing ribald songs. She tried to
keep them out, but they forced the door. They locked her
up in one of the top rooms and then pandemonium reigned
downstairs. They say that her heart was broken that night.
She had left her husband, but the blessing of the people
went with her. It did, indeed.

"I tell you that she brought her sons with her too, but
he took them from her again after instituting legal proceed-
ings. And didn't he rear them well, piously, and properly!
They never went to school and the teaching they got from
their father—well, much good it did them. If their father
killed a man without rhyme or reason they applauded the
deed and said that never was such a fine deed done in Ireland.
It was amazing to see these five young men going mad through
the country scaring man and beast. I saw one of them myself—Redmond he was called—being hanged in Galway. He
had killed his own brother all over a woman.

"He had nine others at home between sons and daughters.
Mind, I don't say that his wife returned. Oh, no! not likely!
But he got another wife—what's this her name was? No
matter. He had three more sons and two daughters by her.
What's the use of talking? People wouldn't have said much,
perhaps, were it not that he was a bad man in other respects.
He never gave anything in charity, and after a night's feasting
it was not to the poor that he gave the leavings next day but
to his dogs. My father told me that, one morning he went
there with a car, he saw the dogs and the poor scrambling
for the remnants of the preceding night's banquet. O'Flaherty
himself was present enjoying the fun. My father struck him.
Were it not that the other man was drunk my father would
not have got a month's imprisonment."

By this time we were approaching the town.

"What was the end of him?" I asked.

"Well, indeed, it's hard to say truly," he answered, "for
there are many versions of the story, but mine is the true

one if it was the truth that Big Jack, the bailiff, told me. As I have already said, he owed thousands throughout the country and there was a law then in force that if a man died in debt his body might be seized. He fell ill. He was not at home when the stroke seized him, but hunting with his sons in the hills. He was taken to a little cottage from which he had evicted the tenants years before. He died very shortly. His sons made a coffin to take him home in and they "keened" him bitterly. While they were "keening" a man walked in— apparently a huntsman. He was really a bailiff and his assistants were not far off. He expressed sympathy with the young men. He gave them a drink out of a bottle he had in his pocket. They fell asleep.

"It was night—a terrible night like this. Five young men were asleep on the floor. An old man lay cold and stiff in his coffin. Four others getting ready to carry away the body. Two candles stuck in bottles gave them light. They took hold of the coffin, lifted it and put it on their shoulders. A peal of thunder burst over the mountain cabin and the wind rose. The door was shattered and the lights went out. The body-snatchers trembled. One of the young men stirred and yawned.

" 'Oh! oh! he's alive. He's alive,' said one of the bailiffs.

"They put down the coffin on the floor. They were terror-stricken. They re-lit the candles and took a swig out of the bottle.

" 'Better wait and see will the night clear up,' said one of them.

"They agreed, and all four sat down on the floor around the body. They had another swig out of the bottle. A pack of cards was produced and they began to play.

"The night calmed down. There wasn't the least sound to be heard anywhere save the snoring of the young men in their heavy sleep and the falling of the cards on the coffin-lid. The bailiffs themselves got drowsy and fell asleep one by one. The two candles which were stuck in bottles at the head of the coffin were still burning. One of the bailiffs moved his hand. The cards were all scattered on the floor except one—the one we call the 'devil's own'—and that one lay, menacing and bright as it seemed—right over the heart of the corpse. Again the bailiff moved his hand. This time it touched the card and the card touched one of the bottles and the bottle and candle were knocked over An odd, shapeless shadow crossed the white wall. The floor about the coffin was littered with dry grass and chips of wood. In a twinkling the place was ablaze. The bailiffs escaped. O'Flaherty's sons also got away, except one who tried to carry off the body. He was burned alive. The body was burned—the cabin was burned. But the people never believed that this was the way O'Flaherty died. The old charred walls of the cabin are still there to prove that it was the devil himself that came to take home his heir with him."

We were now in the City of Galway.

"Where will you sleep to-night?" asked the driver.

"I shan't sleep at all, I fear," said I, and I didn't.

# The Drunkard

✻

It was a terrible blow to Father when Mr. Dooley on the terrace died. Mr. Dooley was a commercial traveller with two sons in the Dominicans and a car of his own, so socially he was miles ahead of us, but he had no false pride. Mr. Dooley was an intellectual, and, like all intellectuals the thing he loved best was conversation, and in his own limited way Father was a well-read man and could appreciate an intelligent talker. Mr. Dooley was remarkably intelligent. Between business acquaintances and clerical contacts, there was very little he didn't know about what went on in town, and evening after evening he crossed the road to our gate to explain to Father the news behind the news. He had a low, palavering voice and a knowing smile, and Father would listen in astonishment, giving him a conversational lead now and again, and then stump triumphantly in to Mother with his face aglow and ask: "Do you know what Mr. Dooley is after telling me?" Ever since, when somebody has given me some bit of information off the record I have found myself on the point of asking: "Was it Mr. Dooley told you that?"

Till I actually saw him laid out in his brown shroud with the rosary beads entwined between his waxy fingers I did not take the report of his death seriously. Even then I felt there must be a catch and that some summer evening Mr. Dooley must reappear at our gate to give us the low-down on the next world. But Father was very upset, partly because

From THE STORIES OF FRANK O'CONNOR, New York, Alfred Knopf.

Mr. Dooley was about one age with himself, a thing that always gives a distinctly personal turn to another man's demise; partly because now he would have no one to tell him what dirty work was behind the latest scene at the Corporation. You could count on your fingers the number of men in Blarney Lane who read the papers as Mr. Dooley did, and none of these would have overlooked the fact that Father was only a laboring man. Even Sullivan, the carpenter, a mere nobody, thought he was a cut above Father. It was certainly a solemn event.

"Half past two to the Curragh," Father said meditatively, putting down the paper.

"But you're not thinking of going to the funeral?" Mother asked in alarm.

" 'Twould be expected," Father said, scenting opposition. "I wouldn't give it to say to them."

"I think," said Mother with suppressed emotion, "it will be as much as anyone will expect if you go to the chapel with him."

("Going to the chapel," of course, was one thing, because the body was removed after work, but going to a funeral meant the loss of a half-day's pay.)

"The people hardly know us," she added.

"God between us and all harm," Father replied with dignity, "we'd be glad if it was our own turn."

To give Father his due, he was always ready to lose a half day for the sake of an old neighbour. It wasn't so much that he liked funerals as that he was a conscientious man who did as he would be done by; and nothing could have consoled him so much for the prospect of his own death as the assurance of a worthy funeral. And, to give Mother her due, it wasn't the half-day's pay she begrudged, badly as we could afford it.

Drink, you see, was Father's great weakness. He could keep steady for months, even for years, at a stretch, and while he did he was as good as gold. He was first up in the morning and brought the mother a cup of tea in bed, stayed at home in the evenings and read the paper; saved money and bought himself a new blue serge suit and bowler hat. He laughed at the folly of men who, week in week out, left their hard-earned money with the publicans; and sometimes, to pass an idle hour, he took pencil and paper and calculated precisely how much he saved each week through being a teetotaller. Being a natural optimist he sometimes continued this calculation through the whole span of his prospective existence and the total was breathtaking. He would die worth hundreds.

If I had only known it, this was a bad sign; a sign he was becoming stuffed up with spiritual pride and imagining himself better than his neighbours. Sooner or later, the spiritual pride grew till it called for some form of celebration. Then he took a drink—not whisky, of course; nothing like that— just a glass of some harmless drink like lager beer. That was the end of Father. By the time he had taken the first he already realized that he had made a fool of himself, took a second to forget it and a third to forget that he couldn't forget, and at last came home reeling drunk. From this on it was "The Drunkard's Progress," as in the moral prints. Next day he stayed in from work with a sick head while Mother went off to make his excuses at the works, and inside a fortnight he was poor and savage and despondent again. Once he began he drank steadily through everything down to the kitchen clock. Mother and I knew all the phases and dreaded all the dangers. Funerals were one.

"I have to go to Dunphy's to do a half-day's work," said Mother in distress. "Who's to look after Larry?"

"I'll look after Larry," Father said graciously. "The little walk will do him good."

There was no more to be said, though we all knew I didn't need anyone to look after me, and that I could quite well have stayed at home and looked after Sonny, but I was being attached to the party to act as a brake on Father. As a brake I had never achieved anything, but Mother still had great faith in me.

Next day, when I got home from school, Father was there before me and made a cup of tea for both of us. He was very good at tea, but too heavy in the hand for anything else; the way he cut bread was shocking. Afterwards, we went down the hill to the church, Father wearing his best blue serge and a bowler cocked to one side of his head with the least suggestion of the masher. To his great joy he discovered Peter Crowley among the mourners. Peter was another danger signal, as I knew well from certain experiences after Mass on Sunday morning: a mean man, as Mother said, who only went to funerals for the free drinks he could get at them. It turned out that he hadn't even known Mr. Dooley! But Father had a sort of contemptuous regard for him as one of the foolish people who wasted their good money in public-houses when they could be saving it. Very little of his own money Peter Crowley wasted!

It was an excellent funeral from Father's point of view. He had it all well studied before we set off after the hearse in the afternoon sunlight.

"Five carriages!" he exclaimed. "Five carriages and sixteen covered cars! There's one alderman, two councillors and 'tis unknown how many priests. I didn't see a funeral like this from the road since Willie Mack, the publican, died."

"Ah, he was well liked," said Crowley in his husky voice.

"My goodness, don't I know that?" snapped Father. "Wasn't the man my best friend? Two nights before he died—only two nights—he was over telling me the goings-on about the housing contract. Them fellows in the Corporation are night and day robbers. But even I never imagined he was as well connected as that."

Father was stepping out like a boy, pleased with everything: the other mourners, and the fine houses along Sunday's Well. I knew the danger signals were there in full force: a sunny day, a fine funeral, and a distinguished company of clerics and public men were bringing out all the natural vanity and flightiness of Father's character. It was with something like genuine pleasure that he saw his old friend lowered into the grave; with the sense of having performed a duty and the pleasant awareness that however much he would miss poor Mr. Dooley in the long summer evenings, it was he and not poor Mr. Dooley who would do the missing.

"We'll be making tracks before they break up," he whispered to Crowley as the gravediggers tossed in the first shovelfuls of clay, and away he went, hopping like a goat from grassy hump to hump. The drivers, who were probably in the same state as himself, though without months of abstinence to put an edge on it, looked up hopefully.

"Are they nearly finished, Mick?" bawled one.

"All over now bar the last prayers," trumpeted Father in the tone of one who brings news of great rejoicing.

The carriages passed us in a lather of dust several hundred yards from the public-house, and Father, whose feet gave him trouble in hot weather, quickened his pace, looking nervously over his shoulder for any sign of the main body of mourners crossing the hill. In a crowd like that a man might be kept waiting.

When we did reach the pub the carriages were drawn up outside, and solemn men in black ties were cautiously bringing out consolation to mysterious females whose hands reached out modestly from behind the drawn blinds of the coaches. Inside the pub there were only the drivers and a couple of shawly women. I felt if I was to act as a brake at all, this was the time, so I pulled Father by the coattails.

"Dadda, can't we go home now?" I asked.

"Two minutes now," he said, beaming affectionately. "Just a bottle of lemonade and we'll go home."

This was a bribe, and I knew it, but I was always a child of weak character. Father ordered lemonade and two pints. I was thirsty and swallowed my drink at once. But that wasn't Father's way. He had long months of abstinence behind him and an eternity of pleasure before. He took out his pipe, blew through it, filled it, and then lit it with loud pops, his eyes bulging above it. After that he deliberately turned his back on the pint, leaned one elbow on the counter in the attitude of a man who did not know there was a pint behind him, and deliberately brushed the tobacco from his palms. He had settled down for the evening. He was steadily working through all the important funerals he had ever attended. The carriages departed and the minor mourners drifted in till the pub was half full.

"Dadda," I said, pulling his coat again, "can't we go home now?"

"Ah, your mother won't be in for a long time yet," he said benevolently enough. "Run out in the road and play, can't you?"

It struck me as very cool, the way grown-ups assumed that you could play all by yourself on a strange road. I began to get bored as I had so often been bored before. I knew Father was quite capable of lingering there till nightfall. I knew I might have to bring him home, blind drunk, down Blarney Lane, with all the old women at their doors, saying: "Mick Delaney is on it again." I knew that my mother would be half crazy with anxiety; that next day Father wouldn't go out to work; and before the end of the week she would be running down to the pawn with the clock under her shawl. I could never get over the lonesomeness of the kitchen without a clock.

I was still thirsty. I found if I stood on tiptoe I could just reach Father's glass, and the idea occurred to me that it would be interesting to know what the contents were like. He had his back to it and wouldn't notice. I took down the glass and sipped cautiously. It was a terrible disappointment. I was astonished that he could even drink such stuff. It looked as if he had never tried lemonade.

I should have advised him about lemonade but he was holding forth himself in great style. I heard him say that bands were a great addition to a funeral. He put his arms in the position of someone holding a rifle in reverse and hummed a few bars of Chopin's Funeral March. Crowley nodded reverently. I took a longer drink and began to see that porter might have its advantages. I felt pleasantly elevated and philosophic. Father hummed a few bars of the Dead March in *Saul*. It was a nice pub and a very fine funeral, and I felt sure that poor Mr. Dooley in Heaven must be highly gratified. At the same time I thought they might have given him a band. As Father said, bands were a great addition.

But the wonderful thing about porter was the way it made you stand aside, or rather float aloft like a cherub rolling on a cloud, and watch yourself with your legs crossed, leaning against a bar counter, not worrying about trifles, but thinking deep, serious, grown-up thoughts about life and death. Looking at yourself like that, you couldn't help thinking after a while how funny you looked, and suddenly you got embarrassed and wanted to giggle. But by the time I had finished the pint, that phase too had passed; I found it hard to put back the glass, the counter seemed to have grown so high. Melancholia was supervening again.

"Well," Father said reverently, reaching behind him for his drink, "God rest the poor man's soul, wherever he is!" He stopped, looked first at the glass, and then at the people round him. "Hello," he said in a fairly good-humored tone, as if he were just prepared to consider it a joke, even if it was in bad taste, "who was at this?"

There was silence for a moment while the publican and the old women looked first at Father and then at his glass.

"There was no one at it, my good man," one of the women said with an offended air. "Is it robbers you think we are?"

"Ah, there's no one here would do a thing like that, Mick," said the publican in a shocked tone.

"Well, someone did it," said Father, his smile beginning to wear off.

"If they did, they were them that were nearer it," said the woman darkly, giving me a dirty look; and at the same moment the truth began to dawn on Father. I suppose I must have looked a bit starry-eyed. He bent and shook me.

"Are you all right, Larry?" he asked in alarm.

Peter Crowley looked down at me and grinned.

"Could you beat that?" he exclaimed in a husky voice.

I could, and without difficulty. I started to get sick. Father jumped back in holy terror that I might spoil his good suit, and hastily opened the back door.

"Run! run! run!" he shouted.

I saw the sunlit wall outside with the ivy overhanging it, and ran. The intention was good but the performance was exaggerated, because I lurched right into the wall, hurting it badly, as it seemed to me. Being always very polite, I said "Pardon" before the second bout came on me. Father, still concerned for his suit, came up behind and cautiously held me while I got sick.

"That's a good boy!" he said encouragingly. "You'll be grand when you get that up."

Before, I was not grand! Grand was the last thing I was. I gave one unmerciful wail out of me as he steered me back to the pub and put me sitting on the bench near the shawlies. They drew themselves up with an offended air, still sore at the suggestion that they had drunk his pint.

"God help us!" moaned one, looking pityingly at me, "isn't it the likes of them would be fathers?"

"Mick," said the publican in alarm, spraying sawdust on my tracks, "that child isn't supposed to be in here at all. You'd better take him home quick in case a bobby would see him."

"Merciful God!" whimpered Father, raising his eyes to heaven and clapping his hands silently as he only did when distraught, "what misfortune was on me? Or what will his mother say? . . . If women might stop at home and look after their children themselves!" he added in a snarl for the benefit of the shawlies. "Are them carriages all gone, Bill?"

"The carriages are finished long ago, Mick," replied the publican.

"I'll take him home," Father said despairingly. . . . "I'll never bring you out again," he threatened me "Here," he added, giving me the clean handkerchief from his breast pocket, "put that over your eye."

The blood on the handkerchief was the first indication I got that I was cut, and instantly my temple began to throb and I set up another howl.

"Whisht, whisht, whisht!" Father said testily, steering me out the door. "One'd think you were killed. That's nothing We'll wash it when we get home."

"Steady now, old scout!" Crowley said, taking the other side of me. "You'll be all right in a minute."

I never met two men who knew less about the effects of drink. The first breath of fresh air and the warmth of the sun made me groggier than ever and I pitched and rolled between wind and tide till Father started to whimper again.

"God Almighty, and the whole road out! What misfortune was on me didn't stop at my work! Can't you walk straight?"

I couldn't. I saw plain enough that, coaxed by the sunlight, every woman old and young in Blarney Lane was leaning over her half-door or sitting on her doorstep. They all stopped gabbling to gape at the strange spectacle of two sober, middle-aged men bringing home a drunken small boy with a cut over his eye. Father, torn between the shamefast desire to get me home as quick as he could, and the neighbourly need to explain that it wasn't his fault, finally halted outside Mrs. Roche's. There was a gang of old women outside a door at the opposite side of the road. I didn't like the look of them from the first. They seemed altogether too interested in me. I leaned against the wall of Mrs. Roche's cottage with my hands in my trousers pockets, thinking mournfully of poor Mr. Dooley in his cold grave on the Curragh, who would never walk down the road again, and, with great feeling, I began to sing a favorite song of Father's.

> *Though lost to Mononia and cold in the grave*
> *He returns to Kincora no more.*

"Wisha, the poor child!" Mrs. Roche said. "Haven't he a lovely voice, God bless him!"

That was what I thought myself, so I was the more surprised when Father said "Whisht!" and raised a threatening finger at me. He didn't seem to realize the appropriateness of the song, so I sang louder than ever.

"Whisht, I tell you!" he snapped, and then tried to work up a smile for Mrs. Roche's benefit. "We're nearly home now. I'll carry you the rest of the way."

But, drunk and all as I was, I knew better than to be carried home ignominiously like that.

"Now," I said severely, "can't you leave me alone? I can walk all right. 'Tis only my head. All I want is a rest."

"But you can rest at home in bed," he said viciously, trying to pick me up, and I knew by the flush on his face that he was very vexed.

"Ah, Jasus," I said crossly, "what do I want to go home for? Why the hell can't you leave me alone?"

For some reason the gang of old women at the other side of the road thought this very funny. They nearly split their sides over it. A gassy fury began to expand in me at the thought that a fellow couldn't have a drop taken without the whole neighbourhood coming out to make game of him.

"Who are ye laughing at?" I shouted, clenching my fists at them. "I'll make ye laugh at the other side of yeer faces if ye don't let me pass."

They seemed to think this funnier still; I had never seen such ill-mannered people.

"Go away, ye bloody bitches!" I said.

"Whisht, whisht, whisht, I tell you!" snarled Father, abandoning all pretence of amusement and dragging me along behind him by the hand. I was maddened by the women's shrieks of laughter. I was maddened by Father's bullying. I tried to dig in my heels but he was too powerful for me, and I could only see the women by looking back over my shoulder.

"Take care or I'll come back and show ye!" I shouted. "I'll teach ye to let decent people pass. Fitter for ye to stop at home and wash yeer dirty faces."

" 'Twill be all over the road," whimpered Father. "Never again, never again, not if I lived to be a thousand!"

To this day I don't know whether he was forswearing me or the drink. By way of a song suitable to my heroic mood I bawled "The Boys of Wexford," as he dragged me on home. Crowley, knowing he was not safe, made off and Father undressed me and put me to bed. I couldn't sleep because of the whirling in my head. It was very unpleasant, and I got sick again. Father came in with a wet cloth and mopped up after me. I lay in a fever, listening to him chopping sticks to start a fire. After that I heard him lay the table.

Suddenly the front door banged open and Mother stormed in with Sonny in her arms, not her usual gentle, timid self, but a wild, raging woman. It was clear that she had heard it all from the neighbours.

"Mick Delaney," she cried hysterically, "what did you do to my son?"

"Whisht, woman, whisht, whisht!" he hissed, dancing from one foot to the other. "Do you want the whole road to hear?"

"Ah," she said with a horrifying laugh, "the road knows all about it by this time. The road knows the way you filled your unfortunate innocent child with drink to make sport for you and that other rotten, filthy brute."

"But I gave him no drink," he shouted, aghast at the horrifying interpretation the neighbours had chosen to give his misfortune. "He took it while my back was turned. What the hell do you think I am?"

"Ah," she replied bitterly, "everyone knows what you are now. God forgive you, wasting our hard-earned few ha'pence on drink, and bringing up your child to be a drunken corner-boy like yourself."

Then she swept into the bedroom and threw herself on her knees by the bed. She moaned when she saw the gash over my eye. In the kitchen Sonny set up a loud bawl on his own, and a moment later Father appeared in the bedroom door with his cap over his eyes, wearing an expression of the most intense self-pity.

"That's a nice way to talk to me after all I went through," he whined. "That's a nice accusation, that I was drinking. Not one drop of drink crossed my lips the whole day. How could it when he drank it all? I'm the one that ought to be pitied, with my day ruined on me, and I after being made a show for the whole road."

But next morning, when he got up and went out quietly to work with his dinner-basket, Mother threw herself on me in

the bed and kissed me. It seemed it was all my doing, and
I was being given a holiday till my eye got better.

"My brave little man!" she said with her eyes shining. "It
was God did it you were there. You were his guardian angel."

# Teresa

✳

On the platform at Dieppe, at a corner so near the sea and the boat as to be part of the quay, there stood a small nun, flanked by three shapeless bags of that old-fashioned kind known as portmanteaux. Lovely as a black wall-flower, large-eyed by nature, her eyes were now enormous: for she was looking across the quays with delight at the sun-blazing confections of houses on the other side. Now and again an old nun came hobbling up to her from the busier end of the platform, muttering something that drew a shadow across the lovely face, and then hobbling away again, head down, to this official and that official, wavering around like a top as each one hurriedly threw a few words at her and rushed past. At last the old nun came back to the novice, with her two hands out in appeal. The novice, followed by the old nun, at once walked straight down to the first official she saw and said in clear English:

"Where is the train for Rouen?"

The official glanced at her, then smiled, then bowed, and said politely, indeed with deference:

"There it is, mademoiselle," and pointed to it.

"Mais non, non," babbled the old nun. "Pas aller à Rouen! Aller à Leesoo!"

"That's all right, Sister Patrick," said the other. "We change at Rouen." And taking charge of the situation, she led the still-protesting nun up to the waiting train, put in the bags,

From THE MAN WHO INVENTED SIN, New York, The Devin-Adair Co.

helped—almost pushed—the old woman before her, and settled herself for the journey. The old woman clambered out again, red with fluster. Once more she ambushed official after official, all of whom said a word so like "Wrong" that she insisted on hauling out her companion.

"Listen, Sister Patrick," begged the novice, with saintly patience. "I know the route backwards. It's Dieppe, Rouen, Elbeuf St. Aubin, Serquigny, and then Lisieux. This is the train."

The guard confirmed this, as far as concerned Rouen, and they clambered in at the last moment, but the old woman was still saying that they would never get to "Leesoo," that they would find themselves landed in Paris in the middle of the night, that she had told Mother Mary Mell not to send her, that thirty-one years is too long out of a country for anyone to remember the language, and so on and so on, while the younger nun gazed wide-eyed out of the window at the passing fields.

"Our pilgrimage has begun," she said in a dreamy voice, almost to herself.

"And what's going to be the end of it at this rate?" snapped the old woman. But then she gave a frightened look at the little face before her. The big eyes had lowered. A tremble was flitting across the red lips. The old woman immediately calmed down, laid a rough hand on the novice's knee, and said, gently, "Sure, don't mind me, Sister Teresa. I'm all of a fluster. We're on the road now. Just as you say. When we get to Leesoo, 'twill be all right, a gilly. Saint Teresa will look after you and . . . Look't, I have no sense. We should be eating our lunch."

"I'd love a cup of tea!" said the girl. "I have a raging headache."

"Tut tut," clucked the old woman, and then she grabbed the girl's flank. "Are ye wearing your double petticoat, Sister Teresa?"

"Yes, Sister," said Teresa, with a blush and a warning look into the corner of the carriage, where an old Frenchman was devouring a roll and slugging red wine.

"Have ye the red-flannel drawers on ye?" demanded the old nun.

"Yes, Sister. Sssh!"

"There's nothing like red flannel next the skin," said the nun, fiddling with the lunch-parcel. " 'Tis a touch of cold you've got."

" 'Twas the heat down under that deck," said Teresa, and big floods of water entered her eyes. Her chaperone did not notice. "I never saw Dieppe from the sea," she whimpered. "And Mother Mary Mell says that it's lovely from the sea."

"Will ye have egg and cress, or tomato?" asked the old woman, too intent on her own appetite to take notice of anything else. "We earned it," she laughed, with a happy look about her and a countrywoman's smile and nod to the old "Clemenceau" in the corner. He just dug a chunk of his roll off with his penknife, wiped the back of his hand right and left across his mustaches, and with an idle glance at her, opened both mouth and eyes simultaneously to devour the chunk.

The nuns began to nibble their food. Two hens could not have pecked more nimbly or neatly. Their traveling-companion finished his lunch almost before they had well begun. He carefully stowed away his bottle, produced a long cheroot, and began to fill the carriage with smoke. Then, to the dismay of the novice, he leaned across and closed the window tightly. By the time she had finished eating, she had already begun to lean her aching head on her palm. In minute imitation of the Frenchman, the old woman rubbed her mustaches and her beard clean of crumbs, leaned back, closed her eyes, began to eat chocolates and to breathe through her nose. She woke with a start to hear Teresa say to the Frenchman:

"C'est assez chaud, monsieur. Veuillez bien ouvrir la fenêtre."

The old tiger-face glared, growled, tapped his chest fiercely, poured out a flood of uncompromising French, and leaned back. His sideward glare thereafter was like a cat ready to pounce.

"What's that?" asked the old nun apprehensively.

"My head," groaned Teresa.

"Offer it up, girl," advised the old woman. "Offer it up to Saint Teresa for the success of your intention."

"I've offered it up on the boat the whole way over," retorted the novice.

" 'Tis a cross," said the old woman easily. " 'Tis put on you by Saint Teresa to try you. Suffer it for her sake."

The girl looked at her coldly. Then she observed that they had a second traveling-companion. He was a cavalry officer, who, with more consideration than their "Clemenceau," was walking up and down in the corridor to smoke his pipe. Each time he passed the door he glanced up at his luggage on the rack. She raised her eyes appealingly the next time he passed. He paused, glanced at her, was about to pass on, paused again to look. A tiny gesture of her hand, a widening of her eyes held him. He came in, sat down, looked around him, and stared at her.

"Monsieur," she begged. "J'ai mal à la tête. La fenêtre. Est-ce que nous pouvons l'ouvrir?"

"With pleasure," he said, in English, stalked over to it and slapped it down.

A raucous argument started up at once between the officer and his fellow-countryman. Sister Patrick sat up, glared at her charge, and drew herself in from the combatants. The argument ended with the abrupt flight of the old man, cursing as he went, a laugh from the officer, and a frightened smile from the novice, accompanied by a glance at her chaperone, who, in the greatest suspicion of the officer, had lowered her head to look crookedly at him, like a duck, out under her coif. He was stroking his little line of mustache and smiling at Teresa. When Patrick slewed full around to survey her charge, Teresa had cast her eyes down demurely on her clasped hands.

Presently the officer got up, and went out to smoke another pipe. Every time he passed, he bowed in to the two nuns. Teresa never looked higher than his knees. When he had passed for about the sixth time, Patrick said:

"Sister, do you realize that officer is bowing to us every two minutes?"

"He is very kind," said the little nun. "Everybody is very kind," she sighed, and began to pray on her beads.

But when he passed again, and bowed, the old nun said crossly:

"I believe you're looking at him, Sister Teresa!"

Teresa shook her head sadly and looked out of her big eyes at her chaperone.

"It is sad," she said. "He will be killed in the wars," and her eyes swam with tears.

"And what's that to you?" whispered the old nun angrily.

"He reminds me of my brother, Jim, in the army," said Teresa. "He will be killed on the battlefield too. Oh, let us pray for the pair of them."

The old nun could not refuse to do this, so they prayed together, and when the officer passed, and bowed, and smiled, the two nuns bowed and smiled back, and went on with their prayers for the repose of his soul when he would be killed in the wars. But he was useful at Rouen. He bought them two lovely cartons of café-au-lait, with buttered rolls, and showed them where the auto-rail would start. Then for the last time he bowed, and smiled, and went away, and they never saw him again.

II

It was the fading hour of day before their little auto-rail came and took the two travellers (and about eight others) trotting out of Rouen. A light haze of rain began to float down through the air. They passed a village deep in trees. There the first lights were beginning to contest the supremacy of the day. Soon the rain shone in rivulets on the lighted windows of the auto. The other travellers leaned closer together in a kind of animal companionship and chattered in loud voices, as if to keep the night at bay.

"I wonder," murmured Teresa, "what are they doing now back in Saint Anthony's?"

"Ah, yes!" sighed the old nun wearily. "It makes England seem very far away to think of Saint Anthony's now."

"And Dublin?" smiled the novice sadly.

"Ha!" said the old nun, with a yawn that dropped the subject into vacancy. Her youth and her friends were too remote for serious reflection.

"I know what my sisters are doing now in Dublin," whispered Teresa. "Having tea and making plans for the night." And she looked out at the evening shower and the thickening night. "I wish I never came," she said suddenly. "I feel terribly lonely."

"Sssh! Tut tut!" chided the old nun; she had begun to eat more chocolates, and did not want to talk.

"It's all right for you," complained the novice. "You're going to meet your aunt. I'll know nobody in Lisieux. And if I find out there that I have no vocation, what'll I do?"

"Now, now, now," grumbled the old woman, "you know you'll get peace and calm in Leesoo. The saint will reveal your heart to you. You'll quieten down. You'll know that all these scruples of yours mean nothing at all. Sure, we all had them!" In spite of herself she became impatient. Her soothing voice gradually took on an edge. "And anyway, goodness knows, you were eager enough to come! And let me tell you it isn't every Reverend Mother would let you. And it's not a holiday you're on, Miss. It's thinking of the holy saint you should be, and not of gillygooseys in Dublin."

The novice withdrew into herself. She was too tired to pray; from sheer repetition the words were becoming meaningless.

Presently the old nun said, as if she were thinking aloud:

"And even if I have an aunt . . . Ha! . . . I suppose she won't know me."

She stopped again and folded her hands deep into her sleeves.

"Thirty-one years," she mused to the window.

The auto-rail rattled along for several miles. Then, Patrick leaned over and said comfortably:

"A terror for the hot milk at night. She'd drink two pints of it. Sure, 'twas enough to kill a plough-horse."

From then on she kept on letting occasional little gasps of laughter escape her. It was as if somebody tickled her every three minutes. Then, after a protracted giggle out of each side of her mouth, she went off into a beatific sleep and the broad smile never left her face until they stopped abruptly in Lisieux.

As they left the station and emerged on the great square, Teresa cried in delight:

"But it's really a big place!"

Through the rain the little town shone into the station like a prismatic waterfall. She saw a green neon light flitting through the wetness over a hotel door. She saw a vis-à-vis crawling shiningly across the Place, and it made the town seem both cosy and intimate, and at the same time enormous and important. But Patrick had flown into a hurry and scurry, fumbling with her umbrella, and clutching her bags, and gazing all around her in a new rush of timidity; the two, in this conflict of absorption, nearly lost one another in the crush. The novice said:

"Oh, Sister Patrick! Couldn't we have one cup of tea in a restaurant before we go to the Hostel?"

"Wh-a-t?" cried Patrick, hunching up her shoulders, and laying her hand on her guimpe like a stage French-woman. "Mon Pethite, que dites vous? Du thé? Vous savez bien . . . Vous savez bien que nous . . . Il faut . . . Il faut . . ." She groaned furiously. "I can't talk French. I told Mother Mary Mell . . . Are you talking about tea? Do you realize, Miss, that you're on a pilgrimage? Gosthering in the middle of the street! Hurry! Hurry!"

They did hurry, under their two black umbrellas, like two ants with top-heavy loads. Suddenly Teresa stopped and sneezed resolutely; once . . . twice . . . four times. Patrick towered over her. She started to gibber at her like a baboon.

"You're after getting a cold on me! That's yourself, and your window, and your fine officer!" Teresa sneezed a fifth time. "Are you sure," demanded Patrick, "that you have the double petticoat?"

The novice's big eyes were directed miserably into a confectioner's window. It was bright with the brightest cakes.

"Dear Sister Patrick!" she wheedled. "Don't you think we could have one small, tiny little cup of tea?"

The nun opened her mouth to say "No," looked at the window, looked at Teresa, and after a struggle said:

"Well! Since you have a cold coming on you, I'll let you have just one hot cup of coffee. Just one, mind you!"

It was warm in the café. Patrick had an éclair. Over their heads a radio kept weaving waltzes that made the novice sway gently on her chair. Patrick had two éclairs. The novice made her coffee last as long as possible. Patrick had a third éclair. Then, in spite of a fleck of cream on her jaw, Patrick's face was unusually forbidding as she looked up and said:

"Well, Miss, I hope you're feeling better now?"

"Thank you very much, Sister," said Teresa, and rose with an air of firm resignation. "We must go to the Hostel."

A bell rang eight o'clock as they emerged. They wasted ten minutes searching for the Hostel, a bald faced house rising plumb from the pavement. Its brass tipped, reed-woven half-screens were damply inhospitable. Its closed door and iron grille were shining with the rain. The lay-sister who drew the slide of the grille spoke in unintelligible, provincial French, of which they understood only one word, "Impossible!"

"Quoi?" squawked Patrick, clawing the grille, as the slide shot to in her face. "What did that wan say?"

The bell jangled down the hall again. This time the lay-sister was even more emphatic, and therefore even less intelligible, and she became still less intelligible as Patrick hung to the grille and blustered in Franco-English. Teresa firmly pushed her aside, with a calm sanity:

"Vous ne comprenez pas. Tout est bien arrangé. Notre mère a écrit une lettre à votre mère. . . ."

The lay-sister interrupted. She said, "Trop tard." She said, "Huit heures." She said these words several times.

She closed the grille with the slowness of a curiosity that commented on the folly of the two foolish virgins who had come too late. Teresa turned to Patrick, and burst into peals of laughter at the look of horror on her face.

"We're too late!" she cried, joyously. "Now we must go to a hotel!"

Patrick rent her.

"You and your tea! You did it deliberately! Wait until we get back to Mother Mary Mell! I'll tell her you're not fit to be a nun! You're a little flitthermouse! You're a gillygoosey! What a pilgrim we have in you! There's your answer for you! You're not fit to be a nun! You're a slip! You're a miss! What're we going to do? What'll my aunt say to me? What'll Mother Mary Mell say to me? What's going to happen to us?"

Teresa began to cry. Patrick at once hushed her tirade, unfurled her umbrella (it was as big as a bookmaker's), dragged up two of the bags and set off, in a mouth-buttoned fury, to find a hotel. The rain was now a downpour. Their bags weighted them down. She halted. She gave the girl a look that was worse than a blow, shoved her into a doorway, and said, "Don't stir from there till I come back." She left the bags in her care, and butted out into the rain.

Men kept approaching the door, and seeing the nun, they would stop dead, and push away. At first this merely frightened her for she did not realize her predicament: but suddenly a cistern flushed noisily behind her and she recognized that she was standing in the doorway of a *cabinet*. Clutching her bags, she fled down the street, down a side street, another side street, and halted panting under a café awning.

The old proprietor came out and looked at her, cocked his head to one side, bowed, considered her, smiled, said that it was a bad night, and wiped his indifference on to the tabletop. Then he gazed around him, looked at her again, shrugged, and went indoors. More men passed her, on their way in or out, always pausing, after the first glance, to smile and bow. Twice she got up to fly, wondered whether Patrick would ever find her, sat again on the damp iron chair. A drunken old man with a beard finally put her to flight by taking off his hat, leaning on the tabletop, and starting a flowery speech. She ran into a gendarme who was accompanying Sister Patrick down the street. Patrick threw her two hands up to the sky preparatory to a tornado of abuse. She was soaked; her guimpe was a rag; her coif hung around her face like lace. Before she could speak, Teresa hurled herself on the old woman's breast and sobbed out all her awful adventures, so that the gendarme and the nun calmed her with difficulty. They took her bag, then, and led her, whimpering, to the little pension-pub that Patrick had chosen for their night's lodging. There Patrick put her into bed, in a cosy little room all to herself, with red stuff curtains and a dusty-looking carpet—it was nearly thread-bare—and with her own two hands Patrick lit a fire, brought an omelette, rolls, and coffee, and tucked her in for the night; and all the time Patrick kept begging her pardon for that outburst at the Hostel. What with the comfort, the kindness, and the vestigial excitement, the little novice was melted to tears of happiness.

"Our pilgrimage is beginning," she whispered happily to Patrick. "Isn't it, dear Sister Patrick?"

" 'Twill begin in the morning," temporized Patrick. "And then the saint will smoothen everything out."

Right cheek touched right cheek, and left cheek touched left cheek, in the way of all nuns kissing. Old fingers laid out her glossy black hair on the pillow. The light went out. A rough palm smoothed her forehead. The door clicked. The flames flickered on the ceiling.

In Kent, at Saint Anthony's, the only sound around the convent at night had been the crackle of twigs in the damp wood, the hoo-hoo of an owl. Here she heard footsteps in the street below, an occasional motor-car swishing over the cobbles, the soft, whispering downfall of April rain. Looking up at the wavering ceiling, she attended to those sounds, whose tumult, and whose unfamiliarity, and whose suggestiveness made England and her convent, Dublin and her home, utterly remote—less part of another country than part of another life. More than anything else they said, "The pilgrimage has begun!" They said, "O dear Saint Thérèse, I

will leave all things in thy hands." They said, "O most omnipotent God, I yield all the world to Thee."

"I want to be a saint!" she cried out, and beat the cover-
let with her palm. And at that she fell asleep, curled up in
bed as softly as a cat.

### III

Only the hens were awake as they walked to first Mass
at Saint Pierre. The sun was glittering in the water between
the cobblestones. Teresa felt that she alone possessed the
town. She felt that all things converged on the forthcoming
visit to the shrine. Even the warm prophecy of the steam
rising from the streets and the cloudless whiteness of the
sky seemed not something general to everybody in the world,
but particular to her life alone. She whispered to Patrick,
"Thérèse is calling! I hear her!" Patrick nodded, too excited
to speak.

After breakfast they began the ritual of Lisieux. Les
Buissonnets, the Martin home (Saint Thérèse Martin), was
exactly as they had foreseen it, just like all the photos and
descriptions in biographies of the saint. They saw the "trim
lawn in front of the house," and "the useful kitchen-garden
at the back." From the attic windows there was the expected "distant view over the plain." Teresa said to Patrick,
with a sigh of happiness:

"It was all made for her. If I had lived here, I, too, would
have been a saint!"

Patrick nodded in agreement with the general proposition.
For the novice to say that she could have been a saint was
merely a way of saying that God had chosen one and could
as easily have chosen another.

" 'Tis Heaven!" she murmured, and clasped Teresa's hand.

It was the same in the sacristy of the Carmelite convent,
where the saint's hair lies strewn under glass in its reliquary,
and the walls are covered by mementoes of those who have
paid honor to her memory—decorations, orders, swords, letters from all over the world. Here, where Patrick became

almost incoherent at the prospect of meeting her aunt, thirty-one years after, now a Reverend Mother in the Carmelites, Teresa filled with sadness.

"The folly of the world!" she murmured, sighing again and again. "They honor her now. They did not know the sorrow of her heart while she was alive."

The two touched cheek to cheek again.

A Carmelite lay-sister next led them to the grave of the saint. From that they would go on to the convent proper to meet Patrick's aunt. They began to palpitate in mutual sympathy. The grave calmed them by its simplicity.

When they rose, the aunt stood beside them. Patrick toddled to her with cries of joy. The aged woman, her head a mere skull, her hands bony and ridged, gave no sign of recognition other than to say, "God bless you, my child." Old Patrick drew back like a frightened child. Timidly she introduced the novice. She explained falteringly why they had come.

"She's not sure if she wants to be a nun, Mother."

The Carmelite looked at the novice. She, too, at once drew back. But the Carmelite smiled to hear the English name, Teresa, and took her hand gently and led her (Patrick following) across the garden to the convent ante-room. On the way she talked of simple things like the budding shrubs and the blessing of the rain. They sat in the ante-room and the Carmelite rang a bell.

They talked of the price of vegetables, until a faint passage of light in one wall drew their eyes to the grille—the last portal of the inner Carmelite hermitage. Behind the grille was a gauze, and presently Teresa's eyes made out, behind the gauze, a still face from which the gauze had eroded all recognizable character. All she could see was the vaguest outline of a countenance. As if she realized in that second how the discipline of the Order must have likewise eroded from the little girl of Les Buissonnets all human emotion, and in a flash of understanding knew what sacrifice really means, she flung herself at the Carmelite's knees and cried out hysterically:

"Ma mère! I have no vocation!"

Patrick intervened hurriedly:

"Pay no heed to her. She's upset and sick in herself. The child doesn't know what she wants."

The aged Carmelite waved her aside and lifted the novice to her feet. Looking into her face with a clear eye, she said, after a frightening silence:

"Could you be a Carmelite?"

"No!" panted the novice, and she drew back, as if she were at that moment about to be imprisoned behind the grille.

"If you cannot be a Carmelite, my child, you can be nothing."

"She'd be happy enough," intervened Patrick comfortably, "in an easier Order."

"She will be happy—we will all be happy—only in Heaven," said the Carmelite coldly. "Could you not even try to be a Carmelite?" asked the aged woman.

"No!" begged the novice. "I couldn't do it!"

"Why not?"

"To be always shut in?" trembled the girl.

"It is an enclosed Order," agreed the Superioress calmly.

"I couldn't stand it!"

"How do you know?" catechized the Superioress.

For answer the girl burst into such a sobbing wail that Patrick drew her to her broad bosom and turned on her aunt.

"Ye have no heart!" she upbraided. "Badgering the poor child! 'Tisn't that we expected from you! Don't heed her," she comforted Teresa. "My poor little girsha! Don't mind her. Sure we can't all be saints. You'll do your best. You can't do more."

"But," sobbed Teresa, "I want to be a saint. 'Tis to . . . to . . . to be a saint I joined the nuns." Her voice came out through her nose, miserably. "If I can't be a saint, I don't *want* to be a nun!"

The old woman comforted her, and finally restored her to a whimpering silence. Looking up, they saw they were alone.

The grille was closed. The veil was hidden. The Superioress had gone.

The two pilgrims went back to their pension. That afternoon, without discussion, they went on to Saint Malo. There the novice was expected to find bodily rest, as at Lisieux she had been expected to find calm of soul.

## IV

Saint Malo faces across a wide estuary the modern watering-place of Dinard. At night they saw the lights in the hotels and cafés, and more colored lights beaded all around the roof of the casino; and sometimes they heard music across the still surface of water. Steamers from Southampton and the Channel Islands floated in the bay at anchor. Patrick was charmed with her room in the convent where they stayed. It looked directly across at Dinard. She wrote to Mother Mary Mell that she had a "grandstand," and that she was thinking of going across in a row-boat some night to gamble in the Casino and make the fortune of the Order. Becoming serious in a postscript, she said that Teresa had not yet made up her mind, but that she was "behaving with the most edifying devotion."

Not only did the novice attend every service in the convent, but she had become pious beyond description, daily spending long hours alone in adoration in the chapel. But when Patrick noticed that she left her lunch untouched on her table on the third day of her arrival, and went up to the novice's cell to ask if this were wise, she made a frightening discovery. She found that the mattress and bedclothes had been rolled up and put away under the bed, and all the girl's flannel underclothing was hanging in her cupboard. At once she went down to the chapel, and hissed at the solitary worshipper to come out, beckoning madly with her bony finger.

"Sister Teresa," she said severely, "you are refusing your food. Is there any reason for this?"

The novice hung her head and said nothing.

"Answer me, Sister."

Still the novice kept her eyes on the parquet.

"I command you, Sister, to answer me."

"There is no reason," whispered the novice.

"Then eat up your food in future," ordered the nun. "Do you want to make a skeleton out of yourself?" And she added more easily, "Don't you know right well I'm supposed to bring you home as plump as a duck?"

The novice raised two large, sad eyes.

"Sister Patrick," she begged, "I will obey if you command me. But I want to do penance for my sins, and for the sins of the world. I feel I have received a higher command."

"What higher command?" blustered the old woman, taken aback. "What on earth are you talking about, Sister?"

Teresa sighed.

"The sins of the world are all about us," she smiled sadly. "I see them every night from my window, across the water, in the dens and gambling-houses. All lit up like the fires of Hell to lure poor souls astray. I dreamed the first night I came here that the Devil lives over there. I saw his red eyes in the air. I saw that this convent was put here specially to atone for the wickedness that surrounds it."

"Holy Mother!" cried the nun. "What are you talking about, girl? Sister Teresa, let me tell you that if you ate a proper supper . . . And by the same token, Miss, no wonder you have dreams if you sleep on the laths of the bed. Do you," she threatened, "sleep on the laths of the bed?"

The novice once more hung her head, and once more she had to be bullied into replying.

"I do, Sister," she confessed unhappily.

"Well, then, let there be an end of it! What right have you to be going on with these andrewmartins off of your own bat? You know right well you must ask permission of your superior before you do the like. And that reminds me," she cried, grabbing the girl's flank, and then standing back from her in horror, with her gummy mouth open. "You haven't a stitch on you! Go upstairs at once, Miss, and dress yourself properly. I'll be after you in two minutes. I'm worn out and

tormented with your vagaries! Ten times I told Mother Mary
Mell . . ."

She pointed upstairs—a figure of Justice.

The novice went, tearful, head-hanging. In two minutes
the old nun followed. She opened the door of the cell. The
girl lay on the ground, her arms stretched out like a crucifix,
her dilated eyes fixed as on a vision over her head. The old
nun entered the room, closed the door, and thundered:

"Get up out o' that!"

The novice did not move.

"Miss!" said the old woman, pale as a sheet, "how dare
you disobey me!"

The novice trembled as if a wind had ruffled her spirit.
With her heart battering inside her, Patrick walked over
and looked down. The big brown eyes, so strikingly dark in
that pale pink-and-white face, stared up past her. Patrick
looked up at the electric light bulb. She looked all about her.
The thick-moted afternoon sun slanted in across the bed. A
hissing suspiration below the window was followed by the
little groan of the gravel dragging back under the wave. Then
she saw a slimy brown insect, with wavering head, creep to
the white ear of the novice, and she screamed:

"An earwig! Climbing into your ear!"

Teresa sat up as if she was stung. The fright passed. The
two looked at each other with hate in their eyes. At the door,
Patrick said:

"I'll wait in the garden."

In complete silence they walked four miles that afternoon.
They did the same the following morning. That was their last
full day. On the final afternoon Patrick spoke:

"We will be in Saint Anthony's to-morrow night. Do you
know, yet, my dear, if you have a vocation?"

"I have decided to join the Carmelites," said the novice.

They halted. They looked across the sea-wall into the blue
of Dinard. A few lights were already springing up over there
—the first dots in the long, golden necklet that already they
had come to know so well. A lone sea-gull squawked over the

glassy water. The sunset behind the blue pinnacles of the resort was russet.

"And what's wrong with our own Order, Sister dear?" asked Patrick of the vacancy before her.

"I feel, dear Sister Patrick," judged the novice, staring ahead of her, "that it is too worldly."

"How is it too worldly?" asked Patrick in a whisper.

"Well, dear Sister Patrick," pronounced the novice, "I see, for example, that you all eat too much."

The little wavelets fell almost inaudibly, drunken with the fullness of the tide, exhausted and soothed by their own completion.

"I shall tell Mother Mary Mell that you think so," whispered the old nun.

"There is no need, dear Sister. It will be my duty to tell her myself. I will pray for you all when I am in the Carmelites. I love you all. You are all kind and generous. But, dear Sister, I feel that very few nuns really have the right vocation to be nuns." Patrick closed her eyes tightly. The novice continued: "I will surrender myself to the divine Love. The death I desire is the death of Love. The death of the Cross."

They heard only the baby tongues of the waves. The evening star blazed in the russet sky. The old nun saw it, and she said, in part a statement, in part a prayer, in part a retort:

"Sweet Star of the Sea!"

Teresa raised her dark eyes to the star and she intoned in her girlish voice the poem of Saint Thérèse:

> *"Come, Mother, once again,*
> *Who camest first to chide.*
> *Come once again, but then*
> *To smile—at eventide."*

The old nun fiddled with her beads. She drew long breaths through her nose. She tried several times to speak. She ges-

tured that they must go back. They turned and walked slowly
back to the convent, side by side; the old nun as restless as if
she were in bodily agony, the novice as sedate and calm as a
statue. After a while Patrick fumbled in her pocket, and found
a chocolate, and popped it into her mouth. Then she stopped
chewing, and threw an eye at her companion. At the look of
intense sorrow in the face beside her, she hunched up her
shoulders and as silently as she could, she gulped the fragments whole.

On the journey homeward they did not speak one word to
each other: all the way to Rouen in the trotting auto-rail; in
the clanking train to Dieppe; on the boat; in the English
train. In silence they arrived at Saint Anthony's, among the
dank beechwoods, now softly dripping, in time to hear the
first hoo-hoo of the owl, and to troop in with the rest of the
community for evening chapel. Mother Mary Mell barely had
time to ask the old nun how she had enjoyed her holiday—
that first holiday in thirty-one years. Patrick's eyes fluttered.
She recalled the lights of Dinard.

"It was lovely, Mother!"

Mary Mell caught the flicker of hesitation. Just as they
crossed the tessellated threshold of the chapel, she whispered
quickly, "And Teresa?"

Patrick who had been waiting for that question ever since
the final afternoon in Saint Malo, and yet had no answer
ready, took refuge behind the chapel's interdiction of silence.
She smiled reassuringly, nodded, smiled, nodded again, and
then, very solemn and pious, she walked in with her head
down. She said her prayers badly. She slept hardly at all that
night. She heard every crackling branch and fluttering night-
bird. For what, in the name of the Most High, was she to say
to Mary Mell? And what was she to say to the community in
the morning? As she tossed and tumbled, she thought of
Teresa sleeping peacefully in her cell, and the old woman
burst into tears of rage.

In the morning there was no Teresa. She had left the convent, through a ground-floor window, before anybody was

awake, and gone on the milk-train to London. She had walked across the city at that hour when the sun emphasizes the position of the East End, and the sleepers in the Parks that she traversed are unwrapping their newspaper-blankets. A sister-in-law coming out to collect the morning post found a nun sitting on the doorstep. She had breakfast, in a tennis-frock, along with the family.

She saw the convent only once again—about two years later when she brought her husband to see it. As they got out of the train she looked up into the familiar beeches at the steam of the engine caught in the branches, and she remembered how every train used to make the woods seem infinitely lonely and the convent darker and more melancholy, because that white steam suggested people traveling, and the luxury of the world she had renounced. Her George, who was a Protestant, and who was much excited by this expedition, nodded solemnly, and began to get an uncomfortable feeling that he was married to a nun. They were entertained politely. Old Sister Patrick did not appear. As they left, the starting train again sent its gushes of steam into the branches, and now those branches again seemed to Teresa to clutch not only at the white smoke but at her own heart. She felt that the woods enclosed a refuge from the world of which she had, irrevocably, become a part. As she snuggled down into her fur collar she gazed out of her big eyes at her husband, and said, with a shake of her little head:

"Ah George! George! You will never know what I gave up to marry you!"

He smiled adoringly at her as, in obedience to a gesture, he leaned over to put a cigarette between her rouged lips.

"My precious Teresa," he murmured softly, and patted her knee.

She shook her head at him again, with a pitying smile.

"Has it upset you, my sweet?" he asked dismally.

Saying never a word, she kept gazing at him fixedly, as if he were a stranger. He huffed, and hawed, and hedged himself behind his newspaper, looking as despondent as he considered proper. For as he explained to his colleagues in the morning, his wife was "a very spiritual woman" and on occasions like this she always made him feel that he had the soul of a hog.

# The Tent

\*

A sudden squall struck the tent. White glittering hailstones struck the shabby canvas with a wild noise. The tent shook and swayed slightly forward, dangling its tattered flaps. The pole creaked as it strained. A rent appeared near the top of the pole like a silver seam in the canvas. Water immediately trickled through the seam, making a dark blob.

A tinker and his two wives were sitting on a heap of straw in the tent, looking out through the entrance at the wild moor that stretched in front of it, with a snowcapped mountain peak rising like the tip of a cone over the ridge of the moor about two miles away. The three of them were smoking cigarettes in silence. It was evening, and they had pitched their tent for the night in a gravel pit on the side of the mountain road, crossing from one glen to another. Their donkey was tethered to the cart beside the tent.

When the squall came the tinker sat up with a start and looked at the pole. He stared at the seam in the canvas for several moments and then he nudged the two women and pointed upwards with a jerk of his nose. The women looked but nobody spoke. After a minute or so the tinker sighed and struggled to his feet.

"I'll throw a few sacks over the top," he said.

He picked up two brown sacks from the heap of blankets and clothes that were drying beside the brazier in the en-

From The Short Stories of Liam O'Flaherty, New York, Devin-Adair.

201

trance and went out. The women never spoke, but kept on smoking.

The tinker kicked the donkey out of his way. The beast had stuck his hind quarters into the entrance of the tent as far as possible, in order to get the heat from the wood burning in the brazier. The donkey shrank away sideways still chewing a wisp of the hay which the tinker had stolen from a haggard the other side of the mountain. The tinker scrambled up the bank against which the tent was pitched. The bank was covered with rank grass into which yesterday's snow had melted in muddy cakes.

The top of the tent was only about eighteen inches above the bank. Beyond the bank there was a narrow rough road, with a thick copse of pine trees on the far side, within the wired fence of a demesne, but the force of the squall was so great that it swept through the trees and struck the top of the tent as violently as if it were standing exposed on the open moor. The tinker had to lean against the wind to prevent himself being carried away. He looked into the wind with wide-open nostrils.

"It can't last," he said, throwing the two sacks over the tent, where there was a rent in the canvas. He then took a big needle from his jacket and put a few stitches in them.

He was about to jump down from the bank when somebody hailed him from the road. He looked up and saw a man approaching, with his head thrust forward against the wind. The tinker scowled and shrugged his shoulders. He waited until the man came up to him.

The stranger was a tall, sturdily built man, with a long face and firm jaws and great sombre dark eyes, a fighter's face. When he reached the tinker he stood erect with his feet together and his hands by his sides like a soldier. He was fairly well dressed, his face was clean and well shaved, and his hands were clean. There was a blue figure of something or other tattooed on the back of his right hand. He looked at the tinker frankly with his sombre dark eyes. Neither spoke for several moments.

"Good evening," the stranger said.

The tinker nodded without speaking. He was looking the stranger up and down, as if he were slightly afraid of this big, sturdy man, who was almost like a policeman or a soldier or somebody in authority. He looked at the man's boots especially. In spite of the muck of the roads, the melted snow and the hailstones, they were still fairly clean, and looked as if they were constantly polished.

"Travellin'?" he said at length.

"Eh," said the stranger, almost aggressively. "Oh! Yes, I'm lookin' for somewhere to shelter for the night."

The stranger glanced at the tent slowly and then looked back to the tinker again.

"Goin' far?" said the tinker.

"Don't know," said the stranger angrily. Then he almost shouted: "I have no bloody place to go to . . . only the bloody roads."

"All right, brother," said the tinker, "come on."

He nodded towards the tent and jumped down into the pit. The stranger followed him, stepping carefully down to avoid soiling his clothes.

When he entered the tent after the tinker and saw the women he immediately took off his cap and said: "Good evening." The two women took their cigarettes from their mouths, smiled and nodded their heads.

The stranger looked about him cautiously and then sat down on a box to the side of the door near the brazier. He put his hands to the blaze and rubbed them. Almost immediately a slight steam rose from his clothes. The tinker handed him a cigarette, murmuring: "Smoke?"

The stranger accepted the cigarette, lit it, and then looked at them. None of them were looking at him, so he "sized them up" carefully, looking at each suspiciously with his sombre dark eyes. The tinker was sitting on a box opposite him, leaning languidly backwards from his hips, a slim, tall, graceful man, with a beautiful head poised gracefully on a brown neck, and great black lashes falling down over his half-closed eyes, just like a woman. A womanish-looking fellow, with that sensuous grace in the languid pose of his body which is found only among aristocrats and people who belong to a very small workless class, cut off from the mass of society, yet living at their expense. A young fellow with proud, contemptuous, closed lips and an arrogant expression in his slightly expanded nostrils. A silent fellow, blowing out cigarette smoke through his nostrils and gazing dreamily into the blaze of the wood fire. The two women were just like him in texture, both of them slatterns, dirty and unkempt, but with the same proud, arrogant contemptuous look in their beautiful brown faces. One was dark-haired and black-eyed. She had rather a hard expression in her face and seemed very alert. The other woman was golden-haired, with a very small head and finely-developed jaw, that stuck out level with her forehead. She was surpassingly beautiful, in spite of her ragged clothes and the foul condition of her hair, which was piled on her tiny skull in knotted heaps, uncombed. The perfect symmetry and delicacy of her limbs, her bust and her long throat that had tiny freckles in the white skin, made the stranger feel afraid of her, of her beauty and her presence in the tent.

"Tinkers," he said to himself. "Awful bloody people."

Then he turned to the tinker.

"Got any grub in the place . . . eh . . . mate?" he said brusquely, his thick lips rapping out every word firmly, like one accustomed to command inferiors. He hesitated before he added the word "mate," obviously disinclined to put himself on a level of human intercourse with the tinker.

The tinker nodded and turned to the dark-haired woman.

"Might as well have supper now, Kitty," he said softly.

The dark-haired woman rose immediately, and taking a blackened can that was full of water, she put it on the brazier. The stranger watched her. Then he addressed the tinker again.

"This is a hell of a way to be, eh?" he said. "Stuck out on a mountain. Thought I'd make Roundwood to-night. How many miles is it from here?"

"Ten," said the tinker.

"Good God!" said the stranger.

Then he laughed, and putting his hand in his breast pocket, he pulled out a half-pint bottle of whiskey.

"This is all I got left," he said, looking at the bottle.

The tinker immediately opened his eyes wide when he saw the bottle. The golden-haired woman sat up and looked at the stranger eagerly, opening her brown eyes wide and rolling her tongue in her cheek. The dark-haired woman, rummaging in a box, also turned around to look. The stranger winked an eye and smiled.

"Always welcome," he said. "Eh? My curse on it, anyway. Anybody got a corkscrew?"

The tinker took a knife from his pocket, pulled out a corkscrew from its side and handed it to the man. The man opened the bottle.

"Here," he said, handing the bottle to the tinker. "Pass it round. I suppose the women'll have a drop."

The tinker took the bottle and whispered to the dark-haired woman. She began to pass him mugs from the box.

"Funny thing," said the stranger, "when a man is broke and hungry, he can get whiskey but he can't get grub. Met a man this morning in Dublin and he knew bloody well I was broke, but instead of asking me to have a meal, or giving me some money, he gave me that. I had it with me all along the road and I never opened it."

He threw the end of his cigarette out the entrance.

"Been drinkin' for three weeks, curse it," he said.

"Are ye belongin' to these parts?" murmured the tinker, pouring out the whiskey into the tin mugs.

"What's that?" said the man, again speaking angrily, as if he resented the question. Then he added: "No. Never been here in me life before. Question of goin' into the work-house or takin' to the roads. Got a job in Dublin yesterday. The men downed tools when they found I wasn't a member of the union. Thanks. Here's luck."

"Good health, sir," the women said.

The tinker nodded his head only, as he put his own mug to his lips and tasted it. The stranger drained his at a gulp.

"Ha," he said. "Drink up, girls. It's good stuff."

He winked at them. They smiled and sipped their whiskey.

"My name is Carney," said the stranger to the tinker. "What do they call you?"

"Byrne," said the tinker. "Joe Byrne."

"Hm! Byrne," said Carney. "Wicklow's full o' Byrnes. Tinker, I suppose?"

"Yes," murmured the tinker, blowing a cloud of cigarette smoke through his puckered lips. Carney shrugged his shoulders.

"Might as well," he said. "One thing is as good as another. Look at me. Sergeant-major in the army two months ago. Now I'm tramping the roads. That's boiling."

The dark-haired woman took the can off the fire. The other woman tossed off the remains of her whiskey and got to her feet to help with the meal. Carney shifted his box back farther out of the way and watched the golden-haired woman eagerly. When she moved about her figure was so tall that she had to stoop low in order to avoid the roof of the tent. She must have been six feet in height, and she wore high-heeled shoes which made her look taller.

"There is a woman for ye," thought Carney. "Must be a gentleman's daughter. Lots o' these shots out of a gun in the county Wicklow. Half the population is illegitimate. Awful bloody people, these tinkers. I suppose the two of them belong to this Joe. More like a woman than a man. Suppose he never did a stroke of work in his life."

There was cold rabbit for supper, with tea and bread and butter. It was excellent tea, and it tasted all the sweeter on account of the storm outside which was still raging. Sitting around the brazier they could see the hailstones driving through a grey mist, sweeping the bleak black moor, and the cone-shaped peak of the mountain in the distance, with a whirling cloud of snow around it. The sky was rent here and there with a blue patch, showing through the blackness.

They ate the meal in silence. Then the women cleared it away. They didn't wash the mugs or plates, but put everything away, probably until morning. They sat down again after drawing out the straw, bed-shape, and putting the clothes on it that had been drying near the brazier. They all seemed to be in a good humour now with the whiskey and the food. Even the tinker's face had grown soft, and he kept puckering up his lips in a smile. He passed around cigarettes.

"Might as well finish that bottle," said Carney. "Bother the mugs. We can drink outa the neck."

"Tastes sweeter that way," said the golden-haired woman, laughing thickly, as if she were slightly drunk. At the same time she looked at Carney with her lips open.

Carney winked at her. The tinker noticed the wink and the girl's smile. His face clouded and he closed his lips very tightly. Carney took a deep draught and passed him the bottle. The tinker nodded his head, took the bottle and put it to his lips.

"I'll have a stretch," said Carney. "I'm done in. Twenty miles since morning. Eh?"

He threw himself down on the clothes beside the yellow-haired woman. She smiled and looked at the tinker. The tinker paused with the bottle to his lips and looked at her through almost closed eyes savagely. He took the bottle from his lips and bared his white teeth. The golden-headed woman shrugged her shoulders and pouted. The dark-haired woman laughed aloud, stretched back with one arm under her head and the other stretched out towards the tinker.

"Sht," she whistled through her teeth. "Pass it along, Joe."

He handed her the bottle slowly, and as he gave it to her she clutched his hand and tried to pull him to her. But he tore his hand away, got up and walked out of the tent rapidly.

Carney had noticed nothing of this. He was lying close to the woman by his side. He could feel the softness of her beautiful body and the slight undulation of her soft side as she breathed. He became overpowered with desire for her and closed his eyes, as if to shut out the consciousness of the world and of the other people in the tent. Reaching down he seized her hand and pressed it. She answered the pressure. At the same time she turned to her companion and whispered:

"Where's he gone?"

"I dunno. Rag out."

"What about?"

"Phst."

"Give us a drop."

"Here ye are."

Carney heard the whispering, but he took no notice of it. He heard the golden-headed one drinking and then drawing a deep breath.

"Finished," she said, throwing the bottle to the floor. Then she laughed softly.

"I'm going out to see where he's gone," whispered the dark-haired one. She rose and passed out of the tent. Carney immediately turned around and tried to embrace the woman by his side. But she bared her teeth in a savage grin and pinioned his arms with a single movement.

"Didn't think I was strong," she said, putting her face close to his and grinning at him.

He looked at her seriously, surprised and still more excited.

"What ye goin' to do in Roundwood?" she said.

"Lookin' for a job," he muttered thickly.

She smiled and rolled her tongue in her cheek.

"Stay here," she said.

He licked his lip and winked his right eye. "With you?"

She nodded.

"What about him?" he said, nodding towards the door.

She laughed silently. "Are ye afraid of Joe?"

He did not reply, but, making a sudden movement, he seized her around the body and pressed her to him. She did not resist, but began to laugh, and bared her teeth as she laughed. He tried to kiss her mouth, but she threw back her head and he kissed her cheek several times.

Then suddenly there was a hissing noise at the door. Carney sat up with a start. The tinker was standing in the entrance, stooping low, with his mouth open and his jaw twisted to the right, his two hands hanging loosely by his sides, with the fingers twitching. The dark-haired woman was standing behind him, peering over his shoulder. She was smiling.

Carney got to his feet, took a pace forward, and squared

himself. He did not speak. The golden-headed woman uttered a loud peal of laughter, and, stretching out her arms, she lay flat on the bed, giggling.

"Come out here," hissed the tinker.

He stepped back. Carney shouted and rushed at him jumping the brazier. The tinker stepped aside and struck Carney a terrible blow in the jaw as he passed him. Carney staggered against the bank and fell in a heap. The tinker jumped on him like a cat, striking him with his hands and feet all together. Carney roared: "Let me up, let me up. Fair play." But the tinker kept on beating him until at last he lay motionless at the bottom of the pit.

"Ha," said the tinker.

Then he picked up the prone body, as lightly as if it were an empty sack, and threw it to the top of the bank.

"Be off, you—," he hissed.

Carney struggled to his feet on the top of the bank and looked at the three of them. They were all standing now in front of the tent, the two women grinning, the tinker scowling. Then he staggered on to the road, with his hands to his head.

"Good-bye dearie," cried the golden-headed one.

Then she screamed. Carney looked behind and saw the tinker carrying her into the tent in his arms.

"God Almighty!" cried Carney, crossing himself.

Then he trudged away fearfully through the storm towards Roundwood.

"God Almighty!" he cried at every two yards. "God Almighty!"

SEUMAS O'KELLY

# Michael and Mary

✳

Mary had spent many days gathering wool from the whins
on the headland. They were the bits of wool shed by the
sheep before the shearing. When she had got a fleece that
fitted the basket she took it down to the canal and washed it.
When she had done washing it was a soft, white, silky fleece.
She put it back in the brown sally basket, pressing it down
with her long, delicate fingers. She had risen to go away,
holding the basket against her waist, when her eyes followed the narrow neck of water that wound through the
bog.

She could not follow the neck of yellow water very far.
The light of day was failing. A haze hung over the great Bog
of Allen that spread out level on all sides of her. The boat
loomed out of the haze on the narrow neck of the canal water.
It looked, at first, a long way off, and it seemed to come in a
cloud. The soft rose light that mounted the sky caught the
boat and burnished it like dull gold. It came leisurely, drawn
by the one horse, looking like a Golden Barque in the twilight. Mary put her brown head a little to one side as she
watched the easy motion of the boat. The horse drew himself
along deliberately, the patient head going up and down with
every heavy step. A crane rose from the bog, flapping two
lazy wings across the wake of the boat, and, reaching its long
neck before it, got lost in the haze.

The figure that swayed by the big arm of the tiller on *The*

From THE GOLDEN BARQUE, Dublin, The Talbot Press.

*Golden Barque* was vague and shapeless at first, but Mary felt her eyes following the slow movements of the body. Mary thought it was very beautiful to sway every now and then by the arm of the tiller, steering a Golden Barque through the twilight.

Then she realised suddenly that the boat was much nearer than she had thought. She could see the figures of the men plainly, especially the slim figure by the tiller. She could trace the rope that slackened and stretched taut as it reached from the boat to the horse. Once it splashed the water, and there was a little spout of silver. She noted the whip looped under the arm of the driver. Presently she could count every heavy step of the horse, and was struck by the great size of the shaggy fetlocks. But always her eyes went back to the figure by the tiller.

She moved back a little way to see *The Golden Barque* pass. It came from a strange, far-off world, and having traversed the bog went away into another unknown world. A red-faced man was sitting drowsily on the prow. Mary smiled and nodded to him, but he made no sign. He did not see her; perhaps he was asleep. The driver who walked beside the horse had his head stooped and his eyes on the ground. He did not look up as he passed. Mary saw his lips moving, and heard him mutter to himself; perhaps he was praying. He was a shrunken, misshaped little figure and kept step with the brute in the journey over the bog. But Mary felt the gaze of the man by the tiller upon her. She raised her eyes.

The light was uncertain and his peaked cap threw a shadow over his face. But the figure was lithe and youthful. He smiled as she looked up, for she caught a gleam of his teeth. Then the boat had passed. Mary did not smile in return. She had taken a step back and remained there quietly. Once he looked back and awkwardly touched his cap, but she made no sign.

When the boat had gone by some way she sat down on the bank, her basket of wool beside her, looking at *The Golden Barque* until it went into the gloom. She stayed there for some time, thinking long in the great silence of the bog. When at last she rose, the canal was clear and cold beneath her. She looked into it. A pale new moon was shining down in the water.

Mary often stood at the door of the cabin on the headland watching the boats that crawled like black snails over the narrow streak of water through the bog. But they were not all like black snails now. There was a Golden Barque among them. Whenever she saw it she smiled, her eyes on the figure that stood by the shaft of the tiller.

One evening she was walking by the canal when *The Golden Barque* passed. The light was very clear and searching. It showed every plank, battered and tarstained, on the rough hulk, but for all that it lost none of its magic for Mary. The little shrunken driver, head down, the lips moving, walked beside the horse. She heard his low mutters as he passed. The red-faced man was stooping over the side of the boat, swinging out a vessel tied to a rope, to haul up some water. He was singing a ballad in a monotonous voice. A tall, dark, spare man was standing by the funnel, looking vacantly ahead. Then Mary's eyes travelled to the tiller.

Mary stepped back with some embarrassment when she saw the face. She backed into a hawthorn that grew all alone on the canal bank. It was covered with bloom. A shower of the white petals fell about her when she stirred the branches. They clung about her hair like a wreath. He raised his cap and smiled. Mary did not know the face was so eager, so boyish. She smiled a little nervously at last. His face lit up, and he touched his cap again.

The red-faced man stood by the open hatchway going into the hold, the vessel of water in his hand. He looked at Mary and then at the figure beside the tiller.

"Eh, Michael?" the red-faced man said quizzically. The youth turned back to the boat, and Mary felt the blush spreading over her face.

"Michael!"

Mary repeated the name a little softly to herself. The gods had delivered up one of their great secrets.

She watched *The Golden Barque* until the two square slits in the stern that served as port holes looked like two little

Japanese eyes. Then she heard a horn blowing. It was the
horn they blew to apprise lock-keepers of the approach of a
boat. But the nearest lock was a mile off. Besides, it was a
long, low sound the horn made, not the short, sharp, com-
manding blast they blew for lock-keepers. Mary listened to
the low sound of the horn, smiling to herself. Afterwards the
horn always blew like that whenever *The Golden Barque* was
passing the solitary hawthorn.

Mary thought it was very wonderful that *The Golden
Barque* should be in the lock the one day that she was travelling with her basket to the market in the distant village. She
stood a little hesitantly by the lock. Michael looked at her, a
welcome in his eyes.

"Going to Bohermeen?" the red-faced man asked.

"Ay, to Bohermeen," Mary answered.

"We could take you to the next lock," he said, "it will
shorten the journey. Step in."

Mary hesitated, as he held out a big hand to help her to
the boat. He saw the hesitation and turned to Michael.

"Now, Michael," he said.

Michael came to the side of the boat, and held out his
hand. Mary took it and stepped on board. The red-faced
man laughed a little. She noticed that the dark man who
stood by the crooked funnel never took his eyes from the
stretch of water before him. The driver was already urging
the horse to his start on the bank. The brute was gathering
his strength for the pull, the muscles standing out on his
haunches. They glided out of the lock.

It was half a mile from one lock to another. Michael had
bidden her stand beside him at the tiller. Once she looked
up at him and she thought the face shy but very eager, the
most eager face that ever came across the bog from the great
world.

Afterwards, whenever Mary had the time, she would make
a cross-cut through the bog to the lock. She would step in
and make the mile journey with Michael on *The Golden
Barque*. Once, when they were journeying together, Michael

slipped something into her hand. It was a quaint trinket, and shone like gold.

"From a strange sailor I got it," Michael said.

Another day that they were on the barque, the blinding sheets of rain that often swept over the bog came upon them. The red-faced man and the dark man went into the hold. Mary looked about her, laughing. But Michael held out his great waterproof for her. She slipped into it and he folded it about her. The rain pelted them, but they stood together, Michael holding the big coat folded about her. She laughed a little nervously.

"You will be wet," she said.

Michael did not answer. She saw the eager face coming down close to hers. She leaned against him a little and felt the great strength of his arms about her. They went sailing away together in *The Golden Barque* through all the shining seas of the gods.

"Michael," Mary said once, "is it not lovely?"

"The wide ocean is lovely," Michael said. "I always think of the wide ocean going over the bog."

"The wide ocean!" Mary said with awe. She had never seen the wide ocean. Then the rain passed. When the two men came up out of the hold Mary and Michael were standing together by the tiller.

Mary did not go down to the lock after that for some time. She was working in the reclaimed ground on the headland. Once the horn blew late in the night. It blew for a long time, very softly and lowly. Mary sat up in bed listening to it, her lips parted, the memory of Michael on *The Golden Barque* before her. She heard the sound dying away in the distance. Then she lay back on her pillow, saying she would go down to him when *The Golden Barque* was on the return journey.

The figure that stood by the tiller on the return was not Michael's. When Mary came to the lock the red-faced man was telling out the rope, and where Michael always stood by the tiller there was the short strange figure of a man with a pinched, pock-marked face.

When the red-faced man wound the rope round the stump

at the lock, bringing the boat to a stand-still, he turned to Mary.

"Michael is gone voyaging," he said.

"Gone voyaging?" Mary repeated.

"Ay," the man answered. "He would be always talking to the foreign sailors in the dock where the canal ends. His eyes would be upon the big masts of the ships. I always said he would go."

Mary stood there while *The Golden Barque* was in the lock. It looked like a toy ship packed in a wooden box.

"A three-master he went in," the red-faced man said, as they made ready for the start. "I saw her standing out for the sea last night. Michael is under the spread of big canvas. He had the blood in him for the wide ocean, the wild blood of the rover." And the red-faced man, who was the Boss of the boat, let his eyes wander up the narrow neck of water before him.

Mary watched *The Golden Barque* moving away, the grotesque figure standing by the tiller. She stayed there until a pale moon was shining below her, turning over a little trinket in her fingers. At last she dropped it into the water.

It made a little splash, and the vision of the crescent was broken.

BRIAN O'NOLAN

# The Martyr's Crown

✳

Mr. Toole and Mr. O'Hickey walked down the street together in the morning.

Mr. Toole had a peculiarity. He had the habit, when accompanied by another person, of saluting total strangers; but only if these strangers were of important air and costly raiment. He meant thus to make it known that he had friends in high places, and that he himself, though poor, was a person of quality fallen on evil days through some undisclosed sacrifice made in the interest of immutable principle early in life. Most of the strangers, startled out of their private thoughts, stammered a salutation in return. And Mr. Toole was shrewd. He stopped at that. He said no more to his companion, but by some little private gesture, a chuckle, a shake of the head, a smothered imprecation, he nearly always extracted the one question most melodious to his ear: *"Who was that?"*

Mr. Toole was shabby, and so was Mr. O'Hickey, but Mr. O'Hickey had a neat and careful shabbiness. He was an older and a wiser man, and was well up to Mr. Toole's tricks. Mr. Toole at his best, he thought, was better than a play. And he now knew that Mr. Toole was appraising the street with beady eye.

"Gorawars!" Mr. Toole said suddenly.

We are off, Mr. O'Hickey thought.

From *Envoy*.

216

"Do you see this hop-off-my-thumb with the stick and the hat?" Mr. Toole said.

Mr. O'Hickey did. A young man of surpassing elegance was approaching; tall, fair, darkly dressed; even at fifty yards his hauteur seemed to chill Mr. O'Hickey's part of the street.

"Ten to one he cuts me dead," Mr. Toole said. "This is one of the most extraordinary pieces of work in the whole world."

Mr. O'Hickey braced himself for a more than ordinary impact. The adversaries neared each other.

"*How are we at all, Sean a chara?*" Mr. Toole called out.

The young man's control was superb. There was no glare, no glance of scorn, no sign at all. He was gone, but had left in his wake so complete an impression of his contempt that even Mr. Toole paled momentarily. The experience frightened Mr. O'Hickey.

"Who . . . who was *that?*" he asked at last.

"I knew the mother well," Mr. Toole said musingly. "The woman was a saint." Then he was silent.

Mr. O'Hickey thought: there is nothing for it but bribery —again. He led the way into a public house and ordered two bottles of stout.

"As you know," Mr. Toole began, "I was Bart Conlon's right-hand man. We were through 'twenty and 'twenty-one together. Bart, of course, went the other way in 'twenty-two."

Mr. O'Hickey nodded and said nothing. He knew that Mr. Toole had never rendered military service to his country.

"In any case," Mr. Toole continued, "there was a certain day early in 'twenty-one and orders come through that there was to be a raid on the Sinn Fein office above in Harcourt Street. There happened to be a certain gawskogue of a cattle-jobber from the County Meath had an office on the other side of the street. And he was well in with a certain character by the name of Mick Collins. I think you get me drift?"

"I do," Mr. O'Hickey said.

"There was six of us," Mr. Toole said, "with meself and Bart Conlon in charge. Me man the cattle-jobber gets an urgent call to be out of his office accidentally on purpose at four o'clock, and at half-four the six of us is parked inside there with two machine-guns, the rifles and a class of a home-made bomb that Bart used to make in his own kitchen. The military arrived in two lurries on the other side of the street at five o'clock. That was the hour in the orders that come. I believe that man Mick Collins had lads working for him over in the War Office across in London. He was a great stickler for the British being punctual on the dot."

"He was a wonderful organizer," Mr. O'Hickey said.

"Well, we stood with our backs to the far wall and let them have it through the open window and them getting down offa the lurries. Sacred godfathers! I never seen such murder in me life. Your men didn't know where it was coming from, and a lot of them wasn't worried very much when it was all over, because there was no heads left on some of them. Bart then gives the order for retreat down the back stairs; in no time we're in the lane, and five minutes more the six of us upstairs in Martin Fulham's pub in Camden Street. Poor Martin is dead since."

"I knew that man well," Mr. O'Hickey remarked.

"Certainly you knew him well," Mr. Toole said, warmly. "The six of us was marked men, of course. In any case, fresh orders come at six o'clock. All hands was to proceed in military formation, singly, by different routes to the house of a great skin in the Cumann na mBan, a widow be the name of Clougherty that lived on the south side. We were all to lie low, do you understand, till there was fresh orders to come out and fight again. Sacred wars, they were very rough days them days; will I ever forget Mrs. Clougherty! She was certainly a marvellous figure of a woman. I never seen a woman like her to bake bread."

Mr. O'Hickey looked up.

"Was she," he said, "was she . . . all right?"

"She was certainly nothing of the sort," Mr. Toole said loudly and sharply. "By God, we were all thinking of other things in them days. Here was this unfortunate woman in a three-story house on her own, with some quare fellow in the middle flat. herself on the ground floor, and six blood-thirsty pultogues hiding above on the top floor, every man-jack ready

to shoot his way out if there was trouble. We got feeds there
I never seen before or since, and the *Independent* every morning. Outrage in Harcourt Street. The armed men then de-
camped and made good their escape. I'm damn bloody sure
we made good our escape. There was one snag. We couldn't
budge out. No exercise at all—and that means only one
thing . . ."

"Constipation?" Mr. O'Hickey suggested.

"The very man," said Mr. Toole.

Mr. O'Hickey shook his head.

"We were there a week. Smoking and playing cards, but
when nine o'clock struck, Mrs. Clougherty come up, and,
Protestant, Catholic or Jewman, all hands had to go down on
the knees. A very good . . . strict . . . woman, if you understand me, a true daughter of Ireland. And now I'll tell you a
damn good one. About five o'clock one evening I heard a
noise below and peeped out of the window. Sanctified and
holy godfathers!"

"What was it—the noise?" Mr. O'Hickey asked.

"What do you think, only two lurries packed with military,
with my nabs of an officer hopping out and running up the
steps to hammer at the door, and all the Tommies sitting back
with their guns at the ready. Trapped! That's a nice word—
*trapped!* If there was ever rats in a cage, it was me unfortunate brave men from the battle of Harcourt Street. God!"

"They had you at what we call a disadvantage," Mr.
O'Hickey conceded.

"She was in the room herself with the teapot. She had a
big silver satteen blouse on her; I can see it yet. She turned
on us and gave us all one look that said: *Shut up, ye nervous
lousers.* Then she foostered about a bit at the glass and walks
out of the room with bang-bang-bang to shake the house going
on downstairs. And I seen a thing . . ."

"What?" asked Mr. O'Hickey.

"She was a fine—now you'll understand me, Mr. O'Hickey,"
Mr. Toole said carefully; "I seen her fingers on the buttons of
the satteen, if you follow me, and she leaving the room."

Mr. O'Hickey, discreet, nodded thoughtfully.

"I listened at the stairs. Jakers I never got such a drop in me life. She clatters down and flings open the halldoor. This young pup is outside, and asks—awsks—in the law-de-daw voice, 'Is there any men in this house?' The answer took me to the fair altogether. She puts on the guttiest voice I ever heard outside Moore Street and says, 'Sairtintly not at this hour of the night; I wish to God there was. Sure, how could the poor unfortunate women get on without them, officer?' Well lookat. I nearly fell down the stairs on top of the two of them. The next thing I hear is, 'Madam this and madam that,' and 'Sorry to disturb and I beg your pardon,' 'I trust this and I trust that,' and then the whispering starts, and at the wind-up the halldoor is closed and into the room off the hall with the pair of them. This young bucko out of the Borderers in a room off the hall with a headquarters captain of the Cumann na mBan! *Give us two more stouts there, Mick!*"

"That is a very queer one, as the man said," Mr. O'Hickey said.

"I went back to the room and sat down. Bart had his gun out, and we were all looking at one another. After ten minutes we heard another noise."

Mr. Toole poured out his stout with unnecessary care.

"It was the noise of the lurries driving away," he said at last. "She'd saved our lives, and when she come up a while later she said 'We'll go to bed a bit earlier to-night, boys; kneel down all.' That was Mrs. Clougherty the saint."

Mr. O'Hickey, also careful, was working at his own bottle, his wise head bent at the task.

"What I meant to ask you was this," Mr. O'Hickey said, "that's an extraordinary affair altogether, but what has that to do with that stuck-up young man we met in the street, the lad with all the airs?"

"Do you not see it, man?" Mr. Toole said, in surprise. "For seven hundred years, thousands—no, I'll make it millions—of Irish men and women have died for Ireland. We never rared jibbers; they were glad to do it, and will again. But that young man was *born* for Ireland. There was never anybody else like him. Why wouldn't he be proud?"

"The Lord save us!" Mr. O'Hickey cried.

"A saint I called her," Mr. Toole said, hotly. "What am I talking about—she's a martyr and wears the martyr's crown to-day!"

JIM PHELAN

# Bell Wethers

✳

"I declare to God, Packy—I mane Mr. Dollan—there isn't a
pound in money on Mullaravogue Mountain. Not wan pound,
among sixty of us." The big round-shouldered peasantman
shuffled awkwardly, glanced at the crowd of others like himself, then looked back, furtive as a frightened child, at the man
before him.

Packy Dollan sat on a barrel of flour, one leg swinging
loosely. He propped an elbow on a box of bacon, and set his
chin in his hand, to watch with a good-humored smile while
the peasant hurried to speak again in growing embarrassment.

"I'm telling ye, Packy, there isn't as much as half-a-crown
between us," the big man emphasised. "Not until after the
June fair. An' that's the truth." Again he glanced at the crowd
for support.

Timid, sheepish, turning from side to side, they still kept
silent. Only huddling a little closer to one another and to the
speaker, they peeped for brief instants, in hope or fear or
incomprehension, at the smiling red-faced man on the barrel.

Dollan stood up slowly, brushed a smudge of flour from
his trousers, and wiped his hands on his white apron. Still
smiling, he hummed a few bars of a song, ignoring the
peasantmen, and glanced out from the window of the store-
room at the wide sweep of heathery mountain outside. Then,
with a short laugh, he whipped an account book from a shelf
and faced the first speaker.

From Bog Blossom Stories, London, Sidgwick & Jackson.

"Wisha God help ye, John Joe Mooley me poor fella," he grinned. "Sure it's the deservin' case that ye are! Not even half-a-crown. Nor none of these others," he went on, with a humorous shake of his head as he surveyed the group of men who filled the store. "Yerra, John Joe," he finished with a succession of admiring grins, "sure it's yerself has the gift o' the gab—but is it a millionaire ye're takin' me for?" He opened the account book, on the top of the bacon-box.

Slowly the men grouped themselves a little nearer, seemingly fascinated by the book. Packy Dollan swept the crowd with a wide intimate grin, nodded with twinkling eyes whenever a man met his gaze for a moment, and toyed with the account book, as if they were all participants in some huge joke.

Gradually his insistent grin forced answering half-smiles from the men around. Dollan paused, with his forefinger between the pages of the book, and sat erect for a second.

"Sixty of ye," he continued, in the same jocular tone. "Sixty-two I make it, be the book—owin' me forty pound each on an average. But sure," he went on quizzically to John Joe Mooley, "sure a hundher' pound, or a couple of hundher' pound, isn't big enough to matter. No, indeed!" He laughed loudly, and again the crowd of peasants, after a few seconds, pretended to share his merriment.

For a minute or more Packy continued to smile at the crowd. Then he opened the book and commenced to read: —"John Joe Mooley, forty-seven pound, twelve shillin's an' thruppence. Am I right or wrong, John Joe?"

The only immediate answer was a long, snorting, animal breath from the group of men. Then, gradually, they drew still closer around the account book, as the reading continued: —"Mickeen MacHugh O'Byrne, thirty-nine pound, eight an' ten. Am I right or wrong, Mickeen?"

Awkwardly and with childish heavings, the men shook their rounded shoulders into a pretence of laughing agreement with Packy, as if an unpleasant and difficult lesson were being read by a popular schoolmaster. Only from time to time they looked out of the window, in sudden pain and fear, at the big heathery tops they called home.

Mullaravogue was three rocky mountain crests and the whole of a smaller hill. Behind, westward, the black unbroken mass of the main mountain range cut off the world, carried no village, not even a hamlet. Westward was no road.

Down in the lower levels, on the east front of Mullaravogue, where the last small byway from civilization petered out, the little town of Barnasleeve clung to the side of the foot-hills. With its main street a mountain pass but thinly disguised, its very name meaning in Irish "the mountain gap," Barnasleeve was the first or last stop on the way out of or into the mountain lands.

A single large pub overlooked the middle of the street, the name "P. Dollan" over the door. Beside it, a smaller shop bore the same name, with the added information, "Transport contractor. Funerals attended with promptness and civility. Cars for hire."

On the other side of the pub four converted cottages made a roomy general shop, with a big grocery store at one end, where the flat, impassive voice of Packy Dollan read slowly:— "Martin Mike Dockery, forty-two pound, four an' eight. Am I right or wrong, Martin Mike?"

Backing the little town, the sprawling stony mountain laid its greenish-brown arms around score after score of tiny peasant holdings. Circling each home was the scrap of tillage, eternally defended against the inroads of gorse and heather and rolling rock. Between and above were the untilled tops of Mullaravogue, peaceful and lovely, cut into chequered patterns by the myriad low stone walls, white fleeces showing here and there in the squares of gold and green.

Inland, the dark, rocky bulk of the chief range separated Mullaravogue from the vaguely-suggested Ireland beyond. There was no peasant home on the heights, not a pass worthy of the name, not a road across the range. Everything went up, or came down, through Barnasleeve. The droning voice from the grocery store seemed to be emphasising the fact.

"Danny Jem Ryan, thirty-eight pound four an' six. Am I

right, Danny Jem? Paddy Gaffney, forty-wan pound nine an'—"

On the mountains around Barnasleeve there was a stock joke about Packy Dollan. Packy, the hillmen would say, was willing to sell you a cradle or hire you a hearse—he got you coming and going. Everything in Barnasleeve was Packy's.

Starting from nothing, Dollan had worked hard all his life. First adding penny to penny, in a tiny shop, then putting pound beside pound as he prospered, later piling the hundreds into Barnasleeve's only bank, Packy had grown.

The story is common enough in Ireland or in any peasant country. Some one man discovers that he can collect the wealth of a region by supplying necessities. Later and inevitably he becomes the dominant commercial force of his district.

The Irish have a word for it. The small-town merchant who gradually achieves a stranglehold on his neighbours is called a gombeen-man. Gomba, in Gaelic, means vaguely a bit or scrap. Gombeen is the diminutive. A textbook of economics might well be condensed into the single word.

Long before he was thirty, Packy Dollan had grasped the importance of Barnasleeve's geographical position. The little town at the foot of the mountains was the only bridge between the hillmen and civilization. There was no way out, from the lofty backlands, into the world of commerce, except through Barnasleeve. While Packy owned the only five shops in the town, the only pub, the only two motor lorries, Packy was the gombeen.

Half wild, sheepish and timid, mostly unlettered, the men from the hillsides had to come out from their heathery tops, sooner or later, to buy and sell. They bought from, and sold to, Packy. The voice inside the store-room was summarising the results.

"An' Dickeen Cullahan, last," Packy was saying, "Forty-wan pound, eleven an' three. Right, Dickeen?" Cullahan nodded and laughed awkwardly. Packy looked around at the crowd, folding his arms with the account book against his chest, a wide grin of comical discomfiture on his face.

The men scraped their feet on the ground, fumbled in their pockets, peered sideways at one another, fidgeted still more, but kept silent. Dollan waited a few minutes, then suddenly opened a back page of the book.

"Two thousand four hundher' an' ninety-five pound eighteen an' eightpence," he said flatly, "of *my* money, is gone up there on top of Mullaravogue, in flour an' bacon an' tobacco an' the rest. Near twenty-five hundher' pound. Twenty—five—hundher'—pound."

A long, loud, combined exhalation came from the men as Dollan named the total. They peeked at one another, and immediately huddled even closer, exactly like a flock of sheep. Packy laughed.

" 'Tis the great jokers ye are," he commented, nodding approval. "The great jokers. Them that has nothin' can pay nothin'. No. So now ye're all that happy—aye, happy—because ye have nothin'. So me twenty-five hundher' pound is gone, up there."

He turned to the window and looked up at the Mullaravogue tops. The peasants followed his gaze, and Dollan turned back on them suddenly. "All happy," he repeated, and his hearty laugh rang out into the little street. "Because ye have nothin' an' can pay nothin'. Aye."

"After the June fair, Packy—" commenced John Joe Mooley. The other grinned and nodded, silencing him. He opened the book at an early page and glanced at it carelessly, then left it down on a box.

"Them debts," he remarked jocularly, "has been pilin' up from the bits an' pieces left over after the June fair or the December fair for the last twenty year. Now they make two thousand five hundher' pound. Yerra, John Joe, will ye stop jokin' about June fairs before ye make me die laughin'.' "

Acute discomfort showed among the peasantmen, while the shopkeeper still smiled. Gradually, in the silence, a guilty, hang-dog expression appeared on each face, as if Packy had caught them out in some mean and sordid conspiracy to cheat him. Then, the silence continuing, the men stared at the gombeen in blank and hopeless calm. They had nothing, could pay nothing, could do nothing.

"There must be seven or eight hundher' sheep up there on the tops of Mullaravogue, John Joe," said Dollan, quietly and in a casual voice, scarcely above his breath. The crowd of peasants drew back in haste, as if the gombeen had suddenly produced a bomb.

On the Mullaravogue tops, where the many small flocks of mountain sheep grazed in common, gross wasteful patches of gorse alternated with vast ragged rocks, with here and there a small patch of grass or a square of temporarily-good grazing where the gorse had been burnt away.

Up here, all the sheep of Mullaravogue herded together, indiscriminately, each with its owner's brand on fleece or ear, until the time came to separate them, for slaughter or sale or shearing. That meant, until they or their fleece went down into Barnasleeve, to Packy Dollan.

To the hillmen, the sheep were eternal and unchanging, as much part of their lives as the thatch in the cottage roofs or the water in the mountain streams. A man might sell two sheep, or five lambs, or ten fleeces—he always had the same number of sheep, nearly enough, never thought of them as property.

All the little farms produced corn, potatoes, turnips and the like, for sale. These were the hillmen's main preoccupation and source of income, such as it was. The sheep were almost a by-product, a means of extracting each year a few pounds from the otherwise-sterile tops of Mullaravogue.

Hardly one of the little peasant homes was without thirty or forty sheep, somewhere on the mountain. Fifteen or twenty pounds a year, no more, came in profit from each small flock. But it was money for practically nothing, money from the patches between the rocks and gorse, and in a district where every shilling counted it was important.

It had never struck any of the peasants that their ragged flocks were capital. The sheep were there. Now and then they yielded a few pounds. But they were still there, like the turf in the bog or the roof on the house. No one had ever thought of them as property. Except Packy Dollan.

On the afternoon that Packy dropped his bombshell about the number of sheep on the mountain, the hillmen's first reaction had been to stare as if the gombeen had uttered some insane, sacrilegious obscenity. Swiftly they had realized that instead he was pronouncing something like a sentence of death. Packy had known his twenty-five hundred pounds were safe. The hillmen had not.

With infuriating stupidity, each peasant had evaded Dollan's questions as to how many sheep he had. Sure a man couldn't say, they explained. Them sheep was up there all together, and indeed 'twould be hard to tell which was whose, until say the June fair.

Sure now Mr. Dollan must understand, they explained, with fear in their voices and eyes. Them sheep was all mixed up, on the mountain, everyone's together, one here and there like. Sure a man never bothered, on Mullaravogue, barring when he went to shear or to sell a few lambs or the like. One here and there.

Packy had snarled for a second, and then the good-humored grin had reappeared. The peasantmen seemed to shrink in height as he spoke.

"Aye faith," Dollan had summed up. "So not one of ye knows where his sheep are, nor how many he has. No. Just one here and there. Ye've all got just one here and there. But when they're all together there's so many that a man can't count his own either! Wisha ye'll kill me with laughin'. Now—what about me twenty-five hundher' pound?"

In the end, the hillmen had shambled out into the street of Barnasleeve, not even looking at one another. Packy had made it all sound so simple, so businesslike. He was coming up Mullaravogue himself, on the following Saturday. Sure they could laugh at him if they liked, jokers that they were. But there must be near seven hundred sheep up there *somewhere*.

"At three pound apiece—that'd be fair; am I right or wrong, John Joe?—at three pound apiece—"

"Sheep is near five pound apiece in Dublin market," Mooley interjected, apologetically and without much hope in his voice.

"Thrue, begob," the gombeen agreed. "Thrue enough. But the tops of Mullaravogue isn't Dublin market, no. At three pound apiece I'll be losin' near five hundher' pound. But sure that's betther than losin' the lot. Saturday, John Joe. Saturday." The hillmen sidled out.

On the Saturday morning most of the men grouped in the mountain track near John Joe Mooley's farm. They made no attempt to discuss the gombeen's coming visit, merely stared in sheepish and stupid abasement at one another, as if some tragedy or blight had descended but had left them speechless.

Dollan was brisk and friendly, when he left his car outside Mooley's where the steep narrow lane ended, and approached the crowd of hillmen on foot. He refused point-blank to go up the mountain until he had had a drink, wherefore the car yielded up four bottles of whiskey. Four other bottles followed, and some at least of the peasantmen's gloom was gone, before Packy would agree to start up the steep rocky track to the tops.

"Begor I'll be a farmer meself wan of these days," he laughed, as he handed John Joe Mooley a tool like a pair of pliers. "Take that, John Joe—sure I'd maybe punch holes in me own ears with it." He added a slightly-exaggerated hiccup, and the crowd started slowly up the track.

Mooley carried the "punch," an instrument for marking the ears of sheep to indicate ownership. He seemed not to notice that the punch-mark was "P.D.", and gradually Dollan became more confidential while they worked their way up the hill. He held the peasant's arm for a moment, as they struggled across a narrow stretch of the path between sheer rocks, then stepped out a little more briskly behind the single straggling file of men ahead.

"I want to be fair, John Joe," he reiterated. "Fair." Soberly and competently he conveyed an impression that the whiskey had been too strong or too plentiful, that he was in an expansive and generous mood. "Sure I don't care if I do lose a few hundher' pound—we're all neighbours together. Y'see, John Joe?"

Mooley made vague noises of assent, with only a single glance at the man who proclaimed his generosity. Dollan caught his arm again.

"Get me enough sheep to cover some of me money, John Joe," the gombeen said loudly. "Some of it. An' don't take too much from anyone. No. Just one here an' there." He laughed whiskily as he repeated the peasantmen's own phrase. "Just one here an' there, John Joe."

The crowd of men strung out up the mountain in a long broken line, each with a sheepdog or two near his heels. Continually they called short phrases to one another, up or down the track, but all their talk was mere practical gossip about rocks or gorse, about tracks and grazing, with no word of the gombeen or his obvious intention to clear the mountain of sheep for the first time in centuries.

Now and then one or two halted, to look back towards Mooley and Dollan at the rear, glancing at John Joe as if he were a leader, although he came nearly last and hardly spoke. Then they shuffled upward again.

The track became steeper, then swiftly steeper still, and Dollan's laughing protests came more often. Up near one of the rocky crests, where the path climbed through a tiny narrow gorge into an open space, the crowd of men and dogs halted, waiting for Dollan and Mooley to come through.

The pass was barely a yard wide, blue ragged rocks closing in sharply on either side, before they fell away at a small flat pasture. Loose boulders here and there had been rolled aside, so that the sheep could pass, and occasionally some steeper "step" had had a few stones hauled into place, by some peasant of the distant past, assisting nature.

Near the top of the narrowest part, a thick flat slab of rock had been tilted out of the way, years ago, that the track might be passable. Propping it, untouched for decades, a small rock-buttress lay almost buried in heather and gorse trodden short by the tiny hooves of generation after generation of sheep.

In the rock-propping, the improvised buttress, the hoof-treading, was the whole story of Mullaravogue, down the centuries. John Joe Mooley drew a long breath, seeming to realize something of the kind, as his eyes took in the familiar details. For a moment he stumbled awkwardly, and the small rock-buttress moved, for perhaps the first time in a century. John Joe stumbled again.

Packy was stating, in jocular pretence at anger, that he would go no farther, when the short slab of rock fell inward. Not big enough to injure Dollan, the slab merely fetched a curse and a grin from him as it held his leg fast, leaving him to stand awkwardly in the middle of the little pass.

"Hey, John Joe," yelled the gombeen man, with a laughing grimace. "Come an' get this bloody rock off me leg. Devil another foot I'll go anyway. Hey, John Joe."

Embarrassed and contrite, sweating in perturbation and shame, the hillman made an immediate attempt to move the rock with his hands. The rock did not rise, and Dollan cursed.

"I'll just find me a log of a tree, Mr. Dollan," John Joe explained apologetically. "Then I can get a couple of the boys to heave that rock back. Besides, ye have no farther to go. The boys'll be getting the flocks down off the tops in the manetime, for ye to mark yer own. Just a minute, Mr. Dollan." He hurried up the track.

The hillmen moved upward and outward. Still their talk was in short practical phrases, about where a log was to be got, where the sheep were likely to be, where was the best place to get them together, which dogs were to accompany which men. Small, short, practical hillside phrases. In a few seconds Packy was alone.

He heard the men calling to one another across the clumps of gorse and rock, as they moved away uphill, spreading and scattering in search of the sheep, shouting to the dogs, venturing guesses as to where a log or stake might be found, up there where there was little but rock and heather. Then there was silence.

Dollan eased himself into position, to wait. Several minutes passed before he heard anything, and he was beginning to realize that logs would be as scarce as diamonds on the tops of Mullaravogue. Then he heard a sound up the path, and looked forward impatiently for John Joe Mooley.

There was a dull clonking, an occasional lonely note from a bell that sounded cracked. From the other side of the clearing a single sheep descended, crossed the open space, and stopped.

Around his neck he carried a rusty bell, and his horns were long although curved and useless as weapons. After a short glance he went back across the open space and stood there, the bell silent. Packy watched him in amusement and pleasure, trying to guess the owner's identity from the faded red brand on the fleece.

Far up the mountain, and away to the right, there sounded a distant halloing and barking of dogs. The bell wether moved a few yards, looking up towards the noise. The bell clonked, flatly, and a few sheep came into the open, to stand huddling near the first. When the noise came again, from the other side of the hill, the big wether crossed to look and listen, clonking his way past the others and returning to stand passively among them.

Scrambling and hurried, a little group of sheep appeared from between two clumps of gorse. Down the rocks in front half a dozen others showed. The flock in the open space was growing, and Dollan noted its size with grim pleasure. He sent an angry shout up the mountain for Mooley, then bent forward in an attempt to free his leg.

There was no answer to his call, but the peasants seemed to be coming nearer, slowly, calling to the dogs, halloing to one another across the mountain. For a moment the gombeen gave way to anger and irritation, then relaxed in something approaching delight as he realized that the flock of sheep had grown to an enormous size.

Two thousand, Packy computed roughly. Two thousand! He would have been satisfied, would have been doing good business, if Mullaravogue had only yielded up a few hundred sheep. The flock before him was worth ten thousand pounds, or more, at the lowest figure.

Ten thousand pounds. While Mooley and the rest were making pretence of being ruined, here was ten thousand pounds on the bare hillside. The gombeen grinned.

He looked up at the clonking of the bell. The big wether came slowly across and looked at him, then clonked his way back to the others. Up and round the mountain the shouting and the noise of the dogs increased. The bell wether moved across the open again, and hurried back, with a rhythmic clonking, while more sheep came in from the heather.

From the rear of the flock there came a sudden movement, as another score of sheep dashed into the clearing, while the barking of dogs came nearer. The bell wether walked slowly towards Dollan again. For a moment the man and the sheep measured glances. The bell clonked once.

Packy was chuckling, at the thought that the bell wether had the same big, quiet stupid face as John Joe Mooley, when the sheep made a sudden frightened spring into the narrow gap. The bell clonked.

Dollan swore laughingly as the wether squeezed past him, straining the trapped leg into a painful position. Then another sheep, and another, sprang to follow the bell wether, and Packy laughed no longer. For the next five minutes he fought desperately, against the thrust of soft fleeces and the drive of strong little bodies trembling with fear, and against the jabbing of small hard hooves.

"Oh, God Almighty preserve us," called John Joe Mooley, half an hour later. "Oh God protect us—who'd have thought sheep could do *that?*"

Peering and blowing, glancing sideways, huddling together, the crowd of hillmen collected in the open space above the gap. One by one, solemnly and with every mark of sorrow, they crossed themselves as they looked down at the place where the gombeen man had waited.

Spread over the gap, mud-like and spongy, with scraps of clothes here and there and with the lower part of a leg still gripped between the rocks, a flattened red-brown mush of blood and dirt bore the marks of many thousand small feet.

# Weep for Our Pride

The door of the classroom was opened by Mr. O'Rourke just as Brother Quinlan was about to open it to leave. They were both surprised and said "Good morning" to one another as they met in the doorway, and Mr. O'Rourke, although he met Brother Quinlan every morning of his life, gave an expansive but somehow unreal smile and shouted his "good morning" with bloodcurdling cordiality. They then withdrew to the passage outside to hold a conversation.

In the interval English Poetry books were opened and the class began to repeat lines. They had been given the whole of a poem called "Lament for the Death of Eoghan Ruadh" to learn. It was very patriotic and dealt with the poisoning of Eoghan Ruadh by the accursed English, and the lines were very long, which made it difficult. The class hated the English for poisoning Eoghan Ruadh because the lines about it were so long. What made it worse was that it was the sort of poem Mr. O'Rourke loved. If it was "Hail to thee, blythe spirit" he wouldn't mind so much. But he could declaim this one for them in a rich, fruity, provincial baritone and would knock hell out of anybody who had not learned it.

Peter had not learned it. Realizing how inadequate were the few minutes left to him he ran his eyes over stanza after stanza and began to murmur fragments from each in hopeless desperation. Swaine, who sat beside him, said,

From THE TRUSTING AND THE MAIMED, New York, Devin-Adair.

"Do you know this?"

"No," Peter said. "I haven't even looked at it."

"My God," Swaine breathed in horror, "you'll be mangled."

"You could give us a prompt."

"And be torn limb from limb?" said Swaine with conviction. "Not likely."

Peter closed his eyes. It was all his mother's fault. He had meant to come to school early to learn it but the row delayed him. It had been about his father's boots. After breakfast she had found that there were holes in both his shoes. She held them up to the light which was on because the November morning was wet and dark.

"Merciful God, child," she exclaimed, "there's not a sole in your shoes. You can't go out in those."

He was anxious to put them on and get out quickly, but everybody was in bad humour. He didn't dare to say anything. His sister was clearing part of the table and his brother Joseph, who worked, was rooting in drawers and corners and saying to everybody, "Where the hell is the bicycle pump? You can't leave a thing out of your hand in this house."

"I can wear my sandals," Peter suggested.

"And it spilling out of the heavens—don't be daft, child." Then she said, "What am I to do at all?"

For a moment he hoped he might be kept at home. But his mother told his sister to root among the old boots in the press. Millie went out into the passage. On her way she trod on the cat, which meowed in intense agony.

"Blazes," said his sister, "that bloody cat."

She came in with an old pair of his father's boots, and he was made try them on. They were too big.

"I'm not going out in those," he said. "I couldn't walk in them."

But his mother and sister said they looked lovely. They went into unconvincing ecstasies. They looked perfect they said, each backing up the other. No one would notice.

"They look foolish," he insisted. "I won't wear them."

"You'll do what you're told," his sister said. They were all older than he and each in turn bullied him. But the idea of being made look ridiculous nerved him.

"I won't wear them," he persisted. At that moment his brother Tom came in and Millie said quickly:

"Tom, speak to Peter—he's giving cheek to mammy." Tom was very fond of animals. "I heard the cat," he began, looking threateningly at Peter who sometimes teased it. "What were you doing to it?"

"Nothing," Peter answered. "Millie walked on it." He tried to say something about the boots but the three of them told him to shut up and get out to school. He could stand up to the others but he was afraid of Tom. So he had flopped along in the rain feeling miserable and hating it because people would know he was poor when he had to wear his father's boots.

The door opened and Mr. O'Rourke came in. He was a huge man in tweeds. He was a fluent speaker of Irish and wore the gold Fainne in the lapel of his jacket. Both his wrists were covered with matted black hair.

"Filidheact," he roared and drew a leather from his hip pocket.

Then he shouted "Dun do leabhar" and hit the front desk a ferocious crack with the leather. Mr. O'Rourke was an ardent Gael who gave all his orders in Irish. Someone passed him up a poetry book and the rest closed theirs or turned them face downwards on their desks.

Mr. O'Rourke, his eyes glaring terribly at the ceiling, from which plaster would fall in fine dust when the 3rd year students tramped in or out, began to declaim

*"Did they dare, Did They Dare, to slay Eoghan Ruadh O'Neill?*
*Yes, they slew with poison him they feared to meet with steel."*

He clenched his powerful fists and held them up rigidly before his chest.

*"May God wither up their hearts, may their blood cease to
flow,
May they walk in living death who poisoned Eoghan Ruadh."*

Then quite suddenly, in a businesslike tone, he said, "You
—Daly."

"Me sir?" said Daly, playing for time.

"Yes, you fool," thundered Mr. O'Rourke. "You."

The rest could have drowned Daly for saying "Me sir?"
It put Mr. O'Rourke in bad humor.

Daly rose and repeated the first four lines. When he was
halfway through the second stanza Mr. O'Rourke bawled
"Clancy." Clancy rose and began to recite. They stood up and
sat down as Mr. O'Rourke commanded while he paced up and
down the aisles between the seats. Twice he passed close to
Peter. He stood for some time by Peter's desk bawling out
names. The end of his tweed jacket lay hypnotically along
the edge of Peter's desk. Cummins stumbled over the fourth
verse and dried up completely.

"Line," Mr. O'Rourke bawled. Cummins, calmly pale, left
his desk and stepped out to the side of the class. Two more
were sent out. Mr. O'Rourke walked up and down once more
and stood with his back to Peter. Looking at the desk at the
very back he suddenly bawled "Farrell."

Peter's heart jerked. He rose to his feet. The back was still
towards him. He looked at it, a great mountain of tweed with
a frayed collar over which the thick neck bulged in folds. He
could see the antennae of hair which sprouted from Mr.
O'Rourke's ears and could smell the chalk-and-ink schoolmaster's smell of him. It was a trick of Mr. O'Rourke's to
stand with his back to you and then call your name. It made
the shock more acute. Peter gulped and was silent.

"Wail . . ." prompted Mr. O'Rourke.

Peter said "Wail . . ."

Mr. O'Rourke paced up to the head of the class once more.

"Wail—wail him through the island," he said as he walked.
Then he turned around suddenly and said "Well, go on."

"Wail, wail him through the island," Peter said once more and stopped.

"Weep," hinted Mr. O'Rourke.

He regarded Peter closely, his eyes narrowing.

"Weep," said Peter, ransacking the darkness of his mind but finding only emptiness.

"Weep, weep, weep," Mr. O'Rourke said, his voice rising.

Peter chanced his arm. He said, "Wail, wail him through the island, weep, weep, weep."

Mr. O'Rourke stood up straight. His face conveyed at once shock, surprise, pain.

"Get out to the line," he roared, "you thick, lazy, good-for-nothing, bloody imbecile. Tell him what it is Clancy." Clancy dithered for a moment, closed his eyes and said,

"Sir—Wail, wail him through the island, weep, weep for our
    pride
Would that on the battle field our gallant chief had died."

Mr. O'Rourke nodded with dangerous benevolence. As Peter shuffled to the line the boots caught the iron upright of the desk and made a great clamor. Mr. O'Rourke gave him a cut with the leather across the behind. "Did you look at this, Farrell?" he asked.

Peter hesitated and said uncertainly, "No sir."

"It wasn't worth your while, I suppose."

"No sir. I hadn't time, sir."

Just then the clock struck the hour. The class rose. Mr. O'Rourke put the leather under his left armpit and crossed himself. "In ainm an athair," he began. While they recited the Hail Mary, Peter, unable to pray, stared at the leafless rain-soaked trees in the square and the serried rows of pale, prayerful faces. They sat down.

Mr. O'Rourke turned to the class.

"Farrell hadn't time," he announced pleasantly. Then he looked thunderously again at Peter. "If it was an English penny dreadful about Public Schools or London crime you'd find time to read it quick enough, but when it's about the poor hunted martyrs and felons of your own unfortunate country by a patriot like Davis you've no time for it. You're the makings of a fine little Britisher." With genuine pathos Mr. O'Rourke then recited,

*"The weapon of the Sassenach met him on his way*
*And he died at Cloch Uachter upon St. Leonard's day."*

"That was the dear dying in any case, but if he died for the likes of you Farrell it was the dear bitter dying, no mistake about it."

Peter said, "I meant to learn it."

"If I can't preach respect for the patriot dead into you, then honest to my stockings I'll beat respect into you. Hand."

Peter held it out. He pulled his coat sleeve down over his wrist. The leather came down six times with a resounding impact. He tried to keep his thumb out of the way because if it hit you on the thumb it stung unbearably. But after four heavy slaps the hand began to curl of its own accord, curl and cripple like a little piece of tinfoil in a fire, until the thumb lay powerless across the palm, and the pain burned in his chest and stiffened in his toes. But worse than the pain was the fear that he would cry. He was turning away when Mr. O'Rourke said, "Just a moment, Farrell, I haven't finished."

Mr. O'Rourke gently took the fingers of Peter's hand, smoothing them out as he drew them once more into position. "To teach you I'll take no defiance," he said, in a friendly tone, and raised the leather. Peter tried to hold his crippled hand steady.

He could not see properly going back to his desk and again the boots deceived him and he tripped and fell. As he picked himself up, Mr. O'Rourke, about to help him with another, though gentler, tap of the leather, stopped and exclaimed, "Merciful God, child, where did you pick up the boots?"

The rest looked with curiosity. Clancy, who had twice excelled himself, tittered. Mr. O'Rourke said, "And what's the funny joke Clancy?"

"Nothing, sir."

"Soft as a woman's was your voice, O'Neill, bright was your eye," recited Mr. O'Rourke in a voice as soft as a woman's, brightness in his eyes. "Continue, Clancy." But Clancy, the wind taken out of his sails, missed and went out to join the other three. Peter put his head on the desk, his raw hands tightly under his armpits, and nursed his wounds while the leather thudded patriotism and literature into the other, unmurmuring, four.

Swaine said nothing for a time. Now and then he glanced at Peter's face. He was staring straight at the book. His hands were tender, but the pain had ebbed away. Each still hid its rawness under a comfortably warm armpit.

"You got a heck of a hiding," Swaine whispered at last. Peter said nothing.

"Ten is too much. He's not allowed to give you ten. If he gave me ten I'd bring my father up to him."

Swaine was small, but his face was large and bony and when he took off his glasses sometimes to wipe them there was a small red weal on the bridge of his nose. Peter grunted and Swaine changed the subject.

"Tell us who owns the boots. They're not your own."

"Yes they are," Peter lied.

"Go on," Swaine said. "Who owns them? Are they your brother's?"

"Shut up."

"Tell us," Swaine persisted. "I won't tell a soul. Honest." He regarded Peter with sly curiosity. He whispered avidly. "I know they're not your own, but I wouldn't tell it. We sit beside one another. We're pals. You can tell me."

"Curiosity killed the cat . . ." Peter said.

Swaine had the answer to that. With a sly grin he rejoined, "Information made him fat."

"If you must know," Peter said, growing tired, "they're my father's. And if you tell anyone I'll break you up in little pieces. You just try breathing a word."

Swaine sat back, satisfied. If a fellow was expelled or anything mysterious happened, Swaine always knew the ins and outs of it.

Mr. O'Rourke was saying that the English used treachery when they poisoned Eoghan Ruadh. But what could be expected of the English except treachery.

"Hoof of the horse," he quoted, "horn of a bull, smile of a Saxon." Three perils. Oliver Cromwell read his Bible while he quartered infants at their mothers' breasts. People said let's forget all that. But we couldn't begin to forget it until we had our full freedom. Our own tongue, the sweet Gaelic *teanga*, must be restored once more as the spoken language of our race. It was the duty of all to study and work towards that end.

"And those of us who haven't time must be shown how to find the time. Isn't that a fact, Farrell?" he said. The class laughed. But the clock struck and Mr. O'Rourke put the lament regretfully aside.

"Mathematics," he announced. "*Ceimseata.*"

He had hoped it would continue to rain during lunch time so that they could stay in the classroom. But when the automatic bell clanged loudly and Mr. O'Rourke opened the frosted window to look out, it had stopped. They trooped down the stairs. They pushed and jostled one another. Peter kept his hand for safety on the bannisters. Going down the stairs made the boots seem larger. He made straight for the urinal and stayed there until the old brother whose duty it was for obscure moral reasons to patrol the place had passed through twice. The second time he said to him, "My goodness boy, go out into the fresh air with your playmates. Shoo—boy,—shoo," and stared at Peter's retreating back with perplexity and suspicion.

Dillon came over as he was unwrapping his lunch and said, "Did they dare, did they dare to slap Eoghan Ruadh O'Neill."

"Oh shut up," Peter said.

Dillon linked his arm and said, "You took an awful packet." Then with genuine admiration he added, "You took it super. He aimed for your wrist too. Not a peek. You were wizard. Cripes. When I saw him getting ready for the last four I was praying you wouldn't cry." They were all praying he wouldn't cry.

"I never cried yet," Peter asserted.

"I know, but he lammed his hardest. You shouldn't have said you hadn't time."

"He wouldn't make me cry," Peter said grimly, "not if he got up at four o'clock in the morning to try it."

O'Rourke had lammed him all right, but there was no use trying to do anything about it. If he told his father and mother they would say he richly deserved it. It was his mother should have been lammed and not he.

"The Irish," Dillon added sagaciously, "are an unfortunate bloody race. The father often says so."

"Don't tell me," Peter said with feeling.

"I mean look at us. First Cromwell knocks hell out of us for being too Irish and then Rorky slaughters us for not being Irish enough."

It was true. It was a pity they couldn't make up their minds.

Peter felt the comfort of Dillon's friendly arm. "The boots are my father's," he confided suddenly, "my own had holes." That made him feel better.

"What are you worrying about?" Dillon said, reassuringly. "They look all right to me."

When they were passing the row of water taps with the chained drinking vessels a voice cried, "There's Farrell now." A piece of crust hit Peter on the nose.

"Caesar sends his legate," Dillon murmured. They gathered round.

Clancy said, "Hey boys, Farrell is wearing someone else's boots."

"Who lifted you into them?"

"Wait now," said Clancy, "let's see him walk. Go on—walk Farrell."

Peter backed slowly towards the wall. He backed slowly until he felt the ridge of a downpipe hard against his back. Dillon came with him. "Lay off, Clancy," Dillon said. Swaine was there too. He was smiling, a small cat fat with information.

"Where did you get them Farrell?"

"Pinched them."

"Found them in an ashbin."

"Make him walk," Clancy insisted. "Let's see you walk, Farrell."

"They're my own," Peter said. "They're a bit big—that's all. They'll shrink after a while."

"Come on Farrell—tell us whose they are."

The grins grew wider.

Clancy said, "They're his father's."

"No they're not." Peter denied quickly.

"Yes they are. He told Swaine. Didn't he Swaine? He told you they were his father's."

Swaine's grin froze. Peter fixed him with terrible eyes.

"Well didn't he, Swaine? Go on, tell the chaps what he told you. Didn't he say they were his father's?"

Swaine edged backwards. "That's right," he said, "he did."

"Hey, you chaps," Clancy said, impatiently, "let's make him walk. I vote . . ."

At that moment Peter, with a cry, sprang on Swaine. His fist smashed the glasses on Swaine's face. As they rolled over on the muddy ground, Swaine's nails tore his cheek. Peter saw the white terrified face under him. He beat at it in frenzy until it became covered with mud and blood.

"Cripes," Clancy said in terror, "look at Swaine's glasses. Haul him off lads." They pulled him away and he lashed out awkwardly with the big boots which had caused all the trouble. Swaine's nose and lips were bleeding so they took him over to the water tap and washed him. Dillon, who stood alone with Peter, brushed his clothes as best he could and fixed his collar and tie.

"You broke his glasses," he said. "There'll be a proper rucky if old Quinny sees him after lunch."

"I don't care about Quinny."

"I do then," Dillon said fervently. "He'll quarter us all in our mother's arms."

They sat with their arms folded while Brother Quinlan, in the high chair at the head of the class, gave religious instruction. Swaine kept his bruised face lowered. Without the glasses it had a bald, maimed look, as though his eyebrows, or a nose, or an eye, were missing. They had exchanged no words since the fight. Peter was aware of the boots. They were a defeat, something to be ashamed of. His mother only thought they would keep out the rain. She didn't understand that it would be better to have wet feet. People did not laugh at you because your feet were wet.

Brother Quinlan was speaking of our relationship to one another, of the boy to his neighbour and of the boy to his God. We communicated with one another, he said, by looks, gestures, speech. But these were surface contacts. They conveyed little of what went on in the mind, and nothing at all of the soul. Inside us, the greatest and the humblest of us, a whole world was locked. Even if we tried we could convey nothing of that interior world, that life which was nourished, as the poet had said, within the brain. In our interior life we stood without friend or ally—alone. In the darkness and silence of that interior and eternal world the immortal soul and its God were at all times face to face. No one else could peer into another's soul, neither our teacher, nor our father or mother, nor even our best friend. But God saw all. Every stray little thought which moved in that inaccessible world was as plain to Him as if it were thrown across the bright screen of a cinema. That was why we must be as careful to discipline our thoughts as our actions. Custody of the eyes, custody of the ears, but above all else custody . . .

Brother Quinlan let the sentence trail away and fixed his eyes on Swaine.

"You—boy," he said in a voice tired but patient. "What are you doing with that handkerchief?"

Swaine's nose had started to bleed again. He said nothing.

"Stand up, boy," Brother Quinlan commanded. He had glasses himself, which he wore during class on the tip of his nose. He was a big man too, and his head was bald in front, which made his large forehead appear even more massive. He stared over the glasses at Swaine.

"Come up here," he said, screwing up his eyes, the fact that something was amiss with Swaine's face dawning gradually on him. Swaine came up to him, looking woebe-gone, still dabbing his nose with the handkerchief. Brother Quinlan contemplated the battered face for some time. He turned to the class.

"Whose handiwork is this?" he asked quietly. "Stand up, the boy responsible for this."

For a while nobody stirred. There was an uneasy stillness. Poker faces looked at the desks in front of them and waited. Peter looked around and saw Dillon gazing at him hopefully. After an unbearable moment feet shuffled and Peter stood up.

"I am sir," he said.

Brother Quinlan told Clancy to take Swaine out to the yard to bathe his nose. Then he spoke to the class about violence, and what was worse, violence to a boy weaker than oneself. That was the resort of the bully and the scoundrel—physical violence—The Fist. At this Brother Quinlan held up his large bunched fist so that all might see it. Then with the other hand he indicated the picture of the Sacred Heart. Charity and Forbearance, he said, not revenge and intoler-ance, those were qualities most dear to Our Blessed Lord.

"Are you not ashamed of yourself, Farrell? Do you think what you have done is a heroic or a creditable thing?"

"No sir."

"Then why did you do it boy?"

Peter made no answer. It was no use making an answer. It was no use saying Swaine had squealed about the boots being his father's. Swaine's face was badly battered. But deep inside him Peter felt battered too. Brother Quinlan couldn't see your soul. He could see Swaine's face, though, when he fixed his glasses on him properly. Brother Quinlan took his silence for defiance.

"A blackguardly affair," he pronounced. "A low, cowardly assault. Hold out your hand."

Peter hesitated. There was a limit. He hadn't meant not to learn the Poetry and it wasn't his fault about the boots.

"He's been licked already, sir," Dillon said. "Mr. O'Rourke gave him ten."

"Mr. O'Rourke is a discerning man," said Brother Quinlan,

"but he doesn't seem to have given him half enough. Think of the state of that poor boy who has just gone out."

Peter could think of nothing to say. He tried hard to word his defence but it was useless. There were no words there. Reluctantly he presented his hand. It was mudstained. Brother Quinlan looked at it with distaste. Then he proceeded to beat hell out of him, and charity and forbearance into him, in the same way as Mr. O'Rourke earlier had hammered in patriotism and respect for Irish History.

It was raining again when he was going home. Usually there were three or four to go home with him, but this afternoon he went alone. He did not want them with him. He passed some shops and walked by the first small suburban gardens, with their sodden gravel paths and dripping gates. On the canal bridge a boy passed him pushing fuel in a pram. His feet were bare. The mud had splashed upwards in thick streaks to his knees. Peter kept his left hand under his coat. There was a blister on the ball of the thumb which ached now like a burn. Brother Quinlan did that. He probably didn't aim to hit the thumb as Mr. O'Rourke always did, but his sight was so bad he had a rotten shot. The boots had got looser than they were earlier. He realized this when he saw Clancy with three or four others passing on the other side of the road. When Clancy waved and called to him, he backed automatically until he felt the parapet against his back.

"Hey, Farrell," they called. Then one of them, his head forward, his behind stuck out, began to waddle with grotesque movements up the road. The rest yelled to call Peter's attention. They indicated the mime. Come back if you like, they shouted. Peter waited until they had gone. Then he turned moodily down the bank of the canal. He walked with a stiff ungainly dignity, his mind not yet quite made up. Under the bridge the water was deep and narrow, and a raw wind which moaned in the high arch whipped coldly at his face. It might rain to-morrow and his shoes wouldn't be mended. If his mother thought the boots were all right God knows when his shoes would be mended. After a moment of indecision he took off the boots and dropped them, first one—and then the other, into the water.

There would be hell to pay when he came home without them. But there would be hell to pay anyway when Swaine's father sent around the note to say he had broken young Swaine's glasses. Like the time he broke the Cassidys' window. Half regretfully he stared at the silty water. He could see his father rising from the table to reach for the belt which hung behind the door. The outlook was frightening; but it was better to walk in your bare feet. It was better to walk without shoes and barefooted than to walk without dignity. He took off his stockings and stuffed them into his pocket. His heart sank as he felt the cold wet mud of the path on his bare feet.

GEORGE   BERNARD   SHAW

# The Miraculous Revenge

✳

I arrived in Dublin on the evening of the 5th of August, and
drove to the residence of my uncle, the Cardinal Archbishop. He is, like most of my family, deficient in feeling,
and consequently cold to me personally. He lives in a dingy
house, with a side-long view of the portico of his cathedral
from the front windows, and of a monster national school
from the back. My uncle maintains no retinue. The people
believe that he is waited upon by angels. When I knocked
at the door, an old woman, his only servant, opened it, and
informed me that her master was then officiating in the cathedral, and that he had directed her to prepare dinner for
me in his absence. An unpleasant smell of salt fish made me
ask her what the dinner consisted of. She assured me that
she had cooked all that could be permitted in His Holiness's
house on a Friday. On my asking her further why on a Friday, she replied that Friday was a fast day. I bade her tell
His Holiness that I had hoped to have the pleasure of calling
on him shortly, and drove to a hotel in Sackville Street, where
I engaged apartments and dined.

After dinner I resumed my eternal search—I know not
for what; it drives me to and fro like another Cain. I sought
in the streets without success. I went to the theatre. The music was execrable, the scenery poor. I had seen the play a
month before in London, with the same beautiful artist in
the chief part. Two years had passed since, seeing her for

From SHORT STORIES, SCRAPS, AND SHAVINGS, London, 1933. First published
in *Time, a Monthly Magazine*, London, 1885.

the first time, I had hoped that she, perhaps, might be the long-sought mystery. It had proved otherwise. On this night I looked at her and listened to her for the sake of that bygone hope, and applauded her generously when the curtain fell. But I went out lonely still. When I had supped at a restaurant, I returned to my hotel, and tried to read. In vain. The sound of feet in the corridors as the other occupants of the hotel went to bed distracted my attention from my book. Suddenly it occurred to me that I had never quite understood my uncle's character. He, father to a great flock of poor and ignorant Irish; an austere and saintly man, to whom livers of hopeless lives daily appealed for help heavenward; who was reputed never to have sent away a troubled peasant without relieving him of his burden by sharing it; whose knees were worn less by the altar steps than by the tears and embraces of the guilty and wretched: he had refused to humour my light extravagances, or to find time to talk with me of books, flowers, and music. Had I not been mad to expect it? Now that I needed sympathy myself, I did him justice. I desired to be with a true-hearted man, and to mingle my tears with his.

I looked at my watch. It was nearly an hour past midnight. In the corridor the lights were out, except one jet at the end. I threw a cloak upon my shoulders, put on a Spanish hat, and left my apartment, listening to the echoes of my measured steps retreating through the deserted passages. A strange sight arrested me on the landing of the grand staircase. Through an open door I saw the moonlight shining through the windows of a saloon in which some entertainment had recently taken place. I looked at my watch again. It was but one o'clock; and yet the guests had departed. I entered the room, my boots ringing loudly on the waxed boards. On a chair lay a child's clock and a broken toy. The entertainment had been a children's party. I stood for a time looking at the shadow of my cloaked figure upon the floor, and at the disordered decorations, ghostly in the white light. Then I saw that there was a grand piano, still open, in the middle of the room. My fingers throbbed as I sat down before it, and expressed all that I felt in a grand hymn which seemed to thrill the cold stillness of the shadows into a deep hum of approbation, and to people the radiance of the moon with angels. Soon there was a stir without too, as if the rapture was spreading abroad. I took up the chant triumphantly with my voice, and the empty saloon resounded as though to the thunder of an orchestra.

"Hallo, sir!" "Confound you, sir—" "Do you suppose that this—" "What the deuce—?"

I turned, and silence followed. Six men, partially dressed, and with dishevelled hair, stood regarding me angrily. They all carried candles. One of them had a bootjack, which he held like a truncheon. Another, the foremost, had a pistol. The night porter was behind trembling.

"Sir," said the man with the revolver, coarsely, "may I ask whether you are mad, that you disturb people at this hour with such an unearthly noise?"

"Is it possible that you dislike it?" I replied, courteously.

"Dislike it!" said he, stamping with rage. "Why—damn everything—do you suppose we were enjoying it?"

"Take care. He's mad," whispered the man with the boot-jack.

I began to laugh. Evidently they did think me mad. Unaccustomed to my habits, and ignorant of music as they probably were, the mistake, however absurd, was not unnatural. I rose. They came closer to one another; and the night porter ran away.

"Gentlemen," I said, "I am sorry for you. Had you lain still and listened, we should all have been the better and happier. But what you have done, you cannot undo. Kindly inform the night porter that I am gone to visit my uncle, the Cardinal Archbishop. Adieu!"

I strode past them, and left them whispering among themselves. Some minutes later I knocked at the door of the Cardinal's house. Presently a window on the first floor was opened; and the moonbeams fell on a grey head, with a black cap that seemed ashy pale against the unfathomable gloom of the shadow beneath the stone sill.

"Who are you?"

"I am Zeno Legge."

"What do you want at this hour?"

The question wounded me. "My dear uncle," I exclaimed, "I know you do not intend it, but you make me feel unwelcome. Come down and let me in, I beg."

"Go to your hotel," he said sternly. "I will see you in the morning. Goodnight." He disappeared and closed the window.

I felt that if I let this rebuff pass, I should not feel kindly towards my uncle in the morning, nor, indeed, at any future time. I therefore plied the knocker with my right hand, and kept the bell ringing with my left until I heard the door-chain rattle within. The Cardinal's expression was grave nearly to moroseness as he confronted me on the threshold.

"Uncle," I cried, grasping his hand, "do not reproach me. Your door is never shut against the wretched. I am wretched. Let us sit up all night and talk."

"You may thank my position and not my charity for your admission, Zeno," he said. "For the sake of the neighbours, I had rather you played the fool in my study than upon my doorstep at this hour. Walk upstairs quietly, if you please. My housekeeper is a hard-working woman: the little sleep she allows herself must not be disturbed."

"You have a noble heart, uncle. I shall creep like a mouse."

"This is my study," he said, as we entered an ill-furnished den on the second floor. "The only refreshment I can offer you, if you desire any, is a bunch of raisins. The doctors have forbidden you to touch stimulants, I believe."

"By heaven—!" He raised his finger. "Pardon me: I was wrong to swear. But I had totally forgotten the doctors. At dinner I had a bottle of *Grave*.

"Humph! You have no business to be travelling alone. Your mother promised me that Bushy should come over here with you."

"Pshaw! Bushy is not a man of feeling. Besides, he is a coward. He refused to come with me because I purchased a revolver."

"He should have taken the revolver from you, and kept to his post."

"Why will you persist in treating me like a child, uncle? I am very impressionable, I grant you; but I have gone round the world alone, and do not need to be dry-nursed through a tour in Ireland."

"What do you intend to do during your stay here?"

I had no plans; and instead of answering I shrugged my shoulders and looked round the apartment. There was a statuette of the Virgin upon my uncle's desk. I looked at its face, as he was wont to look in the midst of his labours. I saw there eternal peace. The air became luminous with an infinite network of the jewelled rings of Paradise descending in roseate clouds upon us.

"Uncle," I said, bursting into the sweetest tears I had ever shed, "my wanderings are over. I will enter the Church, if you will help me. Let us read together the third part of *Faust;* for I understand it at last."

"Hush, man," he said, half rising with an expression of alarm. "Control yourself."

"Do not let my tears mislead you. I am calm and strong. Quick, let us have Goethe:

> *Das Unbeschreibliche,*
> *Hier ist gethan;*
> *Das Ewig-Weibliche,*
> *Zieht uns hinan."*

"Come, come. Dry your eyes and be quiet. I have no library here."

"But I have—in my portmanteau at the hotel," I said, rising. "Let me go for it, I will return in fifteen minutes."

"The devil is in you, I believe. Cannot—"

I interrupted him with a shout of laughter. "Cardinal," I said noisily, "you have become profane; and a profane priest is always the best of good fellows. Let us have some wine; and I will sing you a German beer song."

"Heaven forgive me if I do you wrong," he said; "but I

believe God has laid the expiation of some sin on your unhappy head. Will you favor me with your attention for a
while? I have something to say to you, and I have also to
get some sleep before my hour for rising, which is half-
past five."

"My usual hour for retiring—when I retire at all. But proceed. My fault is not inattention, but over-susceptibility."

"Well, then, I want you to go to Wicklow. My reasons—"

"No matter what they may be," said I, rising again. "It is
enough that you desire me to go. I shall start forthwith."

"Zeno! will you sit down and listen to me?"

I sank upon my chair reluctantly. "Ardor is a crime in your
eyes, even when it is shown in your service," I said. "May
I turn down the light?"

"Why?"

"To bring on my sombre mood, in which I am able to listen
with tireless patience."

"I will turn it down myself. Will that do?"

I thanked him, and composed myself to listen in the shadow. My eyes, I felt, glittered. I was like Poe's raven.

"Now for my reasons for sending you to Wicklow. First,
for your own sake. If you stay in town, or in any place where
excitement can be obtained by any means, you will be in
Swift's Hospital in a week. You must live in the country, under
the eye of one upon whom I can depend. And you must have
something to do to keep you out of mischief, and away from
your music and painting and poetry, which, Sir John Richards
writes to me, are dangerous for you in your present morbid
state. Second, because I can entrust you with a task which,
in the hands of a sensible man, might bring discredit on the
Church. In short, I want you to investigate a miracle."

He looked attentively at me. I sat like a statue.

"You understand me?" he said.

"Nevermore," I replied, hoarsely. "Pardon me," I added,
amused at the trick my imagination had played me, "I understand you perfectly. Proceed."

"I hope you do. Well, four miles distant from the town
of Wicklow is a village called Four Mile Water. The resident

priest is Father Hickey. You have heard of the miracles at
Knock?"

I winked.

"I did not ask you what you think of them, but whether
you have heard of them. I see you have. I need not tell you
that even a miracle may do more harm than good to the
Church in this country, unless it can be proved so thoroughly that her powerful and jealous enemies are silenced
by the testimony of followers of their heresy. Therefore,
when I saw in a Wexford newspaper last week a description
of a strange manifestation of the Divine Power which was
said to have taken place at Four Mile Water, I was troubled
in my mind about it. So I wrote to Father Hickey, bidding
him give me an account of the matter if it were true, and
if not, to denounce from the altar the author of the report, and
to contradict it in the paper at once. This is his reply. He
says—well, the first part is about Church matters: I need not
trouble you with it. He goes on to say—"

"One moment. Is that his own handwriting? It does not
look like a man's."

"He suffers from rheumatism in the fingers of his right
hand, and his niece, who is an orphan, and lives with him,
acts as his amanuensis. Well—"

"Stay. What is her name?"

"Her name? Kate Hickey."

"How old is she?"

"Tush, man, she is only a little girl. If she were old
enough to concern you, I should not send you into her way.
Have you any more questions to ask about her?"

"None. I can fancy her in a white veil at the rite of con-
firmation, a type of faith and innocence. Enough of her. What
says the Reverend Hickey of the apparitions?"

"They are not apparitions. I will read you what he says.
Ahem!

'In reply to your inquiries concerning the late miraculous
event in this parish, I have to inform you that I can
vouch for its truth, and that I can be confirmed not only

by the inhabitants of the place, who are all Catholics, but by every person acquainted with the former situation of the graveyard referred to, including the Protestant Archdeacon of Baltinglas, who spends six weeks annually in the neighbourhood. The newspaper account is incomplete and inaccurate. The following are the facts: About four years ago, a man named Wolfe Tone Fitzgerald settled in this village as a farrier. His antecedents did not transpire, and he had no family. He lived by himself, was very careless of his person; and when in his cups, as he often was, regarded the honor neither of God nor man in his conversation. Indeed if it were not speaking ill of the dead, one might say that he was a dirty, drunken, blasphemous blackguard. Worse again, he was, I fear, an atheist, for he never attended Mass, and gave his Holiness worse language even than he gave the Queen. I should have mentioned that he was a bitter rebel, and boasted that his grandfather had been out in '08, and his father with Smith O'Brien. At last he went by the name of Brimstone Billy, and was held up in the village as the type of all wickedness.

'You are aware that our graveyard, situated on the north side of the water, is famous throughout the country as the burial place of the nuns of St. Ursula, the hermit of Four Mile Water, and many other holy people. No Protestant has ever ventured to enforce his legal right of interment there, though two have died in the parish within my own recollection. Three weeks ago, this Fitzgerald died in a fit brought on by drink, and a great hullabaloo was raised in the village when it became known that he would be buried in the graveyard. The body had to be watched to prevent its being stolen and buried at the cross-roads. My people were greatly disappointed when they were told I could do nothing to stop the burial, particularly as I of course refused to read any service on the occasion. However, I bade them not interfere; and the interment was effected on the 14th of July, late in the evening, and long after the legal hour. There was no disturbance. Next morning, the graveyard was found moved to the south side of the water, with the one newly-filled grave left behind on the north side; and thus they both remain. The departed saints would not lie with the reprobate. I can testify to it on the oath of a Christian priest; and if this will not satisfy those outside the Church, everyone, as I said before, who remembers where the graveyard was two months ago, can confirm me.

'I respectfully suggest that a thorough investigation into the truth of this miracle be proposed to a committee of Protestant gentlemen. They shall not be asked to accept a single fact on hearsay from my people. The ordnance maps show where the graveyard was; and anyone can see for himself where it is. I need not tell your Eminence what a rebuke this would be to those enemies of the holy Church that have sought to put a stain on her by discrediting the late wonderful manifestations at Knock Chapel. If they come to Four Mile Water, they need cross-examine no one. They will be asked to believe nothing but their own senses.

'Awaiting your Eminence's counsel to guide me further in the matter,

'I am, etc.'

"Well, Zeno," said my uncle, "what do you think of Father Hickey now?"

"Uncle, do not ask me. Beneath this roof I desire to believe everything. The Reverend Hickey has appealed strongly to my love of legend. Let us admire the poetry of his narrative and ignore the balance of probability between a Christian priest telling a lie on his oath and a graveyard swimming across a river in the middle of the night and forgetting to return."

"Tom Hickey is not telling a lie, sir. You may take my word for that. But he may be mistaken."

"Such a mistake amounts to insanity. It is true that I myself, awaking suddenly in the depth of night, have found myself convinced that the position of my bed had been reversed. But on opening my eyes the illusion ceased. I fear

Mr. Hickey is mad. Your best course is this. Send down to Four Mile Water a perfectly sane investigator; an acute observer; one whose perceptive faculties, at once healthy and subtle, are absolutely unclouded by religious prejudice. In a word, send me. I will report to you the true state of affairs in a few days, and you can then make arrangements for transferring Hickey from the altar to the asylum."

"Yes, I had intended to send you. You are wonderfully sharp and you would make a capital detective if you could only keep your mind to one point. But your chief qualification for this business is that you are too crazy to excite the suspicion of those whom you may have to watch. For the affair may be a trick. If so, I hope and believe that Hickey has no hand in it. Still, it is my duty to take every precaution."

"Cardinal, may I ask whether traces of insanity have ever appeared in our family?"

"Except in you and in my grandmother, no. She was a Pole; and you resemble her personally. Why do you ask?"

"Because it has often occurred to me that you are, perhaps, a little cracked. Excuse my candour, but a man who has devoted his life to the pursuit of a red hat, who accuses everyone else besides himself of being mad, and who is disposed to listen seriously to a tale of a peripatetic graveyard, can hardly be quite sane. Depend upon it, uncle, you want rest and change. The blood of your Polish grandmother is in your veins."

"I hope I may not be committing a sin in sending a ribald on the Church's affairs," he replied, fervently. "However, we must use the instruments put into our hands. Is it agreed that you go?"

"Had you not delayed me with this story, which I might as well have learned on the spot, I should have been there already."

"There is no occasion for impatience, Zeno. I must first send to Hickey to find a place for you. I shall tell him that you are going to recover your health, as, in fact, you are. And, Zeno, in Heaven's name be discreet. Try to act like a man of sense. Do not dispute with Hickey on matters of religion.

Since you are my nephew, you had better not disgrace me."

"I shall become an ardent Catholic, and do you infinite credit, uncle."

"I wish you would, although you would hardly be an acquisition to the Church. And now I must turn you out. It is nearly three o'clock, and I need some sleep. Do you know your way back to your hotel?"

"I need not stir. I can sleep in this chair. Go to bed, and never mind me."

"I shall not close my eyes until you are safely out of the house. Come, rouse yourself, and say goodnight."

The following is a copy of my first report to the Cardinal:

> Four Mile Water, County Wicklow,
> 10th August

My Dear Uncle,

The miracle is genuine. I have affected perfect credulity in order to throw the Hickeys and the countryfolk off their guard with me. I have listened to their method of convincing sceptical strangers. I have examined the ordnance maps, and cross-examined the neighbouring Protestant gentlefolk. I have spent a day upon the ground on each side of the water, and have visited it at midnight. I have considered the upheaval theories, subsidence theories, volcanic theories, and tidal wave theories which the provincial *savants* have suggested. They are all untenable. There is only one scoffer in the district, an Orangeman; and he admits the removal of the cemetery, but says it was dug up and transplanted in the night by a body of men under the command of Father Tom. This also is out of the question. The interment of Brimstone Billy was the first which had taken place for four years; and his is the only grave which bears a trace of recent digging. It is alone on the north bank, and the inhabitants shun it after nightfall. As each passer-by during the day throws a stone upon it, it will soon be marked by a large cairn. The graveyard, with a ruined stone chapel still standing in its midst, is on the

south side. You may send down a committee to investigate
the matter as soon as you please. There can be no doubt
as to the miracle having actually taken place, as recorded
by Hickey. As for me, I have grown so accustomed to it
that if the county Wicklow were to waltz off with me to
Middlesex, I should be quite impatient of any expressions
of surprise from my friends in London.

Is not the above a businesslike statement? Away, then,
with this stale miracle. If you would see for yourself a
miracle which can never pall, a vision of youth and health
to be crowned with garlands for ever, come down and see
Kate Hickey, whom you suppose to be a little girl. Illusion,
my lord cardinal, illusion! She is seventeen, with a bloom
and a brogue that would lay your asceticism in ashes at
a flash. To her I am an object of wonder, a strange man
bred in wicked cities. She is courted by six feet of farming
material, chopped off a spare length of coarse humanity by
the Almighty, and flung into Wicklow to plough the fields.
His name is Phil Langan; and he hates me. I have to con-
sort with him for the sake of Father Tom, whom I enter-
tain vastly by stories of your wild oats sown at Salamanca.
I exhausted all my authentic anecdotes the first day; and
now I invent gallant escapades with Spanish donnas, in
which you figure as a youth of unstable morals. This de-
lights Father Tom infinitely. I feel that I have done you a
service by thus casting on the cold sacerdotal abstraction
which formerly represented you in Kate's imagination a
ray of vivifying passion.

What a country this is! A Hesperidean garden: such
skies! Adieu, uncle.

*Zeno Legge.*

Behold me, then, at Four Mile Water, in love. I had
been in love frequently; but not oftener than once a year
had I encountered a woman who affected me as seriously as
Kate Hickey. She was so shrewd, and yet so flippant! When
I spoke of art she yawned. When I deplored the sordidness
of the world she laughed, and called me "poor fellow!" When

I told her what a treasure of beauty and freshness she had she ridiculed me. When I reproached her with her brutality she became angry, and sneered at me for being what she called a fine gentleman. One sunny afternoon we were standing at the gate of her uncle's house, she looking down the dusty road for the detestable Langan, I watching the spotless azure sky, when she said:

"How soon are you going back to London?"

"I am not going back to London, Miss Hickey. I am not yet tired of Four Mile Water."

"I'm sure Four Mile Water ought to be proud of your approbation."

"You disapprove of my liking it, then? Or is it that you grudge me the happiness I have found there? I think Irish ladies grudge a man a moment's peace."

"I wonder you have ever prevailed on yourself to associate with Irish ladies, since they are so far beneath you."

"Did I say they were beneath me, Miss Hickey? I feel that I have made a deep impression on you."

"Indeed! Yes, you're quite right. I assure you I can't sleep at night for thinking of you, Mr. Legge. It's the best a Christian can do, seeing you think so mighty little of yourself."

"You are triply wrong, Miss Hickey: wrong to be sarcastic with me, wrong to pretend that there is anything unreasonable in my belief that you think of me sometimes, and wrong to discourage the candour with which I always avow that I think constantly of myself."

"Then you had better not speak to me, since I have no manners."

"Again! Did I say you had no manners? The warmest expressions of regard from my mouth seem to reach your ears transformed into insults. Were I to repeat the Litany of the Blessed Virgin, you would retort as though I had been reproaching you. This is because you hate me. You never misunderstand Langan, whom you love."

"I don't know what London manners are, Mr. Legge; but

in Ireland gentlemen are expected to mind their own business. How dare you say I love Mr. Langan?"

"Then you do not love him?"

"It is nothing to you whether I love him or not."

"Nothing to me that you hate me and love another?"

"I did not say that I hated you. You are not so very clever yourself at understanding what people say, though you make such a fuss because they don't understand you." Here, as she glanced down the road again, she suddenly looked glad.

"Aha!" I said.

"What do you mean by 'Aha'?"

"No matter. I will now show you what a man's sympathy is. As you perceived just then, Langan—who is too tall for his age, by-the-bye—is coming to pay you a visit. Well, instead of staying with you, as a jealous woman would, I will withdraw."

"I don't care whether you go or stay, I'm sure. I wonder what you would give to be as fine a man as Mr. Langan."

"All I possess: I swear it! But solely because you admire tall men more than broad views. Mr. Langan may be defined geometrically as length without breadth; altitude without position; a line on the landscape, not a point in it."

"How very clever you are!"

"You do not understand me, I see. Here comes your lover, stepping over the wall like a camel. And here go I, out through the gate like a Christian. Good afternoon, Mr. Langan. I am going because Miss Hickey has something to say to you about me which she would rather not say in my presence. You will excuse me?"

"Oh, I'll excuse you," said he boorishly. I smiled, and went out. Before I was quite out of hearing, Kate whispered vehemently to him, "I *hate* that fellow."

I smiled again; but I had scarcely done so when my spirits fell. I walked hastily away with a coarse threatening sound in my ears like that of the clarionets whose sustained low notes darken the woodland in "Der Freischütz." I found myself presently at the graveyard. It was a barren place, enclosed by a mud wall with a gate to admit funerals, and numerous gaps to admit the peasantry, who made short cuts across it as they went to and fro between Four Mile Water and the market town. The graves were mounds overgrown with grass: there was no keeper; nor were there flowers, railings or any of the conventionalities that make an English graveyard repulsive. A great thornbush, near what was called the grave of the holy sisters, was covered with scraps of cloth and flannel, attached by peasant women who had prayed before it. There were three kneeling there as I entered, for the reputation of the place had been revived of late by the miracle, and a ferry had been established close by, to conduct visitors over the route taken by the graveyard. From where I stood I could see on the opposite bank the heap of stones, perceptibly increased since my last visit, marking the deserted grave of Brimstone Billy. I strained my eyes broodingly at it for some minutes, and then descended the river bank and entered the boat.

"Good evenin' t'your honour," said the ferryman, and set to work to draw the boat hand-over-hand by a rope stretched across the water.

"Good evening. Is your business beginning to fall off yet?"

"Faith, it never was as good as it might ha' been. The people that comes from the south side can see Billy's grave—Lord have mercy on him—across the wather; and they think bad of payin a penny to put a stone over him. It's them that lives tow'rst Dublin that makes the journey. Your honour is the third I've brought from south to north this blessed day."

"When do most people come? In the afternoon, I suppose?"

"All hours, sur, except afther dusk. There isn't a sowl in the counthry ud come within sight of that grave wanst the sun goes down."

"And you! Do you stay here all night by yourself?"

"The holy heavens forbid! Is it me stay here all night? No, your honour; I tether the boat at siven o'hlyock, and lave Brimstone Billy—God forgimme!—to take care of it t'll mornin."

"It will be stolen some night, I'm afraid."

"Arra, who'd dar come next or near it, let alone stale it? Faith, I'd think twice before lookin at it meself in the dark. God bless your honour, and gran'che long life."

I had given him sixpence. I went to the reprobate's grave and stood at the foot of it, looking at the sky, gorgeous with the descent of the sun. To my English eyes, accustomed to giant trees, broad lawns, and stately mansions, the landscape was wild and inhospitable. The ferryman was already tugging at the rope on his way back (I had told him I did not intend to return that way), and presently I saw him make the painter fast to the south bank; put on his coat; and trudge homeward. I turned towards the grave at my feet. Those who had interred Brimstone Billy, working hastily at an unlawful hour, and in fear of molestation by the people, had hardly dug a grave. They had scooped out earth enough to hide their burden, and no more. A stray goat had kicked away a corner of the mound and exposed the coffin. It occurred to me, as I took some of the stones from the cairn, and heaped them so as to repair the breach, that had the miracle been the work of a body of men, they would have moved the one grave instead of the many. Even from a supernatural point of view, it seemed strange that the sinner should have banished the elect, when, by their superior numbers, they might so much more easily have banished him.

It was almost dark when I left the spot. After a walk of half a mile, I recrossed the water by a bridge, and returned to the farmhouse in which I lodged. Here, finding that I had had enough of solitude, I only stayed to take a cup of tea. Then I went to Father Hickey's cottage.

Kate was alone when I entered. She looked up quickly as I opened the door, and turned away disappointed when she recognized me.

"Be generous for once," I said. "I have walked about aimlessly for hours in order to avoid spoiling the beautiful afternoon for you by my presence. When the sun was up I withdrew my shadow from your path. Now that darkness has fallen, shed some light on mine. May I stay half an hour?"

"You may stay as long as you like, of course. My uncle will soon be home. He is clever enough to talk to you."

"What! More sarcasms! Come, Miss Hickey, help me to spend a pleasant evening. It will only cost you a smile. I am somewhat cast down. Four Mile Water is a paradise; but without you, it would be a little lonely."

"It must be very lonely for you. I wonder why you came here."

"Because I heard that the women here were all Zerlinas, like you, and the men Masettos, like Mr. Phil—where are you going to?"

"Let me pass, Mr. Legge. I had intended never speaking to you again after the way you went on about Mr. Langan today; and I wouldn't either, only my uncle made me promise not to take any notice of you, because you were—no matter; but I won't listen to you any more on the subject."

"Do not go. I swear never to mention his name again. I beg your pardon for what I said: you shall have no further cause for complaint. Will you forgive me?"

She sat down, evidently disappointed by my submission. I took a chair, and placed myself near her. She tapped the floor impatiently with her foot. I saw that there was not a movement I could make, not a look, not a tone of my voice, which did not irritate her.

"You were remarking," I said, "that your uncle desired you to take no notice of me because—"

She closed her lips, and did not answer.

"I fear I have offended you again by my curiosity. But indeed, I had no idea that he had forbidden you to tell me the reason."

"He did not forbid me. Since you are so determined to find out—"

"No, excuse me. I do not wish to know, I am sorry I asked."

"Indeed! Perhaps you would be sorrier still to be told. I only made a secret of it out of consideration for you."

"Then your uncle has spoken ill of me behind my back. If that be so, there is no such thing as a true man in Ireland. I would not have believed it on the word of any woman alive save yourself."

"I never said my uncle was a backbiter. Just to show you what he thinks of you, I will tell you, whether you want to

know it or not, that he bid me not mind you because you
were only a poor mad creature, sent down here by your
family to be out of harm's way."

"Oh, Miss Hickey!"

"There now! You have got it out of me; and I wish I
had bit my tongue out first. I sometimes think—that I mayn't
sin!—that you have a bad angel in you."

"I am glad you told me this," I said gently. "Do not reproach yourself for having done so, I beg. Your uncle has
been misled by what he has heard of my family, who are
all more or less insane. Far from being mad, I am actually
the only rational man named Legge in the three kingdoms. I
will prove this to you, and at the same time keep your in-
discretion in countenance, by telling you something I ought
not to tell you. It is this. I am not here as an invalid or a
chance tourist. I am here to investigate the miracle. The
Cardinal, a shrewd if somewhat erratic man, selected mine
from all the long heads at his disposal to come down here,
and find out the truth of Father Hickey's story. Would he
have entrusted such a task to a madman, think you?"

"The truth of—who dared to doubt my uncle's word? And
so you are a spy, a dirty informer."

I started. The adjective she had used, though probably the
commonest expression of contempt in Ireland, is revolting
to an Englishman.

"Miss Hickey," I said, "there is in me, as you have said,
a bad angel. Do not shock my good angel—who is a person of
taste—quite away from my heart, lest the other be left un-
disputed monarch of it. Hark! The chapel bell is ringing the
angelus. Can you, with that sound softening the darkness of
the village night, cherish a feeling of spite against one who
admires you?"

"You come between me and my prayers," she said hysterically, and began to sob. She had scarcely done so, when
I heard voices without. Then Langan and the priest entered.

"Oh Phil," she cried, running to him, "take me away from
him: I can't bear—" I turned towards him, and showed him

my dog-tooth in a false smile. He felled me at one stroke, as he might have felled a poplar tree.

"Murdher!" exclaimed the priest. "What are you doin, Phil?"

"He's an informer," sobbed Kate. "He came down here to spy on you, uncle, and to try and show that the blessed miracle was a make-up. I knew it long before he told me, by his insulting ways. He wanted to make love to me."

I rose with difficulty from beneath the table, where I had lain motionless for a moment.

"Sir," I said, "I am somewhat dazed by the recent action of Mr. Langan, whom I beg, the next time he converts himself into a fulling-mill, to do so at the expense of a man more nearly his equal in strength than I. What your niece has told you is partly true. I am indeed the Cardinal's spy; and I have already reported to him that the miracle is a genuine one. A committe of gentlemen will wait on you tomorrow to verify it, at my suggestion. I have thought that the proof might be regarded by them as more complete if you were taken by surprise. Miss Hickey, that I admire all that is admirable in you is but to say that I have a sense of the beautiful. To say that I love you would be mere profanity. Mr. Langan, I have in my pocket a loaded pistol, which I carry from a silly English prejudice against your country-men. Had I been the Hercules of the ploughtail, and you in my place, I should have been a dead man now. Do not redden; you are safe as far as I am concerned."

"Let me tell you before you leave my house for good," said Father Hickey, who seemed to have become unreasonably angry, "that you should never have crossed my threshold if I had known you were a spy; no, not if your uncle were his Holiness the Pope himself."

Here a frightful thing happened to me. I felt giddy, and put my hand to my head. Three warm drops trickled over it. Instantly I became murderous. My mouth filled with blood, my eyes were blinded with it; I seemed to drown in it. My hand went involuntarily to the pistol. It is my habit to obey my impulses instantaneously. Fortunately the impulse to kill vanished before a sudden perception of how I might miraculously humble the mad vanity in which these foolish people had turned upon me. The blood receded from my ears; and I again heard and saw distinctly.

"And let *me* tell you," Langan was saying, "that if you think yourself handier with cold lead than you are with your fists, I'll exchange shots with you, and welcome, whenever you please. Father Tom's credit is the same to me as my own, and if you say a word against it, you lie."

"His credit is in my hands," I said. "I am the Cardinal's witness. Do you defy me?"

"There is the door," said the priest, holding it open before me. "Until you can undo the visible work of God's hand your testimony can do no harm to me."

"Father Hickey," I replied, "before the sun rises again upon Four Mile Water, I will undo the visible work of God's hand, and bring the pointing finger of the scoffer upon your altar."

I bowed to Kate, and walked out. It was so dark that I could not at first see the garden-gate. Before I found it, I heard through the window Father Hickey's voice, saying, "I wouldn't for ten pound that this had happened, Phil. He's as mad as a march hare. The Cardinal told me so."

I returned to my lodging, and took a cold bath to cleanse the blood from my neck and shoulder. The effect of the blow I had received was so severe, that even after the bath and a light meal I felt giddy and languid. There was an alarum-clock on the mantelpiece. I wound it; set the alarum for half-past twelve; muffled it so that it should not disturb the people in the adjoining room; and went to bed, where I slept soundly for an hour and a quarter. Then the alarum roused me, and I sprang up before I was thoroughly awake. Had I hesitated, the desire to relapse into perfect sleep would have overpowered me. Although the muscles of my neck were painfully stiff, and my hands unsteady from my nervous disturbance, produced by the interruption of my first slumber, I dressed myself resolutely, and after taking a draught of cold water, stole out of the house. It was exceedingly dark and I had some difficulty in finding the cow-house, whence I borrowed a spade, and a truck with wheels, ordinarily used for moving sacks of potatoes. These I carried in my hands until I was beyond earshot of the house, when I put the spade on the truck, and wheeled it along the road to the cemetery. When I approached the water, knowing that no one would dare to come thereabout at such an hour, I made greater haste, no longer concerning myself about the rattling of the wheels. Looking across to the opposite bank, I could see a phosphorescent glow, marking the lonely grave of Brimstone Billy. This helped me to find the ferry station, where, after wandering a little and stumbling often, I found the boat, and embarked with my implements. Guided by the rope, I crossed the water without difficulty; landed; made fast the boat; dragged the truck up the bank; and sat down to rest on the cairn at the grave. For nearly a quarter of an hour I sat watching the patches of jack-o'-lantern fire, and collecting my strength for the work before me. Then the distant bell of the chapel clock tolled one. I rose, took the spade, and in about ten minutes uncovered the coffin, which smelt horribly. Keeping to windward of it, and using the spade as a lever, I contrived with great labor to place it on the truck. I wheeled it without accident to the landing-place, where, by placing the shafts of the truck upon the stern of the boat and lifting the foot by main strength, I succeeded in embarking my load after twenty minutes' toil, during which I got covered with clay and perspiration, and several times all but upset the boat. At the southern bank I had less difficulty in getting truck and coffin ashore, and dragging them up to the graveyard.

It was now past two o'clock, and the dawn had begun, so that I had no further trouble from want of light. I wheeled the coffin to a patch of loamy soil which I had noticed in the afternoon near the grave of the holy sisters. I had warmed to my work; my neck no longer pained me; and I began to dig vigorously, soon making a shallow trench, deep enough to hide the coffin with the addition of a mound. The chill pearl-coloured morning had by this time quite dissipated the darkness. I could see, and was myself visible, for miles around. This alarmed me, and made me impatient to finish my task. Nevertheless, I was forced to rest for a moment before placing the coffin in the trench. I wiped my brow and wrists, and again looked about me. The tomb of the holy women, a massive slab supported on four stone spheres, was grey and wet with dew. Near it was the thornbush covered with rags, the newest of which were growing gaudy in the radiance which was stretching up from the coast on the east. It was time to finish my work. I seized the truck; laid it alongside the grave; and gradually prized the coffin off with the spade until it rolled over into the trench with a hollow sound like a drunken remonstrance from the sleeper within. I shovelled the earth round and over it, working as fast as possible. In less than a quarter of an hour it was buried. Ten minutes more sufficed to make the mound symmetrical, and to clear the traces of my work from the adjacent sward. Then I flung down the spade; threw up my arms; and vented a sigh of relief and triumph. But I recoiled as I saw that I was standing on a barren common, covered with furze. No product of man's handiwork was near me except my truck and spade and the grave of Brimstone Billy, now as lonely as before. I turned towards the water. On the opposite bank was the cemetery, with the tomb of the holy women, the thornbush with its rags stirring in the morning breeze, and the broken mud wall. The ruined chapel was there too, not a stone shaken from its crumbling walls, not a sign to show that it and its precinct were less rooted in their place than the eternal hills around.

I looked down at the grave with a pang of compassion for the unfortunate Wolfe Tone Fitzgerald, with whom the blessed would not rest. I was even astonished, though I had worked expressly to this end. But the birds were astir, and the cocks crowing. My landlord was an early riser. I put the spade on the truck again, and hastened back to the farm, where I replaced them in the cowhouse. Then I stole into the house, and took a clean pair of boots, an overcoat, and a silk hat. These, with a change of linen, were sufficient to make my appearance respectable. I went out again, bathed in the

Four Mile Water, took a last look at the cemetery, and walked to Wicklow, whence I travelled by the first train to Dublin.

Some months later, at Cairo, I received a packet of Irish newspapers and a leading article, cut from the *Times*, on the subject of the miracle. Father Hickey had suffered the meed of his inhospitable conduct. The committee, arriving at Four Mile Water the day after I left, had found the graveyard exactly where it had formerly stood. Father Hickey, taken by surprise, had attempted to defend himself by a confused statement, which led the committee to declare finally that the miracle was a gross imposture. The *Times*, commenting on this after adducing a number of examples of priestly craft, remarked, "We are glad to learn that the Rev. Mr. Hickey has been permanently relieved of his duties as the parish priest of Four Mile Water by his ecclesiastical superior. It is less gratifying to have to record that it has been found possible to obtain two hundred signatures to a memorial embodying the absurd defense offered to the committee, and expressing unabated confidence in the integrity of Mr. Hickey."

EDWARD SHEEHY

# The Black Mare

\*

Michael Fardy Cullen wasn't drunk when he saw the mare. He was just in the cheerful state of a man who's had six pints running on an empty stomach following the sale of two bullocks and a springer for the tidy sum of thirty-seven pounds. Anyhow, he decided afterwards that even if he'd been cold sober it wouldn't have made any difference.

Her coat was black and glossy; she had three white stockings and a white star on her forehead. In spite of the patched and shabby winkers he could see that she had a fine head, small, with lively pointed ears and a greyey velvet muzzle. He loved looking at her, appraising the depth of her chest and the cleanness of her legs and wondering what she was doing here, tied by a rope reins to a ring in the wall behind Sheridan's pub. A little way down the lane stood a gaudy tinkers' caravan from behind which came the sound of snarling, quarrelling voices, a man's and a woman's. Maybe the tinkers owned her; if they did, God help her.

He looked at the mare again and saw that the reins had become looped around her off foreleg. He was on the point of setting it to rights when two tinkers came out from behind the caravan followed by an oldish striall of a woman who seemed to be dancing mad with rage at them. When they took no notice of her it only provoked her further. Just as the two were within half a dozen paces of Michael Fardy and the mare she darted to one side, picked up a stone the size of a

From *The Dublin Magazine*.

man's fist and hurled it after them. The pair scattered and
ducked, and the stone struck the wall right in front of the
mare's nose. The mare snorted in fright; she reared and
backed. As she came down the tightened reins tripped her
and flung her over on her side. The tinkers ran back towards the caravan leaving the mare as she was with the
mouth nearly torn out of her. Michael Fardy with pity for her
rushed forward and started tearing at the knot; but it was
so hard with the strain of the mare's fall that it wouldn't
yield to his fingers. He thought of the clasp-knife in his
pocket. He had it in his hand with the blade open when one
of the tinkers rushed up with his mouth full of curses asking
him did he want to destroy a beautiful bit of rope for the
want of a little patience. He shouldered Michael Fardy to one
side and started working on the knot himself, saying to the
other:

"That'll cool her now, Nailer. She wanted that. She's
ruined with idleness and good-feeding—that one is."

"I was afeared she might hurt herself," Michael Fardy
said apologetically.

"Devil a fear of that one," the tinker said. He was a
short stocky fellow with the small cruel eyes of a pig and a
wart on his left eyelid. The tinker called Nailer was tall, lean
and foxy.

"She's a fine mare," Michael Fardy said.

"She's all that," the short fellow said, and, with a savage
tug on the bit he jerked the mare to her feet.

"That one has breeding," Nailer said.

"I can see that," Michael Fardy said.

"Now's your chance to pick her up cheap," Nailer said,
smiling. His smile was yellow-toothed and without friendliness.

"Yerra, come away out of that, Nailer," the short fellow
said. "What'd that poor boy be doing with the finest mare
this side of the town of Mallow and she sired by the famous
Flying Rocket and the mother of Romping Rosa that won
the flapper stakes at the Curragh two years back?"

"What are ye asking for her?" Michael Fardy asked, more out of bravado than anything else.

The short fellow looked straight at him; the eyelid with the wart hung a shade lower than the other giving its owner a look of mocking unbelief.

"Listen here to me, boy," he said, as if he had a secret to confide. "You look to me to be a decent boy so I'll be straight and honest with you, as straight and honest as if you were my own brother. Listen to me now. I'm selling that mare cheap if I can get a buyer for her this day in Castletown. She's nine year old; you can see that for yourself. She was hurt once in the hunting field. There's the scar on her off leg there. But she's as sound on it to-day as ever she was. She'll work under a dray or a trap, plough, harrow or anything you like. She's gentle as a lamb; a child could follow her; ask Nailer there and he'll tell you. And she's selling for ten pound, no more no less. She's selling cheap because I bought her cheap. The man that had her couldn't feed her for the winter and with the gentry in such bad case there's small sale for a classy animal like her. I know a man'd pay three times that for her for a brood mare; but he's in the County Meath and that's a long road. Ten pound, boy, ten pound; and God strike me dead this minute if I'm telling you the word of a lie."

"Show him the action of her," Nailer said, and the short fellow started to trot the mare up and down the lane. She moved well, with an easy and supple grace. Michael Fardy trembled with anxiety as he looked at her. When she came to a standstill again he felt her legs and fetlocks, looked at her teeth, walked around her and looked her over from every angle. He did so more for the effect of the thing than anything else and to gain time. He wanted her, to own her; and ten pounds was cheap. But tinkers could fool you up to your eyes about a horse. Still he couldn't see anything wrong with her.

"I'll give ye eight for her," he said, suddenly forsaking all caution.

The upshot of it all was that Michael Fardy bought the

mare for nine pounds with the winkers thrown in, but not the beautiful bit of rope.

II

It was dark night before he topped Mam-a-Casac and the drink he had taken before leaving the town was wearing off. At one moment he felt like a rapparee riding the black mare out on to the hillcrest. The next he was troubled and nervous; troubled when he thought of what old Pats would say; nervous when the mare shuddered in her muscles and curved away, head up and ears cocked, from a white stone that appeared dimly out of the bogland. He was afraid of her, of the proud spirit he was beginning to sense in her. Would she work? Would she go under a cart and haul home their turf from the bog? The fellow with the wart on his eye said she would; but then he was in a hell-sight too great a hurry to get shut of her. She might be doped; it wouldn't be the first time tinkers doped a horse. Even when she slowed down he hardly dared touch her with the crop; but talked to her coaxingly:

"Ho there, girleen! Come on now, girl!"

Nellie was up by the fire waiting for him when he got in. She put by her darning and started blowing the fire under the kettle.

"You're late," she said.

"Yea," he said.

"How was the fair?"

"Good. I got thirty-seven for the three and I bought a fine mare cheap. You'll see her in the morning. We'll be the envy of them all with her for she's a beautiful beast."

"You had no talk with my father about buying a horse?" she asked.

"Well, what has that to do with it? Don't we need one instead of having to beg the loan of that old garrawn of my brothers every time we want to do a hand's turn? And anyway 'tis none of his business."

"That won't stop his tongue; and you know yourself that if she was the finest out he'd find fault with her, because he had no thought himself of buying a horse."

" 'Tis time he knew who's master in this house then," he shouted. "Didn't we make a settlement? Didn't we? And a generous one too for the bloody old cripple? Has he any complaint to make on that score?"

"But, Michael Fardy," she answered patiently, "we don't want trouble in the house."

"Then let him mind his soul, the old codger, for he's finished minding my business. Let him have what he's entitled to; but I won't be bothered with the vagaries and the contradictions of an old doting amadawn even if he is your father."

He looked belligerently towards the room door and felt a lot better for having spoken his mind. Nellie made him a strong cup of tea and gave it to him with some griddle-bread by the fire. After that they went up to their room, softly so as not to wake the child. Without talk they undressed and got into bed where neither of them slept for a long time; she because of a dull resentment at his not having brought her back any present from the town; he with nursing his anger against his father-in-law and thinking that he'd have to take up a stand with him now or never.

There was hardly light to see when he opened his eyes. Nellie was shaking him roughly, telling him to listen. He heard the heavy thud of hooves. The mare must have got out. She was moving round the house. Lucky she hadn't taken to the road. Even so her heavy restless hoofbeats made him uneasy. Then he remembered that he had forgotten to water her. He got out of bed and started pulling on his clothes.

When he opened the kitchen door he saw her standing on the little grassy hillock on the other side of the boreen. She stood there, noble and strange, surveying the grey, misty valley below her. God, but she was lovely! It frightened him how lovely she was there against the morning sky. She turned, trotted swingingly down the slope, and, nimbly as a cat, leaped the low stone wall to land on all fours in the boreen.

"If she sulks," he thought, "there'll be no catching her." But he had no trouble. When he took her by the forelock she came with him willingly to the well where he hauled out two buckets of water for her.

When he got back to the yard there was old Pats at the door, red-nosed and shivering in the rawness of the morning. Usually he had his breakfast in bed and didn't get up until the day was well aired. "Be the holy!" he muttered, stepping forward, screwing up his watery eyes to peer at Michael Fardy and the mare.

"Wisha, good morrow to your honor," he jeered. "Ah, sure," he went on in mock disappointment, "it's only Michael Fardy that's in it and me thinking 'twas some fine gentleman with his hunter. And what'd you be doing with her, Michael Fardy?"

Michael Fardy was too angry to answer. His father-in-law's jeering always gave him that tightening of the throat and an itch in his hands to take the old cripple by the scruff of the neck . . .

"Ah, wisha," old Pats went on, "sure 'tis the beggar on horseback, a proud seat without a prop. Excuse me asking you, sir. But where did you get the mare, sir?"

"I bought her," Michael Fardy said. "Isn't that enough for you?"

"Ah, I see now. So you're thinking of joining the Edenferry hunt and consorting with the gentry."

"You know damn well we want a horse on the farm."

"Aye, indeed."

"And she's a fine mare," Michael Fardy blustered.

"Aye, that she is. And I suppose you've got grazing and stabling for her at the big house down at Edenferry for 'twould be a pity to see a fine beast famished when she'd eaten every bit of grass off the hill. Or maybe you'd liefer spend a handful of sovereigns on a few loads of hay and a couple of barrels of oats and keep her up in the room. But of course you can't expect to be taken for one of the gentry unless you're prepared to lash the money around."

"Look here now, Pats Byrne," Michael Fardy shouted, "I've

had enough of your bloody guff. D'you hear me now? She's staying here and she's working on the farm and I'll feed her all right. And that's my say."

"Oh, have your say, boy, have your say. No one'll begrudge you that. And I suppose now you had a trial of her under a cart and saw her working? Sure, you'd hardly buy her without, a sensible boy like you?"

Michael Fardy didn't answer. Nellie came to the door of the house and called out that the breakfast was ready. He left the mare in the haggard and went in after his father-in-law.

### III

The news spread like wildfire that Michael Fardy had bought a full-blooded hunter of a mare, and in the course of the day the neighbouring men dropped over on one excuse or another. And each one of them walked into the haggard, circled round the mare, eyeing her all over and each one of them with a smile on his puss as if he knew something bloody funny but wasn't going to give it away. And old Pats went on with his litany, telling every one that came how he had a gentleman for a son-in-law whom nothing would do but a sixteen-hand thoroughbred who'd eat as much as an elephant and demand kinder treatment than a Christian. They had a sheaf of stories of this horse and that horse and how tinkers had fooled men up to the eyes. Michael Fardy knew they thought him a fool. She was a fine mare, they admitted, a grand looking mare. And maybe she'd work. But she was a bit big for the country; the country was too poor to feed the likes of her properly. And if one of them was buying a horse he'd rather a smaller, commoner animal. She'd suit Sam Stockwell, now, down at Edenferry; or a gentleman somewhere who could afford to keep a hunter.

Michael Fardy knew that they were right; but all the talk and all the jeering turned him sour and stubborn. When he looked at them, cringing and mean, and looked at the mare, at the clean beauty of her, he didn't set much store by their talk. But he couldn't keep her just as an ornament so he

listened to their advice when they told him to have a couple
of the lads around when he put her under the cart for the
first time. Frankeen Sugrue and Tim Egan, though they
agreed with the others about her being too big and too finely
bred for the country, were full of admiration for her. Michael
Fardy asked them to give him a hand with her the next day.

The morning was bright with sun, but an ice-cold wind
blew down from Knocknagarragh and stripped the first leaves
from the ash-trees in the haggard. As Michael Fardy put the
winkers on the mare, he nearly prayed to her to take it kindly
and put him in the right. He was shivering with fright, even
though the mare was as biddable as anyone could ask; but
he couldn't rid himself of a feeling that some terrible power
lay hidden in those smooth easy muscles. The others were a
bit nervous too and trying not to show it as they took the
tackling down from the pegs in the cowhouse with quick
jerky movements. Old Pats stood over by the kitchen door
with a smile under his wispy, yellow mustache; he looked to
Michael Fardy as if he was wishing for the worst.

She took kindly enough to the tackling, though she looked
insulted by it, like a delicate lady forced to wear the clothes
of a servant-girl. They wheeled the cart around her a couple
of times to get her used to the jangling of the chains and the
sound of the iron-shod wheels on the cobbles. She obeyed the
hand on the bit when Michael Fardy backed her in between
the shafts. She didn't stir while they linked up the traces and
the britchin.

"We'll take her up by the village," he said.

"Yea," Frankeen Sugrue said, "but better lead her a bit
till she's used to the feel of the cart."

They took up positions, one on either side of her head.
Tim Egan stood the length of the reins behind.

"Come on, girl," Michael Fardy said, urging her forward.

She moved across the yard. 'Twas easy to see that she felt
it strange by the way she tried to edge sideways. As they
reached the rough patch in front of the door the wheels and
the chains made an unmerciful clatter. The mare stopped
dead. She didn't look wicked; she just stalled. They urged

her and coaxed her but she gave them no heed. Then without warning Tim Egan gave her a touch of the ashplant across the rump. In a second she was like a mad thing. She reared, dragging the reins out of Frankeen's grip and lifting Michael Fardy off the ground. She came down, her hooves crashing hardly an inch from his feet. She dipped her head and flung her heels against the bottom-boards of the cart. The britchin snapped; the wood splintered.

"Mother of God, she'll be the death of them!" Nellie wailed, and young Jem clinging to her skirts set up a howl fit to wake the dead.

"Hold her ye divils," old Pats croaked, dancing around them as the mare plunged forward dragging the three of them across the yard.

"Shut the gate, you bloody idiot!" Michael Fardy yelled to him so savagely that without a word he hobbled across the yard and got the gate closed just in the mare's nose.

The three of them held her head while old Pats unlinked the traces and the britchin on the side it still held. When they got her out from under the cart she stood there shivering in every muscle but with no sign at all of vice or wickedness.

"You won't get no good out of that one," Frankeen Sugrue said and Tim Egan agreed. The pair of them, at any rate, had had enough of her.

IV

In bed that night his delight in her beauty was mixed with feelings of fear and helplessness. If she was a common animal he knew he'd be able to tame her. But she wasn't and there was some power in her that bested him. He felt that he had no right to her. It was like the gnawing bitterness of a hopeless love.

She must have got out of the field during the night because once when he woke in the darkness he could hear her hooves on the cobbles of the yard, halting now, then stamping sharply as if she were restless. With ears strained and heart thumping he listened to her moving about. He was afraid and couldn't understand his fear. There was nothing to keep her, no ditch in the place that could hold her from the roads and still she kept nosing round the house, restlessly, as if she were seeking something. There must have been some good reason for selling her so cheap. Maybe she killed a man; maybe once she tore a man with that fierce mouth of hers; maybe she pounded a man to bloody pulp under quick savage hooves. There was nothing he could do but get rid of her . . . and be the laughing-stock of the place and give old Pats something to jeer about till the day of his death.

Morning came and she was standing in the yard, quiet and contented in the sun. Old Pats wasn't up and while he and Nellie were at their breakfast she came to the door and stood looking into the kitchen. He could hardly believe it was the same animal that was under the cart the day before. He went over and gave her a crust of bread which she munched contentedly. "It must have been the hullabaloo," he thought, "and old Pats shouting, that frightened her. Maybe if I just try her myself after milking . . ."

He had the idea in his head all the morning. Old Pats had a touch of his rheumatics and would keep to his bed for half the day. But he was afraid when he remembered the wildness of her the day before; and he was ashamed of his fear. He had bought her and he ought to make the best of his bargain. Even if he couldn't keep her she might at least bring home a few loads of turf while she was in the place. In the end he forced himself to put the winkers on her, promising himself that he'd give up at the first sign from her that she was going to take it badly. He got the collar and hames on her without any trouble; but when it came to the straddle she was inclined to wheel away from it. He looped the reins through the staple on the door-jamb of the cowhouse; but when he picked up the straddle and tried to throw it across her back she started with fright, straining wildly on the rein till the door-jamb shook and pieces of rotten thatch began to fall from the cowhouse roof. He dropped the straddle; but before he could take her by the head she had pulled half a ton of thatch, loose stones and rafters down on top of him.

A cut on the forehead and a few aches in his bones was all he had as a result of the collapse of the cowhouse; but old Pats couldn't stop talking about the ruin the mare was bringing on them all and the curse on his old age of a son-in-law who was an idiot born, who bought a mad race-horse for good money from a band of tinkers, a lunatic animal that'd be dear if you got her for nothing. But in spite of the wreck of the cowhouse, which was easily mended anyway, Michael Fardy felt easier in his mind. He couldn't keep her now. He gave in to her once and for all.

He had a fortnight to wait for the fair at Dunsorley and in the meantime he couldn't meet a neighbour without being asked how he was getting on with the mare. He knew they were laughing at him behind his back but he held his peace and let them think what they liked. He worked all day digging out the potatoes and pitting them; opening the drains; mending the fences between his place and Sugrues. When nobody was around he went and looked at the mare, enjoying the beauty generations of breeding had given her. The gentry had made her like that; they had bred her for themselves and she belonged to them. It was the same with their women. They didn't have to care about work, in a woman, a horse or a dog. A poor man couldn't marry one of their daughters; even if she'd have him, she'd eat him up. The poor man could only marry a drudge who was plain and willing. Looking at her made him feel how tied he was to those half-barren, mountainy fields for a life of endless labour, without adventure, without excitement, without anything of grandeur. The people from the towns drove round in their cars and looked at the hills and said how grand it must be to live in a place like Farranroe. But Michael Fardy cursed the hills, cursed the bleak steep face of Knocknagarragh that meant miles of tramping after sheep through the rock and heath. No man should live in a place like it. He should have gone out into the world, to America, to Australia instead of tying himself down to slavery by marrying Nellie Pats Byrne.

He began to hate the black mare and to be impatient for the day of the fair.

v

He was up at four and spent almost an hour combing her and rubbing her down. He put on her the saddle and bridle he had borrowed from his brother, and which, till now, had lain hidden under the hay, and set out for Dunsorley in the chill starlight.

He reached Dunsorley good and early and spent the morning riding the mare through the streets of the town. He saw with a certain amount of pride how the people turned their heads to look after him as he guided her in and out among the tethered horses, carts and groups of men intent on a deal. But it was well after nine o'clock before anyone tried to stop him. He was beginning to feel desperate when he heard a call:

"Hi, you on the black mare!"

He turned. A wizened, bandy-legged little man in knee-breeches and leggings was beckoning him. He was talking to a tall gentleman with a mustache at the rate of a mile a minute. As he came near Michael Fardy heard him saying:

"I'll lay half-a-dollar to a fiver it's her, sir."

"Well then, go ahead, Kelly," the gentleman said.

"Are you selling?" Kelly asked.

"Yea, then," Michael Fardy answered, "if I can get a price." He tried to look surly and unwilling.

"What are you asking?"

"Twenty-five pound," Michael Fardy said coolly.

The little fellow laughed, a thin jeering cackle.

"Have a heart," he said. "Twenty-five shillings'd be more like it. You won't get no twenty-five pound for that broken-down hack."

Michael Fardy looked away, out over the square crowded with horses and carts and people; he looked at the clock on the town hall which said a quarter to ten. He drew gently on the rein and the mare started to turn.

"Hi!" Kelly called, "aren't you in the hell of a hurry?"

"You heard what I said," Michael Fardy said surlily. The gentleman looked on with an amused smile.

"Bring her over to the fair-field till we see how she moves," Kelly said.

The three of them went to the fair-field and Michael Fardy dismounted. Kelly shortened the stirrups and swung into the saddle. The gentleman and Michael Fardy stood side by side watching while he wheeled her, cantered her and trotted her over the trampled grass. Every eye on the field was turned to watch the fine, gallant mare with Kelly perched like a monkey on her back. The gentleman was delighted with her. You could see that by his face. He didn't have to haggle; Kelly was paid to do that for him. Michael Fardy was sorry now he hadn't asked for more. By all the laws of dealing he'd have to come down from twenty-five. When Kelly brought the mare back the gentleman patted her neck and she nuzzled his coat. She looked like his already, as if he was born to own her.

"I'll tell you what," Kelly said, "the Major here'll give you fifteen for her. That's a lot more than you're likely to get for her these times for she's a long way past her best."

"Twenty-five," Michael Fardy said, "and I'll stick to it."

In the end, after leading the mare away and being called back, after being offered eighteen and sticking out for twenty-two, he sold her for twenty pounds, as they all knew from the start that he would.

A few hours later he bought a cob, a sturdy sorrel gelding for eleven pounds after trying her out in every way that he knew. He left her in the stable yard and went out to have a look round the town and to buy a few things. In Edward Street he ran into Tom Egan, Frankeen's brother, and Pats Simon Danagher from home. From the amused look on their faces he knew they were thinking about the mare. He asked them in for a drink. In the pub he could feel that they were itching for information but he didn't volunteer any. They talked of this, that and the other and had drunk two rounds of pints before Pats Simon said with a grin:

"Well, Michael Fardy, and did you sell her?"

"The mare, is it? Sure I did," Michael Fardy said.

"And did you get any sort of a price for her?" Tom Egan asked.

"Well," he answered slowly, "if you call a pound and double the money I gave for her a good price, I suppose I did."

"Glory be to God!" Pats Simon said, "look at that now. Aren't you the clever boyo and they all thinking you was fooled up to the eyes."

"Ah sure that was only old Pats. Sure I never thought to keep her; but I knew she was a bargain."

"Begor, you ought to take up dealing," Tom Egan said.

"Two pounds and double your money, be Japers!" Pats Simon said.

They had several rounds and the praise of Michael Fardy grew with every round. They wouldn't be so quick to laugh at him after this, so they wouldn't. And old Pats'd keep his mouth shut. The drink and the praise nearly made him forget his bitterness in realizing that never again in his life would he own anything so beautiful.

JAMES STEPHENS

# A Rhinoceros, Some Ladies
# and a Horse

One day, in my first job, a lady fell in love with me. It was
quite unreasonable, of course, for I wasn't wonderful: I was
small and thin, and I weighed much the same as a largish
duck-egg. I didn't fall in love with her, or anything like that.
I got under the table, and stayed there until she had to go
wherever she had to go to.

I had seen an advertisement—"Smart boy wanted," it
said. My legs were the smartest things about me, so I went
there on the run. I got the job.

At that time there was nothing on God's earth that I could
do, except run. I had no brains, and I had no memory. When
I was told to do anything I got into such an enthusiasm about
it that I couldn't remember anything else about it. I just ran
as hard as I could, and then I ran back, proud and panting.
And when they asked me for the whatever-it-was that I had
run for, I started, right on the instant, and ran some more.

The place I was working at was, amongst other things, a
theatrical agency. I used to be sitting in a corner of the office
floor, waiting to be told to run somewhere and back. A lady
would come in—a music-hall lady that is—and, in about five
minutes, howls of joy would start coming from the inner office.
Then, peacefully enough, the lady and my two bosses would
come out, and the lady always said, "Splits! I can do splits
like no one." And one of my bosses would say, "I'm keeping

From *Irish Writing*.

your splits in mind." And the other would add, gallantly,—"No one who ever saw your splits could ever forget 'em."

One of my bosses was thin, and the other one was fat. My fat boss was composed entirely of stomachs. He had three baby-stomachs under his chin: then he had three more descending in even larger englobings nearly to the ground: but, just before reaching the ground, the final stomach bifurcated into a pair of boots. He was very light on these and could bounce about in the neatest way.

He was the fattest thing I had ever seen, except a rhinoceros that I had met in the Zoo the Sunday before I got the job. That rhino was *very* fat, and it had a smell like twenty-five pigs. I was standing outside its palisade, wondering what it could possibly feel like to be a rhinoceros, when two larger boys passed by. Suddenly they caught hold of me, and pushed me through the bars of the palisade. I was very skinny, and in about two seconds I was right inside, and the rhinoceros was looking at me.

It was very fat, but it wasn't fat like stomachs, it was fat like barrels of cement, and when it moved it creaked a lot, like a woman I used to know who creaked like an old bedstead. The rhinoceros swaggled over to me with a bunch of cabbage sticking out of its mouth. It wasn't angry, or anything like that, it just wanted to see who I was. Rhinos are blindish: they mainly see by smelling, and they smell in snorts. This one started at my left shoe, and snorted right up that side of me to my ear. He smelt that very carefully: then he switched over to my right ear, and snorted right down that side of me to my right shoe: then he fell in love with my shoes and began to lick them. I, naturally, wriggled my feet at that, and the big chap was so astonished that he did the strangest step-dance backwards to his pile of cabbages, and began to eat them.

I squeezed myself out of his cage and walked away. In a couple of minutes I saw the two boys. They were very frightened, and they asked me what I had done to the rhinoceros. I answered, a bit grandly, perhaps, that I had seized it in both hands, ripped it limb from limb, and tossed its carcase to the crows. But when they began shouting to people that I had just murdered a rhinoceros I took to my heels, for I didn't want to be arrested and hanged for a murder that I hadn't committed.

Still, a man can't be as fat as a rhinoceros, but my boss was as fat as a man can be. One day a great lady of the halls came in, and was received on the knee. She was very great. Her name was Maudie Darling, or thereabouts. My bosses called her nothing but "Darling," and she called them the same. When the time came for her to arrive the whole building got palpitations of the heart. After waiting a while my thin boss got angry, and said—"Who does the woman think she is? If she isn't here in two twos I'll go down to the entry, and when she does come I'll boot her out." The fat boss said—"She's only two hours late, she'll be here before the week's out."

Within a few minutes there came great clamors from the court-yard. Patriotic cheers, such as Parnell himself never got, were thundering. My bosses ran instantly to the inner office. Then the door opened, and the lady appeared.

She was very wide, and deep, and magnificent. She was dressed in camels and zebras and goats: she had two peacocks in her hat and a rabbit muff in her hand, and she strode among these with prancings.

But when she got right into the room and saw herself being looked at by three men and a boy she became adorably shy: one could see that she had never been looked at before.

"O," said she, with a smile that made three and a half hearts beat like one, "O," said she, very modestly, "is Mr. Which-of-'em-is-it really in? Please tell him that Little-Miss-Me would be so glad to see and to be—"

Then the inner door opened, and the large lady was surrounded by my fat boss and my thin boss. She crooned to them—"O, you dear boys, you'll never know how much I've thought of you and longed to see you."

That remark left me stupefied. The first day I got to the office I heard that it was the fat boss's birthday, and that he was thirty years of age: and the thin boss didn't look a day younger than the fat one. How the lady could mistake these

old men for boys seemed to me the strangest fact that had
ever come my way. My own bet was that they'd both die of old
age in about a month.

After a while they all came out again. The lady was help-
less with laughter: she had to be supported by my two bosses
—"O," she cried, "you boys will kill me." And the bosses
laughed and laughed, and the fat one said—"Darling, you're
a scream," and the thin one said—"Darling, you're a riot."

And then . . . she saw me! I saw her seeing me the very
way I had seen the rhinoceros seeing me: I wondered for an
instant would she smell me down one leg and up the other.
She swept my two bosses right away from her, and she became a kind of queen, very glorious to behold: but sad,
startled. She stretched a long, slow arm out and out and out
and then she unfolded a long, slow finger, and pointed it at
me—"Who is THAT??" she whispered in a strange whisper
that could be heard two miles off.

My fat boss was an awful liar—"The cat brought that in,"
said he.

But the thin boss rebuked him: "No," he said, "it was not
the cat. Let me introduce you; darling, this is James. James,
this is the darling of the gods."

"And of the pit," said she, sternly.

She looked at me again. Then she sank to her knees and
spread out both arms to me—

"Come to my boozalum, angel," said she in a tender kind
of way.

I knew what she meant, and I knew that she didn't know
how to pronounce that word. I took a rapid glance at the
area indicated. The lady had a boozalum you could graze a
cow on. I didn't wait one second, but slid, in one swift, silent
slide, under the table. Then she came forward and said a whole
lot of poems to me under the table, imploring me, among a lot
of odd things, to "come forth, and gild the morning with my
eyes," but at last she was reduced to whistling at me with two
fingers in her mouth, the way you whistle for a cab.

I learned after she had gone that most of the things she
said to me were written by a poet fellow named Spokeshave.

They were very complimentary, but I couldn't love a woman who mistook my old bosses for boys, and had a boozalum that it would take an Arab chieftain a week to trot across on a camel.

The thin boss pulled me from under the table by my leg, and said that my way was the proper way to treat a rip, but my fat boss said, very gravely—"James, when a lady invites a gentleman to her boozalum a real gentleman hops there as pronto as possible, and I'll have none but real gentlemen in this office.

"Tell me," he went on, "what made that wad of Turkish Delight fall in love with you?"

"She didn't love me at all, sir," I answered.

"No?" he enquired.

"She was making fun of me," I explained.

"There's something in that," said he seriously, and went back to his office.

I had been expecting to be sacked that day. I was sacked the next day, but that was about a horse.

I had been given three letters to post, and told to run or they'd be too late. So I ran to the post office and round it and back, with, naturally, the three letters in my pocket. As I came to our door a nice, solid, red-faced man rode up on a horse. He thrust the reins into my hand—

"Hold the horse for a minute," said he.

"I can't," I replied, "my boss is waiting for me."

"I'll only be a minute," said he angrily, and he walked off.

Well, there was I, saddled, as it were, with a horse. I looked at it, and it looked at me. Then it blew a pint of soap-suds out of its nose and took another look at me, and then the horse fell in love with me as if he had just found his long-lost foal. He started to lean against me and to woo me with small whinneys, and I responded and replied as best I could—

"Don't move a toe," said I to the horse, "I'll be back in a minute."

He understood exactly what I said, and the only move he made was to swing his head and watch me as I darted up the street. I was less than half a minute away anyhow, and never out of his sight.

Up the street there was a man, and sometimes a woman, with a barrow, thick-piled with cabbages and oranges and apples. As I raced round the barrow I pinched an apple off it at full speed, and in ten seconds I was back at the horse. The good nag had watched every move I made, and when I got back his eyes were wide open, his mouth was wide open, and he had his legs all splayed out so that he couldn't possibly slip. I broke the apple in halves and popped one half into his mouth. He ate it in slow crunches, and then he looked diligently at the other half. I gave him the other half, and, as he ate it, he gurgled with cidery gargles of pure joy. He then swung his head round from me and pointed his nose up the street, right at the apple-barrow.

I raced up the street again, and was back within the half-minute with another apple. The horse had nigh finished the first half of it when a man who had come up said, thoughtfully—

"He seems to like apples, bedad!"

"He loves them," said I.

And then, exactly at the speed of lightning, the man became angry, and invented bristles all over himself like a porcupine—

"What the hell do you mean," he hissed, and then he bawled, "by stealing my apples?"

I retreated a bit into the horse—

"I didn't steal your apples," I said.

"You didn't!" he roared, and then he hissed, "I saw you," he hissed.

"I didn't steal them," I explained, "I pinched them."

"Tell me that one again," said he.

"If," said I patiently, "if I took the apples for myself that would be stealing."

"So it would," he agreed.

"But as I took them for the horse that's pinching."

"Be damn, but!" said he. " 'Tis a real argument," he went on, staring at the sky. "Answer me that one," he demanded of himself, and he in a very stupor of intellection. "I give it up," he roared, "you give me back my apples."

I placed the half apple that was left into his hand, and he looked at it as if it was a dead frog—

"What'll I do with that?" he asked earnestly.

"Give it to the horse," said I.

The horse was now prancing at him, and mincing at him, and making love at him. He pushed the half apple into the horse's mouth, and the horse mumbled it and watched him, and chewed it and watched him, and gurgled it and watched him—

"He does like his bit of apple," said the man.

"He likes you too," said I. "I think he loves you."

"It looks like it," he agreed, for the horse was yearning at him, and its eyes were soulful.

"Let's get him another apple," said I, and, without another word, we both pounded back to his barrow and each of us pinched an apple off it. We got one apple into the horse, and were breaking the second one when a woman said gently—

"Nice, kind, Christian gentlemen, feeding dumb animals—with my apples," she yelled suddenly.

The man with me jumped as if he had been hit by a train—

"Mary," said he humbly.

"Joseph," said she in a completely unloving voice.

But the woman transformed herself into nothing else but woman—

"What about my apples?" said she. "How many have we lost?"

"Three," said Joseph.

"Four," said I, "I pinched three and you pinched one."

"That's true," said he. "That's exact, Mary. I only pinched one of our apples."

"You only," she squealed—

And I, hoping to be useful, broke in—

"Joseph," said I, "is the nice lady your boss?"

He halted for a dreadful second, and made up his mind—

"You bet she's my boss," said he, "and she's better than that, for she's the very wife of my bosum."

She turned to me—

"Child of Grace—" said she—

Now, when I was a child, and did something that a woman didn't like she always expostulated in the same way. If I tramped on her foot, or jabbed her in the stomach—the way women have multitudes of feet and stomachs is always astonishing to a child—the remark such a woman made was always the same. She would grab her toe or her stomach, and say—"Childagrace, what the hell are you doing?" After a while I worked it out that Childagrace was one word, and was my name. When any woman in agony yelled Childagrace I ran right up prepared to be punished, and the woman always said tenderly, "What are you yowling about, Childagrace."

"Childagrace," said Mary earnestly, "how's my family to live if you steal our apples? You take my livelihood away from me! Very good, but will you feed and clothe and educate my children in," she continued proudly, "the condition to which they are accustomed?"

I answered that question cautiously—

"How many kids have you, ma'am?" said I.

"We'll leave that alone for a while," she went on. "You owe me two and six for the apples."

"Mary!" said Joseph, in a pained voice.

"And you," she snarled at him, "owe me three shillings. I'll take it out of you in pints." She turned to me—

"What do you do with all the money you get from the office here?"

"I give it to my landlady."

"Does she stick to the lot of it?"

"Oh, no," I answered, "she always gives me back threepence."

"Well, you come and live with me and I'll give you back fourpence."

"All right," said I.

"By gum," said Joseph, enthusiastically, "that'll be fine.

We'll go out every night and we won't steal a thing. We'll just pinch legs of beef, and pig's feet, and barrels of beer—"

"Wait now," said Mary. "You stick to your own land-lady. I've trouble enough of my own. You needn't pay me the two and six."

"Good for you," said Joseph heartily, and then, to me—

"You just get a wife of your bosum half as kind as the wife of my bosum and you'll be set up for life. Mary," he cried joyfully, "let's go and have a pint on the strength of it."

"You shut up," said she.

"Joseph," I interrupted, "knows how to pronounce that word properly."

"What word?"

"The one he used when he said you were the wife of his what-you-may-call-it."

"I'm not the wife of any man's what-you-may-call-it," said she, indignantly—"Oh, I see what you mean! So he pronounced it well, did he?"

"Yes, ma'am."

She looked at me very sternly—

"How does it come you know about all these kinds of words?"

"Yes," said Joseph, and he was even sterner than she was, "when I was your age I didn't know any bad words."

"You shut up," said she, and continued, "what made you say that to me?"

"A woman came into our office yesterday, and she mis-pronounced it."

"What did she say now?"

"Oh, she said it all wrong."

"Do you tell me so? We're all friends here: what way did she say it, son?"

"Well, ma'am, she called it boozalum."

"She said it wrong all right," said Joseph, "but 'tis a good, round, fat kind of a word all the same."

"You shut up," said Mary. "Who did she say the word to?"

"She said it to me, ma'am."

"She must have been a rip," said Joseph.

"Was she a rip, now?"

"I don't know, ma'am. I never met a rip."

"You're too young yet," said Joseph, "but you'll meet them later on. I never met a rip myself until I got married—I mean," he added hastily, "that they were all rips except the wife of my what-do-you-call-ems, and that's why I married her."

"I expect you've got a barrel-full of rips in your past," said she bleakly, "you must tell me about some of them to-night." And then, to me, "tell us about the woman," said she.

So I told them all about her, and how she held out her arms to me, and said, "Come to my boozalum, angel."

"What did you do when she shoved out the old arms at you?" said Joseph.

"I got under the table," I answered.

"That's not a bad place at all, but," he continued earnestly, "never get under the bed when there's an old girl chasing you, for that's the worst spot you could pick on. What was the strap's name?"

"Maudie Darling, she called herself."

"You're a blooming lunatic," said Joseph, "she's the love-liest thing in the world, barring," he added hastily, "the wife of my blast-the-bloody-word."

"We saw her last night," said Mary, "at Dan Lowrey's Theatre, and she's just lovely."

"She isn't as nice as you, ma'am," I asserted.

"Do you tell me that now?" said she.

"You are twice as nice as she is, and twenty times nicer."

"There you are," said Joseph, "the very words I said to you last night."

"You shut up," said Mary scornfully, "you were trying to knock a pint out of me! Listen, son," she went on, "we'll take all that back about your landlady. You come and live with me, and I'll give you back sixpence a week out of your wages."

"All right, ma'am," I crowed in a perfectly monstrous joy.

"Mary," said Joseph, in a reluctant voice—

"You shut up," said she.

"He can't come to live with us," said Joseph. "He's a bloody Prodestan," he added sadly.

"Why—" she began—

"He'd keep me and the childer up all night, pinching apples for horses and asses, and reading the Bible, and up to every kind of devilment."

Mary made up her mind quickly—

"You stick to your own landlady," said she, "tell her that I said she was to give you sixpence." She whirled about, "There won't be a thing left on that barrow," said she to Joseph.

"Damn the scrap," said Joseph violently.

"Listen," said Mary to me very earnestly, "am I nicer than Maudie Darling?"

"You are, ma'am," said I.

Mary went down on the road on her knees: she stretched out both arms to me, and said——

"Come to my boozalum, angel."

I looked at her, and I looked at Joseph, and I looked at the horse. Then I turned from them all and ran into the building and into the office. My fat boss met me—

"Here's your five bob," said he. "Get to hell out of here," said he.

And I ran out.

I went to the horse, and leaned my head against the thick end of his neck, and the horse leaned as much of himself against me as he could manage. Then the man who owned the horse came up and climbed into his saddle. He fumbled in his pocket—

"You were too long," said I. "I've been sacked for minding your horse."

"That's too bad," said he; "that's too damn bad," and he tossed me a penny.

I caught it, and lobbed it back into his lap, and I strode down the street the most outraged human being then living in the world.

MAURICE WALSH

# Come Back, My Love

✳

They were a young couple, and six months married, and they should have been as happy as the day was long; and the day was long, for it was in the very heart of June—a slumberous Sunday in June, early in the afternoon, with a gentle warmth in the sun, and a tenuous haze over the orange glory of the furze on all the hillsides.

The thatched cottage nestled securely halfway up the slope at the head of a small valley. A hundred paces below, a spring bubbled from the limestone roots of the hill into a miniature pool; and the overflow went singing down the hollow between clumps of sally and bracken. And far away, in a deep notch of the mountains, the Atlantic sea shimmered under the sun.

Maire Dhu—dark-haired Mary—sat on a straw hassock at the hearthside where the remnants of a peat fire were deeply smoored in white ashes. She was a long-limbed young woman, who, later on, would be a veritable matron and matriarch—nobly busted, placid-eyed, with long strong bones padded in firm flesh. She was knitting placidly and sometimes she smiled softly at a thought of her own.

Manus Boy—yellow Magnus—sat on a rush-bottomed chair at the other side of the fire, his face as solemn and hard as justice, his eyes, unseeing, looking through the open door across the valley, and the rich somber yellow of his eyes matching the golden glory of the furze over there. He was

From TAKE YOUR CHOICE, New York, Lippincott.

feeling his first touch of discontent, and he was frightened as well as unhappy.

He was a man of no more than middle height, but mighty-shouldered, deep-chested, flat-flanked, with a bush of yellow hair and a lean aquiline face, eagle-eyed. And, for the first time, he felt chained like a chained eagle.

Maire lifted slow blue eyes, and looked at her husband—a long, deep, considering look—and then she smiled wisely as a woman will, but there was a trace of wistfulness in her smile too.

She spoke, as if to herself, in her soft Western voice, "So it has come then."

"What has come then?" There was a quick startle in her husband's voice.

"What my mother told me to look for—sooner than I thought, my sorrow!" Maire's voice half mused.

There was a resonant timbre in Manus' voice and he made it deeper, "A wise man told me one time that a wife's mother is apt to be an interfering woman. I believe it."

"Not my mother," said Maire, and went on in the same quiet strain, as if musing to herself. "She told me that a live man and him married would be feeling the halter in the first year."

"Whatever are you talking about?" Manus wanted to know, though well he knew.

Maire gave him her slow, direct gaze. "You are a live man, Manus Boy, and you were lively, too; a seeing man and a doing man, and your hand on more than one girl. And now you feel tied and bound and spanceled to a strange woman's daughter."

"You are my wife whoever your mother is," said Manus gruffly.

Maire went on equably. "Man that you are, you will have to get over it in your own way, for myself can't help you; but if you don't get over it, that will be God's will, too—or my blame, for I have not yet the power over you."

"Who is to blame you, foolish girl?" Manus chided.

Maire leaned toward the long-thighed tongs. "Leave it be,

boy," she said cheerfully enough. "Look! I'll light a furze
root from the embers, and we'll make a cup of tea to ourselves. It is a comforting thing, tea, and might restore you for
a short while. Will you go down to the spring for a pail of
fresh water?"

"I will and welcome," said Manus, promptly on his feet.
He picked up the zinc-hooped wooden pail from below the
dresser and bent below the lintel into the drowsy sunlight.

"Don't be more than an hour anyway," Maire called after
him.

"Five minutes and I'll be back," Manus called over his
shoulder.

"Mother o' God, send him back to me—all of him!" prayed
Maire, and her voice was no longer equable.

Manus put the pail down on a flat slab close to the water.
A circle had been worn on the surface of the slab by the many
pails that had rested there over the centuries. He thrust his
hands deep into the pockets of his gray flannels, looked down-
headed into the crystal pool, and sighed. Gloom was in him
and around him. After a while he sat himself on a knee-high
boss of rock, and after another while he shook his yellow head
and murmured to himself:

"It is true for her; indeed, it is true for her, and damn her
mother's eyes! Tied to the one woman all my life! Oh, the
times that were, the great times that were—and the times
that will never come again, for, bad as I am, there's an honest
streak in me. I do, I must love that girl up there, but it is a
tame love now, and no wild ecstasy any more. But I'll get used
to that, too, and grow sluggishly content. And she will be the
mother of my sons, and hold me in one place stagnant as a
rain splash in a rut. Never again the loose foot and the woman
not kissed before, never again rain on the brae and the wind
blowing. Heigh-ho!"

It was then, in the heart of that mood, that a strange, waiting hush came about Manus. The tinkle of the inlet runlet,
the sighing song of the streamlet down the valley grew remote
as in a dream; no bird sang in these dead hours of the day,

the goldfinches no longer flitted from whin to whin. Everything was hushed and waiting.

And then a new sound got through to Manus in his remoteness. It was the sound of someone or something softly splashing the water at the end of the pool not ten feet away. Manus let his eyes drift, and what he saw stilled his heart and changed his mood utterly.

It was as if a wand had touched him; it was as if the solid land of Ireland about him had become unreal; it was as if himself and what his eyes saw were in a dimension of their own in a dream world. He was under a spell, though he did not know it.

What his eyes saw were a pair of shapely small feet, toes spread and lifted, softly churning the water. They were creamy-white feet, pink-toed, and an entrancing blue vein went delicately aslant an instep into the curve of an ankle. The old devil, never far under the surface, lifted head in Manus, and the skilly use of words had not forsaken him. His voice was as vibrant as a bell. "They are made to tread on a man's heart, and the heart wanting more torment."

And a silver, mocking voice made answer, "So it has been said."

"Ay, and an ankle like that I once saw in a dream."

"That dream I made you dream."

His hand moved in an upward curve. "And that gentle, slender, flowing line—"

A mellow tinkle of laughter stopped him. "That is as far as you need go, golden man."

"But one could be thinking," said Manus softly.

He lifted eyes then, and was pleased by what he saw.

She was a brown girl and dainty—shining brown in the hair, lustrous brown in the eyes, golden-tanned in neck and breast and slender arms. She was wearing a low-necked, short-sleeved, flowing, diaphanous dress the color of ripe corn, with a wide sash studded with topaz, and her brown hair was held loosely by a wheaten ribbon.

The whole blending of her colors and coloring gave her an extraordinary vividness, a strange, other-world vividness.

Her eyes sparkled at him, her mouth smiled at him, showing the tips of small white teeth, and her smile was of heart-stirring sweetness and extraordinary gaiety—a gaiety outside time and space.

Manus smiled back at her, and lifted a sweeping arm in salute.

"Under your feet, Princess."

She crowed delightedly. "Princess! But that is my name. How did you know, golden man?"

"What other name could you have in all the world?" said Manus.

"And your own name, it is Golden?"

"I am known as Manus Boy, which means Yellow Magnus."

"Not yellow! Golden, golden! Golden is your name."

"Whatever you say, Princess," said Manus agreeably.

She, in one deft motion, swung her feet aside out of the water and under the billowing hem of her dress. Then she leaned aside on one brown hand and contemplated Manus seriously. But the seriousness was not genuine.

"You did not live in this place always, Golden?"

"Not always, Princess. That is our—my summer cottage up the slope."

"A good choice for summer."

"Surely," said Manus complacently. "For in this place I meet a princess, and, besides, it is the sweetest valley in all the west."

Again her laughter mocked him.

"No-no! Not the sweetest. The valley where I live—my Queen Mother's valley—is the loveliest of all the valleys."

"It will be some distance away," said Manus politely.

"It is but over there." She lifted a curving arm and pointed a finger southward. "Over that small hill."

Manus knew that over that small hill was a wilderness of stone outcrops in a broken country of moorland spreading twenty miles to the Mountains of Maam. He had hunted over it, and there was no valley in it anywhere.

He made judicious answer, "Where you live, Princess, such a valley would be."

She shook her head at him and grimaced in impish, pretended anger. "You do not believe me. But it is there, there." Again she swung her arm and stabbed a finger. "Up the valley and through the gap, and there is my valley below you." She was impulsive now. "Look! Let me show you. I dare you to let me show you. Come!"

She lifted off the stone lightly as a bird, slipped her feet into flat brown sandals, and flitted to him tiptoe, her hand out. And the two of them, hand in hand, went down the hollow of the little valley by the stream. It was as easy as that.

He never looked back, never looked up toward the house where his young wife waited for her pail of spring water. In his present mood that old tame life was as dim and unsure as a dream remembered.

A bare quarter mile down the valley a gap opened in the slope to the left, and to the draw of her hand he turned in with her. Manus knew that gap. It finished in a steep chorrie of boulders, and he had often been up and over into the wild country beyond.

They came to the face of the chorrie, but did not climb. She drew him to the right along the front of it, where, as he knew, was only a bounding wall of stone. He was wrong, for there was now a narrow opening between chorrie and cliff that he had not noticed before, but that did not surprise him in the least. Through that opening she led him, in and on and up and up, in a half shade, the rock walls towering on either hand, and the sky far overhead.

And then the gorge widened, the walls lowered, and, after one final stiff pinch, they came out into the open at the head of the pass. There the little eager pressure of her palm halted him.

"Look, oh, look!" She was on tiptoe and tugging at his hand. "That is my very own valley where my mother reigns."

"I knew in my heart it was there all the time," said Manus. "And beautiful?"

"There is no small valley anywhere so beautiful."

The valley that he had forsaken had now no objective

reality in his mind, but this new valley was solidly real. It was a big, bowl-shaped green hollow in the hills. The green ran up into brown slopes that rolled over smoothly, and behind rose other slopes a fainter brown, and behind these other slopes turning purple, and behind all the smoky blue ghosts of mountains.

There was a small lake in the flat bottom of the bowl, with a cascade splashing in at one end, and a stream flowing out like a shining ribbon at the other. There were wide demesnes sweeping round the lake, clumped with flowering shrubs, and between the clumps fallow deer and roe deer and gazelles browsed and romped. To the left of the lake was a spread of lawn, emerald green, with a border brilliant with the flowers of summer; and at the back of the lawn on a high terrace stood a long, wide, low, lime-white mansion.

But, most important of all, there were many people on the lawn and about the lake; some were reclining on the grass, some slouching on seats of marble, some strolling with linked arms, many running about at some ball game and many swimming in the lake.

"That is my Queen Mother's great house," said Princess, "and these her people and my dear friends."

"Jealous I might be of one here and there," said Manus.

"Jealous! That is a word I do not know. Is it love?"

"The obverse of the medal, brown darling. But you will have love in this delectable place? It is a subject I could tell you about."

"Yes, yes, yes! Love and more love. In this valley there is nothing but love and gaiety."

"Love is not often gay, but I might be jealous all the same."

She released his hand now and slipped an arm inside his elbow. "Golden, dear," she said, softly persuasive, "you will come down and kiss the Queen's hand and meet my friends?"

"What you want me to do, that I will do," said Manus.

"My dear one," she whispered softly.

So they moved down leisurely over the grassy slopes and between fragrant shrubs, and talked and talked—and it was still afternoon, a land in which it seemed always afternoon.

"Are you a champion, Golden?" she asked him.

"Your champion, Princess."

"But a great champion?"

"There might be one or two greater," said Manus carelessly.

"And you fight other champions?"

"I have used my hands," Manus told her, and that was true.

"And a wrestler?"

"A bit collar-and-elbow in the days of my youth."

"Our champions are great champions, Golden."

"I will challenge them for you, one after the other," said Manus.

"No, no!" There was a serious note in her voice for the first time. "There is one, the greatest in all the valleys—"

"There are other valleys?"

She swung an arm gracefully wide. "Valleys without number, and the greatest champion of all is our champion, Cuchulain."

"There was indeed a great hero of that name."

"He is here now."

"And you love him?"

"There is love always."

"I will take a look at your Cuchulain," said Manus soberly.

"But no!" She was urgent. "He would break you in two with his hands."

He pressed her arm inside his, and nudged her softly with his shoulder. "Same as I could break you with my hands?"

"Your dear, ugly, brown hands! They are round my heart already." There was a thrill in her voice and his blood answered it.

So they moved down to the easier slopes, and were seen coming; and many, crying gay greetings, came flocking to meet them. The maidens came first, skipping and holding hands, and swung in an eager, laughing ring around them. They were all daintily lovely, and of all colorings and shimmerings, but, to Manus' mind, none of them had the extraordinary vividness of his Princess.

The men in richer colors, like a garden of peacocks, came more slowly, bustled through the ring of maidens, and faced the two, thrusting heads forward and grimacing at Princess with a ferocity that Manus recognized as make-believe. Himself they ignored.

But Princess brushed them aside with a quick imperious gesture, and cried, "Children, first my Queen Mother."

The crowd swung in behind, and laughed and chattered and wondered about this soberly clad, deep-chested, yellow-eyed stranger who had a somber gravity that they could not assess. And one whispered to another, "Would this hero have what is called a soul?"

Manus and Princess, still arm in arm, skirted round the lake and came up between flower beds to the wide lawn, where the rest of the company made a curve back of a white marble dais whereon a malachite canopy enclosed a wide throne seat of white marble piled with blue and yellow cushions. And among the cushions sat a great lady, a tiara of gold and jewels in her yellow hair.

A golden, noble, mature woman she was, but not old. Indeed, in that valley Manus never met an old man or an aging woman. Nor did he meet any children.

Princess still holding his arm, Manus mounted the steps of the dais slowly and gravely, and Princess cried out eagerly, "Queen Mother Fand, I present my new champion, Golden."

Queen Mother bent her fine head and smiled slowly. "Your new champion is welcome here, little one." Her voice was low-pitched where all the other voices were high and even shrill. And Manus noticed, too, that she was a quiet woman, and grave, and that behind her slate-blue eyes was something that might be melancholy, as if she half knew something precious and would never know the other half. She reached him a slow hand at the end of a molded arm, and Manus took the coolness of it in his finger tips and bent his lips to it.

And Princess made an exultant little boast, "All by myself I found him, Queen Mother."

"You found him when the mood was on him and the gate open, my daughter," said the woman wisely. "He is a quiet man, your champion."

"But he can speak, and his words have a hidden meaning."

"You may find out that meaning if you hold him long enough."

Princess threw up her hands joyously, and cried, "I will keep him forever and ever and ever."

"That has been tried before," said the woman, a sad mockery in her voice. "Go now to your friends and rivals!"

There is no need to go into details. The slow afternoon passed into evening, and evening into gloaming, but at no time did darkness come. Manus, Princess ever at his side, strolled here and there and talked to this one and that one; he looked on at the games and wrestling, and make-believe fighting, and once he swam in the lake, out-pacing Princess and most of the others. When he came out of the water he found that his gray flannels had disappeared, and in their place were a gorgeous silken tunic and trews of Venetian red, with a corn-colored sash studded with topaz. It was Princess' own sash to show whose champion he was. After some hesitation he donned his splendors, and was not even ashamed.

Sometime in the evening Princess whispered to him, a shade of doubt in her voice, "It is the custom, Golden, for a new champion to show his skill. What are you skilled in besides love?"

From what he had seen, the young men were deft at wrestling, but merely playful at boxing, which was his own game. They were tall enough and active but not durable looking, and he felt that a solid right hook might knock any one of them into the middle of next week.

"You will choose a wrestler for your poor champion," he told her.

"That I will do," she said eagerly, "for I will not have you hurt." She put her hand over her heart and frowned. "There is a strange feeling here when I think of it. You will let me choose, Golden, please? You have a devil in your eyes."

Holding his hand, she hopped lightly, skirts awhirl, onto a marble bench, and he stepped firmly up to her side. He was not a tall man, but her brown head was only level with his shoulder.

She clapped her hands and gave a clear, ringing halloo; and the young people came thronging as if knowing what was afoot. She reached a hand so that the back of it touched Manus' breast, and the silver of her voice carried far, "This is now my champion, Golden, and he challenges one of you to wrestle!"

A mighty shout drowned her voice, and the youths pressed forward, hands up, faces fierce, but gaiety in every eye.

"Try me! Try me! Try me!"

Princess' flat-handed, imperious gesture brought silence, and she looked them over to choose a victim. Manus' voice was in her ear, his arm across her shoulder, "Is the hero Cuchulain amongst them?"

"No, no, not Cuchulain," and again her hand came to her heart.

"That is he standing apart?"

"Yes, but he would break you in his hands, that hero. Look, Golden, dear!" And her voice was urgent, "If you are shamed I cannot stand the pain, and I might not have life in me any more."

Manus was not heeding her. He had his eye on this Cuchulain for some time. A man in purple and red, he stood behind the crowd, feet wide-planted, hands on hips and black head forward; a quiet man—dark in the hair, cleanly pallid in face, blue-black in the eyes, not any taller than Manus, but wide as a door.

Manus found a dominance rise in him, not for the first time. He patted Princess' shoulder.

"Your champion chooses the best always, and after that works down to his own level. Stay and see!"

He moved aside her hands that would clutch him and took a long stride off the bench. And Princess stood there forlornly, a constriction about her heart that her hands could not ease.

Manus strode straight at the press and shoved through. Something in the carriage of his head, some other-world savagery in his eyes made these young men move hastily aside to give him room. And there he was, yellow head thrown back and yellow eyes half-hooded, face to face with Cuchulain. For the first time there was a hush.

Cuchulain smiled gravely, but Manus was brusque.

"Are you that Cuchulain who was once the Hound of Ulster?"

"What I once was I do not know," said Cuchulain, heavy-voiced, "but what I am now is well known."

"The champion of all the valleys?"

"That is what I am."

"Or the second best?"

"You would dispute it?" Cuchulain smiled again, but a spark lit behind the black eyes. "I warn you that sometimes I lose my temper and am rougher than is permitted. You will forgive me."

"I might be rough, too," said Manus, "and I will not ask anyone to forgive me."

He thrust his right hand out low and his left high. Cuchulain did the same, and forthwith the two champions grappled. Slowly, link by link, they took the strain, testing each other's strength before trying any feints or clips. And there Manus got the surprise of his life.

Cuchulain was indeed strong, weightily strong, but, somehow, there was no pith in him, no explosive energy of body or soul to oppose the electric explosiveness of a man. He strained heavily, eyes hot and hotter, but Manus held him glued to the ground.

"Let us try it this way," said Manus. He loosed a spurt of energy, swung Cuchulain in half circle, and brought him down on spread feet; and in turn he took Cuchulain's sluggish swing and came down poised. And so at it they went, in half swings, three-quarter swings, full swings, Manus gradually increasing the tempo, so that the young people, crying shrilly, had to scatter and get out from under.

And then, with a sudden resistant wrench, Manus brought that bearlike dance to a dead stop, and Cuchulain's legs buckled and he went down on his knees. But Manus brought him upright again, patted his shoulder and let him go.

"Show you a trick or two sometime, brother," Manus said, and walked away.

Everyone there knew that there was a new champion amongst them, and everyone cheered mightily, forgetting the defeated. But Manus walked on to where Princess waited on her bench, her eyes glistening with something that might be moisture. He lifted arms to her, and she came down into them, and she knew that she was being kissed—for the first time. Her heart would not let her speak.

What is the use of going on? It was evening now, the evening that never darkened, and there was feasting in the white palace, where rose-pink silken curtains moved in the soft air and countless mirrors made endless crystal vistas. Thereafter there was music making on harps and thin-sounding pipes, and arabesque-like dancing, and poetry reciting and song making and song singing, and more feasting and dancing and singing. And Manus sang the one song he wanted to sing, an old passionate song, in his flexible baritone voice:

> "For you I thirst, O Strange Woman's
>     Daughter!
> Give me strong wine of Love, not cool
>     spring water,
> Not pallid joy—red love and its sorrow,
> For my heart you hold in your hands'
>     hollow."

He sang that song for one only, and that one knew.

Need it be said? Manus did not go home that night. He did not even remember that he had any home to go to. And after that night he did not want to go anywhere.

He stayed a week, he stayed a month, he stayed a year. He stayed. And his brown Princess was always with him, and always loving him; and her Queen Mother looked on and smiled sadly.

It was sometime in the seventh year that the change of mood came over Manus. Make-believe gaiety, make-believe fighting began to weary him, and he began to move about by himself on the northern slopes of the valley, avoiding even Princess, in whose company there was a spell no longer. The scene, the people, the spiral of fevered pleasure seeking were losing a sense of reality; and some inner vision was seeing a clean and wholesome world starkly etched under an evening sun. And there was a dark woman—

Princess noted his mood from the very beginning; she saw it bud and burgeon and bloom, and keep on blooming, and a new pain grew and grew in her. But she did not importune him, and some new desolate mood in herself would not let her do what she could do to hold him. She just followed him about at a distance, a woebegone small princess, no longer shimmering with vividness, gay never again.

Came the day when Manus, heavy with gloom, sticky with the soft warmth no longer salubrious, plunged into the lake, battled sullenly against the clinging waters, and came out unrefreshed. He reached for his Venetian reds. They were not there. There, instead, were the gray flannels that he had not seen or thought about for seven years. The roughish texture of them was pleasant to the feel, and the very stiffness of them, compared with silk, was oddly comforting and manly.

Again and heavy-footed he plodded up the northern slopes, where no longer as he well knew, was there a gap leading anywhere—anywhere he wanted to be. Gay voices called after him to join in a game of hurling, but to him they were only voices that were calling in a dream.

Princess watched him go, and herself went to where her Queen Mother sat, as usual, amongst her cushions; and that wise woman moved her fine blond head from side to side.

"So it has come, little one," she murmured sadly.

"And what now, Queen Mother?"

"If you want your Golden he can be held."

"I want him."

"There are spells—"

"And spells?"

"And more and more spells."

"And when he wakes one time, any time, will he want to stay with me for myself, myself only?"

Queen Mother again moved her head slowly. "There is a tie that no spell can kill forever. Listen, little one! You have the one chance that few get in all the valleys, but the pain is too great. Once, long ago, I, too, had that chance. I let my lover go, but you, his daughter, I could not forsake even to win a soul. I know only the half life, but I know all the pain, and that pain I will not let you suffer. I will make a spell."

Princess threw her head up, and her voice was anguished, "No, no, no! I am used to pain, and I will have no spells."

She turned away, and she, too, moved northward, her feet unsure and her eyes blinded.

Manus sat on a shelf of stone close up to the northern rim of the valley, his arms folded firmly across his breast. And he was thinking:

*This is not life; it is only an image of life. Effort is useless, for effort leads nowhere, and all motion returns on one spiral. It is maybe some subtle form of hell. No, not hell. It is life without a soul, and I will have no more of it though I am held here forever. I threw my life away in a blind and selfish hour, the only life worth living. With manhood on, you choose your road and hold by it. Take a wife and cleave to her, and to hell with romantic urges. Work and beget and rear and teach and toil. Leave hostages to fortune; let love renew itself as it will; and let one die unafraid. Oh, love that I threw away in a dark hour. Oh, my dark love.*

A whisper, that he did not know was a whisper, came out of the air, "And she was beautiful?"

"That is only a word," he whispered back. "She had black hair and blue eyes, a generous mouth, and a white nape to her neck. No, not white! White is the color of dread. A smooth and fragrant ivory! And when I used move my hand up from her neck through her hair, her hair used crackle and crisp between my fingers, and the waves of it reached my throat."

"And she had the thing we call a soul?"

"Shining through in day and dark."

"Ayeh me! there is no soul in this valley or in any valley. It is what we seek, and we do not know what it is. My Queen Mother knows, and she tells a story that once in a hundred years one of us wins a soul through a great pain and great sacrifice, and that one is seen no more, ever. I held you as long as I could, Golden."

"You held me a long time."

"Not against your will?"

"Not against my will."

"And I will not hold you against your will now. Pain I know, and if I must know more, I will know it. Come!"

He found himself on his feet, her left hand holding his right as of yore. Head down, he went where she drew him. He found himself in a gap of the hills going downward; he found himself in shade between high stone walls, he found himself through the gut, and a clean cool live air in his face. And there was a final whisper, "You are back now, Golden, and I go, where I do not know. All I know is that I will never see you again, never, never, never."

After a while he had grace enough to lift his head and turn round. Princess was not there, and there was no longer a gap between the chorrie and the cliff.

"And that is the end of that," he said in his throat, and there was neither sorrow nor regret in him.

He went out of the side gap then, and into his own valley, and up by the course of the runlet. He went slow-footed, heart down, head down, not daring to lift his head for fear of what he might see—ruined thatched, gaping windows, broken walls.

So in time he came to the little pool of spring water, and sat him down on the boss of stone where he had sat seven years before. He looked through the shimmering translucency of the water, and went deep into the recesses of his own mind.

It was again a sun-hazed summer afternoon, and stillness was over all that land. The birds were not yet singing, though goldfinches flitted from whin to whin; and the tinkle of running water was in a remote dimension of its own.

After a time Manus sighed deeply, drew in a long breath and stiffened his shoulders. His voice was sad, but not forlorn, "Seven years is a long time, but it is by, and there is nothing I can do about it. I threw the living life away, but there is great life in me still. If it be so willed, and the one woman remains to me still, I will seek her out at the world's end, and put my hands under her feet, and cherish her, and strive for her and her children, so that life shall be always eager and always calling. And if that is not given me, as God made me, I will face whatever life there is."

He shook his head, fiercely resolute, looked about him and stared.

"That is a strange thing," he said. "It looks like our water pail, but our pail will be worn into staves these many days."

A zinc-hooped wooden pail did, indeed, rest on the flag where many a pail had worn a ring. It was a good new pail and there were traces of moisture in the bottom of it.

Manus held his breath, and, for the first time, looked up the slope. Then he exhaled shortly. For the cottage was still there, nestling securely into the breast of the hill. It had not changed at all. The small four-paned windows shone; the walls were still blue-white; the door was still open to the summer air; and the rough-cast chimney out of the brown thatch sent up a thin ribbon of smoke, as if some housewife were burning furze roots to boil a kettle.

Manus smiled, and some of the old dare-devil was back in his smile. He got to his feet.

"Whatever woman is in that house," said he, "she will be having use for a pail of spring water. Very well so! A pail of spring water she shall have, and let it be a good beginning to set my feet on the seeking road."

Firmly, then, he scooped the pail full, and faced the upward path steadily, shelf above shelf amongst the furze and bracken. He stood in the open doorway, and his heart hollowed out, and he drew thin air into a tightened throat.

Maire, his young wife, sat there at the fireside on her hassock. She was placidly knitting, and a last furze root was burning down into white ash. She half turned and smiled her slow smile.

"You took a long time to bring me my pail of water," she said in her quiet, soft voice.

His voice might have broken if he had not kept it vibrating deeply in his throat.

"But in the end I brought it. Was it a long time indeed?"

"A full hour anyway."

"I thought it was longer," said Manus evenly.

"No. You were sitting on the stone hunched over, and brooding to yourself. I thought you were asleep."

"Asleep and dreaming. But at end—in one hour or in seven years—I had only one desire in all the world."

Something in his voice, in his eyes made her heart shake her.

"Yes, Manus?" she said softly.

His voice thickened. "I only wanted to come back to you and put my hands under your feet."

Her heart turned completely over, and her blue eyes were drowned in the glow of his yellow ones.

"Manus Boy, Manus Boy! You are back to me."

"Till time and tides are done, one woman."

He put the pail down at the fireside. He ran his hand from the soft cream of her neck into her black hair, and it crisped and crinkled between his fingers. He bent his cheek to hers and whispered, "Let us not boil the kettle for a small while yet."

And she turned her mouth to his.

But what of the fairy Princess? Was she only the vision of an hour to show a man the definite road he must take? It could be. Yet there is a tradition in that countryside of a sad and lonesome small song that comes out of the hillside in the gloaming of a June evening. Words have been put to that song, and here are a few of them:

> *When I see the plover rising*
> *Or the curlew wheeling,*

> *Then I hope my mortal lover*
> *Back to me is stealing.*

It is not easy to win a soul.

# The Happy Prince

✳

High above the city, on a tall column, stood the statue of the Happy Prince. He was gilded all over with thin leaves of fine gold, for eyes he had two bright sapphires, and a large red ruby glowed on his sword-hilt.

He was very much admired indeed. "He is as beautiful as a weathercock," remarked one of the Town Councillors who wished to gain a reputation for having artistic tastes; "only not quite so useful," he added, fearing lest people should think him unpractical, which he really was not.

"Why can't you be like the Happy Prince?" asked a sensible mother of her little boy who was crying for the moon. "The Happy Prince never dreams of crying for anything."

"I am glad there is some one in the world who is quite happy," muttered a disappointed man as he gazed at the wonderful statue.

"He looks just like an angel," said the Charity Children as they came out of the cathedral in their bright scarlet cloaks and their clean white pinafores.

"How do you know?" said the Mathematical Master, "you have never seen one."

"Ah! but we have, in our dreams," answered the children; and the Mathematical Master frowned and looked very severe, for he did not approve of children dreaming.

One night there flew over the city a little Swallow. His friends had gone away to Egypt six weeks before, but he

From The Happy Prince and Other Tales, London.

had stayed behind, for he was in love with the most beautiful Reed. He had met her early in the spring as he was flying down the river after a big yellow moth, and had been so attracted by her slender waist that he had stopped to talk to her.

"Shall I love you?" said the Swallow, who liked to come to the point at once, and the Reed made him a low bow. So he flew round and round her, touching the water with his wings, and making silver ripples. This was his courtship, and it lasted all through the summer.

"It is a ridiculous attachment," twittered the other Swallows; "she has no money, and far too many relations"; and indeed the river was quite full of Reeds. Then, when the autumn came they all flew away.

After they had gone he felt lonely, and began to tire of his lady-love. "She has no conversation," he said, "and I am afraid that she is a coquette, for she is always flirting with the wind." And certainly, whenever the wind blew, the Reed made the most graceful curtseys. "I admit that she is domestic," he continued, "but I love travelling, and my wife, consequently, should love travelling also."

"Will you come away with me?" he said finally to her, but the Reed shook her head, she was so attached to her home.

"You have been trifling with me," he cried. "I am off to the Pyramids. Good-bye!" and he flew away.

All day long he flew, and at night-time he arrived at the city. "Where shall I put up?" he said; "I hope the town has made preparations."

Then he saw the statue on the tall column.

"I will put up there," he cried; "it is a fine position, with plenty of fresh air." So he alighted just between the feet of the Happy Prince.

"I have a golden bedroom," he said softly to himself as he looked round, and he prepared to go to sleep; but just as he was putting his head under his wing a large drop of water fell on him. "What a curious thing!" he cried; "there is not a single cloud in the sky, the stars are quite clear and bright, and yet it is raining. The climate in the north of Europe is really dreadful. The Reed used to like the rain, but that was merely her selfishness."

Then another drop fell.

"What is the use of a statue if it cannot keep the rain off?" he said; "I must look for a good chimney-pot," and he determined to fly away.

But before he had opened his wings, a third drop fell, and he looked up, and saw——Ah! what did he see?

The eyes of the Happy Prince were filled with tears, and tears were running down his golden cheeks. His face was so beautiful in the moonlight that the little Swallow was filled with pity.

"Who are you?" he said.

"I am the Happy Prince."

"Why are you weeping then?" asked the Swallow; "you have quite drenched me."

"When I was alive and had a human heart," answered the statue, "I did not know what tears were, for I lived in the Palace of Sans-Souci, where sorrow is not allowed to enter. In the daytime I played with my companions in the garden, and in the evening I led the dance in the Great Hall. Round the garden ran a very lofty wall, but I never cared to ask what lay beyond it, everything about me was so beautiful. My courtiers called me the Happy Prince, and happy indeed I was, if pleasure be happiness. So I lived, and so I died. And now that I am dead they have set me up here so high that I can see all the ugliness and all the misery of my city, and though my heart is made of lead yet I cannot choose but weep."

"What! is he not solid gold?" said the Swallow to himself. He was too polite to make any personal remarks out loud.

"Far away," continued the statue in a low musical voice, "far away in a little street there is a poor house. One of the windows is open, and through it I can see a woman seated at a table. Her face is thin and worn, and she has coarse, red hands, all pricked by the needle, for she is a seamstress. She is embroidering passion-flowers on a satin gown for the loveliest of the Queen's maids-of-honour to wear at the next Court-ball.

In a bed in the corner of the room her little boy is lying ill. He has a fever, and is asking for oranges. His mother has nothing to give him but river water, so he is crying. Swallow, Swallow, little Swallow, will you not bring her the ruby out of my sword-hilt? My feet are fastened to this pedestal and I cannot move."

"I am waited for in Egypt," said the Swallow. "My friends are flying up and down the Nile, and talking to the large lotus-flowers. Soon they will go to sleep in the tomb of the great King. The King is there himself in his painted coffin. He is wrapped in yellow linen, and embalmed with spices. Round his neck is a chain of pale green jade, and his hands are like withered leaves."

"Swallow, Swallow, little Swallow," said the Prince, "will you not stay with me for one night, and be my messenger? The boy is so thirsty, and the mother so sad."

"I don't think I like boys," answered the Swallow. "Last summer, when I was staying on the river, there were two rude boys, the miller's sons, who were always throwing stones at me. They never hit me, of course; we swallows fly far too well for that, and besides, I come of a family famous for its agility; but still, it was a mark of disrespect."

But the Happy Prince looked so sad that the little Swallow was sorry. "It is very cold here," he said; "but I will stay with you for one night, and be your messenger."

"Thank you, little Swallow," said the Prince.

So the Swallow picked out the great ruby from the Prince's sword, and flew away with it in his beak over the roofs of the town.

He passed by the cathedral tower, where the white marble angels were sculptured. He passed by the palace and heard the sound of dancing. A beautiful girl came out on the balcony with her lover. "How wonderful the stars are," he said to her, "and how wonderful is the power of love!"

"I hope my dress will be ready in time for the State ball," she answered; "I have ordered passion-flowers to be em-broidered on it; but the seamstresses are so lazy."

He passed over the river, and saw the lanterns hanging to

the masts of the ships. He passed over the Ghetto, and saw the old Jews bargaining with each other, and weighing out money in copper scales. At last he came to the poor house and looked in. The boy was tossing feverishly on his bed, and the mother had fallen asleep, she was so tired. In he hopped, and laid the great ruby on the table beside the woman's thimble. Then he flew gently round the bed, fanning the boy's forehead with his wings. "How cool I feel!" said the boy, "I must be getting better"; and he sank into a delicious slumber.

Then the Swallow flew back to the Happy Prince, and told him what he had done. "It is curious," he remarked, "but I feel quite warm now, although it is so cold."

"That is because you have done a good action," said the Prince. And the little Swallow began to think, and then he fell asleep. Thinking always made him sleepy.

When day broke he flew down to the river and had a bath. "What a remarkable phenomenon!" said the Professor of Ornithology as he was passing over the bridge. "A swallow in winter!" And he wrote a long letter about it to the local newspaper. Every one quoted it, it was full of so many words that they could not understand.

"To-night I go to Egypt," said the Swallow, and he was in high spirits at the prospect. He visited all the public monuments, and sat a long time on top of the church steeple. Wherever he went the Sparrows chirruped, and said to each other, "What a distinguished stranger!" so he enjoyed himself very much.

When the moon rose he flew back to the Happy Prince. "Have you any commissions for Egypt?" he cried; "I am just starting."

"Swallow, Swallow, little Swallow," said the Prince, "will you not stay with me one night longer?"

"I am waited for in Egypt," answered the Swallow. "To-morrow my friends will fly up to the Second Cataract. The river-horse couches there among the bulrushes, and on a great granite throne sits the God Memnon. All night long he watches the stars, and when the morning star shines he utters one cry of joy, and then he is silent. At noon the yellow lions come down to the water's edge to drink. They have eyes like green beryls, and their roar is louder than the roar of the cataract."

"Swallow, Swallow, little Swallow," said the Prince, "far away across the city I see a young man in a garret. He is leaning over a desk covered with papers, and in a tumbler by his side there is a bunch of withered violets. His hair is brown and crisp, and his lips are red as a pomegranate, and he has large and dreamy eyes. He is trying to finish a play for the Director of the Theater, but he is too cold to write any more. There is no fire in the grate, and hunger has made him faint."

"I will wait with you one night longer," said the Swallow, who really had a good heart. "Shall I take him another ruby?"

"Alas! I have no ruby now," said the Prince; "my eyes are all that I have left. They are made of rare sapphires, which were brought out of India a thousand years ago. Pluck out one of them and take it to him. He will sell it to the jeweler, and buy firewood, and finish his play."

"Dear Prince," said the Swallow, "I cannot do that"; and he began to weep.

"Swallow, Swallow, little Swallow," said the Prince, "do as I command you."

So the Swallow plucked out the Prince's eye, and flew away to the student's garret. It was easy enough to get in, as there was a hole in the roof. Through this he darted, and came into the room. The young man had his head buried in his hands, so he did not hear the flutter of the bird's wings, and when he looked up he found the beautiful sapphire lying on the withered violets.

"I am beginning to be appreciated," he cried; "this is from some great admirer. Now I can finish my play," and he looked quite happy.

The next day the Swallow flew down to the harbor. He sat on the mast of a large vessel and watched the sailors hauling big chests out of the hold with ropes. "Heave a-hoy!" they shouted as each chest came up. "I am going to Egypt!" cried the Swallow, but nobody minded, and when the moon rose he flew back to the Happy Prince.

"I am come to bid you good-bye," he cried.

"Swallow, Swallow, little Swallow," said the Prince, "will you not stay with me one night longer?"

"It is winter," answered the Swallow, "and the chill snow will soon be here. In Egypt the sun is warm on the green palm-trees, and the crocodiles lie in the mud and look lazily about them. My companions are building a nest in the Temple of Baalbec, and the pink and white doves are watching them, and cooing to each other. Dear Prince, I must leave you, but I will never forget you, and next spring I will bring you back two beautiful jewels in place of those you have given away. The ruby shall be redder than a red rose, and the sapphire shall be as blue as the great sea."

"In the square below," said the Happy Prince, "there stands a little match-girl. She has let her matches fall in the gutter, and they are all spoiled. Her father will beat her if she does not bring home some money, and she is crying. She has no shoes or stockings, and her little head is bare. Pluck out my other eye, and give it to her, and her father will not beat her."

"I will stay with you one night longer," said the Swallow, "but I cannot pluck out your eye. You would be quite blind then."

"Swallow, Swallow, little Swallow," said the Prince, "do as I command you."

So he plucked out the Prince's other eye, and darted down with it. He swooped past the match-girl, and slipped the jewel into the palm of her hand. "What a lovely bit of glass!" cried the little girl; and she ran home, laughing.

Then the Swallow came back to the Prince. "You are blind now," he said, "so I will stay with you always."

"No, little Swallow," said the poor prince, "you must go away to Egypt."

"I will stay with you always," said the Swallow, and he slept at the Prince's feet.

All the next day he sat on the Prince's shoulder, and told him stories of what he had seen in strange lands. He told him of the red ibises, who stand in long rows on the banks of the

Nile, and catch goldfish in their beaks; of the Sphinx, who is as old as the world itself, and lives in the desert, and knows everything; of the merchants, who walk slowly by the side of their camels and carry amber beads in their hands; of the King of the Mountains of the Moon, who is as black as ebony, and worships a large crystal; of the great green snake that sleeps in a palm-tree, and has twenty priests to feed it with honey-cakes; and of the pygmies who sail over a big lake on large flat leaves, and are always at war with the butterflies.

"Dear little Swallow," said the Prince, "you tell me of marvellous things, but more marvellous than anything is the suffering of men and of women. There is no Mystery so great as Misery. Fly over my city, little Swallow, and tell me what you see there."

So the Swallow flew over the great city, and saw the rich making merry in their beautiful houses, while the beggars were sitting at the gates. He flew into dark lanes, and saw the white faces of starving children looking out listlessly at the black streets. Under the archway of a bridge two little boys were lying in one another's arms to try and keep themselves warm. "How hungry we are!" they said. "You must not lie here," shouted the watchman, and they wandered out into the rain.

Then he flew back and told the Prince what he had seen.

"I am covered with fine gold," said the Prince, "you must take it off, leaf by leaf, and give it to my poor; the living always think that gold can make them happy."

Leaf after leaf of the fine gold the Swallow picked off, till the Happy Prince looked quite dull and grey. Leaf after leaf of the fine gold he brought to the poor, and the children's faces grew rosier, and they laughed and played games in the street. "We have bread now!" they cried.

Then the snow came, and after the snow came the frost. The streets looked as if they were made of silver, they were so bright and glistening; long icicles like crystal daggers hung down from the eaves of the houses, everybody went about in furs, and the little boys wore scarlet caps and skated on the ice.

The poor little Swallow grew colder and colder, but he

would not leave the Prince, he loved him too well. He picked up crumbs outside the baker's door when the baker was not looking, and tried to keep himself warm by flapping his wings.

But at last he knew that he was going to die. He had just enough strength to fly up to the Prince's shoulder once more. "Good-bye, dear Prince!" he murmured, "will you let me kiss your hand?"

"I am glad that you are going to Egypt at last, little Swallow," said the Prince, "you have stayed too long here; but you must kiss me on the lips, for I love you."

"It is not to Egypt that I am going," said the Swallow. "I am going to the House of Death. Death is the brother of Sleep, is he not?"

And he kissed the Happy Prince on the lips, and fell down dead at his feet.

At that moment a curious crack sounded inside the statue, as if something had broken. The fact is that the leaden heart had snapped right in two. It certainly was a dreadfully hard frost.

Early the next morning the Mayor was walking in the square below in company with the Town Councillors. As they passed the column he looked up at the statue: "Dear me! how shabby the Happy Prince looks!" he said.

"How shabby, indeed!" cried the Town Councillors, who always agreed with the Mayor: and they went up to look at it.

"The ruby has fallen out of his sword, his eyes are gone, and he is golden no longer," said the Mayor; "in fact, he is little better than a beggar!"

"Little better than a beggar," said the Town Councillors.

"And here is actually a dead bird at his feet!" continued the Mayor. "We must really issue a proclamation that birds are not to be allowed to die here." And the Town Clerk made a note of the suggestion.

So they pulled down the statue of the Happy Prince. "As he is no longer beautiful he is no longer useful," said the Art Professor at the University.

Then they melted the statue in a furnace, and the Mayor

held a meeting of the Corporation to decide what was to be done with the metal. "We must have another statue, of course," he said, "and it shall be a statue of myself."

"Of myself," said each of the Town Councillors, and they quarrelled. When I last heard of them they were quarrelling still.

"What a strange thing!" said the overseer of the workmen at the foundry. "This broken lead heart will not melt in the furnace. We must throw it away." So they threw it on a dust-heap where the dead Swallow was also lying.

"Bring me the two most precious things in the city," said God to one of His Angels; and the Angel brought Him the leaden heart and the dead bird.

"You have rightly chosen," said God, "for in my garden of Paradise this little bird shall sing for evermore, and in my city of gold the Happy Prince shall praise Me."

# Red Hanrahan

✳

Hanrahan, the hedge schoolmaster, a tall, strong, red-haired young man, came into the barn where some of the men of the village were sitting on Samhain Eve. It had been a dwelling-house, and when the man that owned it had built a better one, he had put the two rooms together, and kept it for a place to store one thing or another. There was a fire on the old hearth, and there were dip candles stuck in bottles, and there was a black quart bottle upon some boards that had been put across two barrels to make a table. Most of the men were sitting beside the fire, and one of them was singing a long wandering song, about a Munster man and a Connaught man that were quarrelling about their two provinces.

Hanrahan went to the man of the house and said, "I got your message"; but when he had said that, he stopped, for an old mountainy man that had a shirt and trousers of unbleached flannel, and that was sitting by himself near the door, was looking at him, and moving an old pack of cards about in his hands and muttering. "Don't mind him," said the man of the house; "he is only some stranger came in awhile ago, and we bade him welcome, it being Samhain night, but I think he is not in his right wits. Listen to him now and you will hear what he is saying."

They listened then, and they could hear the old man muttering to himself as he turned the cards, "Spades and Dia-

From STORIES OF RED HANRAHAN, New York, The Macmillan Company.

monds, Courage and Power; Clubs and Hearts, Knowledge and Pleasure."

"That is the kind of talk he has been going on with for the last hour," said the man of the house, and Hanrahan turned his eyes from the old man as if he did not like to be looking at him.

"I got your message," Hanrahan said then; "he is in the barn with his three first cousins from Gilchreist," the messenger said, "and there are some of the neighbours with them."

"It is my cousin over there is wanting to see you," said the man of the house, and he called over a young frieze-coated man, who was listening to the song, and said, "This is Red Hanrahan you have the message for."

"It is a kind message, indeed," said the young man, "for it comes from your sweetheart, Mary Lavelle."

"How would you get a message from her, and what do you know of her?"

"I don't know her, indeed, but I was in Loughrea yesterday, and a neighbour of hers that had some dealings with me was saying that she bade him send you word, if he met anyone from this side in the market, that her mother has died from her, and if you have a mind yet to join with herself, she is willing to keep her word to you."

"I will go to her indeed," said Hanrahan.

"And she bade you make no delay, for if she has not a man in the house before the month is out, it is likely the little bit of land will be given to another."

When Hanrahan heard that, he rose up from the bench he had sat down on. "I will make no delay indeed," he said, "there is a full moon, and if I get as far as Gilchreist to-night, I will reach to her before the setting of the sun to-morrow."

When the others heard that, they began to laugh at him for being in such haste to go to his sweetheart, and one asked him if he would leave his school in the old limekiln, where he was giving the children such good learning. But he said the children would be glad enough in the morning to find the place empty, and no one to keep them at their task; and as for

his school he could set it up again in any place, having as he
had his little inkpot hanging from his neck by a chain, and
his big Virgil and his primer in the skirt of his coat.

Some of them asked him to drink a glass before he went,
and a young man caught hold of his coat, and said he must
not leave them without singing the song he had made in
praise of Venus and of Mary Lavelle. He drank a glass of
whiskey, but he said he would not stop but would set out on
his journey.

"There's time enough, Red Hanrahan," said the man of the
house. "It will be time enough for you to give up sport when
you are after your marriage, and it might be a long time
before we will see you again."

"I will not stop," said Hanrahan; "my mind would be on the
roads all the time, bringing me to the woman that sent for
me, and she lonesome and watching till I come."

Some of the others came about him, pressing him that had
been such a pleasant comrade, so full of songs and every kind
of trick and fun, not to leave them till the night would be
over, but he refused them all, and shook them off, and went
to the door. But as he put his foot over the threshold, the
strange old man stood up and put his hand that was thin and
withered like a bird's claw on Hanrahan's hand, and said: "It
is not Hanrahan, the learned man and the great songmaker,
that should go out from a gathering like this, on a Samhain
night. And stop here, now," he said, "and play a hand with
me; and here is an old pack of cards has done its work many a
night before this, and old as it is, there has been much of the
riches of the world lost and won over it."

One of the young men said, "It isn't much of the riches of
the world has stopped with yourself, old man," and he looked
at the old man's bare feet, and they all laughed. But Hanrahan
did not laugh, but he sat down very quietly, without a word.
Then one of them said, "So you will stop with us after all,
Hanrahan"; and the old man said: "He will stop indeed, did
you not hear me asking him?"

They all looked at the old man then as if wondering where
he came from. "It is far I am come," he said, "through France

I have come, and through Spain, and by Lough Greine of the hidden mouth, and none has refused me anything." And then he was silent and nobody liked to question him, and they began to play. There were six men at the boards playing, and the others were looking on behind. They played two or three games for nothing, and then the old man took a fourpenny bit, worn very thin and smooth, out from his pocket, and he called to the rest to put something on the game. Then they all put down something on the boards, and little as it was it looked much, from the way it was shoved from one to another, first one man winning it and then his neighbour. And sometimes the luck would go against a man and he would have nothing left, and then one or another would lend him something, and he would pay it again out of his winnings, for neither good nor bad luck stopped long with anyone.

And once Hanrahan said as a man would say in a dream, "It is time for me to be going the road"; but just then a good card came to him, and he played it out, and all the money began to come to him. And once he thought of Mary Lavelle, and he sighed; and that time his luck went from him, and he forgot her again.

But at last the luck went to the old man and it stayed with him, and all they had flowed into him, and he began to laugh little laughs to himself, and to sing over and over to himself, "Spades and Diamonds, Courage and Power," and so on, as if it was a verse of a song.

And after a while anyone looking at the men, and seeing the way their bodies were rocking to and fro, and the way they kept their eyes on the old man's hands, would think they had drink taken, or that the whole story they had in the world was put on the cards; but that was not so, for the quart bottle had not been disturbed since the game began, and was nearly full yet, and all that was on the game was a few sixpenny bits and shillings, and maybe a handful of coppers.

"You are good men to win and good men to lose," said the old man, "you have play in your hearts." He began then to shuffle the cards and to mix them, very quick and fast, till at last they could not see them to be cards at all, but you would think him to be making rings of fire in the air, as little lads would make them with whirling a lighted stick; and after that it seemed to them that all the room was dark, and they could see nothing but his hands and the cards.

And all in a minute a hare made a leap out from between his hands, and whether it was one of the cards that took that shape, or whether it was made out of nothing in the palms of his hands, nobody knew, but there it was running on the floor of the barn, as quick as any hare that ever lived.

Some looked at the hare, but more kept their eyes on the old man, and while they were looking at him a hound made a leap out between his hands, the same way as the hare did, and after that another hound and another, till there was a whole pack of them following the hare round and round the barn.

The players were all standing up now, with their backs to the boards, shrinking from the hounds, and nearly deafened with the noise of their yelping, but as quick as the hounds were they could not overtake the hare, but it went round, till at the last it seemed as if a blast of wind burst open the barn door, and the hare doubled and made a leap over the boards where the men had been playing, and went out of the door and away through the night, and the hounds over the boards and through the door after it.

Then the old man called out, "Follow the hounds, follow the hounds, and it is a great hunt you will see tonight," and he went out after them. But used as the men were to go hunting after hares, and ready as they were for any sport, they were in dread to go out into the night, and it was only Hanrahan that rose up and that said, "I will follow, I will follow on."

"You had best stop here, Hanrahan," the young man that was nearest him said, "for you might be going into some great danger." But Hanrahan said, "I will see fair play, I will see fair play," and he went stumbling out of the door like a man in a dream, and the door shut after him as he went.

He thought he saw the old man in front of him, but it was only his own shadow that the full moon cast on the road before him, but he could hear the hounds crying after the hare over the wide green fields of Granagh, and he followed them very fast, for there was nothing to stop him; and after a while he came to smaller fields that had little walls of loose stones around them, and he threw the stones down as he crossed them, and did not wait to put them up again; and he passed by the place where the river goes under ground at Ballylee, and he could hear the hounds going before him up towards the head of the river. Soon he found it harder to run, for it was uphill he was going, and clouds came over the moon, and it was hard for him to see his way, and once he left the path to take a short cut, but his foot slipped into a boghole and he had to come back to it. And how long he was going he did not know, or what way he went, but at last he was up on the bare mountain, with nothing but the rough heather about him, and he could neither hear the hounds nor any other thing. But their cry began to come to him again, at first far off and then very near, and when it came quite close to him, it went up all of a sudden into the air, and there was the sound of hunting over his head; then it went away northward till he could hear nothing more at all. "That's not fair," he said, "that's not fair." And he could walk no longer, but sat down on the heather where he was, in the heart of Slieve Echtge, for all the strength had gone from him, with the dint of the long journey he had made.

And after a while he took notice that there was a door close to him, and a light coming from it, and he wondered that being so close to him he had not seen it before. And he rose up, and tired as he was he went in at the door, and although it was night time outside, it was daylight he found within. And presently he met with an old man that had been gathering summer thyme and yellow flag-flowers, and it seemed as if all the sweet smells of the summer were with them. And the old man said: "It is a long time you have been coming to us, Hanrahan the learned man and the great song-maker."

And with that he brought him into a very big shining house, and every grand thing Hanrahan had ever heard of, and every color he had ever seen, were in it. There was a high place at the end of the house, and on it there was sitting in a high chair a woman, the most beautiful the world ever saw, having a long pale face and flowers about it, but she had the tired look of one that had been long waiting. And there was sitting on the step below her chair four grey old women, and the one of them was holding a great cauldron in her lap; and another a great stone on her knees, and heavy as it was it seemed light to her; and another of them had a very long spear that was made of pointed wood; and the last of them had a sword that was without a scabbard.

Hanrahan stood looking at them for a long time, but none of them spoke any word to him or looked at him at all. And he had it in his mind to ask who that woman in the chair was, that was like a queen, and what she was waiting for; but ready as he was with his tongue and afraid of no person, he was in dread now to speak to so beautiful a woman, and in so grand a place. And then he thought to ask what were the four things the four grey old women were holding like great treasures, but he could not think of the right words to bring out.

Then the first of the old women rose up, holding the cauldron between her two hands, and she said, "Pleasure," and Hanrahan said no word. Then the second old woman rose up with the stone in her hands, and she said, "Power"; and the third old woman rose up with the spear in her hand, and she said, "Courage"; and the last of the old women rose up having the sword in her hands, and she said, "Knowledge." And everyone, after she had spoken, waited as if for Hanrahan to question her, but he said nothing at all. And then the four old women went out of the door, bringing their four treasures with them, and as they went out one of them said, "He has no wish for us"; and another said, "He is weak, he is weak"; and another said, "He is afraid"; and the last said, "His wits are gone from him." And then they all said, "Echtge, daughter of the Silver Hand, must stay in her sleep. It is a pity, it is a great pity."

And then the woman that was like a queen gave a very sad sigh, and it seemed to Hanrahan as if the sigh had the sound in it of hidden streams; and if the place he was in had been ten times grander and more shining than it was, he could

not have hindered sleep from coming on him; and he staggered like a drunken man and lay down there and then.

When Hanrahan awoke, the sun was shining on his face,
but there was white frost on the grass around him, and there
was ice on the edge of the stream he was lying by, and that
goes running on through Daire-caol and Druim-da-rod. He
knew by the shape of the hills and by the shining of Lough
Greine in the distance that he was upon one of the hills of
Slieve Echtge, but he was not sure how he came there; for all
that had happened in the barn had gone from him, and all of
his journey but the soreness of his feet and the stiffness in his
bones.

It was a year after that, there were men of the village of
Cappaghtagle sitting by the fire in a house on the roadside,
and Red Hanrahan that was now very thin and worn and his
hair very long and wild, came to the half-door and asked leave
to come in and rest himself; and they bid him welcome because it was Samhain night. He sat down with them, and they
gave him a glass of whiskey out of a quart bottle; and they
saw the little inkpot hanging about his neck, and knew he
was a scholar, and asked for stories about the Greeks.

He took the Virgil out of the big pocket of his coat, but
the cover was very black and swollen with the wet, and the
page when he opened it was very yellow, but that was no
great matter, for he looked at it like a man that had never
learned to read. Some young man that was there began to
laugh at him then, and to ask why did he carry so heavy a
book with him when he was not able to read it.

It vexed Hanrahan to hear that, and he put the Virgil back
in his pocket and asked if they had a pack of cards among
them, for cards were better than books. When they brought
out the cards he took them and began to shuffle them, and
while he was shuffling them something seemed to come into
his mind, and he put his hand to his face like one that is trying
to remember, and he said: "Was I ever here before, or where
was I on a night like this?" and then of a sudden he stood up
and let the cards fall to the floor, and he said, "Who was it
brought me a message from Mary Lavelle?"

"We never saw you before now, and we never heard of Mary Lavelle," said the man of the house. "And who is she," he said, "and what is it you are talking about?"

"It was this night a year ago, I was in a barn, and there were men playing cards, and there was money on the table, they were pushing it from one to another here and there—and I got a message, and I was going out of the door to look for my sweetheart that wanted me, Mary Lavelle." And then Hanrahan called out very loud: "Where have I been since then? Where was I for the whole year?"

"It is hard to say where you might have been in that time," said the oldest of the men, "or what part of the world you may have travelled; and it is like enough you have the dust of many roads on your feet; for there are many go wandering and forgetting like that," he said, "when once they have been given the touch."

"That is true," said another of the men. "I knew a woman went wandering like that through the length of seven years; she came back after, and she told her friends she had often been glad enough to eat the food that was put in the pig's trough. And it is best for you to go to the priest now," he said, "and let him take off you whatever may have been put upon you."

"It is to my sweetheart I will go, to Mary Lavelle," said Hanrahan; "it is too long I have delayed, how do I know what might have happened her in the length of a year?"

He was going out of the door then, but they all told him it was best for him to stop the night, and to get strength for the journey; and indeed he wanted that, for he was very weak, and when they gave him food he ate it like a man that had never seen food before, and one of them said, "He is eating as if he had trodden on the hungry grass." It was in the white light of the morning he set out, and the time seemed long to him till he could get to Mary Lavelle's house. But when he came to it, he found the door broken, and the thatch dropping from the roof, and no living person to be seen. And when he asked the neighbours what had happened to her, all they could say was that she had been put out of the house, and had married some laboring man, and they had gone looking for work to London or Liverpool or some big place. And whether she found a worse place or a better he never knew, but anyway he never met with her or with news of her again.

# Notes on the Authors

PAUL VINCENT CARROLL was born July 10, 1900, at Black-rock near Dundalk. A schoolteacher and a playwright of first rank, he is best known in America for his plays, *Shadow and Substance* and *The White Steed,* both of which had successful Broadway runs.

DESMOND CLARKE was born in 1907. His short stories have appeared in the *Manchester Guardian, New Writing, Dublin Magazine, The Bell, Irish Writing,* and elsewhere. Some of his stories have been listed by Martha Foley among the best for the years 1949, 1950, 1951. He has written a life of Thomas Prior which was published in 1951, and has recently completed a life of Arthur Dobbs, Governor of North Carolina (1754-1766). He is Librarian of the Royal Dublin Society and Editor of the *Journal of the Library Association of Ireland.*

DANIEL CORKERY was born in 1878 in Cork City and has spent his life there as a schoolmaster and Gaelic teacher. He has written a novel, four volumes of short stories and two critical works. Three plays were produced at the Abbey. His influence on younger Irish writers, especially O'Connor and O'Faolain, has been considerable.

ERIC CROSS was born in Ireland in 1905, the son of an English father and Irish mother. Professionally he is a research chemist specializing in food and "organotherapy"; his hobbies include writing short stories, broadcasting from Radio Eireann and touring Ireland from his home in Co. Mayo.

LORD DUNSANY Edward John Moreton Drax Plunkett has produced some sixty volumes of novels, short stories, poetry and plays. Born July 24, 1878, he was educated at Eton and Sandhurst, served with the Coldstream Guard in the Boer War and was wounded in World War I. He spends his time between Dunsany Castle, Co. Meath; Kent, England, and the west coast of the United States searching for the "lost times and vanished regimes" that haunt his imaginative stories.

ST. JOHN ERVINE's stories, plays, and novels are generally considered excellent expressions of the Ulster mind, if a bit on the aggressive side. A member of the Irish Academy of Letters, he has had plays produced at the Abbey, which he managed for a time, and written a powerful novel, *Mrs. Martin's Man*, depicting Ulster types. He lives in Devon.

PADRAIC FALLON was born in Athenry, Galway, in 1906. He is a customs official at Wexford, where he writes excellent poetry and an occasional story for the *Dublin Magazine* and other periodicals.

ARNOLD HILL writes of the same middle-class Belfast individuals that engage St. John Ervine. Born in Belfast in 1918, he has had stories published in various English and Irish periodicals and plays produced by the B.B.C. and other broadcasting companies. Like most Irish writers, he is "working on a novel."

DAVID HOGAN (Frank Gallagher), a veteran of Ireland's war of independence, has served long terms of imprisonment, engaged in protracted hunger strikes, (the shortest 3 days, the longest 41 days) been an official of the first Dail Eireann and founder-editor of the *Irish Press*. He has written a history of these events and called it *Four Glorious Years*. He has also written *Day of Fear*, the journal of a hunger strike.

JAMES JOYCE was born in Dublin, February 2, 1882, and died at Zürich, Switzerland, January 31, 1941. His influence on modern literature is very great indeed, and his stature seems to be gaining with the years.

PATRICK KAVANAGH was born on a farm in Co. Monaghan in 1905. He has published an autobiography, *The Green Fool,* a novel, *Tarry Flynn,* and some fine poetry in a slim volume called *A Soul for Sale.* He lives in Dublin, where he has become something of a legend.

MARY LAVIN lives in Co. Meath on a farm. She was born in Boston, Mass., in 1912, but was raised and educated in Ireland, where she was graduated from the National University, Dublin. She has published several books of short stories and two novels.

DONAGH MacDONAGH was born in Dublin in 1912, son of the 1916 poet Thomas MacDonagh. Educated at University College, Dublin, he is a barrister who writes as a hobby. Two volumes of verse and a verse play, *Happy As Larry,* have been published.

MICHAEL MacGRIAN is the pen name of C.A.M. West of Anglesey, N. Wales. He was born in 1910 "in the sweet County Down." In 1930, he visited the U.S. and Canada for five years, served another five with the RAF as Pathfinder Navigator. In 1946, he won a Rockefeller Award in literature and moved with his family to Wales. He has written a number of stories and is working on a novel.

MICHAEL McLAVERTY was born in Co. Monaghan in 1907 and was educated at St. Malachy's College in the city of Belfast. He has lived there ever since and teaches school. His novels (six to date) have enjoyed increasing popularity in America. *The Game Cock,* a collection of short stories, achieved great critical acclaim when published here in 1947.

BRYAN MacMAHON first made a hit with his book of stories, *The Lion Tamer,* published here in 1949. It was followed by a successful novel, *Children of the Rainbow,* 1952. He was born in Listowel, Co. Kerry, and now teaches school there. A second book of stories, *The Red Petticoat,* was published in 1955.

GEORGE MOORE was born in 1852 in Co. Mayo, spent much of his adult life in London, where he died in 1933. He spent the years 1901-1910 in Dublin, however, and there wrote his book of short stories, *The Untilled Field*. He is best known for his three-volume history of the Literary Revival, *Hail and Farewell,* and for his somewhat ostentatious conversion to Protestantism.

VAL MULKERNS (Mrs. Maurice Kennedy) was born in Dublin and educated at the Dominican College there. She has taught school and written a successful novel, *A Time Outworn,* which Frank O'Connor has praised as "the most interesting and significant to have come out of Ireland in 25 years." She now lives in Dublin and is working on a second novel.

BRIAN O'NOLAN is better known by his two pseudonyms, Flann O'Brien (author of *At Swim-Two-Birds*) and Myles na gCopaleen (columnist of the *Irish Times*). He was born in Strabane, Co. Tyrone, in 1912, studied in Berlin and holds a degree of M.A. from the National University, Dublin. He is equally at home in Irish and English. Married and lives in Dublin.

PADRAIC O CONAIRE, our only Gaelic author, was born in 1882 in Galway City. Educated by the Christian Brothers, he taught Gaelic classes in London. Two books of stories and sketches have been translated into English. He died in Dublin in 1928. A statue, subscribed for by Gaels the world over, was unveiled in Galway in 1935.

FRANK O'CONNOR (Michael O'Donovan), Ireland's best-known contemporary writer, has had six selections of his stories published here. Born in Cork City in 1903, he has taken part in "The Troubles," been a librarian, a director of the Abbey Theatre, translated various poems from the Gaelic, written several novels and a travel book and is presently living in the United States, where he has been giving courses in the short story at various universities.

SEAN O'FAOLAIN was born in Dublin in 1900, and raised in Cork. He was graduated from University College, Dublin. He has done his stint with the I.R.A., taught school, edited *The Bell*, is perhaps Ireland's most prolific writer. Three novels, five full-length biographies, three travel books, three volumes of short stories plus a book on writing, a study of the Irish temperament and a collection of translations from the Irish have appeared to date. He has studied at Harvard and given a series of graduate lectures at Princeton.

LIAM O'FLAHERTY was born in the Aran Islands in 1897 and early studied for the priesthood. After a short time at University College, Dublin, he joined the Irish Guards and spent six months in France, returning shellshocked to Ireland, where he has lived, off and on, ever since. He has written 14 novels, the best of which are *The Informer* and *Famine*. His various short-story selections have been combed and a volume of the best of them, *The Stories of Liam O'Flaherty*, was published in 1955 by Devin-Adair.

SEUMAS O'KELLY was born in Galway. His first book of stories was published in 1906. It was followed by three others and by a novel, *The Lady of Deer Park*. Several of his plays were produced at the Abbey. He died prematurely in 1918.

JIM PHELAN is a tramp by profession, in the tradition of Jack London and Jim Tully. About 35 years ago, he "took to the road and quite suddenly felt at peace and at home." He has published a book of tramp stories and another of Irish stories, as well as two books of autobiographical sketches. Born in Ireland, he presently lives in England.

JAMES PLUNKETT (Kelly) was born in Dublin. He was educated by the Christian Brothers, is a trade union official and plays the viola professionally. His first book of short stories, *The Trusting and the Maimed*, was published in 1955 by Devin-Adair. He is married and has three children. His trip to Russia in 1955 created a sensation in Dublin.

GEORGE BERNARD SHAW published the altogether remarkable story (remarkable that Shaw should have writtten it) included here, in 1885. Born in Dublin in 1856, Shaw died in England in 1950. He was a charter member of the Irish Academy and one of the great playwrights of all time.

EDWARD SHEEHY was born in Tralee, Co. Kerry, some forty years ago and holds an M.A. degree from the National University. He has contributed stories to different magazines, taught school and presently lives in Co. Wicklow with his artist-wife and two children.

JAMES STEPHENS was born in Dublin in 1881. He died in London in 1950. A novel, *The Crock of Gold*, has become a classic. His collected poetry was recently reissued by Macmillan. He died before completing his autobiography, from which "A Rhinoceros, Some Ladies and a Horse" is taken.

MAURICE WALSH was born May 2, 1879, in Co. Kerry on a farm. He became a customs officer and traveled widely through the British Isles. His *Saturday Evening Post* stories became very popular in the U.S. He has published some 14 novels, served as president of the Irish P.E.N. and now lives outside Dublin. He has three sons and two grandsons.

OSCAR FINGAL O'FLAHERTIE WILLS WILDE was born in Dublin on October 16, 1854, and died in Paris on November 30, 1900. He was buried in the cemetery of Père Lachaise. In 1951, St. John Ervine published *Oscar Wilde: A Present Day Appraisal*. The *Complete Works* have recently been made available through Dutton & Company; also *The Epigrams of Oscar Wilde* (John Day) and the autobiography of Wilde's son, Vyvyan Holland.

WILLIAM BUTLER YEATS was born near Dublin, June 13, 1865, and died January 28, 1939, while visiting in France. His genius is universally recognized and his reputation increases with the years.